UNDEAD IN L.A.

A Comedy

Whip Lipsey

Etherege & Wycherley

UNDEAD IN L.A.

NIGHT OF THE PINCHED MAN

Down a dreary street, in the fading light of dusk, walked a thin man. The man's name was not Victor Drakan, but in L.A. everyone has a story and he meant to stick to his. Born of an English aristocrat and a Russian spy, he had lived first in Macao and later in ports and capitals all over Europe. Though he showed prodigy-like skill at music as a young boy, his parents had refused to hand him over to the maestros who occasionally asked after young Drakan. Instead, they had taught him at home, or rather in the embassies of the world where his father served as a diplomat. He mastered first the great Greek and Roman classics and later the natural sciences. He read the great minds in the original: Plato, Descartes, Newton, Kepler, Lovecraft. While in his late teens, and living in Marseille, he had wounded a powerful man's son in a sword fight over a woman. To escape the authorities, and the man's father, young Drakan had joined the Foreign Legion. After fighting in several of France's colonial wars, he had gone to South Africa hunting diamonds. In the course of time he had moved on to mine gold in the mud pits of Brazil and to hunt big game in West Africa. In the United States he finally got around to college and stunned the professors of first Princeton, and then Harvard, with his prodigious intellect. Soon he held half a dozen patents and had, in his spare time, stolen several major paintings from the Boston Museum of Art—just for the fun of it.

Now, while *not one word* of this fanciful biography was actually true, these self-told lies filled the head of Victor Drakan as he approached the Marion Wright Museum of Cultural History. Drakan had his story, and his image. And he knew that in L.A. at least, a story and an image could go from lie to fact to legend before the ink of the lie had dried. You just need a little capital.

Drakan usually walked fast, his shoulders locked up and his head thrust forward. This evening he took obvious pains to walk slowly. His shoulders still locked up, and his head still thrust forward, but his feet hit the ground in a ponderous, slow stride. He wore all black, including a black scarf around his neck. He carried a black gym bag. His pale skin shined like a florescent light against the black of his clothes. His hair receded in the classic v pattern, revealing a long, furrowed brow that pointed down to thin, pursed lips and a sharp chin. He looked like a man perpetually sucking a lemon. Thus ponderous, pursed and pinched, he headed for the back of the museum.

Only a single guard and a very old alarm system stood between any prospective thief and the treasures of the Marion Wright. The most difficult task of any would-be felon lay in finding something worth the trouble to steal. Artifacts of cultural history rarely garner top dollar at Sotheby's. In fact, they rarely garner bottom dollar at Mic's All-Night Pawnshop. Still, one might find treasures in the small museum, if one knew where to look.

Victor Drakan knew where to look. As dusk settled into night, Drakan halted his stilted progress across the street from the museum's back lawn. He stared intently at the Marion Wright Museum in what he assumed was a nonchalant manner. Drakan knew nothing about looking nonchalant. He looked, instead, rather like a black fish hooked by the museum's flagpole—head thrust forward, lips tightly pursed.

The main building of the Marion Wright has the feel of nineteenth century elegance (build date: 1942). It had housed the original Mrs. Wright. In converting the old house into an exhibition space, some mad architect with a grudge against museums had attached a nearly windowless brick addition. The resulting edifice looked like an old Victorian mansion being mugged by a brick oven. Inside, the museum sported non-weight bearing Doric columns, rooms lined with wood paneling, and in the center, an atrium open to the air. Architecturally sensitive epileptics had been known to fit-out upon touring the Marion Wright.

The museum's permanent collection consisted mostly of porcelain dolls, period clothing, and turn of the century cutlery. Mrs. Wright simply could not get her hands on enough tableware. Unless you had a fetish for doilies and silver spoon sets, you could enjoy Mrs. Wright's contribution to cultural history in just under twenty minutes. So the curators gave over most of the museum's exhibition space to temporary exhibits. Outside, in the rising light of the moon, Drakan could read the sign announcing the current exhibit: "Commerce with the Dead: A History of Human Journeys into Hope."

Drakan stood on the street corner, hooked to the flagpole, watching the small parking lot next to the museum. When the last car but one pulled away, he knew his hour of destiny had arrived. The yellow Buick still remaining in the lot belonged to the single night guard—the Marion Wright lay empty and ready for ravishing.

Before crossing the street, Drakan took a black stocking cap from his pocket and pulled it over his head. He raised the black scarf to cover his face below his close-set eyes. He looked about. Seeing no one, he headed across the street to the lawn leading up to the Marion Wright.

Earnest in his larceny, Drakan failed to see or hear Mrs. Martha Talbert Pembroke walking her dog just behind him as he jaywalked to destiny. Mrs. Pembroke watched the strange man in black rush across the street and through the short stretch of grass to the back of the museum. While her dog *Toffle* christened the lamppost behind her, she saw the man in

3

black struggle to put on kneepads, elbow pads, chest pads, and gloves. Walking on, she thought how very like an octopus he finally looked.

◆ ◆ ◆

Drakan began his ascent to the second floor. He had practiced using his suction cups by climbing the walls of his apartment. Proper adhesion required a clean and slightly damp surface. Drakan used a spray can and a collapsible mop to prepare the surface of the museum wall. His way cleared of grime, Drakan rammed home the first of the suction cups. Somewhat to his surprise, it stuck. Off he went. By smashing his knees one at a time into the wall, and holding on to another suction cup with his left hand, he could use his right hand and the rest of his body to ram home the suction cups on his chest. After just his first attempt he had blooded his nose and bruised both knees. But the suction cups held. He aimed to place them, and thus himself, progressively higher up the building. Getting one cup loose without detaching them all proved no mean trick. Further, the loud *pop* each cup emitted when dislodged sounded to Drakan like an artillery shell. Still, he climbed on, ramming himself up the wall.

Looking rather like some exotic leech mating out of species, Drakan maneuvered himself to the second floor window of the backside of the Marion Wright. Secured by several suction cups, he planned now to cut a hole in the window just above the latch. He had practiced with a diamond-edged glasscutter on car windows in his neighborhood. Now, however, the suction cups held him too close to the window to get proper leverage. Rather than the graceful cut of the cat burglar he had envisioned, he sawed away at the glass as if he had some personal score to settle with it. Glass dust covered his face and clothes, and desperation rose in the sunken, sallow breast of Victor Drakan. Trying to re-adjust himself, he sent an elbow through the weakened glass, smashing it loudly. Drakan froze.

He need not have. The museum's sole guard sat a floor below at the front of the building watching a portable television. If Victor Drakan accidentally pulled the fire alarm, the guard *might* run out of the building to find help; but this was the extent of the threat he posed.

Hanging from the broken window, half suctioned to the wall, Drakan did not know this. Drakan was a man of many vices, but he was not a coward. Destiny called, and broken glass or no, Victor Drakan would answer. With some pain, and much popping of suction cups, Drakan hauled himself into the museum.

Drakan had tried to find out what sort of alarms might protect the Marion Wright. Though a simple matter in the movies, it had been impossible in real life. He imagined electric eye beams piercing the dark in every direction, so he had planned to use an aerosol spray can whose mist could reveal the hidden light of laser alarms. In fact, aerosol proved hard to find, so he now tried the trick with a perfume-mister. Since the security budget of the Marion Wright Museum did not allow even for alarms on the windows, Drakan had little to fear from laser beams. Nonetheless, as he made his way through the museum to his final destination on the third floor, he periodically stopped and sprayed a mist of slightly perfumed water vapor at the odd doorframe. By such misty stealth did Victor Drakan finally arrive at the display case that held his reward.

Within the case lay a book. Drakan set to cutting a hole in the glass case in close imitation of those society cat burglars he had so recently studied in old movies. His diamond-edged glasscutter made scant impression on the tempered glass protecting his prize. Nor could he lift the glass. In frustration, Drakan pounded on the glass yelling "Arrrr! Arrrr!" But *arrr-arrr* launched no magic, and the glass remained defiant.

Drakan looked around. Across the room a large mummy's sarcophagus stood looming beside another display case. He walked (actually crept—he had been creeping everywhere, so why stop now?) behind the sarcophagus. With effort he started it rocking. Back and forth, from its left to its right side; its right to its left side. Thus did the dead of Egypt walk again towards the resistant glass of the case enclosing Drakan's prize. A few feet from the case Drakan halted the sarcophagus. He checked his distances and returned to the back of his battering ram. Drakan pushed the sarcophagus toward the display case. With a crash, Amenhatet's final resting place freed the book from its crystal captivity.

Drakan thrilled at the success, but the sound of the crash deafened his ears and dampened his joy. He snatched the book and ran, not crept, but ran, back to the broken window on the second floor. Here he found the rope he had tied to a pedestal that displayed a particularly nice knife and fork set. He had ascended on the suction elevator; he would descend on the rope. Two seconds and two rope-burned hands latter, Drakan hit the ground. He ran to his car clutching an old black book to his chest as if it were the Lindbergh baby. Joy filled his heart— he was a success at last.

A VERY VERY WOMAN

Tom Delaney liked big hooters and he liked what he saw now. Even though she wore a karate gi, Delaney could tell that the woman standing before him was stacked. She was Hispanic, with thick shoulder-length black hair, brown eyes and a dark complexion. She had it. Tom wanted it.

Tom said, "Hey, I'm Tom."

The hooters replied, "Yolanda Vasquez," and took an attack posture.

"What? You want to fight?" Tom asked.

"Sparring. It's called sparring in class," the hooters answered.

"Well, I'd like to tussle with you," Tom said, "but maybe after class." Tom thought this subtle—the hooters would be impressed.

"What's the matter?" the hooters taunted, "afraid I'll embarrass you?"

Taunting hooters! Imagine that. "It's just that you're a woman," Tom reminded the hooters.

"You've never worked out with a woman before?" the hooters asked.

"Yeah, but you're a very ... very ..." Tom searched for the right word.

"Woman," the hooters said.

Tom thought to himself, I'll knock her around a little bit, just enough to show her who's boss. After that, maybe I give a compliment on how well she held up. Then it's just a matter of the right word in the right place. The hooters will be mine. Tom took his attack posture.

He still had a stupid, condescending grin on his face when a foot hit him square in the nose.

"Ouch!"

The hooters kicked him! Hooters should not kick. Tom put on his serious face—his game face—his war face. These hooters will be taught a lesson.

The hooters threw three punches. Tom deftly blocked the first two. The third knocked the wind out of him. Tom was mad at the hooters. Though big, round, lovely, and showing their cleavage though the gi, they were not being friendly. Tom vowed he would show them how to treat a man.

While Tom vowed, the hooters kicked him in the side. This time Tom kept his head. He immediately threw an over-hand right, and if it bruised the head on top of the hooters it would be a good lesson for Ms. Vasquez.

Half way to teaching the hooters a good lesson, Tom noticed that his arm had gotten caught in something—other arms apparently—and that his face was heading with unseemly haste to the padded mat. Had the hooters taken him down face first to the floor? This seemed quite impossible. But what other explanation could account for the pain in his nose and the fact that all he could see now was a tear in the mat?

"Maybe you should take some more lessons." It was the hooters again, speaking from high above. "And you should maintain better eye contact." The hooters trailed off now. They were leaving. Going off to ruin some other poor slob's day.

◆ ◆ ◆

Yolanda Vasquez showered in the basement locker-rooms of the LAPD's Fountain Avenue Division precinct house. Looking at herself in the mirror, she had to agree that she was, indeed, a very, very woman. Other men before Tom What's-his-name had underestimated her, and would again. She would have to take them to the mat as well. Yolanda dressed for her first day at this new assignment. Slacks, sensible shoes, and a top and jacket that she hoped would minimize her "hooters."

She had made detective just six weeks ago and had spent all the time since then on hooker detail. She and several other policewomen would cruise a street trolling for lonely, randy men out to spend the steak money on some sweaty companionship. Detective Vasquez had obvious talent at this particular decoy assignment. She averaged about two minutes and two seconds of actually standing on the street. Twice men had fought each other on the sidewalk for the privilege of taking her to a sleazy motel room. It made her feel like the Belle Star of Hollywood Boulevard. About the only fun she had on the job came from bidding her price up. Initially the detail supervisor had advised the policewomen to ask for twenty-five dollars—crack money. By the end of her six weeks, Yolanda Vasquez would not accept less than five hundred dollars.

They never turned her down.

But the captured perpetrators of illicit lust received nothing more than a citation. When the vice boys leapt out of the bathroom at the perps, the once randy men panicked. (Yolanda called the vice cops the "Erection Busters.") The perps assumed life as they knew it had ended. Within twenty minutes they realized the worst of it would be staking out their mailboxes to see that the wife didn't get the ticket first. So for all the division chief's talk of saving marriages, cleaning up neighborhoods, and stopping the spread of embarrassing diseases, the whole thing amounted to red faces and a ticket. Worse yet, Yolanda had become the butt of jokes, most of them starting with the phrase, "If you ever give up police work..."

Yolanda considered herself a serious woman, and she intended to be taken seriously. Walking up the stairs to meet her new supervisor, she practiced how she should introduce herself. Should she be friendly? Cooperative? Feisty? She hated feisty. Coldly professional would at least put off the leering innuendo. But Yolanda was not by nature a cold woman, only a determined one.

The detective room of the Fountain Avenue Precinct looked

nothing like those described in gritty stories of hard-boiled detectives and world-weary policemen. Not grim, nor grimy, nor full of noir. White walls, desks, cubicles, and lots of bulletin boards filled with signs and notices. On the boards she saw signs covering union regulations, policy declarations on race-profiling ("Don't"), and departmental memorandum on maintaining good community relations ("Do"). Also, lots of post-it-notes reminding the detectives to feed the fish. Yolanda noticed that for a police precinct the place had a lot of aquariums. But one thing it did not have a lot of was mysterious atmosphere. You could mistake it for an insurance office. The Hollywood location director would reject this place as "inauthentic" and move on to some dark room with a swinging gate for his men-of-action to leap over. These days real detectives worked in standard office space, and rarely leapt at all.

The half-glass door ahead of her read *Lieutenant Sam Washington*, and the large black man behind the desk inside bid her enter. She entered. Lieutenant Washington finished a phone call while Yolanda waited.

Lieutenant Washington looked up from a folder on his desk. "Vasquez," he said.

"Washington," replied Vasquez.

"Oh," said Washington, "so you *are* a detective."

Yolanda had the impression she had not starting out well. Though, perhaps, Lieutenant Washington was trying out one of those crusty-boss-with-a-heart-of-gold images.

"You're assigned to robbery/homicide," the Lieutenant said, "You'll be doing robbery."

"I prefer homicide," Yolanda said.

"So does everyone else," said Washington. "It's a sick world out there. Detectives claw at each other to get homicide cases —then they do nothing but complain at all the sick crap they have to endure on the job. Everything's blood and body goo, but will they hang it up and take burglary or bunco? No. It's a sick world."

Lieutenant Washington no longer looked at Vasquez. She wondered if she should leave. Instead she said, "Mostly, I'd just like to avoid more decoy work," Yolanda added in what she thought was a tone of compromise.

"You'll do decoy if you're assigned it!" yelled Washington. His tone startled her at first, then Yolanda put on her war-face. Definitely the cold professional here.

Lieutenant Washington's features softened a bit. "I know I yelled. I am sorry about that. But high blood pressure makes a man yell and you should get used to it. Still." Washington shuffled some papers on his desk to no apparent purpose. "It so happens you are not on decoy. I have your first case right here," Lieutenant Washington threw her a thin folder. "You'll work it with MacGriffin. He's a twenty-year veteran. You watch. You listen. You learn the ropes from MacGriffin. Do what he does and let him take the lead at all times. He's your partner. You work with him. Got it? You follow MacGriffin at all times."

"Where's MacGriffin?" Yolanda asked.

"He's out sick—maybe a week or two," replied the Lieutenant. He had turned away from Yolanda and seemed busy with something else. After a moment or two, Yolanda took it she had been dismissed and left the office. A confusing start, but she had a case and she was not on decoy. She opened the folder Washington had given her. Inside she saw a single piece of paper. On it were written an address and the words: *Marion Wright Museum of Cultural History. Burglary. Science book.*

Well, she thought, everyone has to start somewhere.

Yolanda twice drove past the Marion Wright Museum before realizing that the coy building with the awkward addition was her destination. Upon finding the parking lot to the museum, she noticed the broken window—clearly the entry point. No, one mustn't jump to conclusions; perhaps it was an inside job. Yolanda Vasquez would not let this case get past her.

Yolanda entered the museum to find a bustle of activity.

Several uniformed officers had already arrived, and four old ladies, a security guard, and a representative of the Already Alarm Company tripped over each other explaining matters to the policemen. Yolanda approached one of the harried officers and said, "Detective Vasquez, I'm in charge here." And, indeed, she was.

Like a single organism the pack turned on her.

"It's terrible! They destroyed the mummy case!"

"I didn't hear a thing, they must have had mufflers or something."

"The warranty on this alarm expired years ago, we have no liability here."

Yolanda turned to the officer, "Arrest them all," she said. She turned to the pack, "This officer will take statements from all of you. I'll meet with you a little later. No one leave without giving a statement and seeing me first." Turning to the officer she said, "Take the security guards' statements first."

"Okay, there was just one on duty," the officer replied.

Yolanda left the babble of excuses behind and made her way through the museum to the broken window on the second floor. Had it been a murder, the LAPD would have filled the building with science-types dusting and tagging everything. Being just a burglary, a single uniformed officer fumbled with fingerprint dust near the broken window while badly wishing the department would cancel it's program in patrol officer cross-training.

"Anything?" Yolanda asked.

"I'm not too good with this stuff," the officer replied.

Yolanda showed him how to do it, and in the end mostly did it for him. On a more important crime scene a photographer would have taken a picture prior to the print lifting, but mere burglary rated no photography. The officer watched as Yolanda lifted the print and tagged it on the evidence card.

"What did they take?" Yolanda asked him.

"Just some science book on the floor above," he replied.

Yolanda heard a voice from behind her, "The museum didn't

own it. We borrowed it as part of the visiting exhibit." The voice belonged to one of the old ladies from below. She had followed Yolanda up the stairs and to the broken window. "This is very grave trouble for the museum. It damages our credibility."

"And you are?" Yolanda asked.

"Mrs. Cartwright. I'm the museum director," the woman said.

"I thought they were called curators?" Yolanda said.

"The curators handle the exhibits, I'm in charge of the museum's day to day operation."

"The thieves took only one item?" Yolanda asked.

"Yes, but they maliciously destroyed another. We may never be trusted with an important exhibit again," Mrs. Cartwright said.

Yolanda turned back to the window. Smashed through. On the floor she noted the shards of glass. A large one had heavy scratch marks on it. It looked as if the perp had cut it up with a glasscutter. Why cut it if you were going to smash it?

"How did he get up here," Yolanda asked to no one in particular.

"He climbed the rope," Mrs. Cartwright said.

"So what—he smashed the window from below and lassoed the spoon set?" Yolanda said.

Mrs. Cartwright replied in a huff, "I don't know much about detective work, but I am quite sure the Los Angles Police could put more men on this matter."

Yolanda noted the way Mrs. Cartwright put an emphasis on *men*. "Can you take me to where the item was stolen?" Yolanda said as Mrs. Cartwright recovered from her huff.

Mrs. Cartwright led Detective Vasquez through the museum. Yolanda passed the Marion Wright's extensive collection of porcelain dolls, and its not quite famous exhibit of dresses from the 1930s through the 1940s (all once owned by Mrs. Wright herself). Yolanda saw a room filled with "workman's equipment," apparently from the forties and used on some notable construction project in L.A. at that time. Yolanda followed Mrs. Cartwright up the stairs to the third floor. The museum gave over half of this floor to exhibits containing costume jewelry of the 1920s and pictures of rotund flappers. The other half housed visiting exhibits. Yolanda noted the sign announcing the current exhibit, "Death and Hope?"

"Yes," Mrs. Cartwright replied as they walked slowly up the stairs, "I believe Mr. Sabernail said it has something to do with putting a positive spin on the end of existence."

"Sabernail?" said Yolanda.

"Yes, Mr. Sabernail curates the visiting exhibits," said Mrs. Cartwright, "I've heard he is very well thought of in certain circles back East."

"What kind of name is *Sabernail*?" asked Yolanda.

"I asked him about that once ..." Mrs. Cartwright seemed to hesitate.

"Well, what did he say?"

"He said he had it changed from *Sabertooth*. Here we are, Detective Vasquez."

They had arrived at the main room of the exhibit on the hopeful prospects of death. Detective Vasquez walked through the room. The exhibit included torture devices, racks, thumbscrews, death masks, embalming liquids, framed obituaries, mourning clothes (black from Europe, white from Korea), prayers for the dead, hieroglyphs for preparing Pharaohs for the afterlife, a CIA assassination manual, a hand grenade, a bowie knife, a shot gun, cigarettes, Tibetan prayer wheels, a coffin, a miniature hearse, scenes from a slasher film, a painting of the after-life as envisioned by a "rightwing Buddhist death-cult leader," a picture of a cadaver, another of an autopsy being performed, an advertisement for a funeral parlor, and a large oven. That last took Vasquez by surprise until she read the sign next to it. A cremation oven. It pleased Yolanda to see that pictures and costumes of the Mexican Day of the Dead hung on a sidewall.

At the back of the long exhibit room, a large painted box, roughly in the shape of a person, lay in a field of broken glass. Yolanda knew the box once held an Egyptian mummy. Clearly the thieves used it to break the glass case.

"Where did you keep the mummy case before it fell?" she asked Mrs. Cartwright.

"It did not fall. We had it secured to the wall over there," Mrs. Cartwright indicated a place about ten feet from the shattered glass case.

"Secured with what?" Yolanda asked.

"Just a hook. My point is that it did not fall. We have earthquakes in California, so we secure things."

Yolanda wondered where Mrs. Cartwright thought that Detective Vasquez came from, but she let it pass.

Mrs. Cartwright stared at the broken glass saying only, "How did it get over here?"

"The perp walked it over I suppose," replied Yolanda as she looked more closely at the damaged case. "What did this display case contain?"

"You should ask Mr. Sabernail about items in the exhibit," Mrs. Cartwright replied. She seemed a bit wary about the case's former occupant.

"Where is Mr. Sabernail?"

"He took the weekend off, working on his investment portfolio he said. I left several messages on his answering machine. But he is not always easy to find on his time off."

Yolanda thought about the absence of the curator. Interesting. She said, "But you do know what the glass case contained."

"Yes," replied Mrs. Cartwright.

"Well, what was it?" asked Yolanda.

"It is written on the case," Mrs. Cartwright offered.

Irritated by the woman's reticence, Yolanda looked at the small sign on the base of the broken case. It read: *"The Compendium of Necromantic Sciences."*

A NICK IN TIME

"A loser."

Though the dealer referred only to Nick Sabernail's latest hand, the phrase had a rather summary sound to it. For the last eight hours, Nick had sat at the ten-dollar minimum blackjack table of the Lucky Eleven Casino in Las Vegas. He had watched his fellow players come and go. His chips had just gone.

Nick held the seat to the dealer's far left, allowing him to observe the other players and pay only scant attention to his cards. Blackjack requires concentration only if you are good at it. To the dealer's far right sat a squat man with hairy ears and a *Born To Porn* t-shirt. The cards had been kind to him—up two hundred in the last two hours. Mr. Born-to-Porn had noticed that Nick Sabernail had not been doing so well and shouted at him from across the table, "Guess I got your money over here."

Funny. Nick said quietly back, "Guess I'll just follow you out to the parking lot." That shut up Mr. Born-to-Porn and earned Nick another nasty stare from the floorwalker.

Next to the gnomish wise-cracker sat an attractive woman of about twenty-five or so. On arriving at the table she had declared her name to be "Skye" and that she had come to "party like a rock star." Nick assumed this meant she intended to bang groupies, shoot heroin, and pass out drunk in her own excrement. Instead she played blackjack; circling her fist over her head and whooping with every win. For a while she won a lot, and kept Mr. Born-to-Porn transfixed with her antics. An hour into the performance the hairy gnome tried a subtle seduction: "I got a pole in my pocket if you want to try some pole dancing."

"She'll lose her grip on anything less than three inches," Nick said.

"Loser," the woman said. With that she jinxed herself. An hour later she whooped no more and just watched sullenly as her money flowed to the house like the Nile to the sea.

Next to Mrs. Party-Like-A-Rock-Star sat your classic blue haired old lady. She wore an *Elvis Lives* T-shirt and smelt so strongly of tobacco you could roll her up and smoke her. She didn't smoke at the table but her blackjack play did. She had won over a thousand dollars in the last half hour. She ordered drinks but didn't drink them. The shot glasses just stacked up next to her chips. She committed only one sin at a time, but did that one well. Not that she enjoyed it. She was so tense she snapped chips in her clinched fingers. She shouted her instructions to the dealer. "Hit me!" she screamed. A temptation the dealer resisted. He fed her cards instead. Good ones.

Next to Old-Lady-Elvis-Lives had sat a Japanese man flanked by two pretty Japanese women. He had bet the maximum every hand and never failed to double down. Nick felt so bad at the guy's losses he considered giving Mr. Double-Down some gaming advice. Nick made a suggestion, but the fellow didn't seem to understand, and at this stage, Nick giving advice on blackjack felt rather like the captain of the Titanic recommending restaurants in New York. Mr. Double-Down departed with two thousand dollars less, and two women fewer, than he'd had on arrival.

Then there was Nick Sabernail.

"A loser," the dealer said.

The words jolted Nick Sabernail from his lethargy. He looked down and saw he had only one chip left. He pitched it to the blue-haired lady, "Invest this for me," Nick said as he rose to go. Mr. Born-to-Porn smiled a wicked grin at Nick and started to say something. The glint in Nick's eyes made the words catch in the hairy gnome's throat, and the fellow started a coughing fit instead.

Nick walked through the Lucky Eleven, taking in the scene as he left it at last. The air hummed with buzzes, beeps, and chirps from the slot machines, as if filled with the mating calls of impatient birds. Loud *ding-a-lings* announced winners and suppressed the groans of the silent majority. Lights flashed the promise of lucre. Asian women stood patiently behind their Sic Bo tables offering exotic Far Eastern ways of getting fleeced. The Lucky Eleven small timers sat hunched over their cards, looking up at the croupiers as if at Tarot dealers. Tell me my fortune. Please. "A loser!"

Between desert and air conditioning, the air of the Lucky Eleven was so dry that sweat evaporated before staining your clothes. Nick licked his lips, but his ration of body moisture had left him with his last bourbon. His dry tongue licked sandpaper lips.

In the air hung a faint smell of urine; someone unwilling to break his lucky streak for a potty break. Isn't Vegas grand?

Nick Sabernail knew he was no longer a part of this pathetic scene. He had hit bottom, and he was on his way back. His only bets now would be with the road back to L.A.

Sabernail stepped out of the air-conditioned discomfort of the casino, into an August dawn in Vegas. Dawn? Had he been here that long? No matter. He strode confidently to the valet parking attendant. The Lucky Eleven might be the last stop for losers on the way to being beat up by pawnbrokers, but they still insisted on parking your car for you. Nick saw his man: a twenty-year-old kid in a red vest. The kid had the look of someone who drove fine automobiles fifty feet at a time.

Sabernail approached the valet; the kid dropped a quarter. As the kid reached down for it, a foot flashed in front of his face covering the coin. Nick's foot.

"Fifty dollars it's tails," a voice said. It was Nick's voice, but the words had come so fast to his lips that he looked around for a moment to make sure no one else had spoken them.

The valet looked up at the thirty-something man with the quick feet. "Right, fifty," the kid said. Nick moved his foot.

After paying the snot-nosed little runt his fifty dollars, Nick waited for his car. He endured the snickers of the other valets, whose yearly income he now guessed to be several times his own. The kid drove up in Nick's 69 Thunderbird convertible. A classic car whose paint job and general state of repair suggested ownership by a compulsive car abuser. The kid exited the car with a snicker on his face. As Sabernail reached into his pocket for a tip, the kid shoved a fist inches away from Sabernail's face.

"A hundred dollars you can't guess if I got one or two keys in my hand," the kid said.

The phrase *your on: two!* galloped hard from the back of Nick's head, but he only said, "No bet."

So Nick Sabernail was back on track. He rode top-down in the opening of day along the road back to Los Angeles. He had bottomed out, but he was on his way back. He had said no to the kid's bet, and that had to be a good sign. Okay, so the kid *did* have two keys in his hand; it still had to be a good thing he turned the bet down. Nick Sabernail rode back to L.A. as the sun rose behind him. With light traffic, and doing a hundred and twenty most of the way, he beat his own personal best back to his L.A. apartment.

Still, he would be late to work again.

Nick opened his door to find his answering machine impatiently flashing its *messages waiting* light. The first four he could safely ignore—these were from bookies to whom Nick owed so much money they could only be calling to inquire about his health. Such messages all started with violent obscenities and ended with pleas about their kids orthodontic work. Nick's favorite bookie, Sid Pauli, had called at two o'clock in the morning. Nick figured Sid would have been pleased to know that Nick hadn't been just jerking around when he missed the call, but rather trying to win some money to pay Sid off. Nick almost returned Sid's call to tell him that. Almost.

Of more concern were the calls that had started around seven thirty that morning (while the new—reformed—Nick Sabernail drove back from Vegas) and had come in every ten minutes or so, like telephonic chimes to rouse the dead. The first one came from Mrs. Cartwright: "Oh it's terrible, it is just terrible. You must come in at once." She had declined to say what was terrible, and Mrs. Cartwright was prone to panic, so Sabernail fixed his breakfast and listened to the other messages.

The second came from Mrs. Cartwright: "Mr. Sabernail, please pick up the line! We have an emergency here. It's terrible! Glass is everywhere. If you can't come in at least call."

Terrible and glass everywhere. The third, fourth, and fifth messages all hailed from Mrs. Cartwright, all equally earnest, and all just as informative. Nick took a long shower. Mrs. Cartwright emergencies required a clear head. She had once called the police to report a picture stolen from its frame, only to find out from Nick that the frame itself was the artwork on display. It had taken Nick almost an hour of explaining the post-modern concept of "art-that-is-the-absence-of-art" before the Mrs. Cartwright let the police go. Mrs. Cartwright had some old-fashion ideas about art. She liked frames with *pictures* in them. If she called five times in one hour—and to report terrible seas of glass at that—then Nick certainly needed a shower.

Nick needed a long hot shower, but he hadn't paid his gas bill in three months, so he took a short, cold one instead. After toweling off with his one good towel (originally one of the Marriott Hotel's many bad towels), Nick dressed for work in sneakers, jeans, a black T-shirt and a florescent green leisure jacket. Not his idea of style, and not anyone else's— but sometimes Vegas doesn't leave you with much. Nick drank some cold coffee and headed out the door.

On his way to work in his Thunderbird, he listened to his tape of *Simon Diverge and the Wild Homunculi.* Although already ten o'clock in the morning, the traffic plodded along as if just girding up for rush hour. Most of the drivers in the cars around Sabernail spoke into cell phones as they made their meandering way. Several consulted in-car computers. Nick wondered what useful traffic intelligence such devices could pick up. Could any driver stuck in this steel molasses actually extradite himself to some alternate route? And if one could do one's business in the car, why not keep the car in the garage? With a laptop, a mobile phone, a pager and an air-conditioner one practically had an office in the car already. Put a mini fridge next to the driver side window, a fax machine under the seat, and a carbon monoxide detector on the hood, and the garage would serve better than a downtown office. Or at least better than the downtown streets. Nick considered a marketing plan for his new "stationary-mobile office of the future." The trick lay in luring prospective buyers into an L.A. commute.

A rather too cheerful fellow in grubby clothes bounded toward Nick's car wielding a squeegee and water squirter like God's answer to Man's faults. Nick flicked on the window washers and shot the man a look that said, "I got water, thanks." The Squeegee Man offered Nick a look reeking of accusation and woe. Where lived charity in this cold town? A man offers a service, not begging mind you, offering a service —clean, sterile windows, done with natural, biodegradable water—and does the world offer its hand? No, the world does not. The world flicks on the windshield wipers and gives a nasty look. The Squeegee Man began a little dance there in the traffic, spraying his precious supply of water over his head. Maybe a show. The nasty world craved entertainment. Nick considered chucking a quarter at the guy, then looked for something bigger. Quarters being unable to do much damage, and manhole covers being too heavy to lift, Nick had to just sit and watch. So Squeegee Man continued his Dance Against the Unjust World without critical response from Nick Sabernail.

"Hey! Hey!" Squeegee Man shouted at a blonde woman in a

Jeep Cherokee Sport Utility Tank, "I got movement baby! You want some movement?"

The panicked looking woman hit an "additional feature" button on her land-crawler, setting off a siren loud enough to wake the dead. The siren's sound consisted of a greatest hits selection of car alarm noises and so startled Squeegee Man that he dropped his equipment. Still, ears covered, he continued his dance.

"Tunes! Tunes!" he said, "I got tunes now."

Nick creeped on past this street theater in the steel and glass sludge of L.A. traffic. In these streets Nick belonged. Here he lived, nearly every morning, in a community of immobility. If the cars ever stopped completely, really stopped—no more movement at all so forget about it—then the members of this community would abandon their rolling cubicles and actually speak to each other. They would say things like, "so it finally happened," and "traffic really sucks," and such things. Not the stuff of vivid conversation, but still face-to-face contact. This never happened though. The city planners kept the crawl just fast enough, and the dead-in-your-tracks stops just brief enough, to keep everyone pinned to their seats, safely belted in place. So instead of pure human speech, the little community of the perpetually road-bound spoke to each other in dueling radio stations. Pop tunes emanated from each car announcing the inhabitant's favorite musical variety. Each selection a message. The message always: *this is me; I'm someone who listens to the Crack Divers at ear splitting decibels.* Or, if not the Crack Divers, then Hank Williams Jr., or The Aztec Hitmen, or even Mozart. Real loud on Mozart, to show that you are educated, cultured, rich, and were deafened at Woodstock. Every now and then a low-rider flowed through the slow steel river, playing a song whose lyrics remained forever unnoticed, but whose base beat could be heard in Cayuga Canyon. All the other radios turned down in deference to the loudest irritant on the street, each driver wondering, "What does that guy want to prove anyway?"

22

And Nick? When he really wished to establish his presence in the tribe, he put on his special recording of Alistair Cook's Introductions to Masterpiece Theatre punctuated by audio enhanced balo-balo-bird mating calls. Turned up to window-bending volumes. Not much to listen to, but boy the heads did turn.

Today, though, Nick just creeped along. Foot on the brake; foot off the brake. Is that my car squeaking? No, that's the guy in front of me. No, it is my car! And so on. Off to the side of the road, at a corner under a sign promising either tattoos or tacos, two cars had collided. Their drivers alternated screaming at each other with yelling into their cell phones. Suddenly, one of them grabbed the other's cell phone and hurled it towards the street. It landed on the seat beside Nick. He picked it up.

"Hello?" he asked.

"Norman? Hit him Norman! Just hit him! I'll call the lawyer!" a woman's voice said over the phone.

"Norman will have to call you back," Nick said. He looked around and noticed the car stopped next to him had an open passenger window. Nick tossed the cell phone onto the driver's seat where it landed beside the driver's phone. Looking back just behind him, Nick could see the two men still arguing on the side of the road. They apparently fought now over the one remaining cell phone. One had lost the contents of his briefcase—an act of vengeance for the earlier cell phone shot-put. Looking to his left, Nick saw the man in the car next to him talking into the wrong cell phone. He seemed very confused. Inching along on roads threatening to turn into parking lots, Nick Sabernail could not help but think that everyone in this town would be better off if they could just move where they were going next to where they were now.

Approaching the parking lot of the Marion Wright, Sabernail noticed several police cars. Since fewer than twelve patrol cars occupied the lot, he assumed that no one had been shot. Since he could see no ambulance, he assumed Mrs.

Cartwright had not stroked out. One police car denoted a traffic stop. Three meant a traffic stop on a bicycle. Four police cars indicated assault and battery. Twelve cars meant murder. Fifteen cars warned of a domestic dispute. Over twenty must be a murder at a donut shop. What about two? Had to be a robbery. But what could anyone have stolen in the Marion Wright?

Nick entered the building. Joe Freener, the night guard, approached, "Mr. Sabernail! Did you hear what happened?"

"What? Someone sold Mrs. Cartwright into white slavery?" Nick replied.

"I had nothing to do with it, I didn't hear a thing," Joe said.

Nick barely noticed him as they walked toward the stairs. "You know, Joe, I'm not sure that line works for the security guard. You're supposed to have something to do with it when the place gets robbed. Unless you mean that you weren't the one who sold Mrs. Cartwright into white slavery."

Finding no joy here, Joe pealed away as Nick started up the stairs. Then she appeared. Coming down the stairs in sensible shoes, slacks and a .38 pistol. A very, very woman indeed.

"The museum is closed this morning," the pistol-toting woman said to Nick as he climbed the stairs. Behind her, Mrs. Cartwright appeared.

"That's him! That's him! That's Mr. Sabernail!" she said. It sounded like an accusation—and the look on the armed woman's face suggested that she had taken it that way.

"This is Detective Vasquez of the LAPD," Mrs. Cartwright said.

"I'm Nick Sabernail of the Five and Dime," Nick said, offering his hand.

"Where have you been Mr. Sabernail?" asked Yolanda, "I understand Mrs. Cartwright has been trying to get a hold of you."

For just a moment Nick's mind flashed on the image of Mrs. Cartwright clutching him in passion's embrace—a bit scary that.

"Call me Nick," Nick said.

"So where have you been Mr. Nick Sabernail?" Yolanda asked.

"Well," said Nick, "in bed, then the shower, a few minutes in the kitchen, and then on the road to work."

"Didn't you get my messages?" asked Mrs. Cartwright.

"Yes," Nick said. "And let me just say you have a lovely phone voice; though you were a bit sparse on informative content." Nick noticed Detective Yolanda Vasquez sizing him up. Was she admiring him, or just looking for a good place to hit him with a baton? Nick rather wished at this moment that he had pawned the fluorescent green jacket and kept the black leather one. But then he would have had to go without electricity as well as hot water. Still, Nick figured the detective must be warming up to him. Nick was an optimist like that.

"Perhaps you could just tell us where you were when the museum was robbed," Yolanda said.

"Sure," Nick said. In the long ensuing pause Nick noticed how fixed Yolanda's eyes remained. She looked at him dead on, nothing shy about her. Well, she wouldn't be shy, not as an LAPD cop. The thin blue line has to crack gang-banger heads and all. Nick noticed her hair too. Nice hair. Dark as night; and thick. Nice shoulder-length cut as well.

"Well?" Detective Vasquez asked. For a moment Nick worried that she had been reading his mind.

"Well what?" asked Nick in all innocence.

"Where were you at the time of the robbery?"

"Oh. What time did it occur?"

Detective Vasquez looked at Nick as if trying to tell if he was cagey or just plain dim-witted. "Why don't you just tell me where you were last night?"

"Okay," Nick said, "but then can I ask a question?"

"Let's start with where you were."

"Vegas, then the road from Vegas, then my apartment," Nick said.

"Were you seen in any of these places?" Yolanda asked.

"Sure, lots of people saw me."

"Do you have their names?"

"No," Nick said, "they were all driving past me to Vegas at ninety miles an hour." Yolanda stared at him for a moment. Nick continued, "now my question: What got stolen?"

Before Yolanda could answer Mrs. Cartwright jumped in. "Oh Mr. Sabernail, it is terrible, just terrible!"

"I guessed that from your messages," Nick said, "but just which terrible things did we lose?" Mrs. Cartwright turned and headed towards the main exhibition hall. The other two followed after her.

"You're the curator, Mr. Sabernail?" Yolanda asked.

"Nick, I'm Nick the curator," Nick said.

"Your collection has a lot of silverware," Yolanda said.

"And dolls, lots of dolls, you might like the dolls." Yolanda said nothing, so Nick continued, "I mean, women sometimes like … I mean they often have dolls. That is, had dolls, before they were women—that is girls, when they were girls." At that moment Nick Sabernail flashed on a thought: If he had worn his other shoes today he would now have a steel-toed boot to chew through.

"You like working with dolls, Mr. Sabernail?" Yolanda asked.

"Nick. Like a scratch, only small," Nick said. "Dolls are fine, not what I'd fill a museum with if it were up to me, but I like dolls fine. The fact is, I'm only the visiting exhibits curator. Linda Tanish keeps the spoons and dolls."

They entered the main exhibit room. Through the ghoulish exhibit they walked, stopping at last in front of the smashed display case. They all stood for a moment. Mrs. Cartwright seemed ready to cry. Nick pointed to the sarcophagus, "He's out of place for a start."

"I'll put that down as a clue then," Yolanda said.

Mrs. Cartwright turned on Nick, "Mr. Sabernail, you assured us that our security was adequate."

"Actually," Nick said, "I assured you nothing would get stolen—and that because we couldn't get anything someone might want."

Yolanda turned to Mrs. Cartwright, "Am I to understand that you consulted Mr. Sabernail on increasing security, and he advised against it."

"That's right," Mrs. Cartwright said, sensing suspicion turning towards another, "he advised against it."

"Yes," Nick added, "so we re-invested the security improvement fund into another coffeemaker instead." Nick looked at the glass case. His reputation lay shattered in that glass. It wasn't much of a reputation. Nothing you'd pay cash for. But you could get credit on it from time to time, and it was all gone now.

"The item missing," said Yolanda, "it was worth a lot?"

Nick stared at the case.

"Mr. Sabernail?" Yolanda said, "Nick?"

"Right." Nicked snapped out of his thoughts. "Worth a lot? Who would buy it? I'm sure it is not on any under-world collector's to-steal list."

"But they passed up everything else to get to it," Yolanda said.

"Oh yeah, they passed up a hundred and forty spoon sets and a cremation oven to get to it," Nick said.

"You can sell spoons," Yolanda said.

She had him there. You could sell spoons. But why would anyone want that book? "Well, it is rare—I suppose you could sell it on that account alone," Nick said.

Yolanda looked at Nick Sabernail for a long moment. "You won't be leaving town, will you Mr. Sabernail?"

Nick looked at her, "Well, not unless I go to Vegas for a weekend and ..." Detective Vasquez just stared at him. "That is to say," Nick continued, "no ... not ... no, right here, in town, that's where I'll be." He looked at Mrs. Cartwright's hard stare. "I'll be right here, looking for work."

THE LONG HOURS

Victor Drakan lived in a single giant room on the second floor of a small building in the warehouse district. Although the city of Los Angeles zoned the area exclusively for light industrial use, it served principally as a holding pen for poor immigrants of ambiguous legal status working in the garment business. If their "employers" would let them out at night, the citizens of this village of warehouses would form an impressive international community: Guatemalans, Salvadorans, Mexicans, Koreans, Vietnamese, and most recently a wave of Chinese families. But even the few who had keys to their "homes" dared not venture out often onto the streets. The only thing they feared more than living in a sewing factory in the United States was the prospect of returning to their country of origin.

Drakan just liked a quite place to work. Within his warehouse apartment he lived in a maze of glass. Glass beakers from the Scientific Equipment Manufacturers of Lawrence, Ohio filled tables and shelves throughout the large empty space. The collection included every shape and size of glass beaker imaginable. Some used the English system of content notation, others the metric; some had no markings at all. A few had biohazard warnings, others names of chemicals stenciled on them. They had all been stolen from the manufacturers' trucks in the last four months.

Glass tubes and large metal vats lay in the south side corner of the large room. Across from these lay two battery operated generators and enough electrical equipment to keep half of the L.A. building inspectors busy for a year should they stumble into the home of Victor Drakan. Although to the unappreciative eye it might appear a random mess, in fact, Dr. Frankenstein himself could learn a thing or two about space management from Drakan. In the north corner of the room, partitioned by a few portable screens, Drakan had arranged his actual living quarters. This consisted of a single chair, a cot covered by two sheets, a hot plate, two small shelves lined with tomato soup (Drakan's only food), an industrial size bottle of antacid, and a desk covered in papers. Books lay all over the floor. When Drakan walked in the living section of his apartment, his feet never touched the floor. He strode majestically on three uneven layers of books.

On this evening Drakan sat on his swivel chair, which sat on the three layers of books, which sat on the floor of his apartment/workshop. He read solely by the light of a desk lamp; all the other lights fed into a *clapper* which allowed Drakan to illuminate or darken his workshop with two claps of his hand. He called this a security measure, but in truth he just liked to play at Moses. On his most noble day he hardly struck a Moses-like figure, but tonight he looked like a pale, naked, hunched ferret. For three days straight he had read from the book so recently liberated from the Marion Wright. He had barely turned his blood-shot eyes away from the tome long enough to grab a few hours sleep and force down a can of cold tomato soup. He lived now like some confused bibliophile vampire. Yet not in vain had he studied his pilfered book. A horrible truth had finally come to light. Drakan spoke of this into his tape recorder.

"August 20, I have made the most portentous discovery," Drakan spoke into the darkness, "a discovery I can only credit to my brilliant coup of emancipating the *Compendium*. As I have long suspected, animal blood will not react sufficiently with the sub-chemical base I had previously discovered. Just like alchemist of yore, I too have now found the missing element to the process of hypto-reanimation diatronics. I stand now as the last in the long line of unheralded greatness

—and I shall finally realize the promise of the un-sung science by—damn!" The tape recorder stopped—out of tape.

Drakan fidgeted with it a moment, then searched his desk for another tape. Most were already filled with past ruminations, but he found a blank tape in the bottom drawer. He excavated two layers of books to open the drawer and wrestled for several minutes with the manufacturer's packaging before freeing the cassette and putting it into his recorder. By that time he had lost his train of thought.

"Hypto-reanimation diatronic process," he spoke again into the recorder, "has been discovered by me, as by other ... uh, wait." Drakan re-wound the tape, and spoke again: "Now again I can make my bid for the eternal verity of ... of ... the un-stuck science—I mean ... damn!"

Well, even Einstein occasionally misspelled his lecture notes. Newton sometimes forgot to carry the two. Darwin once up-chucked on his book proofs. Drakan put down the recorder. He sat in the dark. The full weight of what was now required of him finally came to sit upon his tightly pinched shoulders. Neither animal fluid, nor fluid from a dead person, nor fluid from a living person would do. Undeath lay between life and death, and only in that space could its means be found.

In the waning hours of evening a day later, Janet Giallo walked home from the coffee shop where she worked. She had missed her bus and did not feel like enduring the leers of the two men still waiting at the bus stop. They knew her from the neighborhood, and they knew what she did on the side to make the rent money. Janet had changed from her waitress uniform at work, and, yes, she had changed into something, well, nice. Or more exactly something that suggested that she could be very nice herself, for a slight fee. Janet thought she might be up to making a bit of quick money tonight, but a few minutes on the street and a few knowing sneers from the local guys had put the mood right away. Her feet hurt and she did not feel like company—especially the company that pays for company. Besides, she was trying to give it up. She had a regular job now. And while the Indigo Street Family Restaurant had not yet proven a launch pad to better living for its servers, even her most intrusive customers stayed completely outside her body. That was worth a cut in income.

So Janet Giallo walked fast and held tight to her virtue; and if she had walked just a little faster, or held on just a little tighter, she would have made it home safe. But as she was about to cross Ortega Street, just a block from her apartment complex, she was nearly trampled down by a skinny, pale man wearing all black. When he ran into her he jumped back three feet in shock. He then looked her up and down as if trying to picture from what planet she might hail. This pinched little man offered the most ineptly obvious scrutiny Janet had ever suffered.

"And I can help you, how?" Janet asked with all the irritation of a waitress with sore feet.

The man stood stock still for a moment. Apparently, he had not expected language skills from this particular form of life. "I'm looking for a woman," the pale man said hurriedly, "that is, I'm looking for women. I mean I'm not looking for more than one—I just need one—just no particular one. I mean, I just want one woman." He seemed triumphal in this finish.

"So?" asked Janet, slightly amused.

The pale man just waved his hands palm up in front of her as if to say "see—see." When Janet just smiled, he tried speaking again. "I need a woman who might be like you. I mean, I don't know which street I should actually be on. I want the right street, where I can find something like ..." at this point he just waved his hands up and down before Janet again, as if genuflecting to some strange new idol.

Janet laughed beneath her breath. The pale man's face looked like it had been too close to a slamming door that had squished all his features into a triangle. Still, looks were not really the issue, turnover rate mattered more at the moment. Janet saw this newcomer as good for two minutes at the most. Perhaps he would even take her advice on the standard fee-structure.

"New at this?" Janet asked in what she knew to be a rather comic version of the seductive voice.

"Oh no," the pale man assured her, "I've been driving around for almost two hours."

"I meant," Janet continued, a bit less seductively, "that you're looking for some action and you're new at trying to find any." She studied his perplexed look for a moment. "Did you break your piggy-bank before you came out here?" Janet asked in a voice normally reserved for very young children.

Her question seemed to confuse the pale man. "Pigs won't work, I need a human," he said.

Janet began to feel that the initiation process might not be worth the trouble. "I'm glad to hear there won't be any pigs, but I meant: did you bring a lot of money?"

The man reached into his black coat and pulled out a great handful of cash. "I'm not sure of the usual price. I'd like to pay the usual price," he said.

Janet stared at the money. Gas, electricity, a day off from filling coffee cups; it all lay right there in the pale man's hands. Janet gathered herself. "Did you have any particular place in mind?" she asked the pale man.

"I have a van," he said.

"Well, that's coming prepared. You're practically a Boy Scout."

The two of them, the tired semi-pro and the unlikely Boy Scout, walked together around the corner to the back doors of a black van. Janet watched carefully as the pale man opened the doors. She could still run away if anyone tried to leap out at her. The van proved empty and the pale man had the nervous jitters, so Janet entered the van as the pale man followed and closed the door behind them.

In the pitch dark of the van, Janet realized that the windows admitted no light at all. The pale man clapped twice and bright light illuminated the van from the floor. In the odd yellow light the pale man looked suddenly sinister. From a bag by the door he produced a long shaft like a cattle prod.

"You ain't sticking that in me!" Janet shouted.

"For science!" the man yelled as he lunged for her.

Janet managed to dodge the cattle prod. The tip of the long shaft hit the side of the van. Janet saw sparks fly and heard a *zzzaaaap!* Nobody had to tell her twice that the time to get was now. She lunged for the door.

The pale man spun around so fast he stepped on the cattle prod giving himself a major hotfoot. "Owwww!!" he screamed.

Janet echoed his cry with "You crazy freak!" She tried the door, but it would not open. She looked behind her. The man, looking desperate in the strange light, raised the metal shaft above his head to strike down at her. It's tip hit the roof of the van and sparks flew. He jumped back in surprise. Janet put her weight to the door. Still it would not budge. She looked behind her again. Again the man held the shaft up—this time high and to his right. Janet yelled and put her spiked heel right into the middle of his forehead. The man fell backwards; sparks flew. Janet gave up on the door. She grabbed the bag that had hidden the man's weapon. It felt heavy. As the man righted himself, now with the impression of a heel in his forehead, Janet lunged at him with the heavy bag. She hit him square on, but the tip of the cattle prod caught her mid-section. The electricity coursed through her body. Her mouthed gapped open. She had put up a good fight. Now it ended.

ALL ALONG THE WATCHTOWER

Detective Yolanda Vasquez had worked for all of three hours on the Case of the Missing *Compendium* before Lieutenant Washington informed her that that was one hour and fifty minutes too long. L.A. is a busy town and a lot of the persons in it are busy stealing things. So Yolanda quickly received further assignments. A woman on Downy Street had the entire contents of her bedroom stolen over the weekend by her lover —also a woman. The girlfriend had further complicated The Case of the Lesbian Looter by leaving the stolen bedroom in a U-Haul outside her own apartment, and it too had been stolen before morning. The paper work on cases like this can drive a sane woman to drink.

The very day Yolanda met Nick Sabernail she also meet Hunter Coyote, a homeless man robbed of over $5,000 cash by two street thugs. Apparently, without rent to pay, he had managed to save a considerable sum of L.A.'s generosity. The Case of the Prudent Panhandler soon moved over for a more serious crime. Joy riders stole Lieutenant Washington's car, leaving it near a shopping mall. There, a group of thieves re-stole it and drove it through the display window of Channel's House of Lingerie, whereupon the thieves rushed the shop's stock, making off with enough frilly nothings to clothe several cable television casts. Such did the Case of the Ironic Joy Riders seamlessly segue into the Case of the Underwear Underworld.

Upon finding the good Lieutenant's car, Yolanda proceeded

to investigate a grave robbery at the Happy Endings Estates. Someone had dug up one Leonard Spitzkouski after he had rested peacefully, if not permanently, for almost ten years. The Spitzkouski family had no enemies, nor could they recall any dispute over Leonard's interment. The manager of Happy Endings thought "corpse lovers" had done the deed. This seemed unlikely to Yolanda, but then so did the idea that somewhere in L.A. one could find a market for dead bodies.

These represent only the more colorful of Detective Vasquez's first week of cases on the robbery desk of the Fountain Avenue Precinct. Most of her duties did not rise to this level of excitement. Her daily task required that she fill out crime reports so that the victims could make an insurance claim. She might have thought this a useful occupation at least, until she noticed the same young men returning time and again to report robberies. Being a detective she looked into the matter and discovered that they patrolled their neighborhoods finding out what might have been stolen, and then filed police reports on those items so that they could make claims against the recovered property room of the LAPD. All in all, Yolanda's first week made her feel like a mid-level functionary of some giant swindle.

◆ ◆ ◆

At home, Yolanda's work did not end. She lived alone in a two-bedroom apartment. Upon arriving back from the Fountain Avenue Precinct she changed clothes and set to cleaning the apartment. Sometimes Yolanda left the apartment tidy but un-cleaned for weeks; sometimes she cleaned it top to bottom twice in the same day. It all depended on how she felt. Tonight, Yolanda cleaned. She took the rug covering the hardwood floor to the balcony and beat it mercilessly with her police baton. Two hands on the baton, she pounded the rug. What little dust it had collected since the day before flew off the rug only to settle on it again. After this she vacuumed the floor where the rug had lain and replaced the rug. She took the glasses out of the cupboards and placed each one in the dishwasher. Halfway through this ritual it occurred to her that music might be nice. She went to her stereo and turned on some nondescript local pop-music station. She returned to the glasses. The dishwasher filled, she turned it on. She returned to the stereo and switched the station to KAZZ, a local jazz station.

Yolanda remade her bed, seeing to it that the sheets stretched tight across the mattress. You could bounce a quarter off of that bed. She turned off the stereo. She thought about dusting the windowsills but decided she hadn't the heart for it. She thought about dusting the picture frames. This would be easy since all her pictures but one still sat on the floor, each leaning against the wall below the space she had selected for them four months ago when she had first moved into this apartment.

Yolanda turned on her TV set. She sat in the chair across from the set and thought she should be hungry. She was not hungry. She got up and went to the refrigerator. She removed a tray of strawberries and a bottle of compressed whipped cream. She returned to the chair across from the television. She carefully sprayed a top hat of whipped cream onto the pointed head of a strawberry. She ate the strawberry, from the side, careful to get half strawberry and half whipped cream leaving an equal sized selection of strawberry and whipped cream for the next bite. She took a second bite of strawberry and prepared the next with whipped cream. She noticed something. Something very different tonight from last night. She put down the strawberries and whipped cream and walked over to the television. She turned the sound completely down and returned to her chair. The soundless blue light of the television played off her face and illuminated the room around her in its incandescent blue glow. Yolanda sprayed a top hat of whipped cream onto the pointed head of a strawberry. She took another half bite. Yolanda ate strawberries at home.

♦ ♦ ♦

At the office Yolanda threw herself into her work. Just two weeks on her new assignment and she finally had her stride. The District Attorney had requested some twenty-five interviews relating to a case in preparation. Yolanda set about gathering the evidence needed to convict one Jerome Blankly of Simi Valley. By the day's end Yolanda had interviewed seven persons by phone, and five more in person, and typed the notes from each interview. At five minutes to four that afternoon the assistant DA assigned to the Blankly case called to say thank you very much, but Mr. Blankly had pled to a lesser charge and, no, he would not need those interviews done.

The next day Yolanda received another set of interview requests from the DA's office. She took her time with these.

Had Yolanda taken stock of her career in the two-weeks since her first day at her new assignment, she would have judged that the market was active but that her portfolio was under-capitalized and trading below its worth.

Then a great blessing for the career-minded detective occurred. The same person, who was likely a stranger to them both, had killed two women, strangers to each other. That meant serial killer. Yolanda, though a lowly pusher of paper, nevertheless attended Chief Detective Harmon's general briefing.

Harmon was a big round man and he spoke to a large room of cops. "We have two victims so far," the detective began, "we expect to find more. The first one found was one Juniper Beth Conners of Hollywood by way of Yorba Linda. Twenty-eight, five foot one and a professional street walker." Harmon spoke before a bulletin board. As he described the case he periodically pointed to one picture or another on the board. His pointing seemed to correspond to nothing in particular on the board since he stood well in front of it and always pointed at something as he had moved onto another topic. Yolanda found this distracting, but being a fine detective she sorted matters out as he went.

"She died nasty," Detective Harmon continued, "or at least she got nastied up shortly after death. We've established she died between nine p.m. and midnight on August 16. The other victim is a thirty-four year old semi-pro prostitute named Janet Giallo. She went missing on the evening of August 14. Both victims died of heart failure brought on by loss of blood. Both showed signs of a struggle, and burn marks, possibly made by an electrical device used to immobilize them. Maybe a tazar-gun or a cattle prod. Both show rope burns indicative of having been restrained, probably by hospital straps, or something of the like."

"Any sign of rape?" asked one particularly green detective, obviously bucking for attention, promotion, the admiration of his peers, and ultimately a studio contract as a technical advisor. Harmon looked at the man as if torn between shooting him and spanking the little runt.

"I'll give the briefing, you take notes and ask questions if I miss anything, okay sonny?" Harmon said. Gathering his forces he continued, "No signs of rape. Now get this; this is the good part. The perp drained them of all their blood. I mean, they were all shriveled up after death. The medical examiner says it was done with a pump—like doctors use or something. We have two of them sucked dry, so that means serial killer. The killer, he dropped them both in a high-powered cleaning solvent prior to ditching the bodies, so we have no forensics."

"Do we know the killer was male?" asked the bullish young detective of the rape question. Yolanda answered him without ever looking up from her pad. "Almost all serial killers are men," she said.

"But that's a presumption. And do we know there was only one—one perp?" the young detective asked.

Detective Harmon looked on wishing he had an Uzi. What can you do with aggressive young detectives but strangle them at birth? His ulcer was kicking acid all the way up to his tonsils while these little puck-hounds compared F.B.I. seminar notes. Harmon cleared his throat to regain the attention of the room. It was like churning acid with a blender, and his face turned beet red. When he spoke next his voice squeaked for a moment. "You got the particulars in the briefing folders," someone laughed at Harmon's cracking voice, "the bit about the blood draining is departmental information only." Harmon paused for effect. "We got some sort of weirdo vampire loony-bird serial killer here. We got two bodies dead inside a week with no clues. Research suggests that if we don't catch this guy … or guys … or folks, or whatever—real soon—then we are going to get a lot more bloodless bodies. This case is top priority. Check your own case files. See if anything you've covered recently might connect to loony doctors, vampire lovers, blood sucking or anything else weird like this."

Returning to her paper packed desk Yolanda thought about Harmon's instructions. She knew of a case involving something strange in a vampire-like way. Coincidentally enough, it also concerned a rather strange individual. Yolanda took her lunch bag out of her desk drawer. She had earlier turned down several offers to join fellow detectives for lunch. They had each said they wanted to go over the new serial killer case with her, but she worried that the topic might stray. One group had included Tom Delaney and that had been enough to encourage eating at the desk. Truth to tell, Yolanda found it hard to deal with the come-ons and innuendo that always accompanied shoptalk among the mostly male detectives. The same had held true as a patrol officer. She put up a tough front. No one ever knew they had worn down Yolanda Vasquez. No one ever thought of her as a spoilsport or a girl scout either. Her peers knew her as tough and thick-skinned. She gave as good as she got and could take care of herself just fine, thank you.

But the suggestive patter and locker room humor wore her down all the same. She might answer an off color remark with a well-placed jab, of wit or an elbow, but after the twentieth time of the day she jabbed like a punch drunk fighter. Somewhere inside her a voice asked why she had to fight the felons of Los Angeles *and* her peers. She had by now lost her bearings. She could not tell: was she hypersensitive, over-stressed, or just living in the land of the louts? The worst of it lay in second-guessing herself. She wondered constantly if she still perceived her social world correctly. Did she still understand what people were saying when they spoke to her? Often it seemed easier to eat alone.

So Yolanda ate a tuna fish sandwich alone at her desk and reviewed her notes on the Marian Wright robbery. One item taken: a book on *necromancy*. A quick internet search had revealed that *necromancy* concerned the study of death, particularly in terms of bringing back the dead. The word shared the same root as *necrophilia*. Yolanda had no other information on the content of the book or on its market value. She did have a suspicion as to who stole it—the visiting exhibits curator: Nick Sabernail. She had found his name included in the department's criminal records database. But when she tried to access his file she only received the message: IMPROPER ACCESS REQUEST. Data Base Management told her that this message failed to follow inquiry failure protocol. This being an exotic way of saying that she should not get IMPROPER ACCESS REQUST on her screen when asking to see Mr. Sabernail's police file. The computer whiz at Data Base Management (she used to call them "computer-nerds," but they held the reigns of power now and preferred "whiz") suggested that someone had "monkeyed with" the file. The whiz's elaboration of "monkeyed with" left Yolanda with a headache the size of Kansas, so she dropped that line of inquiry. A hard copy search for Sabernail's file came up empty. However it was that Nick Sabernail had offended against the people of Los Angeles, she saw no way of finding out about it now.

Still, Mr. Sabernail had done something to merit departmental attention in the past—his name could be found in the database. On top of this, Yolanda considered these facts. He had ordered a copy of the stolen book for the exhibit. He had no alibi for the night of the theft. He had a gambling problem according to the museum director. He had recommended against a new security system. His wardrobe, as revealed the one time Yolanda had met him, manifestly revealed his need for cash.

Yet, if Mr. Sabernail stole the book for money, why not steal the spoons too? Mrs. Cartwright had told Yolanda that Mr. Sabernail had insisted on an exhibit about death. No one else on the board fancied it much. Mr. Sabernail had selected the book on death. Now someone had gone to a great deal of trouble to steal the book on death, and nothing else. Detective Yolanda Vasquez finished her sandwich. Her mind lingered on the image of Nick Sabernail. Not a bad looking fellow, but maybe a thief, or worse. Definitely, she needed to find out more about this man.

In the meantime, the department kept a complete news blackout on the Vampire Killer case. Thus it took the local newspapers all of two days after the formation of the task force to have, and print, most of the relevant details. This leak so embarrassed the District Attorney that he called a press conference to deny that any leak had occurred, or that the police had meant to suppress any information beyond that necessary for the investigation.

After this, the Chief of Police held a press conference to dispute the notion that the DA had any business saying what had, or had not, been suppressed by the police department. He also held that only the Chief of Police had authority to authoritatively deny anything concerning the Vampire Killer case. Further, he confirmed that it had been LAPD officers who had dubbed the killer the "Vampire Killer," and no, he would not say why, nor confirm or deny any sucking of blood or draining of bodies. But if anyone *could* confirm such a thing it would be him.

Then the Mayor held a press conference expressing full

confidence in the DA's Office, and in the Chief of Police, but advising both to avoid future press conferences on the subject. He chided the press for attending such press conferences and wished they would stick to attending *his* press conferences, which in future would be held more frequently. He also would not confirm or deny any sucking of blood or draining of bodies, but he would confirm that such confirmation could only come from the Chief of Police—though hopefully only in a joint press conference with the Mayor himself. He could definitely confirm that the LAPD indeed dubbed the Vampire Killer as such—though he knew for a fact that the office of the District Attorney approved the name whole-heartedly. He would not confirm his intention to run for re-election at this press conference, but might at a future one.

The L.A. County Sheriff then held a press conference to affirm that the Sheriff's Office intended to investigate the so called Vampire Killer. Further, he vigorously denied the Chief of Police's claim that the LAPD named the Vampire Killer, not withstanding the Mayor's confirmation. In fact, the name originated with the County Sheriff's Office. Though the correct name was "Vampire Slayer," not "Vampire Killer." The County Sheriff's Office had no intention of cooperating with any "Vampire Killer" task force at the LAPD. However, if the police department would form a "Vampire Slayer" task force, the Sheriff's Office would be glad to cooperate with *it*. After all, they would then be working on the same case.

The Chief of Police held another press conference to deny that the killer was named "Vampire Slayer" and further to assert his right to hold any press conferences he liked. Of course the Mayor would be invited to attend and participate in any such press conferences. No, the Mayor had not been invited to this one.

Finally, Detective Harmon, head of the Vampire Killer Task Force, held a press conference to say that the police had no suspects.

And that last was true at least. The police had no real

suspects. Though at least one junior detective had a possible suspect in mind.

"That's Nick Sabernail ... at the Marion Wright." Nick had been on the phone for several hours now, with the result that he hated phones. "No, *Sabernail* ... that's me ... the Marion Wright, that's the museum I work at." The problem wasn't actually with the devices themselves; fine examples of human ingenuity they were. The problem lay with the persons at the other end of them. "Right. Exactly right. Except take out the 'knot' in 'Saberknot' and replace it with a 'nail'; then replace 'Mic' with 'Nick' and it's perfect." In fact, the problems with persons on the other end of telephones were so extreme they cast doubt on the very idea of the device itself. "I'm calling about a Compendium ... of Necromantic Sciences ... C..O..M..P ... right. Of Necromantic ... N..E... look, is there someone else there I can talk to? Someone without a hearing aid?" For one brief moment Nick feared that the woman on the end of the phone had left to find a *completely* deaf person to take his call. "Hello?"

In the weeks since the unfortunate loss of the *Compendium,* Nick had assessed his alternatives and found that they reduced to two. He could either find a *Compendium of Necromantic Science,* or he could invent and patent a perpetual motion machine and retire to glory. After several days work on perpetual motion he had given up on science and turned to option one. Unfortunately, Compendiums of Necromantic Science did not lie thick on the ground.

In the silence of his wait for some equally indifferent conversational partner, Nick reflected on how he had found himself in this dilemma. The problem, he decided, lay in working for a museum of cultural history; an institution no one would open but for lacking anything worthwhile to build a museum around. All the great paintings by the old masters hang in prestigious national collections, or on hidden walls in the haciendas of Colombian drug lords. All the bad paintings of old masters hang in middling national collections or in the waiting rooms of old New England bluebloods. Italy had plenty of largely unseen old masters, but most remained immovably plastered on the walls of nunneries and such. Europe could export medieval triptychs and finger-pointing saints to upstart museums, but how many of those will the average tourist want to view in the two hours they allot to a museum visit?

Once, the Impressionists could be bought up with Paris mad-money, but now the elites loved them, and the public had no sense at all that they should think them scandalous. Even a bad Picasso could still fetch a fortune, and no new museum could afford enough of them to make a mark as a center of cubist worship. A new museum could buy plenty of more recent modern art, but such works did not really put one on the map the way an established figure would. You could still break into postmodern art, especially if you wished to patronize new artists. Unfortunately, postmodern works had the habit of slipping into modern works in the ever-shifting sands of fashion. Nothing would be worse than buying a postmodern masterpiece only to find it had turned into a mundane bit of modernism before your budget had recovered.

So if you meant to establish a museum on the cultural map at the turn to the new century you did not have a lot to choose from in the way of big-deal art works. How could you establish your presence among the serious art set? Cultural history provided the answer. The whole point of cultural history rested in its capacity to take mundane, boring, ordinary objects—past or present—and turn them into valuable, intellectually important, ordinary objects. Any old chair would do, so long as you accompanied it with postmodern verbiage and fashionable political posturing. The object need not be rare, nor valuable, nor nice to look at. The curator's story counted, and the object served only to move that story along. The look of utter incomprehension on the part of the ordinary patron, staring at an common coffin and four columns of text on its meaning, confirmed to any art school graduate the validity of postmodernism and the functional brilliance of cultural history. It was a sort of alchemy, turning base exhibits into gold.

Nick had to admit he thought it all a kind of scam—but he appreciated a good scam. For his part, Nick thought he could make a great museum out of famous art forgeries of history. The works could be got on the cheap too—and no worry that some snot-nose little natural scientist with an x-ray machine and a grudge against the humanities will turn your five million dollar Rembrandt into a five dollar "school of Rembrandt" in the blink of an eye. So far though, Nick had not found funding for his own museum.

Nick thought he heard a voice on the phone at last. "Hi," Nick said to the new voice, "I'm Nick Sabernail at the Marion Wright Museum of Cultural History, and I was wondering if you had … a *Compendium of Necromantic Science* … lying around … for sale." Auction houses, museums, private collectors; Nick had a lot of ground to cover. "A Compendium; it's a sort of summary of the science of … uh … necromancy." What was so funny about all this? "Sure necromancy's a science, I took it in college; Necromancy 101—I had it on Tuesdays and Thursdays right after my pyramid power class." There must to be a better way of finding a *Compendium of Necromantic Science* than this; maybe an ad in the paper.

"Mr. Sabernail?" a voice called from the door of Nick's office.

"That's Saberknot," Nick replied to the voice, "no, wait, you got it right—Sabernail."

Nick turned around to see the striking form of Ms. Detective Yolanda Vasquez standing alluringly at his door. In point of fact, she was just standing—but this woman allured just standing. Nick hung-up on the forty-second call of the day. "I was just looking for Compendiums," he said.

"Don't you have one already?" Yolanda asked.

"No," said Nick, "and if I don't find one to replace the one we lost soon, Mrs. Cartwright is going to have the board tar and feather me prior to termination."

"Tarred and feathered, I didn't realize museum directors had that kind of authority," Yolanda said.

"Well I have a rather unique contract. They can actually pull my fingernails out with channel locks if they want to," said Nick. "Would you like to sit down?" Nick began moving papers off the only other chair in the office. "I'm sure I have another chair under here someplace," Nick said as he re-organized his files. Nick's office resembled a paper mill after a terrorist attack.

"I'll stand, thank you," said Yolanda. This seemed to be her only real option anyway.

"Right," said Nick, "you stand, I'll sit; strong command of the elevated position, dominance, control; just the thing for the detective. I'll just sit here and squirm like a junkie." Nick looked up at her affecting an air of innocence.

Once again Yolanda didn't know what to make of the strange patter of Nick Sabernail. Was this a psychopath or just a pathological oddball? "I wanted to ask you a few more questions," she said.

"Any clues on the missing book?" asked Nick.

"That would be *you* asking questions," said Yolanda.

"Right, you're the boss, I'm the victim of the third degree, go ahead," Sabernail said.

Yolanda gathered her thoughts and started, "I called the Lucky Eleven. No one seems to remember you there. Could you give me the names of anyone there you talked to?"

"What are the first and second degrees?" Nick said. "Do you always start at the first and move on?" Nick looked as if he were thinking for a moment. Then he looked about the room. "Shouldn't there be another cop here? The bad cop. Or the good cop, or whichever one you're not?" Nick knew he was rambling, but why stop a good ramble?

"Mr. Sabernail, maybe you don't take this theft seriously, but I assure you the LAPD does," Yolanda said.

"Not take it seriously?" said Nick, "my job's hanging by a

thread over this."

"Then maybe you don't take me seriously," said Yolanda in a voice to be taken seriously.

"I always take armed women seriously," Nick said.

Yolanda took a deep breadth preparing to forge ahead when Sabernail shot out of his seat towards the door.

"Let's walk," he said. They walked. Sabernail spoke again, "I wasn't making a lot of friends at the Lucky Eleven. You have to win to make friends at a casino. I don't even think I could *describe* anyone there—unless *desperate looking reprobates* is a helpful description. I know I look good for this robbery, and after several days calling around I can attest that Compendiums of Necromantic Science are rare. But believe me, if I were going to steal something, even from this museum, I could do better than that damn book."

Through a forest of silverware they walked. Yolanda had to decide how to handle her suspect. How much should she treat him? Should she try charm or bring on the heat? She tried charm. "So you admit you've thought about robbing the Museum?" she said.

Okay, so charm is not her forte.

"Should you be reading me my rights?" Nick asked.

"Should I?" replied Yolanda.

Nick thought a moment, then said, "This is what they call cat and mouse, right?" Yolanda just looked at him. Nick said, "I'm the ... mouse, right?"

Yolanda had to laugh. He might be a thief and a psycho killer, but he had a silver tongue. The two made their way to the exhibit that had so recently been looted. They passed the death masks and voodoo dolls and stood before the display case that had once housed the missing book. They looked at this for a moment in silence.

"The place just seems empty without it, don't you think?" Nick said.

Now Yolanda really did try a different tack. She said, "Mr. Sabernail, I don't know if you stole this book or not—probably not—but you do know something about it. That could help. What was this book about, Mr. Sabernail?"

Nick looked her dead in the eyes. She asked a serious question and Nick owed her a serious answer. He could see in her eyes that she was serious. Her eyes were deep brown, like two pools of caramel. Nick loved caramel.

"Mr. Sabernail?" she said.

"Huh? Oh." Nick said, "You asked me something." Nick's voice had a note of triumph in it.

"The contents of the book, Mr. Sabernail, what was the book about?" Yolanda asked, trying very hard not to be attractive.

"Ah, yes," said Nick, "a bit of a problem there. See, I never actually read the book."

Yolanda's expression did not inspire confidence.

"I saw it in a loan catalog," Nick continued, "the title fit the theme. When it arrived I took a few pictures of the inside pages for the display and put the book under glass. I didn't actually sit down and read it over a few glasses of wine."

"You're supposed to be an expert on this stuff," Yolanda said.

"On what? Death?" Nick said, "I specialize in modern conceptual art. Necromancy is outside my area."

Or, thought Yolanda, just your thing.

An old woman carrying a small dog approached Nick. She looked Sabernail up and down and somehow managed to inject every word she spoke to him with a tinge of disapproval, "Do you work here young man?"

"No," Nick said, "I'm the boss, I watch everyone else work."

"I know who stole your book—from that display case right over there," the woman said.

Both Nick's and Yolanda's eyes opened wide; they looked at each other for a moment, then at the woman. She waited patiently for something. Nick and Yolanda waited impatiently for her to spill the beans. Finally, Nick asked her, "So, who took the book?"

When she spoke, she spoke as would some grand dame from another era, "I am Mrs. Martha Talbert Pembroke. I knew Mrs.

Wright when she was alive. I spoke to her often about her plans for this museum. It was her house at one time you know." She spoke this last sentence to Yolanda with a knowing nod, and then continued addressing Nick, "They've added rooms since then. I don't think Mrs. Wright would have approved of that, incidentally. I could have told them that, if I had been asked. No one asked me. Many times Mrs. Wright told me she meant for her home to be preserved as a museum and her fortune to finance the housing of her doll collection in it." Again she looked at Yolanda and smiled, "I didn't approve, of course," she said and spoke again to Nick, "I thought she should have given me her dolls—have you met Toffle, my dog?" This she asked of Yolanda. She waved Toffle's paw at the detective and pressed on with her tale to Nick, "I can bring Toffle in here because I am an old friend of Mrs. Wright. Mrs. Wright knew Toffle. Not this Toffle, the original one. This is Toffle VIII." She said it just like that, as if it had to be written in Roman Numerals.

"Mrs. Pembroke," Yolanda broke in, "you said you knew who robbed the museum. Could we just hear about that?" Yolanda said this kindly, and Mrs. Pembroke took it well considering it had interrupted the start of her soliloquy on her favorite subject: Toffle the First.

"Certainly. An octopus man stole it," she said.

Nick let out a disappointed sigh. Yolanda caught her eyes in mid-roll. Mrs. Pembroke did not let either of them disturb her in the least. "I knew you wouldn't believe me. That's why I told you about being a friend to Mrs. Wright. Mrs. Wright would not have a friend who wasn't trustworthy."

"It's not that we don't trust you," said Nick, "It's that octopuses typically live in the ocean. On dry land they just crumple to the ground and dry out."

"I said an octopus *man*. A black octopus man."

"Are you saying," asked Yolanda, "That you saw a black man breaking into the museum?"

"A black *octopus* man."

"And what did he do?" asked Nick.

49

"Why he climbed the building, just under the broken window I saw the next morning. I don't know what he did after that. Toffle had to eat." She looked at Yolanda, "He likes his meals just on time."

Nick looked at Yolanda whose expression indicated she had no further interest in Toffle's digestive habits. Nick thanked Mrs. Pembroke and pointed out the Pet Cemetery Photo Gallery on the back wall. Mrs. Pembroke left with no higher esteem for Mr. Sabernail than she had had when she entered.

"Well," Nick said, "there you have it: the octopus man did it. I feel better already. You couldn't ask for a more distinctive description. How many could there be? You know, now that I think about it, I did detect a slight odor of calamari the day after the theft." Nick sniffed the air. "Still smells a little fishy in here."

Yolanda smiled. She asked, "Mr. Sabernail, where were you on August 14th?"

The question took Nick back a little. "Ah, I think that was another Vegas weekend."

"And August 16th?"

"I spend a lot of time in Vegas. There's the gambling, the losing, the loan sharks, the waking up in a pool of your own blood—I'm kidding of course," Nick said, since Yolanda did not seem amused.

"Mr. Sabernail, do you have any witnesses to your presence in Vegas on these dates?" Yolanda asked.

"Am I missing something? Did someone rob the museum three times? They only told me about the one." Nick looked a bit peeved now.

"I am not at liberty to disclose that aspect of my investigation," said Yolanda. She thought of asking about the missing police file, but decided not to.

"I don't have an alibi for those dates—I will be keeping a close log of all my contacts from here on out. I had no idea my life would require such documentation before today."

Yolanda changed the subject, "I am interested in the content of the missing book. You haven't read it, but do you know anyone who has?"

Nick didn't, and he said so.

"Thank you Mr. Sabernail, I'll be in touch," Yolanda said as she turned to walk away.

Nick watched her go. She was trouble, and it was best to let trouble go. Nick decided to let her walk right out of his life for good. "Detective?" he called after her. She stopped and turned to him. Nick said, "I could research it for you. We could even look into it together. I do know some people. I could call around." Who said that?

"Alright," Yolanda said.

"Maybe we could get together tonight … or Thursday night, yes, Thursday night, for dinner, and I could tell you what I found out," said Nick.

"Alright," Yolanda said.

"Anyplace special you'd like to eat?" asked Nick.

"Your place, around seven," Yolanda said, and she walked away.

THE SOUNDS
OF SCIENCE

The labors of Hercules were as nothing to the toils of Drakan. Killing may come easy to blood-lust sex lunatics who orgasm with every thrust of the knife, but it was pure chore to Drakan. And then hauling the unconscious bodies of his victims up to his warehouse apartment! And down again; nothing but drudgery. The first, Janet Giallo, had been far too heavy. After the trouble of carrying her up two flights of stairs, Drakan vowed to use only petite woman from then on. Thus did the challenge of finding ladies of loose virtue increase to the further challenge of finding small ones.

For all that, dealing with the living had proven much easier than dealing with the dead. The dead had to be dug up. In the movies they always *cut to scene* just as the spade touches the dirt. No more digging to see till the shovel hits coffin wood. In reality you have to heave every shovel-full of dirt. And the hole. It had to be almost twice the size of the coffin to get anything out. And the coffin! Trying to open a modern high-end coffin involved more work than cracking most safes. Once retrieved from the ground, the dead were no less heavy than the living, and they smelled bad. They also had to be drained of preserving fluid and re-prepped with Drakan's chemical cocktail from the age of the apothecary.

The dead offered at least one advantage; they would just lie there on the work table. The living liked to squirm. You needed straps, gags, ropes, and a television mounted on the wall. Drakan thought the television would help distract them during the initial preparation phase. Drakan put a lot of thought into just what shows might interest a person strapped to an examination table about to have their blood sucked out. Nothing too serious, he thought. Deep drama might depress the soon to be drained. Soap operas had continuing plot lines that would hold little interest to those about to greet the eternal void. Comedy seemed in bad taste all things considered. Drakan thought current events might work. In any event, once the process began in earnest, TVs were of no help.

The initial experiments had not gone well. The living subject kept ripping out the tubes used for draining her blood. The cyclotron broke when she put a spiked heal through it. The gags kept coming loose. And Drakan went through almost twenty tubes trying to finish the job. He would have loved to drug her, but the *Compendium* insisted that "only through agony, terror, and hopeless pain can undeath be born." There had been plenty of all that, but far too much kicking and squirming. For some reason, the woman could not be soothed by Drakan's assurance that someday she would be famous; just like the rats in Pasture's experiments.

The problems presented by uncooperative experimental subjects paled beside those of a purely technical nature. Many of the traditional ingredients were impossible to find. Drakan had to guess at industrially produced substitutes. Much of the instruction, even in the great *Compendium*, consisted of useless ritual. Still, one could never be sure what had real utility without proper experimentation and detailed records. So Drakan had smeared himself with pig's blood, on the off chance that it might mix with body sweat to emit some essential chemical into the local atmosphere during the process. He had chanted ritual incantations, on the remote possibility that these created rhythmic vibrations that facilitated the chemical interactions. Victor Drakan was the last man on earth to doubt the wisdom of the ancients.

Still, the first experiment had gone poorly. He had seen

not a glimmer of undeath. If only he could have used the previously living subject as the recipient subject in the next experiment. But the sources spoke clearly on this: The process of preparation of the living subject precluded its later use. Likewise for the recipient subject, if chemical injection actually took place. So on his initial failure Drakan had to return again to the Paramount Cemetery and to the busy streets of L.A.

His second round of experiments faired no better. Drakan chose his new living subject mindful of his stairs, but lacking x-ray vision he had to catch-as-catch-can on the body of the recipient subject. Just his luck, the cavernous hole revealed a heavy aluminum coffin filled with the fattest man Drakan had ever seen. Wrestling the big man's body out of the hole, he kept cursing under his breath that cemeteries should keep a public record of the corpse size and coffin type of all of their occupants. The key to any successful human endeavor lies in keeping proper records.

Thanks to his development of a superior strapping method, and the smaller size of the living subject, the second attempt included far less effective squirming. But, in spite of these improvements in technique, Drakan found no sign of undeath.

Now he sat in the dark of his large room clapping his lights on and off. His newest living subject lay unconscious, strapped to an inclined table. This time Drakan prepared to drain a small Korean man he had found out walking alone. Drakan waited for him to awaken.

Slowly, the Korean gentleman awoke to a scene of absurd horror. All around him lay instruments of torture. His arms, legs, head and torso strapped down to the table, he could hardly move at all. A gag nearly suffocated him. Tubes ran from his arms and his neck to a diabolical looking machine that churned slowly at his side. To his left he saw a Frankenstein's laboratory of beakers and potions. To his right, he saw a fat dead man, lying in a large tub of liquid. Above him a television blared the ten o'clock news. The lights flicked on and off to the clapping of unseen hands.

Into this vision of hell thrust a pinched pale face. It loomed over the poor man and spoke the ominous words: "Just watch a little TV, this won't take long."

What wouldn't take long was truly unspeakable, but Drakan noted, the man didn't find it un-screamable. Though little noise escaped, the man gave it all he could. Drakan proceeded with the extraction of blood. The blood flowed from the terrified Korean, through the pump, to the cyclotron, to the vats filled with Drakan's formula, to a centrifuge, to another pump, and finally into the tub where the dead fat man lay. Tubes fed the mixture into the body itself. The slow process left Drakan time to take notes, adjust knobs, and catch up on the news.

The news. He had no doubt that someday it would record his greatness. Not this particular episode perhaps, but some of what would come after it. The little Korean man flailed around violently now. The pumps swished and whirred. The liquid in the vat gurgled, and the chipper newscasters flirted innocuously on the TV. These, thought Drakan, are the sounds of science.

The little Korean man's desperate struggle slowly ended as death took him at last. Drakan watched with rising hopes. The secondary suction pump kicked in to fully desiccate the body. Then the automated shut-down system started, signaling the end of the extraction. The cyclotron cut off. The agitators in the vat cut off. The pumps stopped. Quiet descended on the small dark room. Drakan watched the fat man's vat. Not a sound, not a stir, emerged. Defeated again.

Drakan cursed his soul. He had done everything right. He had followed the book. He deserved success. He considered his options, and the best of them seemed to be to pack it in and find some other road to the success, fame, and wealth that destiny had laid up for him. How could so careful a plan have gone so wrong? Drakan turned off the TV and clapped his hands, pitching the room into darkness. In that darkness

Drakan sat; a defeated failure once more.

The air stood still. Not a sound to hear. Then. A splash. Not a big one; more like a bird cleaning its beak. Then another. Drakan clapped his hands just as the fat man's tub erupted in churning water. Leaping to his feet, Drakan jumped to the tub and looked in. The once dead man's arms hurled about underwater. His eyes were open! He had broken the stitches the undertaker had used to close them in death. To Drakan he looked like a drowning man frantically trying to reach the surface of life.

Quickly Drakan collected himself. He ran to a table and retrieved his camcorder. As the fat man churned the liquid of his eerie bath, Drakan fumbled with the camcorder's shutter.

"Open! Open, Damn it!" Drakan shouted. The defiant shutter opened as Drakan tried to remember how to record. He had not, till now, had anything to film. Drakan read the instructions he had carefully tied to the camcorder: "Congratulations on your purchase of the Zenith Com-Max 2000 camcorder—damn it!" He skipped a few paragraphs and read on. As he rehearsed the camcorder's instructions to himself, the churning water died down. Finally, the camcorder's light went on and took its first picture: Drakan's confused and angrily pinched face. Drakan turned the camera about to the tub. It recorded only the body of a fat dead man; eyes still open, but no sign of life.

Drakan cheered nevertheless. Success! Crowning glory. This one moment confirmed his destiny. He had much to do. Notes to consult. Records to make. Next time, and now he knew there would be a next time, he would do better.

◆ ◆ ◆

Drakan's days now blurred into his nights. A dusk of murders; a twilight of digging. He laid up new extraction subjects and new bodies for reanimation. Soon he could keep a dead body suspended in undeath for several minutes; then several hours. He found that the average undead person quit thrashing about once you lifted the head out of the fluid. The newly undead could not drown, but they seemed to retain the fears and instincts they had in life, though in a muted form.

Drakan's first zombies proved very unexciting. The first he ever kept undead after removing the tubes was Juan Alverez, died 1987, according to the tombstone. Or, as Drakan now called him: Juan the Zombie. Juan the Zombie did not last long. He received the blood of Bambi the Prostitute, augmented by Drakan's reanimation cocktail. Drakan had lifted Juan out of the tub and dried him off. No sooner had the quasi-corpse dried than he returned forever to death. Drakan could have screamed.

Still, he could see the problem: too many leaks. Dead bodies are less watertight than living ones. The glowing green reanimation fluid leaked out of the cuts on the body —especially those made by morticians and opened up in the struggle from darkness to undeath. Fortunately, Drakan had in his busy life not only mastered the dark arts of raising the dead, but the more mundane craft of stitching. He learned to secure the weak points in a corpse prior to reanimation and promptly plug up any holes.

From then on he managed to keep the newly minted undead ghoul sitting dry in a chair, and securely undead, for hours. They looked a pathetic sight. Dead yellow eyes bugging out and apparently incapable of blinking. These denizens of undeath resembled the classic cliché more than Drakan liked to admit. For some reason, most kept their mouths agape and walked rather stiff-legged. Death did not do a body good.

Nor did the undead converse much. Clyde Forstal, died 1993, aka Clyde the Zombie, managed to say his name, barely: "Ca … Ca … Clyyy … Clyyyyd … da … da …" This thrilled Drakan so much he forgave the zombie spitting up green gunk after the last "da." The Clyde experiment proved another point. The powers of chemical necromancy could repair the wounds caused to flesh by death. Many of the zombies seemed to fall apart just sitting in a chair, but Clyde's general level of *stick-togetherness* improved as he sat in place. He managed a healthier color than the others as well—provided that gray-yellow can ever be a healthy color. Principally, the case of Clyde showed that the undead did not have to remain loose bags of useless flesh. Proper formulation of the reanimation fluid, and care with the subject, could work wonders in making them functional ghouls.

Alas, for all his promise, Clyde lasted only three days. This proved the limit of endurance for the reanimation fluid. After that the zombie had to have a new fix. If you caught them before complete shutdown, a fairly modest "booster-shot" could perk them up. Even if they fell down dead to the world (again), a quick re-treatment in the necrotic fluids brought them back to full, if necessarily limited, vigor. Clyde proved, however, that after more than a few hours of renewed death, they could never be re-animated again.

The procedure for producing optimal zombies continued to elude Drakan. His latest ones worked better than his earlier tries, but inexplicable variation in results remained. Perhaps some folks are just destined to be better zombies than others. A particularly bad time trying to work with a zombie named "Yang-Fung" soured Drakan on "oriental" corpses altogether. Too bad, he thought, since they were generally smaller to carry about.

After a while, Drakan created, or recreated, or quasi-recreated, a specimen that could not only walk, but follow simple instructions. He was Drakan's greatest triumph to date: Walter the Zombie. Dried off, and redressed in the tuxedo that Mrs. Walter had buried him in, he stood ready to answer his master's voice.

"Arise, my servant, hear the voice of thy master and answer to the call of thy destiny!" Drakan intoned. Or at least he attempted to intone. It may be that intoning is, strictly speaking, impossible for a high-pitched voice, prone to squeaking. In any event, Walter the Zombie sat staring at

Drakan while pushing a thumb thru a tuxedo buttonhole.

"Arise to your glory! Arise to my destiny!" Still not a move. "Get up Walter!"

At this Walter arose. Drakan reasoned that the limited cognitive ability of a corpse nine years dead did not allow for dramatic modes of instruction. No matter, Drakan would keep it simple.

"Walk there Walter." Drakan said, pointing across the room. Walter the Zombie began his stiff-legged, bug-eyed way. Drakan marveled at his balance. Drakan himself could not have walked pounding his legs into the ground, without falling over. Walter was a marvel indeed. Drakan rushed to find the camcorder so that he could record the moment for history. While retrieving the camcorder from its case, he heard a crash of glass hitting the floor. Turning around, he noticed that Walter's sleeve had caught on a beaker and knocked it over. "Watch the beakers," said Drakan, returning his attention to the camcorder. The playback feature of the device confirmed that that the current tape contained the full documentation of Roseanne the Zombie's gunk gurgling episode. He needed a fresh tape.

While looking for the tape he noticed he had not heard any legs pounding on the floor since his warning to Walter. Looking around he saw the zombie staring wide-eyed at the beakers on the table. "No," said Drakan, "go that way," and he pointed again to the far wall. Walter headed out, ramming his legs like post-hole diggers into the floor. Drakan loaded a new cartridge into the camcorder. Suddenly his warehouse apartment erupted in the sound of breaking glass. Drakan whirled around to find Walter plowing through a table of beakers and jars.

"What are you doing?" he yelled.

Walter answered with "Goooooaaa," and plowed right on ahead, indifferent to glass and noise.

"Stop!" demanded Drakan.

Walter stopped. Drakan raced over to inspect the damage.

A complete loss on the beakers. Walter seemed all right. Dead skin could not easily be pierced. Drakan made a note: zombies tended to be rather literal minded.

◆ ◆ ◆

Walter the Zombie proved a great help digging and carrying. The carrying in particular proved a godsend. For some reason the undead come gifted with inhuman strength. For all that, Drakan still had a lot of carrying to do himself—he now dug up at least two bodies a night. He needed plenty of bodies for his experiments.

One experiment he chose not to repeat concerned the driving ability of the undead. Drakan noted that Walter the Zombie had a great fixation on the plumbing in Drakan's bathroom. If left to his own devices he would find his way to the toilet, stare gape-mouthed into the bowl, and flush till Drakan screamed for him to stop. Drakan judged this interesting enough to invest a bit of research into the phenomenon. He discovered that in life dear Walter had been a plumber. A bit of experimentation on the sink showed that Walter the Zombie could follow instructions much better when working with pipes than even with the simple act of walking across the room. You wouldn't want to just set him loose on your leaky faucet, but he clearly retained in undeath the skills acquired in life—if not the will to execute them independently.

This gave Drakan an idea. Why not have Walter the Zombie serve as chauffeur? Drakan had hoped to be rich enough at this stage in his work to afford one. Unfortunately, since killing the living proved a necessary means to producing the undead, Drakan had yet to convert his discovery into fame and wealth. But why not a *zombie* chauffeur? Walter's legs were far less stiff now, and his work with the pipes had been exemplary.

So that very night found Walter the Zombie in the driver's seat. "Start the van, Walter." Drakan said. Walter turned the key and Drakan's van fired up. Drakan could not have been more pleased. Walter the Zombie clearly understood the concept of van starting! Drakan had not had to explain that he needed to turn the key to accomplish the task. Great. In the midst of his revelry, Drakan noticed a high-pitched grinding sound coming from the front of the van. Looking over he found that while the engine now hummed along, Walter the Zombie still turned the key forcibly to the start position.

"You'll burn out the starter!" yelled Drakan. Walter the Zombie jerked his head at the Necro-master and listed forward shoving his nose to within an inch of Drakan's. Drakan found this habit of the undead particularly nauseating. The starter grinded on. "Stop turning the key!"

Walter stopped. The van purred nicely now. Only a faint hint of smoke hung in the air. Drakan made a note to himself: dig up a mechanic tonight.

"Put the van in drive," Drakan commanded. Walter the Zombie did so, and they began to move slowly forward. "Now, drive to the stop light." Walter hit the gas so hard the acceleration nearly shot Drakan into the back of the van. He righted himself to find Walter following instructions perfectly: he had aimed the van straight at the pole holding up the stop light and now raced toward it like a man already dead. Drakan almost said *stop* and thought the better of it. "Take your foot off the gas pedal," he said. Walter did, leaving them headed to destruction a bit slower now. Drakan noticed cars crossing their path as they neared the intersection. He yelled, "Turn the wheel to the right!" Walter lurched the wheel to the right. "Not that far!" Drakan yelled. The cars in the intersection slammed on breaks. The Necro-master needed to get out of the intersection fast. "Hit the accelerator!" Drakan yelled.

Walter disappeared under the steering wheel and Drakan thought that his own last living thought would be, *how on earth had the reanimation fluid run out so soon?* At the last moment before being hit, the van lurched forward. Drakan grabbed the wheel to direct the car and only then noticed that

Walter was punching the accelerator pedal with his fist. "Use your foot—not too far down—sit up!" The ghoul sat up and took command of the steering wheel. Drakan saw cars coming in their path. "Ease to the right!" To his great delight, Walter remembered "ease" from his days among the sentient, and nudged the car back into the proper lane of traffic.

Drakan had a brainstorm. He told Walter the Zombie what speed to keep the car. Initially this caused the ghoul to stare solely at the speedometer, only turning the wheel to Drakan's frantic commands. After a bit, Drakan could instruct him as to when to look at what, and gave him constant updates as to what speed they should travel, including "zero" which, thankfully, Walter understood to mean *stop slowly*. Drakan found that he had to give turning and speed commands some three seconds prior to wanting them executed if his undead driver was to time the maneuver correctly. Three seconds may sound like plenty of time, but it made choosing the order of instructions a constant challenge. After all, one mistiming could send you through a shop window.

After a bit, Drakan got the knack, "Keep your speed at twenty—now ten—foot off the pedal—slow breaking—full stop—speed at one—five—twenty—forty—avoid the truck!—twenty—right turn now—less speed—go straight at thirty—go straight at forty—slow to twenty." And so on. He felt like Captain Kirk directing a particularly stupid helmsman.

Drakan nearly died of fear on the freeway.

After forty minutes of heart-in-the-throat zombie driving, Drakan and Walter the Zombie arrived at Pleasant Hovel Cemetery. Drakan decided not to let the undead drive in future. He and Walter broke into a crypt, but found the body too badly off to use and had to break into another to finally retrieve two subjects for the night's experiments. Drakan badly hoped at least one of these would turn out well. He could really use a good zombie right about now.

CHARLEY SPARROW

Charley Sparrow stood outside the Palace Theater in Hollywood, reading the L.A. Times. The paper showed the date as October 14, 1937. The headlines mostly concerned war scares and depression news. Charley had slim interest in the headlines. Long ago he had come to realize that his influence on international affairs and economic reconstruction amounted to flat zero. Some top-hat downtown might be able to push world events one way or the other, not Charley Sparrow. Charley was a big man, six foot five, and 310 pounds. He had a good idea what he could push. He could not push Europe back from the brink of war. He pushed punks, and deadbeats, and over zealous fans. Charley read the racing news.

He wore an ill-fitting suit over his large and muscular form. No tie. He sat against the side of a car. Not his. Charley Sparrow once wore a tie and owned his own car. A big black car with running boards and polished silver door handles. People paid good money to have Charley Sparrow put on a tie and drive them around in that big black car with the running boards and the silver door handles. Important people. Celebrities and such. Many times he drove up to the Palace Theater for an opening—driving the star or co-star of the picture. And he was not just a driver either, but a bodyguard as well. And not just a bodyguard, but a fix-it man. And to be a fix-it man in Hollywood in the 1920s was to be a man indeed. But those times were dead and gone. He dropped off no one at the Palace today. He leaned on someone else's car, and read the racing news, and thought of better times.

And what times they were. Charley had made the short

trip from San Juan Capistrano to Hollywood in order to break into the movies. The wife of his football coach told him he could convert his rugged good looks into a career and stardom. Turned out that his looks were more rugged than good, and he got nothing but bit parts playing goons and thugs. Besides, Charley hated putting on make-up, and he disliked the suspiciously effeminate leading men he had to let beat him up in the pictures. Charley could out-fight and out-shoot them, but on the screen they were the men, and Charley was just a big target.

One day the star of a big three-reeler—Lawrence Touway —failed to make the call at location. Touway hailed from the London stage, but in the silent picture days he could just as easily play a cowboy. He hated doing it, preferring to play wounded-hearted, drunken poets in search of love and meaning. But the fans didn't go for poets, so Mr. Touway launched into cowboy roles. Charley used to rope cattle in the hills past the San Juan Mission, and he thought Lawrence Touway looked the dandiest, most girl-faced cowboy he had ever seen. Sparrow knew damn well that any western steer spying Lawrence Touway charging after him in that ten gallon hat, covered in face-cake, would turn round and gore the silly fancy-pants. But when Charley read the script, sure enough, there stood Touway blazing away, killing Charley Sparrow dead as a doornail. Charley knew he had about as much a chance of being a real movie star as that Marion Morrison fellow he drank with at the Adobe Kitchen Café. No chance at all.

That day—the day Touway turned up missing—put Charley on a different track all together. The director of the picture fell into a pure panic. Seems he knew where Touway had taken off to, and if Touway could not be enticed back, the studio would fire the director. Sparrow thought directing had to be the most humiliating job in Hollywood. Even bit players like him had more creative input than the director. At least Charley got to pick his hat; he liked the Mexican sombrero. The director couldn't crap biscuits but that the producer didn't look them over. This being the case, Charley remained mystified as to why the director prized his job so much as to panic over the absence of that pain in the ass-area, Lawrence Touway.

But panicked he was, and not for not knowing where the star might be found. He knew very well that Touway had headed off to Madam Beauregard's House of Plenty; a whorehouse frequented by Hollywood stars, stuntmen, and real estate developers (another poor lot). For all that, the pitiful director could find no one willing to drag the star back. The leading lady refused to go near the place (she had once worked there and did not fancy a return) and no one on the crew would take up the charge of trying to bring the star back from love's embrace. Least of all the set guard, whose job it should have been to see to stuff like that.

Charley might have just sat the day out, picking up his pay, but Charley despised timeservers. He asked the director what delayed the work.

"Touway's holed up drunk as piss-water at Madam Beauregard's, surrounded by that Tito gang, and won't come out for love nor money," the director said.

Charley offered to bring him back if the director would at least let him be the last to take a bullet from the effete cowpoke.

"Those goons of Tito's will cut your nuts off Charley, they don't take to interference."

Charley allowed that they had slim scruples but offered to take the task on in any event. The director hollered for joy and promised to set flowers on Charley's grave—if it should come to that.

Charley found Touway at the whorehouse, drunk as a skunk, singing old Irish drinking songs with two of the mangiest looking women Charley had ever laid his young eyes on. He also found Tito Valvano and three big goons lapping up all the Hollywood glamour that Touway gave off, when he wasn't throwing up in Madam Beauregard's antique spittoon.

Charley waited until Touway finished a little ditty about needing a drink on a boat and then approached him about his contractual obligations.

"You're wanted," Charley said to him.

"My boy," said Touway, "my good, big boy, I must be the most wanted man west of the Mississippi—a dreadful river by the way—and I'll be wanted all the more for my absence than my presence, I'd wager. For in my absence the want grows greater as the absence increases, while in my presence the want grows quieted as my presence extends."

As he spoke, Touway flung his hands about like a cow swatting at flies. And spoke he did, at length and to the unaccountable amusement of Tito and his friends, "Further, when I am wanted when absent, I feel the want of those absent from, and the want of those present," as he said this last he smiled knowingly at one of the scraggy whores, who smiled back at him knowingly. She didn't have the first idea what he meant, but when smiled at a good whore smiles back. "But when wanted and present," he continued, "the want of the absent is absent and the want of the present is all too ... there." At that the star appeared to have run out of steam.

Charley said: "You gotta come with me."

Tito spoke up, sly and full of vinegar, "Rick, you better explain to the cowpoke who owns the world."

Rick, a very big man with a scar on his right cheek, smiled and grunted and took a step toward Charley, preparing the explanation. Charley kept looking at the drunken form of Touway until Rick was just about on him.

"It's like this kid," began Rick. He didn't get past the beginning because Charley took out his Smith and Wesson and cracked him upside the head with the grip so hard the whore on Touway's lap screamed at the sound. Not stopping there, he pistol-whipped the big man back against the wall drawing a sea of blood. Charley knew that had he just punched the man he would have had to fight all four of them—but seeing a man pistol-whipped tended to freeze the blood. After all, at any moment the fellow could turn to shooting.

Tito and the others just stood and watched the frenzied assault. Big Rick crumpled onto the ground with a whimper, and Charley Sparrow turned back to the picture star and put the revolver back away under his coat. He said, "You gotta come with me." He said it just as he had before, without the least change of expression or composure. This chilled the blood of one and all more than anything else. Touway got on his feet like a puppet with its strings pulled taut. Charley looked at Tito who wolfed down his drink and turned his eyes away. Charley left with the star.

Back at the set the producer had shown up and fired the director. Upon Charley's return with the picture-star, the producer re-hired the director. Though barely sober, Lawrence Touway gave his most convincing performance to date (and his last, he died three weeks later when a horse he had been feeding brandy fell on him). More importantly, Charley became known as a fix-it guy.

A fix-it guy. When Rita Malone gets knocked up by some second set stunt man who wants ten thousand dollars (absurd amount, thought Charley) not to spill the mess to the gossip hounds, then you have a problem that needs fixing. Charley went to talk to the fellow. He beat him down to two hundred and boat passage to Brazil.

When some kook sends Sara Bernhard dirty letters, full of sex drawings and such, Charley wrote him back pretending to be the actress and arranged a meeting. There, Charley told the guy a story about old war wounds—and gave him a reason to need it.

And a lot more besides. Charley handled blackmailers, gambling debt collectors, nasty boyfriends, crazy girlfriends, opium dealers, drinking problems—you name it. If something had to be covered up; Charley Sparrow covered. If someone had to have a bit of persuasion laid on them; Charley Sparrow persuaded. If you worked in Hollywood, and had any problem that a little craft, a little muscle, and a lot of guts could solve,

Charley Sparrow could fix your problem.

Charley figured to buy a ranch someday but bought a car first. After ferrying drunken starlets around in it, he decided to buy a bigger car, black, with running boards, and charge money for the trouble. Charley drove the stars, drunk and sober, and they paid for the privilege, since even when stars passed out drunk, Charley Sparrow did not steal their jewelry or drive them to some alley and have a friend take pictures of them in the nude. Charley did not take advantage. He fixed problems, he didn't make them.

One day, back in '29, Charley went out after some new starlet the studio wanted back. She called herself Lilly Luvley for the screen, and she had progressed from background dancer to lesser love interest. She had a contract but refused to work. She wanted out of the contract, but the studio said no. Charley searched the speakeasies for her but found her, on a tip, and much to his surprise, waiting tables in Redondo Beach.

Charley said, "You gotta come with me."

"And who am I, that so mountain of a man must bring me in?" she said, pouring him coffee.

"You're Lilly Luvley. No lies, you gotta come with me."

The woman laughed. "I was never Lilly Luvley. Someone thought that was cute and called me that on the credits. But my mother named me Edith, and Edith I shall always be." Edith smiled at him. She seemed to Charley more beautiful than any woman or steer he had ever seen.

"You have to come with me," Charley said.

And come with him she did. She came with him to the Palace for openings, riding in the front seat while Charley drove. She came with him to meet his ailing mother down in Capistrano. She came with him to the ranch he said he wanted to buy. She came with him everywhere.

And the studio contract? Charley fixed that.

They married. They had a daughter, Dorothy. The depression hit, and Charley lost the big black car with the running boards and polished silver door handles. And no one needed Charley to fix problems anymore. Things still got broken, but other people fixed them, and Charley could not find a job. For years he could not find a job.

So now he sat, without a tie, on someone else's car, across from the Palace. But this time he looked away from the theater, at the bank across the street. Waiting for an armored car that should have arrived at least ten minutes ago. Charley looked fine reading the paper, but Joey, and Joey's dumb friend, paced back and forth by the bank entrance like they were waiting for something. Very dumb. Charley looked at the car on the corner. He didn't remember the driver's name. Old What's-His-Name looked jumpy. Charley cursed at himself for getting in so deep. He didn't even know the driver's name. Stupid, Charley, stupid.

The armored car drove up and stopped in front of the bank. Charley had a simple task. Cross the street, clunk the guard that stood by the rear car door, and grab the loot while Joey and the dummy clunked the other two. Then away in the car. With the no-name driver.

Charley put the paper under his arm and crossed the street. He didn't hear the cars pulling up to the left and right of the bank's side of the street. He just stayed focused on the guard. He heard a scuffle from the other side of the truck. Joey had jumped too soon! Charley ran to get the guard now drawing his gun. Just as Charley arrived the guard sensed something behind him and spun around to see the big man bearing down on him. The guard had no time to level the gun at Charley but fired anyway.

Charley took a slug in the leg as he hit the guard, sending the man down hard. He heard more shots. He looked up and saw Joey and his dumb friend blowing holes in two armored car guards lying on the ground. One guard held a hand up at them, either pleading for his life or trying to ward off bullets, Sparrow couldn't tell. Charley felt sick to his stomach. Joey had a smile on his face as he shot round after round into the guy holding up his hand. Charley heard more shots, but he did not look to where they came. He just wanted all this to end. He grabbed a bag from the back of the van and started walking across the street, to the car he had been leaning on. He saw the no-name guy drive past him fast and heard gunshots. He heard the car crash. He headed for the parked car.

Charley felt something hit his back, and then something else hit his back. He took another step, and then another, and then he felt his legs give way. He felt the earth come up to greet him, and something hard hit his face. Not the pavement, but the bag he had taken. It was full of coins. Charley heard more shooting, and cars screeching, and people shouting and screaming. But it all grew dimmer, and he cared less and less. He thought of Edith … and Dorothy … and he died there in the street.

But not forever.

◆ ◆ ◆

From the not-quite-eternal darkness, eyes again hailed the light. They saw dimly through a film of murky liquid. They sat in the head of a drowning man. Then a hand reached down and plucked the head containing the eyes from the dreary deep. The drowning ended, and the light grew clearer. Ears upon the head heard: "This is the voice of your master—obey me. Do not thrash about."

Somewhere that was nowhere in particular, the eyes, and the ears, and the once drowning lungs, participated in a feeling of relief. They were mastered and would obey. The master's voice spoke again, and the ears radiated the words to all parts near and far: "Your name is Charley Sparrow—you remember that." A name! The parts collect now under a name! Not eyes, and ears, and lungs, independent; but eyes of Charley Sparrow, ears of Charley Sparrow, lungs of Charley Sparrow! A rebirth of parts into a whole. Glorious unity. A united identity.

The master's voice spoke again: "Get out of the tub." A tub. The parts of Charley Sparrow, now unified under a name, had a task. They lay in a tub. They had to get out. Legs floundered, arms flailed, and liquid splashed. They remained in the tub.

Not they—it: a singular. Hold to the unity. The eyes saw the edges of the tub. Fingers had reached for the edge and fell short. The eyes watched the hand grope again, and the hand groped in the path of the eyes. The back twisted and the legs flailed. The ears heard the flailing, and the eyes saw it did not help. The legs stopped pitching water and braced against the side of the metal tub instead. They pushed as the arms pushed, but the unity under the name of Charley Sparrow remained in the tub.

"Get out!" demanded the master's voice. Out! All parts must get out. The eyes observed, as the arms, and legs, and back coordinated, missing a beat now and then, but improving against the observation of the eyes and the command of the master's voice. Then the legs kicked, the arms pulled, and the back of Charley Sparrow left the tub into the world, falling to the floor in a clump. Charley Sparrow was reborn to undeath.

CRAZY DATE

Cattle prods. She had to look for cattle prods, Yolanda reminded herself. It would not be an easy thing to work into conversation. "So have you any blood-covered cattle prods around the house?" No, not easy to work in. But Lieutenants Washington and Harmon assured her that she had developed a lead. They had admired her moxie in arranging a date with a suspect. As per departmental procedure, she wore a wire. "Testing ... one, two, testing," she said as she walked down the street to Nick Sabernail's apartment, in the waning light of the day. A car ahead of her flashed its lights, indicating they could hear her. Glad though she felt at having the backup, she didn't like who backed her up. But you can't always pick your partners. She saw the door to Nick's apartment.

However well educated in the art history it's occupant might be, the décor of Nick's apartment looked to Yolanda less like the quarters of a man who knew his way around a Rembrandt than of one who knew he would not spend much time at home. Being generous, you might allow that the beanbag chairs lay in just the right place to offset the dented coffee table in the middle of the living room. You might concede that the three-colored track lighting gave a *day at the races* feel to the room. And you might agree, with reluctance, at the thought that no one but a decorative genius would risk black-light posters in ultra-modern L.A. But you would only make such allowances and concessions after a good meal and several glasses of wine. On the other hand, you could immediately acknowledge that Sabernail's rooms lacked corpses and blood extraction equipment. You might find that discouraging, but you had to acknowledge it.

And no cattle prod; disappointing that.

Nick gave her the grand tour, lasting almost three minutes, including a rather elaborate explanation for why all the pictures hung upside down. (Something about "striving to see things in a new way," but ending in an admission that he had not paid much attention when he strung the wire on the frames.) The highlight of this brief tour: his dissertation project. This consisted of a sculpture of a pair of human lungs —made entirely of pipe cleaners.

"Reeked of irony," Nick said, "the professors just love irony."

"It just plain reeks," said Yolanda.

"Soiled pipe cleaners," Nick said, "enhances the irony."

They ate in the kitchen. The apartment had no dining room and the living room, which did have a cluttered table, did not encourage one's appetite. During her briefing Lieutenant Washington had warned Yolanda that she might steer clear of actually eating anything offered by the subject, in case he meant to poison her. Yolanda had not credited the poisoning idea, but she was not exactly struggling to avoid the food.

"You cooked this?" asked Yolanda.

Nick said, "I cooked everything. From scratch."

"No, I mean did you *cook* it? It tastes raw or something," Yolanda said.

"Well it's tamzuli—sort of the sushi of Greece," Nick said.

"This is fish?" said Yolanda, "it doesn't taste like fish."

"It's not fish," Nick said a bit testily, "don't worry about ingredients, just savor."

Yolanda ate on, her face suggesting endurance rather than savoring. Yolanda thought Nick's cuisine aesthetic matched his interior design sensibility.

"Any progress with the case?" Nick asked as Yolanda braved the feast.

"Not unless you have a confession to make," she replied.

"I do. The brazilles—those nut-tasting things you seem to

like—I didn't make those. I bought them from the market on the corner. I made everything else from scratch." Nick watched Yolanda finish the brazilles with relish. He got up from the table to retrieve a cream-romole for desert. If all else fails, hurry to desert. He set the cream filled pastry down beside her.

"It's a cream-romole," he said, "very good."

She looked on with skepticism, "Did you cook this from scratch too?"

"I cooked everything from scratch—except for the brazilles and the cream-romole." Yolanda ate the cream-romole. She liked it.

"So where do you come from?" she asked in place of a question about cattle prod ownership.

This was just the sort of first-date question Nick could not abide; besides, she clearly preferred cream-romole to a discourse on the Sabernail family tree. Nick got up and went to the stereo in the next room. A moment latter his apartment filled with the sounds of Juan Martinex and the Salsa Kings. In triumph he returned to the kitchen only to be met with raised eyebrows.

"I don't care much for salsa bands," Yolanda said.

"Really? And here I was going to impress you with my love of the Hispanic heritage. I was even going to try out a little Spanish on you." Nick saw not a glimmer of amusement and returned to the stereo. A moment later Leadbelly played a plaintive blues tune, and Nick returned to what he now accepted as inevitable failure in the seductive arts.

For her part, Yolanda was torn between treating the evening like a date and trying to beat information out of this strange man. Perhaps the direct approach. "So what did you find out about the book?"

"Well, necromancy isn't really a science for a start," said Nick, "and as pseudo-sciences go, it lags well behind spoon-bending in popularity. Would you like to sit on the couch? We could talk on the couch."

Yolanda seemed reticent, "I don't want to get too

comfortable here."

"Well, you're in luck," Nick said. "My couch is down right unpleasant to sit on. Makes my back hurt just to think about it."

Yolanda gave Nick a look usually reserved for mimes who have just stubbed their toe and hollered bloody murder. Really, you can't resist sitting on a couch with a man trying this hard to be charming while failing so badly.

"If we sit on the couch can we stick to talking about the book and not wander off into any new territory? You have found out more about the book, right?" said Yolanda.

"My couch awaits."

Outside Nick's house, in a 1984 Beaumont Sedan, Detectives Tom Delaney and Pat MacGriffin sat listening to a radio receiver. From it came the metallic echo of conversation between Yolanda and Nick. Delaney smiled the smile of a man liking his work more than was healthy.

"He's got her on the couch," said Delaney. "That woman belongs on a couch. Belongs on my couch, you know what I mean?"

MacGriffin knew what he meant and wished all the more that his sick-leave had not expired the night before, "We're back-up, not an audience at one of your rain-coat movies."

Delaney smiled, "I worked the porno squad for five years, best five years of my life."

"It's called the vice squad," said MacGriffin.

"I like what I like," said Delaney.

MacGriffin sighed. A partner who likes what he likes. How kind of the world, two weeks before retirement. Only two weeks and Pat MacGriffin could fish every day. Not that MacGriffin would fish—he hated fishing. What he really liked was painting miniature soldiers—especially Napoleonic soldiers. He had a collection of over two thousand painted soldiers in his basement, reenacting the Battle of Waterloo, and this time the French would win, goddamn it. Only by pure bad luck had Napoleon lost the original battle, and luck did not reign in Pat MacGriffin's basement. So in two weeks he could devote himself full-time to painting and arranging miniature combatants. But as far as anyone in the department was concerned, he was retiring to fish. Cops just didn't understand miniatures.

"What was the signal again?" Delaney asked, "To bust in?"

"Christ," said MacGriffin, roused from his visions of mini-Napoleonic glory, "what kind of back-up are you, you don't even know the signal for going in?"

Delaney laughed, "I was staring at her tits when she told us what she'd say—you have to admit, it can be hard to concentrate with those tits in your face."

MacGriffin wanted to tell this foul-mouthed, sexist asshole what a blight on the blue uniform he was. He wanted to tell him about the two grown daughters he had, and how much he wished they never had to deal with the Tom Delaneys of the world. All of this he wanted to say to his temporary partner. But MacGriffin didn't say any of it, because MacGriffin feared one thing above all else: irony. Two weeks to pension, only irony really threatened him. Every night as he slept, L.A. Times headlines danced in his head. "Officer Gunned Down One Week to Retirement," "Colleagues Say Slain Officer Looked Forward to Days of Fishing," "Army of Miniatures Found in Basement of Mortally Wounded Officer." Yes, irony was far too dangerous a thing with which to fool. So MacGriffin would make nice with asshole Delaney because he refused to stir up any irony.

"We go in on *rosebud*," MacGriffin said.

◆ ◆ ◆

"Now your leading expert on Medieval Occult Sciences is Dr. Dantelani of ULV," said Nick.

"ULV?" asked Yolanda.

"University of Las Vegas—big occult sciences school."

"You're kidding me."

"Oh no," said Nick in a voice that failed to reassure, "ULV once had a program in Parapsychology."

"When?"

"Closed it down in '59 I think, something to do with the cold war." Nick shifted uncomfortably on the sofa, the only way, in fact, to shift on his furniture. "As I recall, a certain Professor Montperk received government funding in the mid-fifties for research into mental mediation of Soviet strategic intelligence operations." Yolanda looked blankly at her crazy man. "Are you following this?" Nick asked.

"They wanted the Professor to read Khrushchev's mind," she said.

"Wow, you are good," said Nick in honest admiration.

"Get on with it," said Yolanda in obvious impatience.

"Right, well, it seems the good professor set up about two tons worth of electronic equipment in the basement of the science building and began channel-surfing the minds of Russian military planners. He told everyone that all the wires and buzzers helped him to amplify the thoughts of the Russians. And in his defense, Russia is a long way from Las Vegas. A little bit of amplification couldn't hurt, especially when you consider how softly some Russians think."

Nick looked for some sign of incomprehension on Yolanda's part, but saw only skepticism, and pressed on. "Professor Montperk gathered some of the finest minds in parapsychology to his program. Given the dearth of funding to that noble sport, he had no trouble recruiting. They researched the physics of spoon bending, spirit channeling—especially Russian spirits—and telekinesis. They did double blind experiments with psychics straining to read minds and affect pulse rates in distant rooms. The CIA hoped the psychics could become a new super weapon. Give heart attacks to distant world leaders insufficiently sympathetic to the American Way of Life. Unfortunately, the psychics couldn't perform under double blind conditions, so Montperk lowered the bar. He sat about creating the sort of *nurturing atmosphere* conducive to psychic phenomenon. He allowed the research subjects to affect anyone's pulse rate they wanted, and the researchers would find out later who got zapped. This brought real results. Montperk credited at least seven heart attacks on campus to his psychics. This impressed the spooks. Demonstrable results and seven fewer useless academics in the world—what's not to like?

"They did better with the mind reading too, when Montperk relaxed the rigorous controls. Being watched all the time disturbs the flow of psychic energy. Once the scientists loosened things up, the psychics registered statistically significant results. Hell, after a while they were busting the charts. Moving objects with the mind became a snap too, once the researchers quit putting cellophane over the yellow pages and checking the psychics for hidden strings. The psychics in Montperk's program could bend spoons, forks, keys, you name it; any small light metal object, and they could bend the bejesus out of it. They had a bit more trouble un-bending stuff, but who can fathom the strange ways of psychic energies?"

"The university put up with all this?" asked Yolanda.

"Well, the government paid for it all, and in the fifties who knew that spoon bending belonged on Johnny Carson rather than in the basement of the University of Las Vegas? Anyway, the whole thing came crashing down. For a start, Montperk's electrical channeling doohickeys shut down the Vegas power grid seven times and forced folks to gamble in the dark. The casinos disapprove of this since the pit boss likes to keep an eye on people when they play. Also, it seems that some of the parapsychology professors made a sideline of using E.S.P. to aid players at the card tables."

"It worked well enough to anger the casinos?" asked Yolanda.

"Actually, it failed badly enough to endanger the lives of the professors. One will find few animals as dangerous as a pissed off blackjack player two grand down. But the beginning of the end came when the federal government stuck its long nose into things. Seems the Professor had twice predicted eminent attacks, sending the military into DefCon 2. Also, he had assured the CIA that Soviet counter-psychics controlled Eisenhower's mind every other Tuesday and that Soviet scientists had developed the two inch atom bomb."

"Two inch atom bomb?"

"Yeah, very portable. You can smuggle it into the enemy country inside a diplomatic pouch and deliver it to a target with a wrist-rocket."

"You're making all this up," Yolanda said.

"Not at all. It is all true. I found it on the Internet. Anyway, the government took the unreasonable position that since *they* were paying for everything, Professor Montperk ought to either deliver worthwhile intelligence results or lose his grant. That's the arrogance of the federal government for you."

"What are you, some sort of raving conservative?" asked Yolanda with a smile.

"I'm not really political. I just hate getting my grants pulled," Nick replied.

"You get grants?"

"Sure, I'm really a performance artist. Death exhibits are just a side-line. Frankly, I think if you look at Montperk's whole operation as performance art, it works rather well."

"Channeling Khrushchev from a Vegas basement?" Yolanda said, "just what *wouldn't* work as performance art?"

"I think you have hit on the beauty of my chosen medium," Nick replied as he looked at Yolanda. She sat on the couch like a model in a magazine: half off the cushion, back arched, shoulders back and feet crossed. No one could comfortably sit otherwise on Nick's couch, but she managed to make it look good.

"So finish the story," Yolanda said with a light laugh. She had gotten used to Nick's rather distracted manner around her.

"The fiendish government canceled his ticket, and the university sent poor Montperk packing. He wound up as a carnival barker, I think. After Montperk, the government ended all of its parapsychology funding. We all know what happened after that."

"We do?"

"Sure, the Cuban missile crisis, the Kennedy assassination, Vietnam, OPEC."

Yolanda had to laugh, "All that because Montperk lost his grant?"

Nick smiled and shook his finger at Yolanda like a parent scolding a wayward child, "Pulling grants hurts everybody, and don't you forget it."

Yolanda laughed. She rested her head on her palm covering her eyes and gently shook her head in something between amusement and exasperated disbelief. "So," she said, "what has any of this got to do with Dr. Dantelani and ULV's occult sciences school?"

"I wondered when you'd ask me that," Nick said.

"I wondered when you'd ask me that," repeated Yolanda with a laugh.

"The Feds funded Montperk out of the black-book. That's the espionage accountancy equivalent of a shoulder shrug. No one admits to spending anything. You can imagine how hard it is to keep the books with a system like that. I understand the CIA has some of the worst accountants in government. Who, after all, wants to keep track of budgets for departments that always show up in the ledgers with giant black magic-marker lines obscuring the names? So when the CIA cut Montperk's funding, they must have missed a source. ULV kept getting checks for 'Research Into Strange Phenomena' from some front company in Peoria. No college in the country sends a grant check back. Since they had already kicked out the Professor and his staff of loonies, they decided to change the program to something a bit less far out and hire a guy to collect the money, do the research, and stay out of the way."

"So they went with Medieval Occult Sciences?"

"You have to admit, it is a strange phenomena. In addition,

it can be almost respectable if you find a willing scholar of medieval history. Most important, the Middle Ages were long ago and have nothing to do with politics."

"Like the old Soviet scholar of ancient China said: to be safe your topic must be a thousand miles away and a thousand years ago," Yolanda said.

"Exactly. So that is how the University of Las Vegas obtained the finest, and only, program in Medieval Occult Sciences in the country. Not that it is much of a program at all. Currently, it has just one scholar. Dr. Dantelani. I understand he still works out of a corner in the basement of the science building."

"But of course," Yolanda said, "where else would you put the occult *sciences* program? Surely not the basement of the humanities building."

"Okay," Nick said, "mock if you want, but the good doctor has a program and tenure, and these days a specialist in the occult practices of the Middle Ages can do a lot worse. And remember, he may be the key to solving your little problem."

Yolanda's problem flashed through her head. Finding a killer, not a book. That was no amusing matter. Nick noticed the change in her demeanor, but he had no idea what caused it.

"So what does Dr. Dantelani say about the book?" Yolanda asked.

"Uh, well, I haven't talked to him," Nick said.

"After all this?"

"He doesn't like phones. I can hardly blame him, they haven't done me any favors lately."

"What do you mean he doesn't like phones? Phones aren't to be liked or disliked, they are to be answered and talked into."

Nick squirmed under the heat of Yolanda's question, and squirming hurts on Nick's couch. "Look," said Nick, squirming, "I've tried to get a hold of him on the phone. But obscure scholars with tenure don't have to answer the phone if they don't want to. It took me two days to link up with somebody who knew who he was—and that guy was a janitor working in the science-building basement. I almost got him to bring

Dr. Dantelani to the phone. No dice. The doctor does not do phones. The janitor did say the doctor would happily receive a personal visit. The doctor likes to watch the person to whom he speaks."

This peeved Yolanda. She sat back hard onto the cushion of the couch. A spring caught her between the shoulder blades, doing nothing to help her mood. "So after all this you still know nothing?"

"I know lots of things, it's just that most of them haven't to do with books of necromancy," Nick offered. "But on the bright side," Nick continued, brightening, "I do know where to find out about books on necromancy." Yolanda's doubtful expression took some of Nick's shine off. "It's just, uh, I have to go to Vegas to find out … the stuff … about necromancy books." Nick now knew what a bug on a pin felt like being looked at by a hexapodalist.

Yolanda sat frustrated on the very uncomfortable couch. Nick Sabernail seemed always to tell the truth when the truth didn't help. So far as she could see, the night was a bust. No information on the missing book, no further insight into the motives of Nick Sabernail, no blood-caked cattle prod in sight. The fact that Nick made amusing company only made matters worse if he killed women successively. Serial killers could be charming. But not charming enough to date. Serial killers could be disarmingly charming. But Yolanda was not about to be disarmed by this fellow's charm. Though he was charming. As first-dates-in-the-fellow's-house went this one wasn't half bad. Even the couch proved safe from any temptation to put the moves on—no one could make out on this thing. Yolanda realized that these thoughts were inconsistent with her mission and that pissed her off all the more. "Why do you think it is that Dr. Dantelani doesn't talk on phones?" Yolanda asked.

"Who knows? Maybe his mother beat him with one as a child. Maybe he's afraid of germs. Maybe years of study in medieval history has dulled his skills with modern devices.

Maybe he likes an air of mystery."

"An air of mystery?" Yolanda said.

"Sure, every Citizen Kane needs his rosebud. This is Dantelani's rosebud. His inscrutable signature. Hell, maybe he thinks it will impress the women on the third floor. Who knows?"

◆ ◆ ◆

"Rosebud!" yelled Tom Delaney, nearly deafening MacGriffin. "That's the signal! Let's go!"

"Wait," said MacGriffin, "he said it, not her." But Tom had already leapt out the door. Tom was ready for action. Tom was ready to kick ass. Tom was ready for anything that wasn't more of this weird conversation about colleges and stuff.

MacGriffin bolted out of the car. "Hold it!" MacGriffin shouted, this time in a voice Tom could not ignore, "I gotta get stuff." MacGriffin ran to the rear of the car. He labored to open the car trunk.

"Damn it! Come on, she could be in trouble," Tom shouted.

"That is why I'm not going in unprepared," said MacGriffin. The trunk opened, and from the arsenal inside MacGriffin grabbed a huge bulletproof vest.

"You're already wearing a vest!" pleaded Tom.

"That little thing under my shirt can barely stop rounds from a BB gun. I'm going in covered," said MacGriffin.

Tom watched a moment as MacGriffin wrestled with the vest. Tom looked at the house where this instant Yolanda Vasquez might lie helpless at the mercy of a serial killer. Tom looked back at MacGriffin, almost in the body armor. Tom shrugged. "Got any shotguns in there?" Tom asked.

◆ ◆ ◆

Yolanda started a bit when Nick used the *go-code*, but she quickly settled. After all, *she* had not said it. And no one listening to their conversation could possibly think she faced any danger. When nothing happened for a few minutes she settled completely. Nick went to the kitchen to fetch some coffee while Yolanda fought the couch springs to a draw. She had just found a way to sit back without the couch stabbing her when Nick returned with two cups of coffee.

"You like your coffee like your men: sugary, right?" Nick said.

At that moment both heard a loud thumping on the door.

"Kids?" Sabernail said.

Then two loud gunshots made both of them jump. Yolanda pulled the gun from beneath her pant leg just as the door flew off its hinges. Two men stormed into the room. One wearing a wicked grin and carrying a smoking shotgun. The second in full body armor, wearing a riot helmet and carrying a pistol in one hand and a steel riot shield in the other.

Yolanda did not believe her eyes.

"Drop it!" yelled the man in riot gear. Nick dropped the coffee.

"The gun! Drop the gun now!" yelled MacGriffin through the helmet visor.

"I'm the cop!" yelled Yolanda in disbelief.

The riot-helmeted head jerked forward. MacGriffin pried his visor up with his pistol.

"Jesus!" yelled Tom ducking out of MacGriffin's line of fire, "watch that thing!"

MacGriffin held up the visor and surveyed the scene clearly for the first time.

"Oh," he said.

Nick looked at the two cops. Then at his date with the drawn service revolver. Then at the coffee stain on his imitation Persian rug. Finally back again at his date. "And you act like you don't know anything about performance art," he said.

HIRING THE HELP

Vinnie the Squid sat drinking a Long Island Ice Tea in the Cock-Tails Cocktail Lounge. The lounge took its name from the sign overhanging the road that passes the strip-mall in whose corner the little bar nestled. Said sign read *Cock* at the top and *Tails* at the bottom, and between the two half-words it presented the drawn picture of a woman's derriere. Very clever. The name and picture made promises the bar could not keep, for while a few cocks sat about sucking booze, not a woman's tail, nor an exposed derriere, could be found in the bar. It was the kind of place lonely guys go to pick up gorgeous super-models, fully anticipating that, finding none, they will instead drink themselves into a stupor and sleep it off in the vacant lot across the street. Not that Vinnie was a booze hound. Vinnie the Squid was a man who got things done. A man of action. A virtual poor man's James Bond. Except that mostly, he stole things.

Vinnie drank in this dump only to meet with a guy about steady work. The guy had seemed strange over the phone and the job description even stranger. Fact was, Vinnie did not really know what a "henchman" did. Still, the caller had good references. Big Al Bigdoviwich had vouched for him. The guy knew Big Al (though he did not say how) and Big Al had called from San Quinton Prison—using one of his rare calling privileges, Vinnie noted to himself—to confirm that the guy might be a kook but not a cop. Vinnie needed the work. Whatever the work, Vinnie needed it. He had pretty well blown his cat burglar career falling out of the second floor window of a house and twisting his knee to kingdom come. Considering

California's *three-strikes-and-your-out* sentencing laws, he was damn lucky the house turned out to be a halfway home for the mentally disturbed. The orderly who found Vinnie screaming on the driveway had just been hired. He mistook Vinnie for a patient and called a paramedic instead of the police. Had someone with more than two hours of experience with the marginally insane found the screaming cat burglar, Vinnie would have been in deep trouble. Vinnie had more than three strikes on his record. In fact, if California's mandatory sentencing laws retreated to a modest *thirteen-strikes-and-your-out* policy, Vinnie would still be walking a razor's edge as a professional thief.

In light of all this, Vinnie happily drank in a strange bar on the hope of a cushy job with a connected organization. Big Al said this fellow had real connections. That's what Vinnie needed. Some protection. And no climbing.

◆ ◆ ◆

Victor Drakan sat in his van watching the door of the *Cock-picture-of-a-woman's-butt-Tails* cocktail lounge. He had watched for this "Vinnie the Squid" fellow to show up, and Drakan wanted to be sure he didn't walk into a trap. Not that Drakan knew what a trap would look like. His research for this particular venture had consisted entirely of watching re-runs of the *Mod Squad*. Not seeing any grungy, hip, twenty-year-olds pretending to repair a car nearby, he felt safe. Now though, Drakan considered that not only did he not know what a trap looked like, he also had scant idea what Vinnie the Squid looked like either. Drakan tried to imagine a professional crook that resembled, or behaved in the manner of, a squid. This proved unhelpful at sorting out the universally downtrodden looking clientele entering the bar. Not knowing what Vinnie looked like, and thus not knowing whom to approach in the bar when the time came, merely reaffirmed that building a criminal empire turned out to be harder than it looked.

Drakan's image of a proper crime organization floated again in his mind. Dr. No on his island. Dr. No combined elegant table settings, steel-doored holding cells, nuclear reactors (complete with death-rays), all in a tropical paradise easily accessible by commercial airplane flights. How does one pull off a thing like that? Islands can be bought or rented. Steel doors can be ordered from steel door manufacturers. Even nuclear reactors can be obtained from small countries these days. Drakan didn't even care about the table settings. But the problem of recruiting henchmen puzzled him no end. How did Dr. No get all those people working for him? Exactly how does one get in touch with reliable, seven-foot, bald-headed, ironhanded thugs? How do you recruit astrophysicists willing to work with a criminal entrepreneur on a death ray? Can you put an ad in the paper? *Wanted: Ph.D. in particle physics, must have locked lips and flexible morals, English speakers preferred.* How can you insure that the guy driving the speedboat, or working the decontamination center, or guarding the steel door, will do the job right and keep his mouth shut? What's the pay scale for a thug? Do they need social security cards? In *You Only Live Twice*, the super-villain Blofeld had once operated a volcano sized underground rocket launching and space mission control center on the coast of Japan. How did he hire the people to build such a thing? You can't just tell the contractor what you're up to. Someone might call the police or the newspapers. What do you say? "Oh, rocket science is a hobby of mine. We're just going to blast a few monkeys up there and see what comes down." Drakan knew that these movies were only fiction, but he assumed that they were based in real life. But how do you recruit henchmen in real life?

So this problem too, Drakan solved all by himself. He had signed up with a prison pen-pal group and laboriously written out over a hundred letters to criminals serving sentences in California's penal system. Drakan selected his correspondents carefully. A great number of California's prisoners sat in stir for drug consumption or low-level drug peddling offenses.

These crooks were of no use to Drakan since he needed reliable crooks with underworld experience, not unlucky drug addicts. Nor did he write to killers, wife-beaters, rapists, pedophiles, or political extremists. Drakan wanted professionals. But not too professional. Drakan avoided writing to mafia members, as they already worked for an extensive criminal enterprise, and Drakan intended to build his from the ground up. He wanted no one with divided loyalties. Unfortunately, it can be hard to tell who is in the mafia, so Drakan avoided writing to any prisoner whose last name ended in a vowel. This left a list of car-thieves, fences, bookies, cat-burglars, confidence men, bank robbers, counterfeiters, bad-check passers, jewel thieves, embezzlers, phony psychics, muggers, deserters, pimps, gun-runners, moon-shiners, extortionists, diamond smugglers, money-launderers, transporters of stolen goods, numbers-runners, riot-inciters, home-invaders, pickpockets, forgers, arsonists, plagiarists, kidnappers, bigamists, blackmailers, poachers, celebrity impersonators gone bad, shop-lifters, hired enforcers, joy-riders, crooked cops, peeping-toms, vandals, Ponzi schemers, loan-sharks, tax evaders, parole violators, hijackers, carjackers, racketeers, inside traders, jury-tamperers, price-fixers, smugglers of illegal immigrants, get-away drivers, compulsive gamblers, three-card Monte hustlers, junk-bond dealers, and former politicians. It sounds like a lot to say, but actually the pickings can get slim.

To each of his hundred prospective pen-pals, Drakan sent a letter that subtly suggested that he, Drakan, might make it worth the recipient's while to either join in an "illicit" enterprise upon release, or failing this, to suggest a reliable fellow on the outside who would. In fact, the first letter to each was innocence itself, barely suggesting crime and profit. Only after a correspondence began in earnest did Drakan intend to really suggest criminal partnership. Drakan had expected reticence and downright suspicion on the part of his prison pen-pals. Surely they would suspect a trap, or at least worry about incriminating themselves in writing. Contrary to

Drakan's expectations, the crooks not only leapt at the chance to commit further crimes, they even suggested ways Drakan could aid them in committing further felonies while still in custody. Most of these involved Drakan sending them stolen credit cards, though he could not figure out what they might charge while in prison. One con wanted Drakan to smuggle women into his maximum security prison, writing, "I press the assurance that me and you, we can make millions with this. Millions of cigs that you can trade for your share as cash."

Drakan's biggest problem proved keeping the crooks' interest once he had turned down their scams. After some time (he had fortunately begun this effort even before stealing the *Compendium*) Drakan had settled on an inmate of San Quinton named Alan Bigdoviwich, apparently called "Big Al" either because of his last name or his physical presentation. (Some of Drakan's pen-pals had been oddly interested in giving detailed descriptions of their bodies—along with fluid samples. Fortunately, Big Al had not engaged in such escapades.) After Drakan sent several cash payments to Big Al's sister in San Diego, and promised to send more, the large Polish car-thief set Drakan up with this "Squid" character, promising to "vouch" for Drakan, whatever that meant. But now Big Al's reluctance to broach the topic of appearances forced Drakan to go into the *Cock-picture-of-a-woman's-butt-Tails* cocktail lounge and just guess who would be the first to join his empire of crime. At least now Drakan was pretty sure no one would trap him.

In the bar, Vinnie waited with growing impatience. He looked for a "Mr. Big" type, complete with pinky rings and two dumb goons. Truth to tell, Vinnie knew no more about the mafia than he had seen in the movies. He had known a guy from Vegas who his friends said was connected. The guy did an uninterrupted imitation of Al Pacino. Vinnie's friends said he had only gotten that way after seeing *The Godfather*.

So Vinnie figured either movies got the look from real life, or the wise-guys watched the movies. In any event, as far-sighted as Vinnie was, looks weren't going to matter much. Obviously Vinnie couldn't wear his glasses. One has to make the right first impression.

As Vinnie watched the door, waiting for Mr. Big to appear, he noticed a thin, pale man with pinched features slowly walking from one bar patron to the next, looking each up and down in turn. The man wore a black jump suit, a black neck scarf, and a beret of the same color. He looked like a comic rendering of an old time movie director. He'd stand some five feet away from someone and look the person over slowly, starting with the fellow's shoes, and craning his head around while keeping his feet planted, in order to see the rest. Each bar patron he inspected noticed him but sat stock-still, hoping the loony-bird man would go away. Each time, the loony-bird man did, only to stalk another drinker. Vinnie just hoped Mr. Big got here before the loony-bird man got to Vinnie.

Drakan inspected them each carefully. Shoes were very important. The man, Vinnie, burgled houses in the manner of a cat, and so would have exotic footwear. Given his own success at the art of climbing-to-pilfer, Drakan regarded himself as something of an expert at cat-burglar footwear. Though obviously this Vinnie the Squid person would not be wearing suction cups, he might have spikes on his shoes, or at least a lot of straps. So shoes were important to look at. On the other hand, Vinnie might be incognito and not wear his regular shoes. So Drakan sized up each man's physique and asked himself, could this fellow fit through a small window? And the eyes were important. A cat-burglar had to have keen night vision. Drakan figured it helped his search that the bar was dark—a real test of night vision. In spite of all this, Drakan still could not tell his man.

Drakan had earlier decided that Vinnie received the moniker, *squid*, for the sound he made to signal his cat-burglar partners. This just stood to reason. *Squid* couldn't refer to cat-burglar's suction cups, since all cat-burglars had these (why not call them *squid-burglars*?), nor could the name have anything to do with a squid's many arms. Had Vinnie been a pickpocket, then *squid* might refer to how many hands he could get in on someone, but Vinnie did not pick, he burgled. Squids did not terrify and had no reputation for toughness—except for giant squids in Jules Verne's tales, and Vinnie had not been named *Vinnie the Giant Squid*, and, as he was a cat burglar, he could not be a giant anyway—so Vinnie had not been named a squid on account of his toughness. No one refers to squids as the owls of the sea, so squids had no great intelligence. Squids shot non-lethal dye and ran away when in trouble. They had no great courage. Thus, the only reason his fellow felons could have named Vinnie after the multi-armed aquatic animal must be that he used a squid-like call in the night to signal his confederates that the coast was clear. So much, at least, Drakan knew.

Drakan meant to use this fact to identify Vinnie. Drakan would make a squid call and let Vinnie know that, indeed, the coast was clear. Unfortunately, even after three hours of research on squids the night before at the Los Angeles County Library—Main Branch, Drakan still had no idea what noise a squid made. He had meant to call the Long Beach Aquarium this morning to ask a marine biologist, but circumstances had forced him to sew flesh on a new corpse instead, and as usual these days, the time had just flown by. Now Drakan had to just guess at what a squid sounded like.

Drakan approached a new prospect: a skinny, smelly man wearing tan colored Chuck Jones All Stars sneakers with untied laces. The unkempt man drank at the bar, nursing a brown liquid that reminded Drakan of the pictures of squid dye he had seen in the Encyclopedia Britannica last night. Drakan drew in his breath; it was now or never.

"Squiiiipp! Squiiiipp!" Drakan said at the man.

The man froze in his seat. Though his head remained stock still, Drakan noticed the man's eyes pressing against their sockets, trying to get a look at him. This could be the guy.

"Squiiipp! Squiiipp!" Drakan repeated, proud of how close he must have come to the correct sound.

The scruffy man turned his eyes back to his drink. He breathed fast and shallow now. Drakan took a step closer expecting the man to *squiiipp* in return.

"Get away from me," the man said, so under his breath Drakan barely heard him. "Get away from me or I'll scream. I'll scream and I'll hit you with something," the man said, still just barely audible.

Drakan jumped back. This could not be Vinnie the Squid. Drakan walked carefully over to a man at the end of the bar who wore gray hiking boots.

"Squiiipp! Squiiipp!" said Drakan.

"Stop that," the man said softly, "go away."

Frustrated, Drakan backed away and looked around the bar. In the musty, stale, beer-smelling darkness only one face seemed to notice Drakan. It belonged to a skinny, nervous, squinting fellow sitting in a corner booth. Drakan couldn't see his shoes. The squinter kept darting a look at Drakan and darting his eyes away again. Drakan thought a moment about the corner booth and decided that that might mean something. Drakan headed towards the squinter. As Drakan slowly approached, the man's darting, squinting glances increased in frequency and intensity. He looked like a man desperately trying to stare into the heart of the Antarctic sun.

Drakan stood at the corner of the table as the man tried to turn his eyes into laser beams. "Squiiipp! Squiiipp!" Drakan said, this time with less conviction than before.

"What? What?" said the squinting man, either trying to focus on, or obliterate, Drakan, with his eyes.

Fed up, Drakan just came out and asked, "Are you Vinnie the Squid?"

Suddenly the squinting ended. The man's eyes flew open in a look of shock. "Yes," he managed to say.

Drakan heaved an irritated sigh and plopped into the booth, "Then why didn't you answer the call?"

Vinnie scratched his head. No one told him about a call. He puzzled over the matter for a moment. Then he just figured this fellow must have assumed he knew more about organized crime than Vinnie actually knew. Still, Vinnie planned to keep up appearances. "Sorry," said Vinnie, "I forgot about ... the ... call thing."

Drakan looked Vinnie the Squid over. His first henchman; if he got the job. Drakan jerked his head underneath the table to have a gander at Vinnie's shoes. Penny loafers? Drakan pulled his head up and looked Vinnie square in his eyes. Once again the prospective hireling squinted for all he was worth. Looking at him, Drakan started to squint right back. Drakan's face pinched up so tight it threatened to implode.

The two men squinted across the table at each other as if piano wire stretched between their eyelids.

Vinnie broke the spell, "Would you like a drink, sir?"

A drink. Bars are for drinking. Drakan didn't drink, except for Chablis Rothschild 1807 and Concord Royal Port after dinner, neither of which he had ever had in his life. "Business first," said Drakan, "do you have your resume?"

"Resume?" answered the cat-burglar, "that's like a rap sheet?"

Drakan's anus tightened as he wiggled into the seat. Should this man have a resume? Drakan didn't know. "Very well," Drakan continued, "do you have your rap sheet?"

Vinnie squirmed too. He had never realized that organized crime was so, well, organized. "Uh ... uh, well, uh, the police keep mine."

Drakan squeezed tighter into his seat. He looked at Vinnie in silence for a moment then shot him with a fire hose of words, "I'm putting together a project, an important project, that may have a place for a man like you. Eventually, I'm not saying today or tomorrow, but eventually, our organization may have retirement benefits, healthcare plan, 401K, a standard package, whatever would be standard and expected. But we have a ground floor now. The place to start and we start there and work up to 401K. You don't have to have a resume or your rap sheet. Social security card is optional. But records will be kept. We need to record you. So be prepared to provide the appropriate details to our records. Experience, career projection, where you think you'll fit in the long-term scheme. I just bought a book on this: *Starting a Business for Unlimited Growth.* Page thirty-five so far, no further. We'll have everything sorted out in a week or two. Just two hundred and forty pages in the whole book. Good book. You understand there is no drinking on the job? Vacation time has not been allowed. We will be very busy. *Start-ups require twenty-five hour days and eight day weeks.* Page twenty-six. I'm not saying *no* days off. We'll see. Unlimited growth, that's what I see. You could take over operations some day. I'd do the interviews, handle the paparazzi, you handle day to day. I could see it going that way. All depends on you. Depends on you. Depends on you."

The boss seemed to be winding down, so Vinnie jumped in with what he hoped this fellow would receive as an intelligent question, "Uh, what should I call you, sir, you didn't introduce yourself."

The question so stunned Drakan his sphincter quit tightening. Drakan hadn't counted on this line of inquiry. He didn't want to give him the Drakan name in case things didn't work out. Drakan pulled out of the air what he thought would be an appropriate but inconspicuous name. "You may call me Dr. Baron Victor von Finkelstein," Drakan said. That sounded about right. It sounded to Drakan just the sort of name he would have. Not as good as *Drakan* of course, but good.

"You're a baron?" asked Vinnie.

"Uh, yes." Drakan had not expected this complication. Why must everything one says be taken so seriously?

Drakan pressed on to an explanation, "My family comes from Carpathia, in Eastern Europe. We're the oldest branch of the von Finkelsteins. The Archduke of Carpathia knighted the earliest Finkelstein for his valor at the battle of, uh, Katuhwayustin. That established the main branch of our already distinguished family," Drakan now warmed to the tale, "my great, great, great, great, great … how many greats did I say?"

"Four I think."

"Great, great, great grandfather achieved the rank of baron for his invention of spurs. The family has since produced both warriors and scientists. My great, great, great, grandfather immigrated to this country from the Old World and became the first scientific frontiersman—doing science on the frontier at the frontiers of science—and established the family fortune in the New World. Still, we keep in touch with matters back in the old country."

Vinnie looked impressed, "So we're international—I mean you are—I mean *we* just if I'm in."

Drakan had no idea what being *international* could mean, but the idea appeared to have excited the little thief so Drakan grabbed it. "Very international," Drakan said, "and very national too." This Vinnie person seemed pleased, so Drakan smiled. "Now, Mr. Squid—" Drakan had barely gotten this out before Vinnie the Squid interrupted him.

"About the Squid thing," Vinnie began, in a voice suggesting embarrassment, "see, the thing is, I hoped not to have that name in, well, in the organization. See, I only got that name cause I called myself *Vinnie the Rat*, and a friend said one time I looked more like a squid than a rat, on account of I was sort of awkward—this was before, when I was a kid—and the others laughed, and so I was *The Squid*. But I'd rather lose the name now." Vinnie looked on at his prospective boss hopefully.

Drakan considered for a moment the implications of this new revelation that rats stood higher on the criminal hierarchy than squids. Drakan gave Vinnie what he hoped would appear to be a look of intense concentration. Vinnie just squinted at him. Finally in a portentous voice—one that barely squeaked at all—Drakan said, "I'm sure after a suitable probationary period we can promote you from squid to rat. Indeed, with hard work, you can become Vinnie the Bat, or Vinnie the Gopher. Indeed, if you really work hard, Moose and Wolf are not out of the question. It is all a matter of loyalty and hard work. Are you ready to work hard?"

"Yes, Dr. Baron. I assure you I am a get-the-job-done guy. I just need to be part of an organization. Get some cover. I'm a good man, no squealer. Ask anybody. Well, hell, you know Big Al, he told you. I'm your man."

Drakan smiled so wide that the middle part of his face looked almost un-pinched. "Shall we go see headquarters?"

"Sure," said Vinnie

"Did you drive here?" asked Drakan.

"I took the bus. But I can drive. Would you like me to drive Dr. Baron?"

Drakan leaned back. Dr. No could not have done this better.

Two weeks earlier Drakan had moved his entire operation from the dingy quarters of the warehouse district to spacious digs across from the East Los Angeles Bus Depot. These old warehouses competed successfully in dinginess with his earlier base of operations, but they won hands down in size. Although a bit more urban than Dr. No, his current headquarters could house an industrial size reanimation center.

Vinnie drove the van into the parking lot of this complex, impressed by the scale of what he presumed to be the mob's social club. Vinnie guided his new boss out of the van, acting the experienced valet. Looking around, the little cat-burglar noticed that, though the complex of buildings sat in the middle of a busy city, they enclosed a space unto themselves.

Very much a hide-out. The Baron led Vinnie through a door marked "Entrance—Central HQ." Vinnie thought this sign a bit daring even for a well connected outfit. The door shutting behind him, Vinnie could make out little in the room that had no lights on and with windows smeared over in dark paint. Then the Baron clapped his hands twice, and florescent lights throughout the open warehouse flickered on. The artificial light barely cut the gloom of the immense room. After a moment or two, Vinnie made out a human figure standing against the nearest wall. Vinnie approached the man, offering his had.

"Hi, Vinnie the ... uh, new guy. Just signed up. I drive the Baron."

Closer now, Vinnie saw clearly that decaying flesh covered the figure leaning against the wall. Dead as dented dentures, no doubt about it. Vinnie jumped back and let out a squeal. "Christ! I mean, I know we get hardcore and all, but shouldn't you at least bury them or something? I mean, leaning them up as decoration? Christ. We should bury 'um at least."

Having just three days ago spent five hours unburying the corpse against the wall, Drakan did not take well to the suggestion. Drakan had already begun laying out Vinnie's jumpsuit and utility belt on a card table in the center of the room and no longer watched Vinnie as the cat-burglar looked at the corpse.

"Shake his hand," Drakan said.

Vinnie thought this a pretty sick ritual, but he reached for the corpse's hand anyway. Just an inch away he saw the hand move up. Vinnie jumped back, "Whoa shit!" The dead man's eyes opened. The hand moved up further as if offering to shake. Vinnie leapt back again, tripping on his own feet, and fell to the floor. "Jesus! Jesus! Jesus!" Vinnie screamed.

"There," said Drakan, pleased with himself, "I have your uniform ready." Drakan turned around to find his undead minion chasing his new henchman about headquarters. "Stop that now!" he shouted. The corpse stopped dead in its tracks.

Vinnie slowly regained his composure.

"That thing's dead!" Vinnie said.

"Undead," replied Drakan.

"What?"

"Not dead, *un*dead. You had better get used to undeath. You will see a lot of it."

Vinnie looked on in horror at the flesh-hung corpse. The zombie stared back with dead yellow eyes that showed no hint of thought or will. Vinnie swallowed hard. He looked back at the Baron expecting to see fangs, and a cape, and to become the vampire's next meal at any moment. Instead, he saw the Baron holding up a purple jumpsuit and a soldier's helmet painted bright yellow.

"This is the henchman uniform," he said proudly.

THE SECOND DEGREE

MacGriffin had his man. Under the hot lights, in a windowless room of concrete blocks painted prison gray, he had his man. The suspect sat at the table across from MacGriffin, who stood watching the pathetic little weasel squirm. At least he would squirm, once MacGriffin got done with him, the little weasel.

"You're all through Saberson, it's all up for you."

"Nail," said the weasel.

"That's right," MacGriffin continued, "Your ass is nailed to that seat, your hide is nailed to the wall, and I got a nail for your head."

"No. Saber*nail*, not Saber*son*."

MacGriffin looked at this perp hard. How to crack this nut? No Bullshit. That way worked. "Your Saber-who-I-say-you-are son, that clear?"

"Okay," said the perp-weasel, "You've arrested someone named Saberson whose head you have nailed to this chair. Since I am not he, can I go now?"

When this room had been called an *interrogation room*, years ago, it had been illuminated by a single light set above the suspect's head. Now they called it an *interview room*, and in the interest of giving it a warmer feel, and allowing everyone more light by which to take notes, the department had added a bank of florescent bulbs crackling an office-light glow. The good old days were well and gone, MacGriffin thought. Still, he met this punk-perp alone, mano a mano. Except for officer Tom Delaney who sat just behind him. And backup from Detective Vasquez, Detective Harmon, and Lieutenant Washington all waiting outside the room and down the hall. But apart from them, MacGriffin faced this killer alone. Curled fists, clenched jaw, and a tight ass, he sat mano a mano against this Sabernut. "No bullshit from you mister."

"I want my lawyer," said the Sabernut.

Shit.

Not five minutes, and the nut-perp wants his lawyer. MacGriffin curled his fists tighter, and clenched his jaw firmer. He felt his blood pressure rise and recalled a departmental flyer on stress as an occupational hazard. A Napoleonic era replica belt buckle he had always wanted flashed briefly before him. Was this guy really named Sabernail instead of nut—or son?

Tom grunted. MacGriffin realized he had been staring, rather plaintively, at the suspect. MacGriffin straightened his back and resumed jaw clenching. Otherwise, he had run out of ideas. Fortunately, Tom charged to the rescue. He walked up to the suspect and leaned into the light beam emanating from the overhead fixture. The effect of this would have sufficed to chill the blood of a guilty man, were it not for the gross illumination given off by all those fluorescent lights above. Tom put his face just an inch away from the perp.

"You want Sabernail? Fine, you're Sabernail," Tom said.

Good start, thought MacGriffin. Give the man a little rope and watch him hang himself.

Tom continued, "But you can kiss your dick goodbye cause your ass belongs to me. And when I'm done humping it, all your gonna have left is a raw bloody hole ripe for infections. We know you killed those girls. You're a class A sleaze, and you are going down. A month from now you're gonna be spending all your time trying to fend off horny black lifers trying to do the rump rumba with you."

"So you will have returned it by then?" the perp asked.

Tom held his tough-as-nails-take-no-prisoners gaze for half a beat before a puzzled "uh?" expression forced its way onto his face.

"My ass," Sabernail continued, "you'll have returned it by

then?"

Tom's face hurt from the sudden change in expression. What the hell was this guy talking about?

"Because I assume that sexually deprived black lifers would not be lusting after an assless man. Although, on your account, by the time you return my ass to me it should be well accustomed to strenuous sodomy."

MacGriffin judged that they had lost control of the interview. Time to regroup. "Tom," he said, "step out in the hall with me for a moment."

MacGriffin pushed open the door of Interview Room One and followed Tom into the hall, letting the door close behind him. Where the interview room had been silent as sweat, the hall buzzed with telephone calls, pagers, snippets of conversation, and the hum of aquarium filters. A recent commission investigating police brutality had recommended placing aquariums throughout the LAPD's precincts in order to "facilitate relaxation and provide a domestic ambience conducive to peaceful feelings." So the hall now hummed. MacGriffin gave a long sigh and turned to Tom. "You're the good cop, *I'm* the bad cop," he said.

"Bullshit," said Tom, "I'm the bad cop. I'm always the bad cop. I hate being the good cop."

MacGriffin sighed. Just once he wanted to be the bad cop. He opened the door and led Tom back into the silent pressure cooker of the interrogation room. The door closed behind the two cops, and they faced again the bored visage of Nick Sabernail—psycho killer.

MacGriffin walked to the table and slid out the chair opposite Sabernail. He sat down and put on his best avuncular expression. This required some effort. He had to force first the right, and then the left sides of his mouth into an up-turn that approximated a smile. He blinked his eyes several times until they felt to him sympathetic, wise, and giving. He relaxed his jaw and folded his hands together, prayer-like, on the table in front of the rat-weasel serial killer. He built up a sigh inside of himself. A sigh filled with the cares of the world. A sigh that knew the pain and desperate needs of night-crawling maniacs. He let that sigh build inside of himself, and then he let it out while shaking his head gently from side to side. That particular angle and speed of headshake he knew spoke worlds of understanding to blood-lust lunatics. He had his man now. Care and human understanding would now do what recent departmental policy had forbidden truncheons to carry out. MacGriffin began his address in soothing words.

"Saberson, I know what you've been through. I'm a man too. I feel a man's needs just like you do. I know what it's like, sitting at home, alone, maybe in your basement, wanting things the world just doesn't give you. You sit there, and you tinker, and you wish. With me it's—fishing; with you … it's a deeper need. A need to go out and find someone. Someone perfect for you. Someone you can spend time with and kill. You're not alone in these needs. I carry a gun every day. I mean, just like you, I meet people; people that need a good killing. Don't you think I've felt the urge? Hell, I get a rude waitress at Denny's and, sure, the first thing I feel like doing is pulling my piece and putting a hole in her chest. You're not alone there, that's a man thing you've got.

"And women, its women you got the problem with, right?" MacGriffin saw only continued boredom on the crazy man's face. "It's women, right? Hell, do you think there's a man alive today who hasn't wanted to stick a knife or a cattle prod into a woman or two? It's cattle prods, right? That you want to stick them with? I always favored bailing-hooks myself, but I can see the cattle prod idea now. The point is, that I'm a man like you. A man with needs. And women, huh!" MacGriffin said this last with what he hoped would sound like a note of outraged conviction, "what are they really for but sex, and making babies, and killing and sucking blood out of? It's not as if we don't have a lot of them around. And whores. It's whores you don't like, right?" MacGriffin surveyed Sabernail's impassive face, "whores are the worst. Or maybe they are just women and easy to get to? The point is that women or whores, its all the same. The point is the killing. I understand that. I feel that. You can talk to me about it. Talk to me about your feelings. One of the guys. You will feel so much better. I can relate. Your demons are my demons and they're not really demons because demons are bad, but these aren't bad. Or maybe they are bad, in a good way. A way I understand. Let it all out to me. One of the guys."

MacGriffin hung on in silence to see what this would bring from the killer before him.

"I want to see my lawyer," said the killer.

Shit.

MacGriffin looked around at Tom and wondered why Tom's jaw had dropped.

◆ ◆ ◆

Yolanda stood in a hall on the detective's floor of the Fountain Avenue Precinct. To the left, and five doors down, Delaney and MacGriffin questioned her date/suspect. Here she faced a pacing Lieutenant Washington. He passed back and forth before her, shaking his head as if the sheer improbability of life had loosened the screws of his neck. He gripped and ungripped his hands, squeezing a ball of wax. The departmental stress-management therapist had told him that wax would have a calming effect on his nerves. So far it had only a waxing effect on his palms. Every time Lieutenant Washington heard a door open around the corner, he stopped his head shaking, and wax mashing, to check if anyone would come round the bend. When no one did, he would continue on, shuffling up and down the hall, shaking his head and squeezing his wax. Yolanda thought he looked like a novelty toy.

"You really screwed this one up," he said.

"How did *I* screw it up?" Yolanda said.

"You gave the go-code; with nothing to go for."

"I didn't say it. Nick, that is the suspect, said it."

"You had nothing. Nothing on him yet."

"That's why I didn't give the go-code."

Washington sighed a sigh of the damned. He looked at Yolanda and shook his head. He tried to explain, "You panicked. The whole thing got to you. I understand. Undercover work is high pressure. No. Don't try to explain to me. I've seen it all before. The atmosphere felt dangerous. The suspect acted creepy. You got bubbles in your blood and panicked. No. Don't offer excuses. I've seen it before. You panicked. Let's not talk about it again."

Washington looked at Yolanda. He smiled a smile of paternalistic forgiveness. When he smiled this smile to one of his wayward daughters, say, after one took the car and bent its fender, letting that damn hip-hop gangsta-wannabe of a boyfriend drive it, well his daughter just melted.

Yolanda did not melt.

"In the first place, Lieutenant Washington, I did not panic. The atmosphere did not seem dangerous, just poorly decorated, and the suspect did not seem creepy, just fashion addled. I did not give the go-code, which was *rosebud*. The suspect said it, and the boys in the car panicked. More likely they hardly listened to what went on at all. The only dangerous event of the night occurred when the partner you assigned me kicked in the door dressed in full body armor and demanded I drop my weapon."

I'm glad *she's* not my daughter, thought Washington. He sighed. "Why the hell did you pick that stupid word, *rosebud*, anyway? That started the problem."

"Obviously, I picked it because I thought it would be memorable but would not come up in conversation."

"Rosebud? Memorable? That doesn't figure."

Yolanda rubbed her temples. A door around the corner opened up again, and both she and Washington heard the muffled voices of Delaney and MacGriffin. After a moment, the two detectives must have re-entered the interrogation room since they did not round the corner. Yolanda heard another door open and close, stilling the voices.

"Are you charging Sabernail?" she asked Washington.

"You let me worry about that."

"It's my case."

"You let me worry about that."

Just now, Yolanda could agree to let him worry about that.

Most persons hauled into the kind care of the LAPD booking system had no lawyer. They came pleading their innocence and confident that the overburdened justice system of Los Angeles would find it much easier to find them not guilty, or at least guilty of a lesser charge, than to actually try to prove that each had done what each had really done. Most of the accused took whatever overworked, uninspired lawyer the Public Defender's Office saw fit to send them.

Most public defenders regarded their work as the ethical equivalent of trash disposal. They got to know their clients through booking cards and long rap sheets—neither tending to endear the accused to a lawyer. The average rap sheet does not suggest roguish daring-do, but rather petty criminality or brutal socio-pathology. Any public defender three days on the job knew that their clients were guilty, or at least guilty of a lesser charge, and that the key to an effective defense lay in work. More precisely, in over-work. For no criminal justice system west of the Mississippi boasted more over-work than L.A.'s. So the average public defender knew that success lay in proving that the client, poor citizen though he may be, would be more trouble to convict than to process without trial on a lesser charge. This pleased everyone. Less work for the prosecutor, less work for the defense attorney, fewer jurors taken away from productive employment, lightened case loads for the judges, less expense to the taxpayers, less burden on the prison system, and, sometimes, the accused gets away with murder. The only thing the system fails to do is inspire public defenders with a sense of mission.

Yet, a few of these servants for the public good had entered the profession inspired by seventies TV shows like *Kazinsky*. Kaz: always the voice of reason in an oppressive world. Kaz assured these idealists that most of those accused by the corrupt criminal justice system were in fact victims of oppression, right-wing politics, or at least of circumstances.

As it turned out, most of those accused by the corrupt criminal justice system were so guilty their fingers would burn if they touched a Bible to take an oath. This fact, that most were guilty, did not arise from any special honesty on the part of the police force. They would railroad people if necessary. It just turns out that L.A. produces more than enough guilty-as-sin criminals to keep the system busy without needing to burden anyone with much in the way of the innocent.

So the accused in the LAPD holding cells took what lawyers the system offered. And why not. The typical occupant of that holding cell had been there before. He knew the system well. He did not need Perry Mason to spring him. Less than five percent of those sent up received a trial by jury. L.A. criminal justice revolved around the art of the deal. You didn't need a great trial lawyer. You needed a deal maker, a plea bargainer, a meat processor. The average public defender knows how to process you through the system. For most, that suffices.

But Nick Sabernail had his own lawyer. Justin Case: *Attorney to the Friends of the Stars.* Justin Case had so far dedicated his legal career, almost two months long now, to defending the honor and income of celebrity best buddies; those high school friends and personal assistants to the stars. Pop musicians and movie stars can afford the very best legal minds, but who looks after their drinking buddies and the shoulders they cry on? Justin Case does. To date, his clients could only marginally be regarded as *best friends* to the stars. They might be more accurately described as, say, companions, or, even more accurately, as chauffeurs and maids, to the stars. In particular, chauffeurs and maids who were suing the stars to whom they had once been companions. Still, Justin Case regarded filing nuisance suits against celebrities on behalf of disgruntled ex-employees as just the first rung on the ladder to representing Friends of the Stars themselves. Justin Case did not mind paying his dues.

Justin Case also did not mind representing his old and dear friend Nick Sabernail. After receiving the okay from the desk sergeant, he made his way through the precinct house, upstairs to the detective's floor. Though almost one o'clock at night now, the precinct house seemed modestly busy. Detectives filed reports, officers booked suspects, janitors cleaned the offices, and a fellow with a yellow armband walked around feeding fish. There sure seemed to be a lot of aquariums for a police station. Justin Case walked on. He found the right room by following the voices of detectives arguing about his client.

"You're supposed to be a good cop, not a psycho cop."

"I was trying to relate."

"Have you two gotten anything?"

Justin Case walked up to the rotund black detective surmising by his harried and panicked look that he must be in charge.

"I'm Justin Case—I represent Mr. Sabernail. I'd like to see my client."

The black detective just grunted. He looked at the other two detectives. The one accused of being a psycho cop shrugged his shoulders and the other opened the door to the interrogation room, now politely designated an *interview room*, Justin Case noted. Case entered and let the door close behind him. He looked at the weary figure of Nick Sabernail. Nick perked up at the sight of his old friend.

"Mike, good to see you."

"It's Justin," said Justin Case.

Nick looked puzzled, "I'm Nick," he said.

"I know that, Nick," said Justin Case helpfully, "*I'm* Justin now. Not Mike. I changed it for the job."

Nick's head hurt. This night would not end. It would just keep going and going. "Why did you change your name, Mike?"

"I'm an attorney now. Justin sounds like Justice, which is what people look for from a lawyer. And get this, I changed my last name too: Case. I'm Justin Case now!" Justin Case took a business card from his wallet. He handed it to Nick. Nick read it as Justin recited it aloud: "Just in case—call Justin Case!"

Nick looked up, so entirely un-amused, it just wasn't funny.

Justin explained further, "It's like a joke or a pun, good for ads, and customers will remember it." Nick continued to look unimpressed. "I'm serious about this job. It's a career, which is just what you call a job you are serious about."

Nick dropped the card on the table and fell hard into the back of his seat. He leaned his head back and closed his eyes. He breathed deep. He straightened up in the chair. He opened his eyes.

Nope, still here.

"Alright Nick," Justin said, sitting down across from Sabernail, "let's get down to cases." Justin could not help smiling a little as he said this. "What are you here for? What did you do?"

"I dated a detective."

Justin thought about this for a moment. "I don't think they can hold you for that."

Nick rubbed his eyes. "They have not actually come out and told me what, aside from being a lousy cook, I am here for. I assumed they suspected me of robbing the museum I work for. But—"

"You work in a museum?" Justin asked.

"I'm a curator now—don't smirk, I really am. I have a degree. Stop smirking—I have a real degree, from a real college. Oh shit, shut up."

Justin controlled his amusement. "So what did you steal?"

"Fine lawyer you are," Nick said, "I didn't steal anything. I assumed they thought I had stolen a book on Necromantic

Science—and don't ask me what that is or I'll split your damn lip!"

Justin held his tongue.

"On further reflection," Nick continued, "I don't guess simple theft would be worth this much trouble. Not in this town. Given the questions they threw at me during the second degree—I can't imagine that could have been a third degree—I surmise they think I killed some women."

Justin's eyes lit up with excitement. "What did they say exactly?"

"Well," Nick went on, "for one thing that older fellow, he needs therapy. I mean someone needs to work out a program with him or something. Twelve Steps to Mental Health. Something like that. I think he's at least fourteen steps away right now. But from what he said, I'm guessing he thinks I cattle-prodded prostitutes, killed them, and then sucked out their blood. I'm just assuming it wasn't all his fantasy, mind you."

Justin hopped out of the seat and paced the room excitedly. "Great! Great! They think you're the Vampire Killer! This is so magnificent! I am made. In this town I will be a god."

Nick did not look nearly so pleased. "Just what," he asked, "is a vampire killer?"

Justin continued his frantic pacing, "Interviews, book deal, Christ—I have to get an agent! Hell, I could be my own agent! A lawyer-agent. What would be a good name for someone like that?"

Nick felt his heart drop to just above his ass. "Tell me it's someone who kills vampires."

Justin looked at his old friend. "What are you talking about?"

"Good question," Nick said, "mind if I use it? What are you talking about? What is a vampire killer? What do they think I've done?"

Justin nodded his head. Tsk-tsk. He sat down again across from his poor friend. "You really need to read the paper more,

Nick. Racing forms alone do not make an educated man. What did you get your diploma in by the way, bad betting?"

"I think," said Nick, "the subject of the day is vampire killers."

"There's a fellow, about your height I think," Justin Case continued, "going about killing prostitutes and then draining out all their blood. The papers call him the Vampire Killer. According to the papers, who have a slightly better than 50-50 chance of being right about these things, the police suspect a Satan-friendly death-worshiper, or some such. Sound like anyone you know? Got any new hobbies I should know about?"

Nick considered his position: sitting uncomfortably in front of a lunatic lawyer facing the death penalty for misplacing a 14th century book on necromancy.

Justin Case popped out of his seat again. "I'm going to be like the next F. Lee Baily." Justin looked off at the ceiling, one arm across his stomach, the other resting on it, holding up two fingers to his cheek. As he thought out loud, he accentuated each point by thrusting the two fingers at a corner of the room, then returning them to rest again on his cheek. "Justin Lee Case." Finger thrust—to cheek rest. "F Justin Case." Stab at the corner—to cheek rest. "J Case Baily."

Nick shook his head in disbelief. "Sorry to disappoint you, but I didn't kill anyone."

Justin didn't even glance at him, just tossed a wave. "Doesn't matter, the LAPD can handle you either way."

Nick got mad. "I've got it! I could name you as an accomplice: The Blood Lust Death Cult! I could play Squeaky Fromm to your Charley Manson. Maybe we could get Vincent Bugliosi out of retirement to prosecute us. Think of the movie deal. We could call the book *Hectic Skeptic*. You are so right! This is the best thing to ever happen to us. Partner."

Justin Case shook himself from his revelry of sudden fame. "I know you didn't do it Nick. I know you. I'm just thinking about the long-term plan for your defense. We have to start early to get the best book deal. These true-crime publishers can turn your ass into shark food if you so much as glance at a contract too long. I'll start researching copyright law as soon as I get home. We should start interviewing ghostwriters immediately. The main thing we do: we manage the publicity from the get-go. Nobody gets the chance to present this thing as anything but your need to kill. Alleged need to kill. Nothing muddies the waters more than some bit player getting a quickie book out before the real killer gets published. Alleged killer gets published. The main thing: we keep the story pointed at you."

"The main thing," Nick said firmly, "is I don't get the electric chair. The only publicity management I want is that I don't get any publicity at all."

Justin Case looked clearly disappointed at Nick's small-minded attitude to his own stroke of good fortune. "You're not looking at this the right way, Nick. Look at this like the Nick of the old days. Look at it like a money making opportunity."

Nick did not look convinced. "And you'll send my share of the take to San Quinton in the form of cigarettes."

"Nobody's going to San Quinton."

"Not alone they're not."

"You need to look at the long term, Nick."

"A long term is what I'm trying to avoid."

Justin Case shook his head at the troubled and confused Nick Sabernail. Tsk-tsk. "I think I know what's best for us."

"I want a public defender."

Panic nearly overcame Justin Case. It started in the pit of his stomach and had made it all the way up to his face, painting it red, and popping open his eye-lids wide, before Justin Case could even get a word out. "Look, look, you don't want to do that. That would really muddy the waters."

"I want out of here, Mike, out now."

Justin studied the determined face of Nick Sabernail. A perfect image for the book cover. Or better, the back of the book; F. Justin Bailey Case should grace the cover. "I'll have you out tonight, Nick, within the hour. Guaranteed."

POLICE PROCEDURES

Yolanda awoke in her apartment. She lay for a moment watching the dust float gently in the beam of early morning light. How could she have let the room become so dusty? She rose from the bed, pulling off the pajama top that alone covered her body. She stepped into the bathroom and turned on the water to the shower. It would take exactly one minute for the water to heat up. She knew this from past experience. She looked into the mirror as she waited. At thirty-one she looked good in the morning. As good as she had looked at nineteen. In fact, she looked better. More mature and wise. A woman past thirty could feel passions a teenager could only read about in books. For all that, Yolanda thought, she still needed a library card.

Yolanda stared at her face. Dark complexion, shoulder length hair. Her features seemed more drawn now than years before. She had very few lines around the corners of her eyes. Laugh lines people called them. Her uncle had once told her that women in the Vasquez family were prone to these at an early age. Part of their Amer-Indian heritage he had said. A good sign, Yolanda thought, that she had so few of these lines. Crows-feet they called these, didn't they? No crow yet had walked on Yolanda's stunning face.

Yolanda looked hard at that face. Her face. Her face to the world. A good face. As she stared at it the face seemed to fade before her. It grew fuzzy and indistinct, as if a veil now cast itself upon its features. Yolanda felt a great sadness welling up in her. She saw the mouth of the face turn to a frown. A fuzzy, indistinct frown. Such sadness came into those eyes as they faded before her. Yolanda reached out to touch that sad face. Her hand touched the wetness of the misted mirror, and the spell broke. The bathroom had filled with steam. More than a minute had passed since she had turned on the water.

Yolanda showered.

◆ ◆ ◆

The crime scene at 1800 Pilot Way reminded George Seeley of some weird work of modern art. Red streaks of blood covered one part of the floor, while jagged pieces of glass and thick-gauge electrical wiring covered the floor on the south side of the single room. Seeley found, stuck in the coagulated blood, bits of electronic gizmos, nuts, bolts, a pair of wire-strippers, two thermometers and two pages torn from a book on herbalism.

Seeley crouched on his knees scrapping he-knew-not-whose-blood from the floor into an evidence vial. He did this job at some twenty different crime scenes every working day. Most had not near this much blood. At some scenes George Seeley's pulse rate quickened at finding so much as a quarter pint of blood, semen, or body goo. Today Seeley knelt in a cornucopia of gruesome riches. Though hardened to this task, he could not shake the feeling that this time, this one, carried a more sinister meaning than all the others.

"Are those wires in that blood?" asked a voice standing above Seeley. Seeley knew it must have come from one of the big-footed detectives lumbering around his crime scene. They might as well spray their shoes with clue-destroying pixie dust and dance the fandango on the floor. He looked to his left at the shoes of the nosey detective. Sensible black Stride-rites. Looking up the leg, he fixed first on a service .38 at the detective's hip and then, looking up still further, he noticed the biggest tits he had ever seen on a cop. How would you get those in a bulletproof vest, Seeley wondered?

"Hello," the cop said, "I'm up here."

Seeley found his feet and stood up to face the detective.

"I'm Vasquez. I just got here. What's the story?"

George Seeley had never so wanted to impress a police officer in his life. "A bloody mess," he began, "blood, feces, chunks of flesh—some of it looks quite old."

"Old flesh?" asked the stunning detective.

"Like partially decayed or preserved. I can't say without further study. I could do this study myself, and I myself could get back to you on this. Myself, I'd say, I could do it pretty quick. And still get good results." But no use; the pretty detective had already turned away to inspect the filth covered ground.

"And the wires? They're mixed in with the blood?"

Seeley watched this Vasquez chick not watching him. Young and pretty, and wanting nothing to do with George Seeley. Could he help it if he had a bit of a belly? His whole day consisted of a series of floor squats, but still he had a belly. This Vasquez woman probably didn't appreciate how few french-fries it took to undo the work of a hundred floor squats. Probably she banged the lead detective on every case she worked. But never anything for the crime scene investigator. The cold hard hand of righteous indignation griped the heart of George Seeley. "I don't do wires—I do blood. You can see for yourself the blood covers the wires. Do you need everything written down for you before you see it?"

"You're dripping blood," the detective said.

And bile too, thought Seeley, and then he noticed he had turned the vial upside down. The detective walked away, again in her own thoughts with no thought for George Seeley.

Yolanda's thoughts, apart from trying to forget the CSI's rudeness, focused on the strange messiness of the crime scene. Detective Washington had sent her here because an old Korean man had disappeared from this area several weeks ago. A tourist from Ohio had found the body just three days ago on a beach. Someone had apparently drained the body of fluid. No one on the task force regarded this as a likely Vampire Killer slaying since all the other victims had been female—usually prostitutes. Serial killers, like scholars, always specialize. They don't move from young prostitutes to old Korean gentlemen.

The old man's body had been bloated by over a week in the water, and fish had feasted on much of it, so no one could be quite sure he had been killed and drained like the others. The task force detectives put him down as a *maybe—probably not*, and let it go at that. Then, yesterday, the owner of the space Yolanda now walked through had come in to throw out a delinquent tenant. Instead of a tenant he found this mess and called the police. Since the old Korean had lived in a unit just around the block, the task force lead detective, Harmon, sent Yolanda to see what she could see. But what she saw made little sense to her. Apart from lots of coagulated blood and a horrible stench, the place just looked a mess. The first detective on the scene had found no sign of people in the adjacent units. The neighbors, mostly undocumented immigrants using warehouse space as living accommodations, had disappeared at the first sign of the cops.

Yolanda saw a very nervous man hectoring a uniformed policeman. Obviously the landlord. Yolanda approached the man, who had just worked himself into a proper tirade.

"I have the cleaners already waiting outside. You have no idea what you have to pay people to clean up a mess like this. The carpet people won't touch it—these are specialists in not barfing I have waiting. And I pay them whether they are cleaning filth or shooting the shit outside the ... well hello there!"

This last remark he directed at Yolanda. She pushed her badge in his face and nodded for the officer to go. "I'm Detective Vasquez. Are you the owner of this unit?"

"I'm Alfredo Gumpton," said Fred, "I make over $700,000 a year on my L.A. properties alone. I drive a Porsche and I own two off-road vehicles, one a Mercedes. I'm thinking about buying a place in Bel Air." Gumpton said all this affecting the air of a man normally reticent about revealing these things about himself. Only two things made Fred Gumpton lose his reluctance to talk about himself, his money, and his cars: (1) beautiful women and (2) anyone who would listen. "In fact, property management is a minor business for me. I travel a lot. The world really. I can't talk about all my business dealings here, but I can tell you whatever you need to know. Mostly I don't do business. I play. I club."

"What? Baby seals?" Yolanda said.

"Uh? Oh. No. I go to clubs. Nightclubs. Do you dance Mrs. Vastkeys?"

"Do you rent the units adjacent to these, Mr. Gumpy?" Yolanda asked.

Gumpton puffed with pride, "It's Gumpton, actually, of the South Hampton Gumptons. I own all these spaces. All the buildings you can see from that door. I thought I might make a club out of some of them. We could use security. Would you be interested in a bit of moonlighting? Or even just a bit of moonlight?" Fred Gumpton, puffed up big as a blow fish, was quite ready to burst with cleverness.

"You realize that the tenants of these spaces use them, illegally, for domestic purposes?" Yolanda said.

A bit less ready to burst, Fred responded, "I don't pry into other people's business."

"Ten to one the tenets have no papers either."

Fred saw his chance at doing a detective evaporate. "The one who signed the lease agreement had proper papers. If he sublet to illegal aliens, he did so against the lease."

"And the man who signed the lease on *this* unit? He had proper papers?" asked Yolanda.

"I faxed the lease to your headquarters. He gave his name as Arthur Tesla. He had identification. He paid cash. I never saw him."

Tesla? A joke?

Yolanda finished her interview with Fred Gumpton of Pales Verdes and interviewed what legitimate business owners she could find in the neighborhood. She ate lunch on the way back to the station and checked in at the task force desk. No new information. She worked on other projects for the rest of the day. She did not call anyone to find out what had happened to Nick Sabernail. But she thought about it.

◆ ◆ ◆

In *The Long Goodbye*, Raymond Chandler's private eye Philip Marlow spent a few days in an L.A. jail. He had a room with two bunks, a lumpy mattress, and a blanket that was "neither dirty nor clean." That was circa 1953. In today's L.A. County Jail only mafia dons and axe murderers enjoy such luxury. Nick Sabernail spent the night on a cot in a massive room occupied by over two hundred fellow inmates. It smelled of body odor, old urine and fresh feces. Few windows aired the giant rooms out. Men coughed, crapped, complained, and cut each other with homemade knives in close citizenship. Morning brings only a better view of the dismal surroundings. Lunatics, only sometimes effectively culled from the general population for special treatment, babbled incessantly in some corners. Drugs, pornography, cigarettes, and weapons changed hands in the vast bizarre of Los Angeles County Central Holding.

In Chandler's book, Marlow just sat in his cell and did nothing. Today's inmate favors such sports as guard taunting, gang knifing, and tattooing. Many occupy the jail awaiting trial, and they would likely await for over six months or more. Nick merely awaited a hearing before a judge. Had his lawyer not insisted that he be either "freed immediately or put in jail," he might now be back at his home. Justin Case showed no mercy on the abusers of the law. He would either see justice done or his client ruined, though the heavens may fall. Nick just wished Case could be here to have a bit of heaven fall on him.

Having no gang, and needing no tattoos, Nick stuck to guard taunting. For this he had the help of an old friend.

"You got nailed, Sabernail, they nailed your hide."

"When do we eat around here?" Nick said.

"When the food is on, boy, when the food is on."

"And what do we do for fun, Hunter?" Nick said.

"If you can't beat the heat on the street, you have to greet the meat at the seat," said Hunter Coyote.

"I saw you doing windows on the street the other day. Is that really a viable scam?" Nick said.

Hunter stretched and yawned and stretched again, just so everyone could see how little he cared. "You got your scam, I got mine. You go for the big con, working for the man. I go for the little con, cause I *am* the man." Hunter stretched again, staring straight at Nick. He stretched his face muscles and danced his head forward and back. Hunter Coyote liked to stay loose in stir.

"You, Hunter, are the foremost practitioner of the micro-scam. Sums too small for ordinary hustlers make your mouth water." Nick stretched his jaws in a yawn to show that he too could punctuate with muscle movements.

"I got big time dough going on," Hunter replied. "them pennies and dimes mount up. They hump up for good money."

Someone screamed bloody murder at the other end of the vast hall. Someone laughed. Nick yelled, "Yo, guards! You're missing a good beating over there." A guard yelled to shut up. Nick noticed a small Anglo man pissing on the wall near him and Hunter. "How did you get in here, Hunter, spit on the commissioner's window?"

Hunter reared back to tell his tale. "Damn conspiracy! They hang just anything on you anymore. Some cop don't like your looks—bang! Drugs in your pocket." When Coyote said *bang* his arms flew out as if each were trying to leave his body in a different direction. "Some rich woman don't want her window squeegeed—bang! Cop busts you for aggravated mischief." Nick wondered how Hunter's arms could take the g-forces. "You walk around, they bust you for vagrancy—you stand still, they bust you for loitering. Stretch too much on the street— bang! It's gang signs, go to jail. The problem is the man has too many easy charges to lay on you. Ain't right they should be able to pick you up on some vague, common old charge they can get on anybody they want."

"So what did they charge you with?"

"Grave-robbing."

Nick had to admit, that would not have been his first guess. "The dead have no money, Coyote. And they smell bad."

"Fact is," said Hunter, "they don't smell that bad. Not like you'd expect. Weren't pretty to look at, but I ain't no bigot."

A team of guards in full riot gear, carrying clubs and tazer guns, passed the two men at a run. The tazer gun is a remarkable invention that allows you to subdue a man without the use of deadly force. Over and over again, if you like. "Somebody gonna get electrocuted," said Hunter. Down the hall, wild cheers went up. Curses flew. Chairs and cots flew back. Another "extraction team" passed Hunter and Nick. The L.A. County Sheriff's office (who ran the jail) used extraction teams to remove especially petulant and uncooperative inmates from their cells. Given the prevailing level of non-cooperation, one had to work hard to merit an extraction team. Someone down the hall had decided that the day's tedium would be nicely broken if five big men in body armor came in and beat him with clubs while shooting his body with electricity. It happened more often than you'd think.

"Why were you digging up bodies?" Nick asked.

Hunter got excited. "It's the latest thing on the street man!" Hunter reached inside his shoe and retrieved a battered bit of newspaper, glued to an equally battered bit of construction paper. "I read this in the paper. Rolled over on the bench and saw it. A sign." Hunter handed the paper to Nick. Nick noticed the Headline: "Grave Robbers Hit Local Cemetery."

"They let you bring this in? They took my magazine away," Nick said as he began to read.

"I shoved it up my ass," Hunter said.

"Jesus Christ!" Nick yelled, flinging the paper back at Hunter. "You sick fuck!"

Hunter gathered up the paper indignantly. "I wiped off the

gunk. What makes you think my ass ain't clean anyway? Just cause a man sleeps on a bench and takes his shower at the beach don't mean his ass ain't clean."

Nick heard screams from down the hall. Some petulant civil disobedient had met Mr. Tazer's invention. "Let's just move on off of your ass, Hunter. Are you telling me you sold dug-up bodies for money?"

For a moment Hunter paid no attention. He strained his ear to enjoy every last bit of painful cry from down the hall. Hunter had spent enough time in mass detention centers to become a connoisseur of pain and cries of humiliation. He knew the quick, sharp "I stubbed my god damn foot!" cries from the slow, building, "This fucker just stabbed me!" ones, to the shocked, scared "this mother fucker just got stabbed!" ones. Hunter Coyote knew them all, and the one down the hall definitely screamed out as "God DAMN! That electricity hurts!" Hunter savored the scream and committed it to memory. He would dream on it tonight. Nothing tasted so sweet to him as the agony another had received instead of him. He turned his attention back to Nick. "I didn't have a buyer. I said it was hot on the street. When the thing is hot on the street, you pick it up, and the buyers will find you."

"So," Nick said, "you just dug up a body and figured someone would show up to buy it."

"God damn worked too! I put the word out on the street and someone showed right up."

"The cops."

"So I'm supposed to know that? I'm supposed to have some sort of cop-detecting vision?"

The extraction team passed by again, hauling a slobbering inmate hanging loosely between them.

"When's dinner?" Nick called out after them.

"My man is hungry here, goddamn it!" echoed Hunter.

"You two better shut up," yelled a walking guard.

"I gots my civil rights," Hunter called back.

"Yeah," added Nick, "he has a *right* to be uncivil."

"Damn knows it."

The guard walked over lightly stroking his tazer gun. "Shut up you two."

Nick stood up and faced the man square on. "You don't scare me with your badge, your mace, and your electric torture device. I have a lawyer so bad that if you lay one finger on me you'll wind up Time Magazine's Cop of the Year, and I'll do one to six for moon-shining." The cop looked at Nick. Some men crack real early, he thought. Hunter dropped his pants and split his butt cheeks between a bar.

"How about this shiny moon?" Hunter said.

Nick pointed down at the butt like a figure in a Renaissance painting. "Now, my man has got shiny butt going *on!*" he said.

Deputy sheriffs at county lockup do not get paid enough.

◆ ◆ ◆

At her desk, Yolanda read the crime scene report for 1800 Pilot Way. CSI had found blood DNA matching four Vampire Killing victims, including the Korean man (now universally recognized as a member of that set). They also found hair and skin from two of the victims. And hair matching one other victim whose blood had not been found there. CSI had found four sets of partial boot prints. These came in at least two different sizes—one quite small, and one very large. This fact set the task force on ear. Vampire Killers? Detective Harmon ordered this fact suppressed from the media. He feared panicky talk about death cults. Angelinos could shrug off two or three independently operating serial killers. But let those killers get together and chant incantations at the moon; gun sales go up.

The rest of the report made no sense. Some of the tissue found at the site showed clear signs of embalming fluid. Harmon assured everyone that the killers had tried to preserve the victims "for future fun," and had failed. Or maybe they had refrigerators full of dead prostitutes at another location. This explanation did not fit, however, as the flesh found positive for embalming fluid had been dead for a long time. Harmon did not like this fact, so he declared it incorrect and chose to ignore it. Harmon liked the idea of cult killers preserving their victims. If Behavioral Sciences had taught us anything, it was that twisted serial killers liked to take trophies. A little something for the memory book. Harman imagined them flipping through their scrap book, pointing at taped in items like little old ladies. "Oh this finger!" they'd say, "I remember where it came from—that lovely girl with the read hair out in Barstow. Oh, those were the days." Something akin to that. Yes, these were victims preserved for a very large scrap book, Harmon was sure of that, and he had made it clear to Yolanda that she should be sure of it too.

What about these items found at the scene: industrial strength cleaning fluid, non-dissolving medical sutures, machine fragments, wiring, glass beakers, fragments from a book on the "zombies" of Haiti, and torn pages from a book of the collected short stories of H. P. Lovecraft. The torn pages intrigued Yolanda. Harmon could not be bothered about them. Behavioral Sciences had established beyond dispute that serial killers did not read short stories. What about the bat droppings and pig parts found at the scene? "Coincidence," said Harmon. Coincident with what he did not say.

The strangest item on the evidence list had to be the eyes found on the scene. Not human eyes. Not pig eyes. CSI found them rolling around on the floor like little marbles. Seeley sent a sample to a lab at the University of Southern California to find out to what animal they once belonged. Whatever animal it turned out to be, the mere presence of its eyes seemed a bit odd. Harmon surmised that they had resulted from some sort of "cannibalistic ritual" that strayed across the species line. This would be a new chapter in B.S. studies.

As lunch rolled around Yolanda recalled that she had a lunch date, and she felt particularly good that she had chosen a vegetarian restaurant to eat at.

Yolanda studied the menu at Hollywood's Three Carrots Café. Nowhere on it could she find a dish whose ingredients included carrots. The "veg-head" plate came closest. It boasted cantaloupes, which are orange, and thus similar to carrots in that respect. Yolanda had a thought. She flagged down a waiter. "Is the veggie burger patty made with carrots at all?" she asked.

The waiter shot her a condescending smile. "I don't know. I could pull one apart for you and see if anything carrot-like falls out." He then cocked his head to the side as if to say: see how little I care about your world, *Missy*.

Yolanda could always tell the gay ones.

Twenty minutes late—to the second—her lunch date arrived. A stunning woman seven years younger than Yolanda. She had a dark complexion, long brown hair, and fingernails you can only get by paying big money on Rodeo Drive. The young woman carried three small shopping bags, each sporting the name of a different Rodeo frilly-nothings shop. She strode breezily up to Yolanda's table and sat with a model's pirouette. She placed her bags on the table at angles to insure that patrons could see the logos from any vantage point in the restaurant. Without looking at Yolanda, she picked up the menu before her and said, "I can't really eat lunch today. I ate breakfast."

Yolanda sighed. "Hello Sis," she said.

Her sister, Antonia Vasquez, looked through the menu, her eyes darting about like a bird's looking for the proper worm to pluck. "I had a meeting with my agent today. He said I need to lose two pounds for an audition on Wednesday. So it's salad with lemon juice on the side."

Yolanda, as has been oft noted, was a beautiful woman. She was not, however, rail thin. Her body had curves and muscles. Her sister Antonia looked as if she wanted to re-ignite the starving imp fashion. "I cannot believe you need to lose two pounds," Yolanda said, "or that leaving lemon juice on the side could help you do it."

Antonia put the menu down and addressed Yolanda in the voice of a determined sprite. "I limit all sweets; even bitter sweets. And I need to lose whatever weight my agent says I need to lose. Besides, Ross thinks I need to lose *five* pounds."

"So you'll come out at an even 70?" Yolanda said. Yolanda did not like Ross, and any mention of his name brought a bitter taste to her words. Antonia just sniffed the air and cast her eyes about the room looking for important people with beautiful hair. A waiter came to their table. He stood over six foot two and had the sort of chiseled features once reserved for cigarette ads.

"Another lovely lady," he said looking now at Antonia, "I feel quite privileged." Antonia perked up at the compliment, which put her perk-quota past one hundred percent. She tucked her long fingernails under her chin and cocked her head. In birds this signaled readiness to mate, in Hollywood it served as preliminary to phone number exchanges.

"I do love a handsome waiter," she said.

The waiter smiled wider, which must have hurt such a chiseled face. "I'm Angus Bronson, I'll be serving you this afternoon," said Angus the waiter.

"You must be an actor," said Antonia.

Angus grew excited. "Have you seen me? I was on the television series *Seattle PD*. I played a cop."

"I missed that one."

"The network cancelled it after two episodes."

Antonia flicked a long fingernail at Angus. "I love the name. Where did you find *Angus Bronson*?"

Angus flushed with pride. "I ran across them in a baby name book. I also hope maybe people will think I'm Charles Bronson's son. It couldn't hurt."

"I'm Debbie Daniel," said Antonia.

This shocked Yolanda. "I thought you were Tricia Tobias?"

she said.

Antonia shot Yolanda a hostile glance—or as close to one as a bumblebee can shoot. "That was over two months ago. I've gotten a part sense then, and I'm Debbie Daniel now. For good this time."

The waiter forced his eyes off Antonia and looked at Yolanda. "And what is your name?"

"Yolanda Vasquez."

"Very pretty," he said.

"Too ethnic," said Antonia.

"Where did you find it?" asked Angus.

"I kept hearing my father and mother repeat it," said Yolanda.

Antonia waved her hands in front of her face; a peacock demanding attention. "Yolanda hasn't a creative bone in her head. Tell me Angus, who is your agent?"

Yolanda endured just five minutes more of whose-who among Hollywood Hopefuls before she produced her badge and told Angus to take their orders or go directly to jail. Angus smiled. Antonia ordered the small salad, lemon juice on the side. Yolanda ordered a tofu chicken sandwich (made by whispering the word "chicken" over tofu as you place the top bun on it) with broccoli chips (every bit as delicious as you imagine them to be) and a side of buttered artichokes. Yolanda had no intention of eating the artichokes. Antonia absolutely loved buttered artichokes.

Antonia excused herself to the ladies room. She stopped at three tables going and four coming back. Her actual restroom time clocked at less than forty-five seconds. The table flitting took fifteen minutes total. She sat down twice when she returned. Antonia liked to sit down just right.

Yolanda sat through most of this looking at other people's plates. She searched for carrots.

When the food arrived, Yolanda smiled while Antonia steeled herself for another exercise in denial.

"You haven't visited Mom in over a month," Yolanda said

to Antonia. Antonia just stabbed at her salad and glared menacingly at the artichokes. Yolanda continued, "She calls me every other night to ask about you."

"Why doesn't she just call me?" Antonia asked.

"You never answer."

"I have a life."

Yolanda ate her tofu chicken sandwich; very slowly and with obvious enjoyment. Antonia stared at the buttered artichokes.

"Maybe you should give Mom Ross's number," Yolanda said.

"I'm out a lot. An actress has to be seen."

Yolanda ate some chips, pretending to relish them. Antonia put down her fork and took out a mirror and a small makeup case. She fine-tuned her face. Yolanda wore no make-up; just a bit of mustard sauce.

"She should remarry," said Antonia, speaking through a dust cloud of face powder.

"After this many years, I don't think she will."

"Still, she should."

"Dad isn't an easy man to replace."

Antonia snapped shut her mirror and sprung her trap, "I didn't know Dad well before he died. People say you remind them of him. That tells me a lot about why Mom isn't looking for any new husbands."

Neither the bitchy tone, nor the attempt to wound, hurt Yolanda. What did hurt? That Antonia thought no more of their father than to use him as a club to beat sister with? "It's too bad you didn't know our father. He might have been able to add a little weight to you."

"I need to lose five pounds, not gain."

"Not that kind of weight, Antonia," said Yolanda. "You're so light, I think sometimes you may just float away on the next breeze, and none of us will ever see you again." Yolanda's voice carried more worry than insult. Antonia looked away to another table. After a moment she waved a little wave to someone in a open-neck sweater and flashed him a half-smile.

She turned back to her sister.

"Maybe I only seem light to you because you're too heavy, and I don't mean *that* kind of heavy. You're the one trying to prove something about father. He was what he was. You can't undo him by being a cop." Antonia picked up her fork and stabbed again at her salad. The buttered artichokes held no appeal for her now. "I'm doing fine, thank you. I have a real part. In a movie."

Yolanda retired the field of battle. "Are you going to be Antonia or Debbie in the credits? I need to know since I probably won't be able to pick you out of the crowd scene."

Antonia ignored the parting shot, "I'm going to be Tina Yamato. Ross thinks that might be my best name. Just for this one picture. I'll change permanently if it's a hit."

"Yamato? You don't look remotely Japanese."

Antonia grew excited again, like a little girl just discovering a use for boys. "That's just the point! Ross says the strangeness of the *juxtapose*, or something, will get people to remember me. He's working out a whole new bio for me!"

Yolanda paid the bill. Antonia kissed her on both cheeks, then Yolanda grabbed her and hugged her tight. Antonia stopped by the hostess podium and exchanged numbers with Angus on her way out. Yolanda walked up after and held her hand, palm up, to Angus. Angus smiled a moment. Yolanda kept her cop face on. Angus handed over Antonia's number. Yolanda left.

❖ ❖ ❖

Outside county lockup, in a parking lot populated by persons completely uninterested in giving him a ride home, and without a cent to his name, Nick Sabernail considered his career options. Museum curation seemed a rapidly fading possibility, and the discharge guard had discouraged application to the Sheriff's Department ("We don't have a Torture Research Department"). So how could an honest man make a decent dollar? More to the point, how could a Nick Sabernail make some quick money?

Las Vegas. Land of loot. Greed made gluttonous. Where the id goes to loosen up a little. Vegas; solution and problem rolled into one. And the really nice thing about Vegas: the money is already there; you don't even need to bring your own. Not if, like Nick, you could make a little crime pay.

ORGANIZED CRIME

Vinnie worked on the roof. He had made it quite clear to the Baron that he had lost his knack for roofs, but to no avail. Zombies just could not handle ladders. The instructions confused them too much. "No, leg up—not out." "Put your foot on a rung." "A rung! A rung! You remember what a rung is!" "No, damn it! Now you're stepping on your hand!" Zombies just could not climb ladders. Except for the big one, and the Baron used him for other things.

Nevertheless, dead bodies could stink to high hell in the September heat, so Vinnie had to work on the roof installing the air conditioners. He almost didn't mind, but for the purple jumpsuit he had to wear. And the stupid yellow helmet. Vinnie had half a mind to quit. Then he thought of zombies tracking him down and turning him over to von Finkelstein, and he put on his yellow utility belt and got busy on the roof. Mostly now he feared falling to his death and having the Baron bring him back as one of *them*.

Them. They numbered now at least three dozen. Some just reeked of the grave. They moved slowly but unstoppably. Given too many instructions they inevitably fouled up whatever they attempted. The Baron had hung a big sign on each one with that zombie's name written on it. If you just gave an order without saying a name, they all did it. Sometimes they didn't remember their names, then the stew got cooked for sure.

Most of them looked pretty bad. Rotten flesh hanging off bones—the Baron worked overtime stitching them back together—smelly gunk flowing from gaping mouths. Either the Baron had the bad luck of unearthing dead morons, or dying effects the brain horribly. Most of the zombies could barely get a word out. They just groaned syllables endlessly. A few carried on better than most. The big one, Mr. Sparrow thank you very much, could just about pass for a normal human. He could talk almost proper too; though he didn't have much to say. Vinnie feared him the most. The Baron called him his "goon." The "goon" could actually shoot a gun and hit something with it. Vinnie tried getting one of the others to use a pistol, one of the less drippy ones, and had almost got his guts shot out for his pains. As it happened, the zombie shot himself twice in the head and once in the foot. Didn't re-kill him though, like in the movies. He just got stupider, if that was possible. And the Baron had hit the ceiling; two extra hours of re-stitching. The Baron hated stitching.

For his part, Vinnie hated just about everything to do with his new job. He had imagined organized crime quite differently. He pictured himself sitting around a poker table, or playing pool most of the day. Air heavy with smoke, wise guys would talk about "whacking" this guy or "busting up" so and so, and always saying "fuhgeddaboudit." Every so often, the Mob Boss would take him aside and give him a quiet instruction. Vinnie would go out and commit a crime, secure in the knowledge that the cops would back off of one of Mr. Big's boys. Then he'd return to the pool table. "That little puke coughed out real quick," he'd say. Or maybe something like, "He tried to pass a *fazool* on me, but I clocked his number." Stuff like that.

Instead, Vinnie dug up bodies, mixed the most noxious reeking fluids he had ever smelled, and installed refrigeration equipment on the roof. More damn roof work. Vinnie looked down the skylight at the huge expanse of room below. The lights flicked on and off. When on, Vinnie could see the Baron sitting in a chair, his body pinched together in a tight little mass. He would clap his hands twice and the lights went out. Two more claps and lights returned. Circling around him, half a dozen denizens of the undead realm carried trays from one desk to another. The Baron wanted to find one good enough to serve as butler. The flickering lights did not distract them. One had to have concentration to become distracted.

Vinnie felt pretty sure he knew what the zombies thought most of the time. Nothing. But what goes through the Baron's head?

◆ ◆ ◆

What would a seamstress name her child? Where would you go to look up something like that? Drakan reasoned that the child of a seamstress would become a seamstress herself. Like mother, like daughter, obviously. If he knew what a seamstress would typically name her daughter, he could find a dead seamstress and dig her up.

Thready? Stitchy? Sewey? Slim chance of finding names like that on a tombstone. Somehow, Drakan had to find someone to do all this flesh sewing. Vinnie had ten thumbs and a weak stomach, and Drakan himself had far better things to do. Science beckoned. The longer he conducted his experiments, the better his undead subjects turned out. His early success with Charley Sparrow had raised his hopes. But Sparrow proved a fluke. Most of the zombies looked and acted like, well, like zombies. And not especially functional zombies at that. Constant effort had brought improvement though. And the more undead he created the more often he got serviceable results. If he could just dig up enough bodies, and capture enough extraction subjects, the odds alone would provide him with plenty of good undead servants.

If only Drakan could devote himself to science alone. Alas, administrative matters took up most of his time. Vinnie and a few zombies could handle the grave digging, but Drakan had to direct Mr. Sparrow personally every night in the search for more living material. Drakan now searched nightly for fat prostitutes. He found that a generous portioned prostitute could be drained to re-animate up to two, sometimes three, dead bodies (depending on the size of the recipient). This efficiency hardly cut into Drakan's schedule. After all, he had to run an undead factory practically single-handed. He considered bringing in his old teacher, but he might be squeamish about the ugly necessities. Vinnie helped a bit, but his constant complaints about his sore knee led Drakan to assign him tasks elsewhere whenever possible. Sparrow and a few others could take the necessary instruction, but one had to give the orders carefully. Drakan hoped one of them might make a good valet at least.

Behind him, Drakan heard a loud crash; silverware hitting the floor. He clapped on the lights and turned around. Norman the Zombie had gotten off track and walked himself into a corner. "Come here, Norman," he said. Too late, Drakan realized that he had spoken the order before the name and had consequently pulled the other five zombies out of formation. Three of them now turned in little circles of confusion, their mouths agape, eyes bugging out, each orbiting his own little "here." Two others just started walking straight toward Drakan, soon to get lost in the vast recesses of the building. "Stop!" yelled Drakan. All of them stopped. "Norman, come here." Norman came and stopped before Drakan. Norman stood six feet four. (Drakan remembered how he had cursed upon opening that coffin.) He loomed over Drakan, eyes open wide, mouth agape, a bit of thick, bright green mucus edging out of his mouth.

"You've knocked your arm out of socket, haven't you?" Drakan asked the zombie.

"Arrghrraa," said the zombie, pushing a great blob of green goo out of its mouth onto the floor at Drakan's feet.

"And you're leaking I see." Drakan pushed at the arm until it returned to its socket and scooped up the green slime off the floor with a dustpan. "No sense letting this go to waste." He put the slime into a large barrel of green slime, and set about lining the zombies up again with their trays. This time without Norman. In ten minutes he had them making their table rounds once more.

Charley Sparrow entered the warehouse through a sliding door to Drakan's right. He carried a large vat of chemicals, far heavier than any living man could carry, Drakan proudly noted, and set it down in the manufacturing end of the operation. Then he left for another. Drakan wished all undead could be like good old Charley. He thought it ironic how disappointed he had felt when he opened Sparrow's coffin that night, seemingly so long ago now. Drakan assumed a man named "Sparrow" would be quite small and light. He had cursed a blue streak to find a six foot five giant in the box. But old Charley proved a good zombie, and an excellent goon. Now, how to make more like him?

Vinnie heard the Baron calling him. He had finished installing the air conditioners long ago, but dallied about on the roof hoping to avoid further work. But the Baron squeaketh, so Vinnie headed down the stairs. Once down, he found the Baron at the center of five orbiting zombies, with the ever-present Mr. Sparrow standing off to one side. The Baron bid Vinnie sit, and Vinnie did. Vinnie nearly jumped out of his seat when a dead man's hand served him a cup of cold coffee.

"Don't jump," said the Baron, "stay still or it will confuse them." The Baron looked at a zombie whose name card read "Howard." Howard the Zombie stood five foot five and had once been about sixty years old; but who knows when that was. "Howard," said the Baron, "give Sergeant Vinnie a sandwich to eat." Vinnie had almost forgotten his recent promotion to sergeant. Twenty zombies had attended the ceremony. The Baron had almost cut his ear off while "dubbing" him with a sword. The Baron had him declare a twenty-minute oath swearing something called "fealty" to something called "the Necronic Empire of Final Keeping of all Undead." Fortunately, the Baron had prepared cue cards.

Howard the Zombie started over with a tray filled with sandwiches. Each had the crust cut off and they looked quite good, but Vinnie would be damned if he would put food a zombie had touched into his mouth. Howard the Zombie walked to Vinnie's chair, grabbed a sandwich with one hand and dropped the tray. It hit the ground with a loud clang that echoed throughout the warehouse. Then Howard the Zombie grabbed the back of Vinnie's head with his free hand and stuffed the sandwich violently into Vinnie's mouth with the other.

"Damn!" yelled the Baron as Howard the Zombie choked Vinnie with ham and cheese on rye. "The simplest thing and they do it all wrong."

Vinnie struggled to breathe. Even he could knock down a little old man, but whatever the Vampire Lord pumped into them to bring them back to "life" also made them inhumanly strong. So Vinnie fought for his life against Howard the Zombie's force-feeding.

Vinnie could hear the Baron jabbering on about what Vinnie considered less than pressing matters. "So much training. So many sandwiches wasted. None of them will make good valets. Except Mr. Sparrow, and I needed him for other things." The Baron paced back and forth to the sound of Vinnie's choking. Vinnie turned blue. Vinnie looked at the Baron with a plea in his tearing eyes. The Baron looked up at Howard the Zombie and Vinnie, death-locked over a ham sandwich. "Vinnie, cut that out, we have to talk," he said. Vinnie choked on. "Howard, go away," Howard the Zombie released Vinnie and started walking. He would keep going till he fell into the sea. As it happened, a wall blocked his route to the Pacific, and he just kept pushing himself into it for three days—when his fluid ran out.

The color returned to Vinnie's face as he spat out bits of ham onto his uniform.

"Sergeant," said the Baron, "I want to try out some names on you." Vinnie thought at first the Baron meant to hit him with them. The Zombie Lord removed a paper from the pocket of his black jumpsuit. "Now look around," he continued, "picture the place a few weeks from now. Full paint job, more lights, some silver table settings, and a long table suitable for large henchmen meetings." Vinnie saw the Baron staring at him and began looking around. Vinnie had absolutely no imagination, so he just pretended to imagine. Vinnie scrunched his eyebrows and nodded a lot. Vinnie supposed that people moved their eyebrows a lot when they imagined. The Baron continued, "I'm going to try out a list of names, see which one fits: *The Lair*." The Baron paused for effect; he looked up to see the effect on Vinnie. Vinnie moved his eyebrows. "*The Dungeon*," pause; look. "*The Hole in the Wall*," pause; look. "*Headquarters X*," pause; look. "*Necropolis*," pause; look. "*The Necro-Lair*," pause; look. "*The Necro-Lair Hole*," pause; look. "*Fort Zombie*," pause; look.

At a certain point a lack of familiar bearings simply leaves one completely out to sea. Without the firm ground of normality, even the abnormal becomes impossible. One merely sails a sea of disconnected sensations. Vinnie suspected insanity had finally descended upon him. He looked forward to the booby hatch. Dribbling lunatics ranting incomprehensible visions could not make for worse living companions than bug-eyed zombie waiters.

The Zombie Lord noticed the panicked expression on his henchman's face. "Names for the headquarters."

Vinnie laughed the laugh of the damned. "Ha ha ha," Vinnie laughed. "Names, yeah, names, of course, names, ha ha ha …"

The Ghoul Master gave up. "All right, never mind. I'll pick one myself. Would you like a drink?"

"Yes, a drink, please Baron."

The Baron looked around. "Uh, Glen, bring Sergeant Vinnie a drink."

Vinnie shot up from the chair. "That's okay Baron! I'm not thirsty anymore!"

The Baron called off the zombie waiter and walked over

to the door leading to a small office. He beckoned Vinnie to follow. "Come in here Vinnie, I want you to see something."

Vinnie followed. As usual, Charley Sparrow came as well. Vinnie found it eerie how much more efficient Sparrow could be compared to the others. In the office, Vinnie saw the Baron's TV and VCR. "Sit down Sergeant Vinnie," the Baron said. Vinnie sat in the chair facing the television. The Baron fooled with a tape, finally getting it loaded into the machine. Vinnie marveled at how the Baron could raise the dead, or at least half raise them, and still not know how to work simple electronic equipment any five year old could steal.

The tape started playing. To Vinnie it looked like an old black and white movie. The Baron straightened up and Vinnie realized that he meant to give a bit of a pep-talk. "Sergeant Vinnie," the Baron began, "the organization is under capitalized. We need an infusion of funds. Robbery remains the simplest method of raising quick cash. Knowing your aversion to further high altitude work, I have eliminated cat-burglaring." Vinnie felt relieved. The Baron continued, "We can't get the undead up the ladders anyway. So it's robbery, not burglary. I considered trains and banks." *Trains?* thought Vinnie. "I'm not sure where they keep the money on trains, so I chose banks. I know you are not experienced in this type of caper, so I found a training film. It's called *The Bank Robbery*. 1923. Very good, I watched it myself. Take notes." The Baron left the room. Vinnie watched the film.

The movie was a western. Vinnie had no idea why he had to watch it. The Baron returned before it ended. He had Vinnie's "civilian" clothes. The film ended and the Baron turned off the TV.

"Sergeant Vinnie, you are going to rob a bank."

Vinnie felt great relief. Stealing things he understood. He could even offer the Baron helpful advice. "I know people for this. I could get us good help."

"People?"

"I know this guy, real tough. I mean, he's black, but he joined the Aryan Brotherhood. That is *tough*, man."

The Baron's face scrunched up. "An Ethiopian in the Arval Brotherhood? They haven't existed since the time of Ancient Rome. Mind you, I've thought of starting a chapter. But no one knows the proper rituals. On the other hand, once I perfect the reanimation formula, we might be able to raise some old Roman from the Brotherhood and learn the ancient ways of the Arvals. We'll have to see. In the meantime, we will use ghoul goons."

Vinnie did not like the sound of that. "Really Baron, I think we need pros for this," Vinnie said.

"Undead is what we have," said the Baron. And Vinnie knew how right he was.

L.A. remains the international daylight bank robbery capital of the world. Experts at the F.B.I. insist that such crimes occur there so frequently because of high population density, easy freeway access, and the large number of small branch banks. Anyone who lives in Southern California knows this to be nonsense. People rob banks in L.A. because the weather is fine, the bills come due, and damn it, those banks have money. In a land with so many Porsches, no reasonable person would choose to walk if he can rob a bank and finance a new car. Understand that these are robberies, not *heists*. A heist requires planning, timing, an original idea, and quite often costumes and special equipment. An L.A. bank robbery requires a gun, loaded or unloaded, and a car; ski mask optional.

Drakan took no chances with his first bank robbery. He briefed his minions carefully. He gave Vinnie detailed written instructions to augment his training film. Drakan then selected three fairly presentable zombies, plus Sparrow, for the assault team. He sat them all down in folding chairs in front of a chalkboard. Drakan had drawn in chalk what he took to be a typical bank layout.

It looked to Vinnie more like a bar scene from an old western movie. Vinnie could not understand why the Baron had drawn in so many decorative items on the boarder of the chalkboard; intricately interlocked dollar signs swirled around the picture of the "bank layout." Rather than stick figures for the guards and tellers, the Baron had drawn fully-dressed, little men and women in a variety of poses. The Baron complained to Vinnie that he did not have enough time to construct a complete diorama of a bank robbery. Whatever that was.

Drakan addressed his seated gang, Vinnie by his side. Drakan pointed at the chalkboard occasionally, at which times the zombies would stare at the tip of his finger. "You will take your orders from Sergeant Vinnie. Do what Sergeant Vinnie says. Leo, you will cover the door. Not now, Leo! When Sergeant Vinnie tells you to. Sit down, Leo. In the chair, Leo. That's better. Now. Sergeant Vinnie will place you—not now, Leo! Sit down, John! You will only get out of the chairs when I say *execute orders,* not when I say *now.* Vinnie will place you each in your proper position in the bank. Leo covers the door, John and Randall will watch the tellers while Mr. Sparrow aids Vinnie in —Randall, push that reanimation fluid back into your mouth, please."

"I think he bit off the tip of his finger," offered Vinnie.

"I'll sew it back on later. Spit out your fingertip Randall. Get that, Vinnie. No! Just Vinnie get it! Everyone back in his seat! That's not your seat, Leo!"

Vinnie retrieved the fingertip and put it in his right pants pocket. That night, while fishing for a lighter, he would pull it out and nearly give himself a heart attack. The Baron managed to get the gang back into proper briefing formation and returned to the blackboard. "When you leave the bank you will go in the brown van. After the robbery everyone returns to the brown van. Does everyone understand that?"

"Aarrhhgaa."

"Aacccaaca."

"Phoopfiff."

This last sound came from the hind end of Randall the Zombie, and Vinnie did not even want to guess what sort of gas he had emitted.

Drakan nodded at Sparrow. "Mr. Sparrow, you will pass out the pistols now."

Vinnie flashed on trouble ahead. "Are you sure they should have pistols, Baron?"

Drakan looked at Vinnie as if the little cat-burglar had lost his mind. "Rob a bank with unarmed zombies? Don't be absurd."

Leo stared down the barrel of his gun. Randall tried to eat the grip of his. Vinnie grew more apprehensive. "Maybe we shouldn't load the guns, uh, Baron?"

Drakan addressed the zombies again, "Do not discharge your weapon without explicit instructions from Sergeant Vinnie," Drakan thought a moment, "or unless someone else fires a weapon. Remember most of all, follow Sergeant Vinnie's instructions." Drakan turned to Vinnie. "The others need not wear masks, but you must. I couldn't decide which worked better, a ski mask or a stocking. I've heard of both being used. I bought you one of each. I suggest wearing the ski mask over the stocking—the stocking might be hard to get on doing it the other way."

With that Drakan returned to his office to write the note. Vinnie could hand the note to the teller, but Drakan thought the writing of it too important to leave to a mere Sergeant. After all, a robber's note had to be given to a teller, and might even be shown to a bank manager. This surely made it a semi-legal document, and so it needed to follow the right formalities. Also, it would eventually end up in the hands of the F.B.I., and the local police, so it should contain false clues and subtle misdirection. This is the note Drakan settled on:

To Whom it May Concern, Which is You,
This note notifies you of an official bank robbery now occurring here. You are it that is being robbed. I, robber of

the first part, require you, victim of the second part, or such agent or agents as your policies require you to delegate such tasks to, to comply with all of my first part instructions. I have a gang of only five men who are all with me but one in the car. My instructions are as follows in the correct order: You, of the second part, or any assisting agents, with or without supervisor approval, are to hand over all money contained here within this financial bank, including that held in the safe, or in any hidden compartments or safes behind pictures or such. All of which I know of, though NOT BECAUSE I HAVE AN INSIDE CONFEDERATE. Such cash is to include all non-traceable money but to exclude such coins as may be too bulky to carry by my accomplices, though not to exclude such rare and valuable coins as tellers are said to squirrel away in their boxes from patrons unsuspecting of their value. Further, you are to drop to the floor and count backward from one hundred—this to be done after handing over the cash. The headquarters of our gang cannot be found on any map and this does not indicate that we are from out of state.

We are not international.

Drakan read the note over three times and thought it could not be better. It only troubled him that he could not think how to sign it. He finally settled on "Robber X," and handed it to Vinnie.

Vinnie sat in a brown van outside the First American Metropolitan Bank of Los Angeles. This would be his first armed robbery. He already wore both the stocking and the ski mask. He could see nothing, and could barely breath. He pulled up his masks and stuffed them under the large cowboy hat the Baron had given him for just such a purpose. Vinnie felt thrilled. He had joined the big time. As a kid, he had often dreamed of leading a gang of hard and mean men on desperate armed robberies. Vinnie looked back at his gang.

Behind him sat the most gruesome collection of human flesh bags ever seen on the earth. Vinnie shuttered. More a vision from his nightmares than his dreams, this was, nonetheless, his gang. Sparrow looked all right; too all right. Unlike the others, Sparrow would look you straight in the eyes, like a real person. For all that, he still looked mostly like a walking dead man. The others were beyond repair. Leo sat leaning forward, eyes cast to the roof of the car, left hand pulling hard at his own tongue. Randall did a sword-swallowing act with his pistol barrel, while John stared at him repeating "Aaaarrrgharrr" over and over again. Fine gang this.

Vinnie wanted to remain inconspicuous while getting out of the van. "Follow me," he said. Vinnie got out of the passenger side and closed the door. For a moment all seemed well. Then he noticed the absence of zombies beside him. Looking back he saw two ghoulish faces pressed hard against the driver's side window. Another body pressed the front windshield. "Christ Jesus," Vinnie muttered.

He waved the gang away from the window so he could open the door. But they just stared at his hand. Vinnie went round to the passenger side of the van and opened the door. "Exit out the back," he said and hurried to the rear doors before he had a pile up there too. Opening the doors, he saw his crew crawling over each other to get to the exit. "One at a time," Vinnie said. Each assuming he was the "one," they all continued their crawl. All but Sparrow, who had not moved through all this. "Leo, then Randall, then John, then Mr. Sparrow," said Vinnie. This sorted things out. Vinnie retrieved the gun from Randall's mouth as he passed.

"Hide the guns," Vinnie said. "In your clothes, not your body, Randall." Vinnie looked them over. They looked fine. For dead guys about to rob a bank. Vinnie put on his game face. "Follow me," he said. Randall stepped on Sparrow's foot; Leo and John hit the side of the van failing to make the turn with

Vinnie. "Spread out some!" Vinnie said. The zombies began to walk randomly away, except for John who tried to pull his ribs apart. "Stop!" yelled Vinnie. For several minutes he arranged his crew in marching order, giving each detailed instructions as to how not to trample his fellow team member. Any number of people saw all this going on as they passed on their way to the bank. But as it was not their business, they did not stop to ask.

Finally confident of not being trampled by the over-earnest undead, Vinnie led the gang into the bank. There Vinnie found something neither he nor the Baron had thought of: lines at the teller windows. Do robbers take priority? Sergeant Vinnie decided he could not push his way to the front while simultaneously keeping good order among the troops. He stationed Leo near the door with instructions to do nothing (a talent with zombies in any case), and lined up between the velvet ropes ahead of the rest of the Dead Eye Gang (as the Baron had taken to calling them before they left). All went well as they creeped along. No one leaked bright green slime and everyone stayed off the heel of the team member in front. Vinnie nearly panicked when a woman approached John and asked if the bank charged for the use of their ATM machine. John the Zombie leaned forward a half-inch from her face and cleared his throat loud enough to wake the dead. The woman sought wisdom elsewhere.

Time seemed to have stopped for Vinnie. Four customers ahead, a woman complained to a teller about false bank charges. Vinnie's head itched like mad under the cowboy hat and double masks. Behind him a group of ghouls concentrated on not trodding over each other. To make matters worse, two armored-car guards had just entered the building, and a bank employee seemed to be taking an unhealthy interest in Leo, who stood doing nothing by the door.

Finally, Vinnie's turn at the teller window came. A friendly blond fellow smiled at him. "How can I help you today sir?" he asked. Vinnie handed him the note. The fellow started reading.

Since Vinnie had a bit of time now, he looked around to see how Leo was getting along. Some crackpot old blue-haired lady was deep in conversation with him. Leo, such a nice old gentleman, just nodded, mouth agape, eyes bugging out.

"I'm not sure what you want me to do with this, sir," the teller said in honest concern.

Well this was just too much! Vinnie pulled out his gun. "Do what the note says!" he told the teller.

The teller, face now flushed with fear, began re-reading the note. Vinnie realized he had not pulled down his mask. He put his gun on the counter, and worked to get both stocking and ski mask over his face. The two became tangled as Vinnie tugged to pull them down. Vinnie couldn't see anything. He felt like a constrictor had coiled around his head.

The teller noticed the sounds of Vinnie's struggle and saw the gun on the counter. For a moment, the thought to grab the gun flashed through his mind. He looked up and saw the cold yellow eyes of Charley Sparrow fixed dead on him. He returned to reading the note.

Vinnie finally tore a hole in the stocking behind one of the eyeholes of the ski mask. The new-torn hole did not align with the eyehole of the ski mask so he had to hold down the ski mask eyehole with the index finger of his left hand in order to see, if not quite breathe. Vinnie grabbed the gun from the counter. How did that get there? He fired a shot into the air (which is to say, through the roof, into the second floor, through the roller of an office chair, and finally into a water cooler on the third floor). The sound of the shot nearly scared him to death. Sparrow never flinched.

"Everybody drop to the ground now!" Vinnie yelled. And they did. The teller disappeared from view. Bank patrons on either side of Vinnie collided heads jumping to the floor. The guard in the back dropped like a bag of sand. Even the blue-haired old lady made a slow progress to the carpet. Vinnie spun in a circle holding the gun over his head with his right hand while his left tugged on the ski mask to keep a view hole open.

Everybody had dropped to the floor. Leo, Sparrow, everybody.

"Shit!" Vinnie yelled. What do you say? Zombies only get up? Vinnie drew a blank on the names. Finally, one came to him. "Sparrow, get the money!" Vinnie yelled. To his great relief, Sparrow got up and sensibly walked around to the half-door separating the lobby from the tellers' section. The locked door shattered as Sparrow went through it. A full door blocked his movement momentarily, but a single blow from the big man's hand broke it in two. Vinnie marveled at the ghoul's strength. Sparrow proceeded to the large safe behind the tellers.

Meanwhile Vinnie had to raise the dead. "Leo get up, watch the door. Pull your gun." Leo got to his feet and tugged at his pistol while staring bug-eyed at the door. "John, get up, pull your gun. Randall, get up, pull out your gun." The others complied. Vinnie saw they stood too close together. "Randall, go over there and—" he almost said "shoot anyone who moves," then realized who the first target would be. Instead he said, "Watch them." He sent John to the other side of the room.

Vinnie went into the tellers' station. He ordered the blond teller to collect the money from the drawers. The man complied, filling a bag Vinnie handed him (with much difficulty since he had to stuff his gun into his armpit in order to retrieve the bag without losing his eye-hole). Vinnie marched down the line of teller drawers like a big-time bandit. He looked up to check his gang. Leo and Randall managed well, but John now stood face flat against a wall trying to walk through it. "Turn around, John," Vinnie yelled. John the Zombie turned and started walking the other way. Sparrow exited the vault carrying a large bag that Vinnie desperately hoped contained money.

Sparrow led the way out into the lobby. Vinnie felt great; high as a kite. Then shots rang out. Two bullets hit Sparrow straight in the chest. The big man did not even pause. Vinnie freaked out. "Return fire!" he yelled, "Shoot! Shoot!"

The zombies banged away. They shot randomly. Twice on his way to the door Vinnie had to hit the ground. The initial shots came from one of the armored-car guards. He did a one-man John Wayne right there in the middle of the room. His partner wanted to live to retirement and stayed huddled to the floor. But Young John Wayne stood in the middle of the room hitting every ghoul in sight. He hit Leo in the chest, Randall in the stomach, and caught John dead center in the back of the head. That boy could really shoot. What he couldn't do was figure out why nobody fell down.

Finally out of bullets, he stopped to reload. Vinnie had half crawled to the exit. "Leo, John, Randall, head for the car!" he yelled. Sparrow had never slowed and now walked out the door onto the street. The other zombies headed for the door, but did not stop the random firing of their weapons. Young John Wayne had almost reloaded now and Vinnie knew that no ghoul would so much as wing him. Vinnie leveled his gun at the gray uniformed guard. He fired. The bullet hit the guard in the arm, knocking him over. That did it for Vinnie. He sprinted for the door. Goodbye gunfight at the OK Corral, hello brown van to freedom.

Outside at last, Vinnie ran to the van. Sparrow had opened the driver's side door and blocked Vinnie's way to the driver's seat. Had he not, Vinnie would have left his gang there and headed for the hills. As matters stood, he had to wait for Sparrow to climb over the driver's seat before he could get in. Sparrow always headed for the driver's seat for some reason. "No! No! I'm driving you smelly bag of puss! Get in the back!" Vinnie looked behind him. Three bug-eyed ghouls filled the street clicking the triggers of now empty guns. What the hell, Vinnie thought. "Get into the brown van!" he yelled. They walked toward him. "Run!" Vinnie shouted. Stiff legged, the three hobbled to the van. Vinnie opened the back door and the three entered. Vinnie climbed into the driver's seat and gunned the engine.

The rest of the escape went like clockwork; until they hit five o'clock traffic and came to a dead stop six miles from the bank. Vinnie saw choppers buzzing about overhead. Traffic helicopters, but Vinnie expected one to land on the hood of the van at any moment. None did. Vinnie began to relax. No cop could identify his van in the metal sludge of L.A. traffic. Vinnie whistled a tune. He took a peak into the bank bag sitting in his lap. The bag exploded. Blue dye #34 covered Vinnie, the window, and two zombies.

"Aaaahh!" yelled Vinnie. The zombies picked up the chant.

"Aaaahh!" yelled Leo the Zombie.

"Aaarraahh!" yelled Randall and John.

Another blue dye pack exploded and the rear window fogged over into azure obscurity. The ghouls continued their howl of the dead. Vinnie felt sanity slipping again. He lost his mind for almost a full two minutes of blue fog explosions and zombie wails. But the traffic would not let up, and Vinnie could not move, and so could find no point of expression for his insanity. Madness un-expressed remains most unsatisfying, so sanity made a reluctant return to Vinnie's mind. The traffic let up a bit. Vinnie found he could drive with one blue head hanging out the window. Leo could put a head out the other one and groan when he saw a space in the traffic. With some effort Vinnie made it safe and sound back to the Necro-Lair. All in all he thought, not a bad effort. He'd never do it again no matter what the Baron threatened, but he had done all right. He didn't lose a man; though the Baron might have some stitching to do.

LAYING THE FLUE

George Murphy, one-third owner of the Southern Illinois Tool Re-Sales Corporation (which re-sells previously re-sold tools), sat in the sports bar of the *Renaissance Fair Hotel and Casino* in Las Vegas, Nevada. The annual convention of the Secondary Use Industrial Tools Association had wrapped up business two hours earlier. Tomorrow morning George would head back home to re-sell tools. Tonight he could play Gypsy King of Las Vegas if he liked.

The Renaissance Fair Hotel, like all the other big hotels in Vegas, had a theme. One can not just sleep and gamble in Vegas today, one must sleep and gamble in an atmosphere. At the Renaissance, this meant rolling dice among Romeos and Juliets, receiving Elizabeth I on progression at your table twice an hour, and having the Bard himself payout the over $1000 slot wins. The maids wore bodices, and the valets pantaloons. At the sports bar, a country and western band played on the "Globe of London" stage, and "Merry Players," reeking of cigarettes, juggled and danced jigs at the food court. Tan and purple ruled the color scheme in both rooms and public spaces. It must have taken some Renaissance scholar years of research to discover that these were the colors of the Elizabethan era.

Most of this theme-soaked elegance passed right by George Murphy. He did wonder why the sports bar menu featured "Macbeth Burgers," and "As You Like It Potato Skins." It also struck him funny that the two bartenders serving the crowd that watched games on the overhead TVs should wear such frilly shirts with puffy-ruffle sleeves. All the drinkers dressed normally. Normal in Vegas encompasses everything from sweatpants to formal wear. George wore a leisure suit.

George sat at the bar sucking on a bourbon. "Barkeep," he shouted, banging his bourbon on the table. "Barkeep. Yee Old Fucking drink is low. Throw another shot at me." The bartender poured another bourbon. He placed it before the big shot from the Midwest, or as corporate office requires them to be called: an honored groundling. George grabbed the bartender's ruffled sleeve. "Listen barkeep, I want to know how come there are so many gook dealers in Vegas? Every time America fights a fucking war, we get more fucking refugees. We win the big one and we re-build fucking France—we ought to own that fucking country—and now the fucking French won't even let us fly over their fucking country to bomb somebody. And these gooks, they wanted fucking Communism, and we let them have it. Now these gooks are dealing at our tables. What the fuck is that?"

The bartender just said, "I don't know, sir," and pulled away. George drank his shot. Back home bartenders knew how to listen. Not that George talked this way back home. But then, who knew him from Adam in Las Vegas? George spied a woman sitting four seats down the bar. He whistled until she turned around. "Hey," he said to her. She looked about thirty-five and had a cell phone to her ear as she turned to face Big George Murphy. "Hey," George said again. "I got a thousand up today. I'm on a fucking howl now." The woman smiled a polite smile. George continued: "I own one third of a tool re-selling company." She smiled again, and turned her eyes down to the bar. George moved over a seat so she could hear him better. "We don't re-sell screw drivers or hammers. It's all big industrial equipment. Presses and such. Hey. Hey! If you don't want to talk to a guy, don't fucking smile at him, uh?"

George ate a peanut. A black man in a business suit and his wife sat down on the two seats still left between George and the phone woman. When George looked up again from his drink, he poked the black man on the arm. "Hey," said George, "You know Sammy? You know Sammy?" The black man seemed in a good mood. Prior to George's poking, he had been laughing at something his wife said.

"Sorry, I don't know what you mean," the man said, still half laughing.

"Yeah," said George, "you forget him pretty quick. He did a lot of good for you people. All his entertaining and all." George wiggled his fingers above the bar, imitating a dance. The black man lost his laughter completely and turned back to his wife. "Hey, I didn't say anything pal," said George. They moved off to a booth. George called after them, "Yeah, I've lost three thousand on the fucking day, and you don't want to talk." George looked for the bartender. He stood at the other end of the bar talking on the phone. George waved for him to come over.

The bartender came over. "How come they dress you in those faggoty shirts? What the fuck is that supposed to be, anyway?" George said to him.

"Just the theme, sir," the bartender said. George asked for another drink and the bartender served him one. George sat a while rolling pennies down the bar. He saw a woman enter the sports bar. A gorgeous, tall blond in a very tight baby-blue dress. She sat down at a table just behind the bar stool at which George sat. She crossed her legs and began applying make-up. George whistled and turned back around to find the bartender standing right in front of him. "Some piece of ass that, uh?" said George. The bartender smiled and walked down the bar to another customer.

After drinking his shot, George turned around to watch the baby-blue blond again. He took her all in. Then a man approached the woman. George could hear their conversation. The man said to the woman, "Oh you are lovely, just like that, lovely."

The woman looked up at him but did not stop dressing her face.

The man continued, "I'd be happy to accompany you tonight, if you'd like some company"

"No thank you," said the woman.

The man reached into his coat pocket and pulled out a wallet. "I'd be willing to pay. I don't mind that."

The woman looked twelve kinds of angry. "You think I'm a prostitute?"

The man smiled, "Hell, you're dressed like a whore. That's alright, I can pay."

The woman put down her compact and picked up a drink someone had left on the table. She flung it at the man, dousing his face in liquid. When she spoke, her voice shot venom, "Get out of here now or next time it will be mace!"

The man backed away wiping his face. George turned back around, laughing to himself. He looked for someone with whom to share the episode. He called to the bartender, but the man took his time with another customer. George ate some peanuts at the bar. He watched a bit of a game on the overhead TV. Then a thirty-something fellow sat down on the stool beside George. George nudged him. The guy looked at George. "What a fucking place," George said.

"Yeah," the man said.

"I'm George," said George, offering his hand.

"Nick," said the man shaking it. "Who's winning?"

"Fuck if I know," said George, "I only keep track if I have a bet on."

"Me too," said Nick, "but I always have a bet on."

George laughed. He liked this guy. A second man, this one in a suit and carrying a brief case, sat down on the other side of George. The bartender came over. "Who's winning?" the man in the suit asked.

"Don't know," said George, "like I was telling this fellow, I only keep track if I bet." George felt good now. In the company of men. The bartender took drink orders from the three of them. Nick introduced himself to the other fellow, whose name was Roy, then introduced George to Roy.

"Glad to meet you," Roy said.

"You going or coming to this meeting?" Nick asked Roy,

referring to the suit, George imagined.

"Both," Roy said, "been doing interviews all day. One hotel room after another. I have three more tonight, if you can believe it."

"Are you looking or giving?" Nick asked.

Roy laughed; one of those *just between us guys* laughs. "I'm looking for a job. My association holds its job fair at the convention. Three days of hell if you're looking."

George wanted in, "You need to own your own. I own one third of a tool re-selling firm. My old lady's dad brought me in years ago. I married the tight-assed bitch for my stake. Her old man hated me, but he had her and two sons and he couldn't just cut her out. I had her turn over the business to me two days after he turned it over to the kids. She's just a homemaker anyway. She didn't know anything about business."

"Did the brothers stay on in the business? Or did they punk out and sell off?" Nick asked. George felt good that this fellow knew how the world worked.

"I pushed them out," George said, "I'd argue with them all the time. Every family gathering, Thanksgiving, Christmas, whatever, I made it a point to talk nothing but the business and how they screwed it to kingdom come. Came to it, the one had enough and wanted to sell. I lined up a buyer. Screwed that asshole good, too. The other sold four years later to a buddy of mine."

"That's the way to do it," Nick said, "you have to be ruthless in this hard world."

"Fucking A plus right," said George. George drank his bourbon. "Let me buy you a drink."

Nick smiled, "We'll pay for the rounds together." Nick pulled out a twenty and put it on the bar, "You want in on this, make it three?" he asked Roy.

"That would put me pretty tight at the interview," Roy said, "but hell, okay."

George liked this a lot. Real fucking men here. Roy opened his brief case and got his wallet. As he turned around he saw something past George's head. He gave a low whistle. "Would you look at that piece of blond fuck-me-please!" Roy said.

Nick and George turned around. The blond woman in the blue dress still sat alone at the small table.

"Fuck me Baby-Blue," Nick said.

George could hardly wait to tell the guys what he had seen earlier. Then Roy said, "I'd bet a hundred dollars she's a whore."

George froze in mid-thought.

"I would too," Nick said, "but who would take the bet?"

George saw his whole night turning around. But should he screw his new friends? Hell, you have to be tough in this ruthless world. "You fellows. She's a nice girl."

Both men laughed. Nick said, "That ain't going to get up her dress, George. It'll take cash to do that."

George smiled. Lord just help me pull the suckers in. "I say she's a nice girl and not a whore."

"But are you willing to bet on that?" asked Nick.

"What kind of man would I be if I said it here and wouldn't put my money where my mouth is?" George said.

Roy looked back at the woman. Nick did too. Both men thought for one hard moment. "Well," said Roy at last, "I'm in for a hundred."

"Is that all?" George asked.

Nick looked long and hard at the beautiful woman in the blue dress. "I'd put five on it that she's a whore," he said.

"Alright, now that's a man's bet," George said.

Roy looked back at the woman. He downed his shot. He let out a sigh. "Okay, five hundred from me too; if you can cover it."

"Sure," George said. He tried hard to keep from bursting from excitement.

Nick pulled out his wallet. He pulled out a hundred dollar bill, four twenties and the rest in tens and fives. George peeled off ten hundred dollar bills, all he had left from his Vegas money, but not all he meant to take home from it.

"We need to put this in something," Nick said.

"Here," Roy said, "I have an envelope in my brief case." He pulled out a small envelope. "I'll have to trade for some of that, I mostly have five hundred dollar bills." Roy pulled out his wallet containing two twenties and six five hundred dollar bills. "I figured I'd gamble less if I kept my travel money in large bills."

Nick laughed, "Guess you figured wrong there."

George worried that the joke might back Roy out of the bet. "That's alright, five hundreds are fine. Can I see them?"

"Yeah," said Nick, "make sure you're not passing counterfeit."

"No, no," said George reassuringly, while checking the bills closely to see that they were real.

"If those are counterfeit I have real troubles," Roy said.

Nick and George looked the bills over carefully. Once satisfied they gave the rest of the money to Roy. Roy gave the envelope to George who put Roy's four bills, one Roy's stake, one Nick's, and two covering his own, into the envelope.

"Here," Nick said, "we'll each write our name on it, so there's no mistaking, and let the bartender hold the bet. Got a pen?" Roy handed over a pen and George handed over the envelope. Nick wrote his name on the back of the sealed envelope, across the seal. He tossed the pen and the envelope back to Roy and called for the bartender, "Hey! Mage of the Magic elixir, come down here."

George felt his excitement growing. This would be one hell of a story to tell back home. Roy passed the envelope and the pen to George. George signed his name under Roy's. The bartender arrived. Nick took the envelope from the counter where George had left it. "We have a bet going, mind holding this?"

The bartender looked at the envelope. "Against the rules," he said and walked away.

"Ah hell," Nick said, "you can keep it George. Put it in your pocket." George took the envelope. "That alright with you Roy?" Nick asked.

"Whatever," said Roy. "Now who asks the whore for a date?"

George figured a thousand dollars worth a drink in the face, "I'll do it." Besides, getting slapped might soften the blow when the boys lost the bet.

"Well should he?" Roy asked, "since he's trying to get her to say no?"

"Oh let him," said Nick, "George, don't insult her or anything, just ask her if she'll come back to your room."

"What if she fancies him?" Roy asked.

Nick laughed. "Right" he said. Roy laughed too.

George didn't much like that turn of things, but pretended to laugh along with them. "I'll ask her, you boys listen up."

George took a shot of bourbon. He screwed on his courage and walked over to the blond. In a loud voice, reeking of feigned politeness, he said, "Honey, you sure are pretty. I wonder if I offered you some money, if you might be willing to come back to my room for a while." He looked over at Nick and Roy, who watched closely.

The blond stood up. She dumped a drink down George's shirt and slapped him hard across the face. "Men are pigs!" she screamed at him. She stormed out of the bar. George's face hurt like hell. But he had secured his fortune. He returned to the bar. Roy looked dejected. Nick seemed philosophical about it; just shaking his head as if to say "yep, a loser again." George tried hard not to look smug as he bellied back up to the bar.

"Shit," Roy said. He closed his brief case and swung around without looking at the other two again. "Shit" he said as he walked away.

George just had to laugh. Nick joined him.

"Guess he don't know how to lose," George said.

"I suspect he does poorly in the rest of his interviews," Nick said.

George liked this Nick guy. A real man. A pal, even if he had to get clipped. Oh well, mess with the best and bleed like the rest. "Let me buy you a drink, soften the blow," George said.

Nick slapped him on the back like a real trooper. "Make it a double, and I'll get the next round. You got guts George. Maybe I'll find a way to take that back from you before the night's over."

George laughed, "I don't bet sports, but lets drink some." George ordered the drinks. Nick excused himself to the restroom for a moment. The bartender brought the drinks. George drank his down. He felt every inch the Vegas sharpie. He pulled the envelope out and examined the scrawled signatures happily. He tore the envelope open and pulled the money out. Four crisp new one-dollar bills.

"Fuck," said George.

CLUES YOU CAN USE

Special Agents Parker and Lansdowne studied the videotape playing on the TV. They had been studying this video, a combination of three originals, for the last two hours. They sat in a sterile office, illuminated by fluorescent lights. They drank cold coffee. They wore suits that proudly proclaimed the moderate income and damaged fashion sense of agents of the F.B.I. Parker sat closest to the TV, right up on it really. Lansdowne watched the action over his shoulder. On the screen they watched black and white images move in slow motion.

"They enter here, as a group," said Parker.

"Mmmm," said Lansdowne. They watched on.

"Cowboy sends bandit #2 to the door," Parker said.

"Mmmm," said Lansdowne.

"They stand in *line*?!?" Parker rubbed his forehead. Parker hit the fast forward button. "For seven minutes they stand in line." Parker let the video proceed at normal speed. "Cowboy hands over the note."

"Mmmm,"

Parker fast-forwards again. "Then he pulls the gun. And *then* he puts on a mask."

"But the others go in masked," offered Lansdowne. They had watched this video seven times, and Lansdowne never failed to make that point here.

"Yeah, the others are already masked," said Parker. "Cowboy puts his gun down for the teller … Cowboy shoots …"

"Witnesses agree he ordered everyone to the floor."

"And Bandits 1 through 4 drop." Parker stopped the tape

and rubbed his temples; hard. Lansdowne drank some coffee. Parker started the tape again. "Nope … nope … it still makes no sense," he said. The tape rolled on.

"Here's my favorite part," said Lansdowne, "everybody starts shooting."

"At everything."

"Maybe they're trying for the cameras?"

"Now?!? Now they shoot for the cameras?"

"Just a thought."

Parker watched the tape. "Down goes Mr. Hero. Out go the bandits."

"And they dance on the street before piling into a van."

Parker stopped the tape. He drank some coffee. Lansdowne backed away and sat in a folding chair at the table. Parker joined him at the table. Both men lose themselves in thought for several minutes. Finally, Parker said, "So, Maverick, what do you think?"

Lansdowne liked it when Parker called him *Maverick*. "Beats me, Hotdog."

Parker stood up. Standing did not help. "Why didn't Cowboy wear a mask like the others?"

Lansdowne drank more coffee. "He had to face the teller, so he couldn't wear the Halloween mask."

"So why not just all go in hard? Why stand in line? With masks on?"

Lansdowne had an idea about this, "Some of the witnesses say they wore no masks—they wore make-up. They stood there over seven minutes, and no one saw they wore masks. They may have worn make-up."

"But Cowboy doesn't believe in make-up?"

Lansdowne nodded, it did not add up. "Then he pulls a mask down, right in front of the camera."

Parker sat down again and buried his head in his hands.

Lansdowne let out a sigh. "Maybe," he said, "maybe they are just real stupid."

Parker pulled out a piece of paper from his pocket. He read

it out loud, "$240,232 taken. They wear full body armor. They know just when the armored truck makes an unscheduled cash drop. And away without a witness to which way they went. These guys were pros past pros.

"So why does Bandit #3 walk face first into the wall for a while?" Lansdowne asked.

"Maybe they mean to fuck with our minds, Maverick. They know we will watch the video. They want to mind fuck *us*."

Lansdowne scratched his chin. "So why do the ones in make-up drop to the floor with everyone else?"

Parker explodes, "I don't know! To … to … throw everyone off. To get into firing position against the armored car guards!"

"So how come they don't shoot back when the guard opens up on them?" Lansdowne asked.

"Fuck it! I hate this case!" Parker felt his sides hurt. He worried that stress would kick up his kidney stones. He wished he could add *causing stress related disorders* to the charge list. If they ever found anyone to charge.

Lansdowne took the puzzles in stride. "Cowboy tells the others to get up—each one, one at a time," he said.

Parker rubbed his sore side. Not a kidney stone, he thought, just not moving enough today. "They are a very disciplined crew."

"The names were obviously phony."

"Obviously phony. Just a red herring."

Lansdowne leaned back and kicked his feet up onto the table. Four hours at the scene, two more reviewing all interviews, another hour on precedent search, and now two hours watching videos. He had logged more time on this case already than on most three he ever worked. "Why did Cowboy put the gun down in front of the teller?"

"I know! I know!" Parker said. "He *wanted* the teller to go for it. Like a gunfight or something. Cowboy wants to be a cowboy."

Lansdowne considered this. "Why did he cover his eyes with the mask?"

Parker let out a huge sigh. This case would not end.

Lansdowne tried a new track, "Are we sure they knew about the armored car delivery?"

"They had to know. They waited in the bank until it arrived. They waited till the two guards were back in the lobby and couldn't hold them off at the vault, and they sprang before the manager had closed the vault. They could only time it like that by knowing when the delivery would be made."

Lansdowne nodded in agreement. "Why did they wait in line?"

Parker kicked a folding chair across the room.

Lansdowne grimaced. He hated seeing Hotdog so frustrated. He thought of something, "Didn't the note say something about an inside man?"

Parker felt acid rise inside his stomach. "I don't want to look at the note again."

Lansdowne walked over to a counter. He picked up a piece of typed paper kept in a clear plastic slip. He returned to the table and sat down. He read for a while. "NOT BECAUSE I HAVE AN INSIDE CONFEDERATE" he read out loud. He looked up at Parker. "Do you think the writer of the note meant to tell us something?"

Parker fumed. He grabbed the note out of Lansdowne's hand. "I *hate* this note. It is the most irritating bank robbery note I have ever heard of! *Not international; safes behind pictures*! What do they take us for?"

"Maybe they worry about extradition."

"I hate this case." Parker gave the note back to Lansdowne.

Lansdowne read the note again. He had to admit it was a pretty clever bit of confusion. He put it down on the table and thought some more. Finally, he said, "Do you think tellers really squirrel away rare coins?"

◆ ◆ ◆

Salamander eyes. Yolanda had learned better than to call

159

them *newts*. The eyes CSI found at the 1800 Pilot Way scene had turned out to be salamander eyes. Yolanda had shown the report to Harmon mentioning "eyes of newt" and been given an icy stare and shown the door. She left him washing down antacid with milk, and wishing she had never used the phrase. Still, newt or salamander, what the hell were they doing at the crime scene?

Twelve victims found so far, and neither the LAPD, nor the L.A. Sheriff's Office, could claim a half inch of progress on the Vampire Killer case. The prevailing theory of the police held that the Vampire Killer (actually *Killers*, but not in front of the press) consisted of at least two and not more than four individuals. They derived sadistic pleasure in torturing and killing women, and occasionally old Korean men. They extracted the blood of the victim as a souvenir and then replaced it with embalming fluid so as to preserve the body. They then did unspeakable sexual acts with the body, either individually or as a group, and kept the defiled bodies somewhere indefinitely.

The F.B.I. Behavioral Sciences Division (The B.S. Division) added further information on the psychology of the killers. They were loners, except when not working alone. They hated and feared women, and apparently Korean men as well. They began expressing their pathology very young by tormenting and killing animals and then progressed to humans—though, evidently, they still liked to kill the occasional pig or newt (sorry, *salamander*). Their neighbors did not suspect them of any foul dealing, but when the perps were captured, those same neighbors would say such things as "He (they) always kept apart." They might be interested in police procedures and try to ingratiate themselves into the investigation. They might try and return to the scene of the crime. They might be related. They would not stop killing until caught.

One thing everyone agreed on: more bodies would turn up. The police suppressed the actual number of slayings from the press to "avoid panic." Yolanda remained unsure what sort of panic might ensue. Riots? Vigilante squads? Villagers with torches and pitchforks? The LAPD handed out fliers describing the danger of blood sucking sex fiends to prostitutes ... and old Korean men.

The Vampire Killer task force divided its operations into several sub-units. One unit checked the background and movements of the victims. Another patrolled areas frequented by prostitutes (and retirement centers in Korean communities). Another set up sting operations where prostitutes had recently gone missing. Another unit searched through files of past sex offenders. Another contacted cult awareness groups. Another attended a seminar at the F.B.I. Behavioral Sciences School at Quantico, Virginia. Yolanda floated between these units doing odd jobs for each. She also pursued her own investigation: searching for a connection between the killings and interest in the occult.

No one else on the task force thought such connections important. The LAPD had no Occult Crime Division for a reason. Local "cults" focused on asset acquisition, not ritual murder. And violent sex killers rarely cared about the metaphysics of their hobby. Even Yolanda had to admit she clutched at straws. Still, they were her straws, and no one minded her clutching at them so long as she got her other work done. So in her spare time she launched her own investigation into the vampire aspect of the Vampire Killer.

Thus far she had found no source for newt eyes in Southern California. One could only get salamanders by catching them oneself. Pigs you could easily buy, but no one kept records on their purchase, at least not when purchased one at a time. When asked about buying bats, the animal suppliers she spoke to suggested she try sneaking into a cave at night with a net and some very thick gloves. One fellow suggested she go to New Mexico. He thought people there ate bats as food and kept them as pets.

Yolanda also interviewed supposed experts on occult practices. Since colleges did not hand out degrees in witchcraft, the status of occult expert remained a bit nebulous. Those "experts" she had talked to fell into two classes: criminologists who studied heavy metal fans lapsing into Satanism, and Gothic posers who promoted the black clothes/white face look. Neither group offered any suggestions as to how newts and pigs might relate to any known occult practice.

She had picked up a few things from occult enthusiasts. For one, vampires were all the rage, and no one outside the Voodoo community had much interest in zombies. (Yolanda had yet to identify the book from which the zombie pages found at 1800 Pilot had come.) Nor did occult and horror lovers read much H.P. Lovecraft. They read Anne Rice; long books, sexy vampires, very Gothic. Zombies had no sex appeal whatsoever. H.P. Lovecraft remained very old school. Yolanda had even tried to get in touch with Dr. Dantelani of Las Vegas University. As Nick had said, the doctor does not do phones.

Yolanda thought about Nick. No one at the department still believed he had anything to do with the killings. CSI had looked over his house and found nothing but cheap furniture and dubious art. Nick's feet did not match the size of any of the boot prints found at 1800 Pilot. Now that the police knew that the Vampire Killer was a collective, recently working out of a warehouse in North L.A., Nick looked less likely—in spite of lacking any alibi for the killings. Mostly though, the list of suspects had grown very large, and Nick Sabernail did not look any better than any of the others. For her part, Yolanda could not see Nick as a sex killer. On the other hand, she had lost none of her earlier reasons for suspecting him. And the devil could take a pleasing shape.

Yolanda tried a different approach. Books. The killers liked occult reading. So Yolanda decided to do a search of the electronic records of the Los Angeles Unified Library System. She searched for records of those who had borrowed a large number of books on the occult and related subjects.

"Occult subjects? What are those?" the librarian asked her.

"Books about vampires, zombies, necromancy, bringing the

dead to life, stuff like that," Yolanda said.

"I can't type in *stuff like that*, I need a complete list of words. We can search by subject, keyword, or titles—fiction or non-fiction or both. But I have to have the actual words or titles for the search."

Yolanda gave him every word connected to the occult she could think of: Death, demons, Dracula, witchcraft, warlocks, ouji boards, ghosts, ghouls, graves, Satan, séance, salamanders, and thirty more besides.

"How far back do I look?"

Yolanda figured four years worth of borrowing records would give her a nice start. The first result gave her over forty-two thousand names. She then limited the search to those that had checked out five or more such books. Eighteen thousand names. Only after limiting the search to those checking out over a hundred books on the subjects did she get a manageable list. One hundred and four names. She stared at the list. Last names, first initials. One name jumped out at her. *Sabernail, N.* In the last seven months he had checked out 117 books concerned with death and the occult. Yolanda kept the list.

The next day Yolanda had a breakthrough. One of the Gothic creepies gave her the name of L.A.'s major supplier of authentic occult and witchcraft paraphernalia. Gene O'Tenisey, aka Grandmaster Ghoul, traded in only *real* items of witchcraft and occult magic practices. Yolanda used a lunch hour to visit his shop on French and Sepulveda.

Outside, the small shop had blackened windows covered in posters, most advertising events long since transpired. Inside, Yolanda walked through a poorly lit series of display cases featuring dioramas from horror movies. Hardly what one would expect in a purveyor of the authentic. Horror movie posters covered the walls. Yolanda called out, "O'Tenisey?"

An older man appeared from behind a curtain concealing a small backroom. "Yes," said the man, "what can I do for you?" He looked quite normal and pleasant—very much the customer satisfaction devotee.

"I wanted to ask you some questions," Yolanda said.

"Chester Chavez, 1944, *El Vampiro*; I can have it for you in two weeks," the man said.

"Sorry?" said Yolanda.

"Just a guess. A game I play," the man said, "a Mexican version of the classic tale. Chavez played Senior Aztecula, really El Vampiro. The posters are rare, but I can get you one. The movie flopped I'm afraid. Quite good, considering the budget, in my opinion. You can see it on one of the Spanish language channels." The man chucked to himself, "But then, I suppose that *is* where you saw it. They don't make dioramas for it, but I can custom make you one myself, if you like. I have to charge quite a bit for that, being custom made and all. On the other hand, I can offer a discount since I haven't done one for that film yet. I love a new challenge. I bet I can do a real good Chester Chavez."

"Are you Gene O'Tenisey?" Yolanda asked.

"Yes," the man said. "Sorry, I just thought … You see, most of the attractive young Spanish girls I get in here have just seen Chavez on a late movie. Handsome fellow. Sorry if I guessed wrong."

Yolanda guessed very few "Spanish girls" ever came in. "I may have been given false information. I'm looking for someone sometimes called *Grandmaster Ghoul*. Someone told me a Gene O'Tenisey went by that name."

At the mention of the Grandmaster, the smile left O'Tenisey's face. In its place a somber expression gazed out at Yolanda. The old man's posture straightened as if someone had called the troops to attention. He raised a single imperious hand to Yolanda and said, "Wait here." He departed through the curtain to the back room. Yolanda heard rustling and chairs scraping along the floor. A few moments passed. Then the curtains opened. The old man wore a swami hat and a fake beard glued to his face. A dark robe covered his clothes. He topped the unlikely outfit off with a cape. The overall impression made Yolanda smile, almost laugh, but the series expression on O'Tenisey's face suggested he meant no joke here.

With great dignity he said, "You may enter the presence of the Grandmaster Ghoul, if you be worthy." He made a sweeping gesture with his left arm indicating Yolanda should enter the backroom. Suppressing a laugh, she did so.

The backroom had two parts. Most of it served as a storage area, but the part O'Tenisey pointed her to looked like a small break room. It had a table and three chairs. A black cloth covered a small TV on a chest. O'Tenisey had lit a candle on top of the cloth and put another on the table. A dark cloth covered a lit lamp on a small chest. Another covered lamp threw dim light from a small desk. O'Tenisey entered and motioned for Yolanda to sit at the chair with her back to the stockroom. He sat opposite her, having to twist rather awkwardly to sit down in the chair without getting his cape caught on the edge of the desk. He looked at her across the tiny table with a grave expression.

"I am the Grandmaster Ghoul," he said. "Heir to secrets old and dark. I have lived many years, longer than you could guess. I am of the Ancient Ones. I know you are worthy of this interview. Only those so worthy could discern my secret identity. Beware with whom you share this secret. I am part of an Ancient Cable of All-Knowers. A curse of *death* rains down upon those who treat lightly with us." When he said "death" he lunged forward at Yolanda flinging his fingers out at her like a cheap magician summoning a rabbit. "This is a day of appointment for you. Who knows what sorts of heart's desires you will find satisfied in me."

Yolanda could not suppress her chuckle.

"Do not laugh sister-initiate to the high secrets!" the Grandmaster said. "The mystic ways can inspire desires the uninitiated can never feel. Do you think the Grandmasters who built the pyramids did not inspire the lusty heart throbbing in the women of Egypt? Ancient is our order and far do our powers extend. Atlantis knew our names. In covens of old England we held our sway."

Suddenly, Yolanda could hear something from the front of the shop, "Hello?" a voice called out. "Hello?"

The Grandmaster seemed a bit kicked off his stride. "Covens we were known at—they knew us there and feared our—"

"Hello? I wanted to pick up a poster."

By now the Grandmaster had lost his place. "A moment adept of the dark way," he said. He turned his back and took off the turban. With the beard still in place he walked out to deal with the customer. Yolanda could hear him trying to finish his business politely, but quickly. And why not, she thought, he had half a spell cast in the backroom.

Yolanda rose to look around the stockroom. She walked back among the stored boxes. Some smelled of incense, most had handwritten words indicating their contents. The boxes contained roots, dried cat-guts, holy water, hangman's ropes, human skulls, cat skulls, dog skulls, wolf skulls, wolf teeth, chicken feet, voodoo rice, and cursed crosses. What those last were Yolanda could not guess. In the very back of the room, Yolanda noticed a small freezer. Stepping over boxes and pushing one out of the way she opened it. Inside she saw mason jars. The contents of most she could not discern, but at least one held a familiar item: salamander eyes. She heard the old man come back.

"What!?!" he exclaimed. "My child, return here."

Yolanda made her way back to the table.

"My child, I know you are curious about the dark arts, but you must not violate the sanctum of knowledge!" He had the turban on again. The Grandmaster raised his hands in righteous indignation and continued his harangue, "A patient acolyte may receive the greatest gifts of terror and might, but sneaking into the sacred places will bring only the curse of *death*!" Again his hands flung forward. He reared back for further curse throwing when Yolanda, who had frankly had enough of the cabaret, pulled open her coat, revealing her service revolver and badge. "Shut up and sit down, swami," she said.

The Grandmasters eyes fixed on the badge. The revelation that his new adept could bust him for illegal possession of unsanitary chicken parts so deflated him that he nearly collapsed into the chair. "Officer, I didn't know they changed those zoning laws. A fellow told me they were okay. I believed him. I believe folks, what they say."

Yolanda stopped his babble: "You sell eye of newt?"

O'Tenisey did not chuckle or roll his eyes as Harmon had done. He just meekly nodded that he did, and wondered silently what spells the police department meant to cast with them.

"Do you keep records of your clients? I mean those for occult items, not dioramas and posters," she said.

"You can't be in the specialty item business without keeping records. Your return customers are your life's blood. You can find stuff for them years after you last see them. They are always grateful for that."

"I'd like to see those records, if you don't mind."

O'Tenisey did not mind. He happily obliged. The records in question consisted of 3x5 cards in several cases, alphabetized by last name. Yolanda found the one she wanted.

"Do you remember this man?" she asked holding up a card.

O'Tenisey looked at the card. "Nick Sabernail? I don't place him off hand."

"Young fellow," Yolanda said, "mid thirties, nicely proportioned. A fast talker."

O'Tenisey thought for a moment. "Is that the fellow that works for the museum?"

"Right. When did you see him last?"

"I got a call from him a week or few back, he wanted a certain book on necromancy—seemed he had misplaced one."

"When did you meet him first?"

"Months before that. He wanted all kinds of things. For an exhibit he said."

"On death?" Yolanda asked.

"No, on witchcraft, he said. Asked about all sorts of occult stuff."

"Did he ask about bats?"

"No, not bats."

"How about those eyes of newts?"

"Yes! He liked those, said they had great *camp value*, whatever that is. Don't know why a man would want to take newt eyes camping."

"Did he buy any?"

"No."

"What did he buy?"

"Nothing. I never sold him anything, and except for the call about his missing book, I never heard from him but that once."

Yolanda thought a moment, "Are those real eyes of newts?"

"Well, they are salamander eyes. Some are from the right species—but you know, some, maybe not."

Not much, thought Yolanda. But another piece had fallen into place.

Yolanda made a third trip to the Marian Wright Museum. Calling ahead, she discovered that Mr. Sabernail had taken an "administrative leave" until certain "questions" could be resolved. At the museum, Yolanda looked the exhibit over more carefully. Nothing in it suggested any special obsession with the occult. But she did notice a collection of electronic torture devices in a display case next to the electric chair exhibit. Several of the early victims had burn marks, probably from a cattle prod or some other electrical device.

Yolanda marveled at the exhibits at the Marian Wright. A hundred years ago the police would have arrested anyone charging admissions to see stuff like this under the banner of a *museum*. P.T. Barnum would have baulked at the scheme. But now you could look at *Spoons Through the Ages*, starting with the 1950's, and call it a museum exhibit. On the other hand, she liked the dolls.

Mrs. Cartwright let her into Sabernail's office, still a mess. She found no newt eyes. She examined his books. The Oxford History of World Cinema lay open on his desk along with a book on Houdini and a manufacture's specification book for handcuffs and other restraints. She saw a number of catalogs and glossy advertisements for touring exhibits. The top shelf of his small bookcase contained fourteen books concerning death. Some dealt with the biology of dying, others with customs of mourning the dead, and others with speculations on the after-life. Sabernail had taken extensive notes in several of them.

The second shelf of the bookcase interested Yolanda even more: five books on the occult. Sabernail had taken no notes in these. Yolanda could make no sense out of the third shelf: a book on gambling in Las Vegas, a collection of books on car-resale values, a mammoth catalog of audio equipment, two law books, and the remains of a Chinese dinner now capable of defending itself. The last shelf contained no books, just papers, most of them concerning the business of exhibit curation. Yolanda left the office and had Mrs. Cartwright take her to the basement of the museum.

Yolanda wanted to look for bodies and cattle prods, and had imagined the basement would be mostly empty, unless it contained a large collection of frozen corpses. In fact, the Marian Wright basement nearly burst with leftovers from the museum's exhibits. You could feed an army of debutants with the cutlery stored there. Mrs. Wright's antique furniture sat in a corner along with a collection of lamps. Mrs. Wright had collected clothes as well as spoons; one section of the space contained nothing but old postal-worker uniforms. Above these, Yolanda could see firemen's hats going back to the nineteen hundreds. Past those, she saw the makings of a Raincoats Through the Ages exhibit. Further in, lay boxes filled with tiaras. Moving these, Yolanda found what had to be the world's largest collection of bathroom slippers.

Escaping the clothes collection, Yolanda found that Mrs. Wright had also fancied chairs. Recliners, office chairs, dining-room chairs; chairs of wood, chairs of steel, chairs no human being could sit in and like it. The basement held drafting chairs and swivel chairs. It had one chair made entirely of glass. Many of these chairs must have dated back over seventy years and more. They lay in a great mountain of potential seatedness, against a wall. Except the glass chair, which sat a bit apart from the others, seemingly cringing at the nearness of the steel and wood monstrosity next to it. Wooden legs and cushioned arms pronged from the chair pile as if reaching out for a new victim to incorporate into its carefully balanced essence. For a moment, in the dim light of the basement, Yolanda imagined it moved. No wonder the glass chair worried.

Yolanda found a coffin—empty. But she found no cattle prods and no bodies. She went home.

◆ ◆ ◆

Yolanda sat at home, legal pad in her lap, television on. Upon the pad she had written, at the very top: Sabernail as Suspect. The television tuned in to Channel Six *Action Power News*, a local broadcast. She wore sweats and sat with her legs folded beneath her. She sank slowly into the thick cushions of her oversized chair. She wrote in black ink and kept a pen with blue ink on the table beside her.

Channel Six boasted more action, with greater power, than any other local broadcast. It competed against *Action News*, *Eyewitness News* and *The Station of the People*, among others. Yolanda had always thought the latter title made the station sound a bit like the Communist Party Broadcast. In fact, little distinguished one station from the next. The *Action Power News Team* consisted of the same chatty male and female anchors, and talking-head-in-front-of-the-burning-blaze remote reporters, as all the others. On Channel Six, Duke Dawson had the male lead at the five o'clock spot, backed up by Jenny Grice, ten years his junior and a scientific experiment in pluckiness. As Yolanda thought on Vampire Killers, they reported on L.A.'s breaking news:

Duke Dawson: "Police found this little fellow, only three years old, hanging by his feet from the third floor of the Tanson Building in the Valley ..."

Yolanda looked up to see the image of a fireman retrieving a monkey from a building ledge.

Jenny Grice: "Now how do you think he got there?"
Duke Dawson: "Just doing a little monkey business."
Jenny Grice: "Ouch."
Duke Dawson: "Stay right there folks, we've got a story on a little dog that may just be able to find your keys for you."
Jenny Grice: "That would be nice."
Duke Dawson: "I know I could use that."

Yolanda wrote the word *killer* under her title on the left side of the paper and the word *innocent* on the right. She chewed on the pen for a moment and thought. Under *killer* she wrote: *interest in death and the occult,* and across from that, under *innocent* she put *research for exhibit.*

Duke Dawson: "Police in Westwood uncovered the bodies of four people slain with a shotgun. Police have no clues in the case as yet. The victims appear to belong to the same family."
Jenny Grice: "The coroner's office released its findings on the Barbecue Butcher slayings. The victims, allegedly killed by Jose Tendez of West Covina, died of asphyxiation, according to pathologists. Police allege that Tendez killed them by locking them into a brick barbeque shack and filling the room with mesquite-flavored smoke."
Duke Dawson: "That'll ruin your appetite."
Jenny Grice: "I'd say."
Duke Dawson: "In other news, twenty undocumented immigrants were found dead in the back of a truck cargo

container in Fountain Valley. Police say they died when they fell asleep while cooking with a propane stove in the closed space."

Jenny Grice: "You just don't realize how dangerous propane can be."

Duke Dawson: "No, you don't."

Jenny Grice: "Stay tuned for more on the Vampire Killer story, and a report on why you may not be safe even after you go to the great here-after."

Duke Dawson: "And after that you'll hear about a little critter who might be making crime-fighting just a little easier —and you'll never guess how."

Jenny Grice: "All that, plus Professor Bob with your Accu-Tota weather forecast—Complete and Guaranteed—and Carl Catum with the Sports."

Duke Dawson: "See how those Angels are doing."

Jenny Grice: "Right."

Below *interest in death and occult,* Yolanda wrote: *why books on the occult if exhibit on death?* She had checked Nick's exhibit carefully and read all the text to each exhibit. Assuming that a discussion on differing cultural expectations on the nature of the after-life did not count as *the occult* (and she had not listed *after-life* on her library word search), then the only piece in the death exhibit related to the occult was the stolen *Compendium of Necromantic Science.* When she first met Nick, that is to say, Mr. Sabernail, he had told her he had gotten it because it "fit the theme." But really it didn't. And he displayed it in a corner separate from the rest of the pieces precisely because it didn't fit anywhere naturally.

"Now back to our Action-Power Team Coverage with Duke Dawson and Jenny Grice, Carl Catum on Sports, Professor Bob with Accu-Tota weather—Complete and Guaranteed—and our man of *Action-Power*: consumer advocate Roy Roundup.

Duke Dawson: "Have you ever wondered why you diet and

diet and just can't take those pounds off?"

Jenny Grice: "I know I have."

Duke Dawson: "Well our reporter, Venus Whimsey, may have the answer for you."

Most of the items in the exhibit included copious amounts of text printed above and to the side, explaining to the poor benighted museum goer just why the item had been placed on display and what edifying lesson might be gleaned from it. But the text for the *Compendium* said only: "Not every belief in bodily resurrection or the after-life rested upon religious doctrines. This reference work from the Middle Ages advocates raising the dead to serve the living without the assurance that the newly gained life will afford joy to the possessor." Nothing more. Yet it did show that Mr. Sabernail had some knowledge of the book's contents after all.

Duke Dawson: "New information today on the Vampire Killer case. For that we turn to Tonya Laratta at City Hall. Hello Tonya!"

Tonya Laratta at City Hall: "Hello Duke. Today the Mayor denied that the investigation into the slayings of local prostitutes has stalled. He congratulated the police on their efforts and on their restraint in dealing with the press ..."

On the left side of the pad Yolanda wrote: *no alibis for any time a victim is known to have been killed (4 cases).* The time spans for these were quite long. Sometimes up to twelve hours. Who doesn't have an alibi for a twelve-hour time span? And to lack one for four different instances. Even winos generally do better than that. Mr. Sabernail says that in every case for which he needed an alibi, for all the times in question, he was gambling in Vegas. He gives no specifics. He only says that he moved from one casino to another. He doesn't keep track of time. "Vegas discourages close attention to passing time, or passing money," he says. On one occasion, however, he does give specifics. For the night of the robbery he has a very definite idea of where in Vegas he was.

Jenny Grice: "Well, it has been unseasonably hot this week."

Professor Bob with Accu-Tota Weather: "Yes it has. Unseasonably hot. Though statistically we are right at average for this time of year."

Duke Dawson: "But it certainly doesn't feel that way!"

Professor Bob: "Well, no it doesn't, but let's get the total and complete picture from our Accu-Tota Weather—Complete and Guaranteed—chart.

The Lucky Eleven Casino. No one remembers him being there. Perhaps he has someone waiting in the wings in case the going gets tough. In any case, he generally suffers from an unusual absence of alibi.

Yolanda looked up and noticed Professor Bob delivering his nightly meteorological lesson. Yolanda wondered why she had to study for a Ph.D. in forecasting science every day, when all she wanted to know was how cold it would be tonight and whether it would rain tomorrow.

Jenny Grice: "Could this be global warming, Professor Bob?"

Professor Bob: "Well today's weather is right at average; but when we have warmer days, those could be the result of global warming."

Duke Dawson: "Well, I know I don't want to have those days!"

Jenny Grice: "Me neither!"

Professor Bob: "They would be warm."

On the left side of the pad Yolanda wrote: *missing file.* No one at the department's Office of Records could find a police file for Nick Sabernail. The F.B.I. had drawn a blank on his fingerprints. Plenty of prints had been found at 1800 Pilot Avenue, but none matched Mr. Sabernail's.

Duke Dawson: "Stay tuned here to find out why some folks just aren't resting in peace anymore."

Jenny Grice: "And then see why this little pup is making some folks rethink e.s.p."

Duke Dawson: "But first, don't miss sports with Carl Catum."

Jenny Grice: "And consumer action with *Action Power's* very own Roy Roundup."

On the right side of the paper Yolanda wrote: *no match on physical evidence at 1800 Pilot.* Not only did they not find Sabernail fingerprints, but no shoe matches, no sightings of Sabernail by neighbors, and no sightings of his car. This might not mean much since few in the neighborhood had cooperated with the investigation. Yolanda had shown Mr. Sabernail's picture to a number of people there the day she visited the crime scene, and no one showed the slightest response.

On the right side of the paper she wrote: *charming.* She scratched it out. Why had she written that? In the first place, Nick Sabernail was less *charming* than disarmingly quick-witted. He seemed roguish, rather than nice, and Yolanda only liked very straight-laced types. Her sister could keep the fast-talkers.

Duke Dawson: "So, those Angels, doing well."

Carl Catum: "Doing well. Yes. Lost today and yesterday. Five game streak now."

Duke Dawson: "But they'll turn it around."

In the second place, some serial murderers could charm the eyes off a snake. Under the scratched out word Yolanda wrote: *a Ross.* This seemed unfair. Nick had been nothing but charming to her, whereas Ross encouraged nymphet weight loss and fooled around on a woman practically living with him. Twice Antonia had landed at Yolanda's door, tear-streaked and fuming at Ross's infidelities; once as Antonia Hammett and once as Tricia Tobias. Yolanda could not stand the idea of Ross changing her sister's name every three months.

Jenny Grice: "Four people died today when a light plane crashed into the ocean off Balboa Pier. Fishermen leaped into the water to lend aid, but could only recover the shoes and watches of the victims before the plane sank. The Coast Guard later raised the plane. Police wish to question those fishing on the pier. No cause for the crash has yet been determined."

The last time she showed up, Antonia had cried herself to sleep after talking till dawn. Two days later she called from Ross's house asking about a lost earring.

Duke Dawson: "A seven year old girl died today in what Police in Compton call a drive-by shooting."

Yolanda found the missing earring after a determined search lasting five hours. It had fallen into the food-disposal, probably while Antonia barfed up the contents of her stomach. Antonia had arrived quite drunk that night. Yolanda fished it out, cleaned it up, cut it into small pieces with the next-door neighbor's wire cutters, and flushed it to the sea from her guest bathroom toilet. She called Antonia at Ross's and left the message that either of them could come over any time to look for it.

Jenny Grice: "If you think that three dollars is not enough money to get burned over, stick around for *Action Power's* very own Roy Roundup's latest quest for justice."
Duke Dawson: "I love those reports."
Jenny Grice: "You know it."
Duke Dawson: "And coming up: you might think your loved ones will stay in place when you bury them; but it ain't necessarily so. Stick around and find out why."
Jenny Grice: "And don't miss our report on this cute little fellow. He might be smarter than you think."
Duke Dawson: "I think so."
Jenny Grice: "That's coming up on *Action Power News*."

It would be just like her sister to make a lateral move from Ross Flintrock (obviously not his real name) to Nick Sabernail. Except Sabernail was the Vampire Killer. Maybe. On the left side of the paper Yolanda wrote: *Sabernail? His real name?*

"Watch Action Power News; L.A.'s number one news at 5:00 and 5:30. With Jenny Grice and Duke Dawson; John Urka with movies, and Venus Whimsey covering Hollywood."

Yolanda shuttered slightly at the thought of her sister with Nick Sabernail. On the other hand, what could he talk about with her? Not art. Sis could not stand any art that did not flicker fast enough to give the illusion of motion. What would Antonia make of Nick's wit? Right past her, no doubt about it. Furthermore, one look at the sorry un-hipness of his apartment, and Antonia would search for a rear exit. Not a bad idea, come to think of it, considering she could be cattle-prodded to death and turned into a blender drink.

Roy Roundup: "I'm Roy Roundup and I fight for *you*! I fight for justice for *you*! Mrs. Gladis Curtis of Encino wrote to tell me that her tortillas from the Happy Hacienda Burrito Buggy had burn spots on them. The Burrito Buggy man said that was normal in fresh cooked tortillas—but I fight for *you*! That means *you*, Mrs. Curtis! We got your three dollars back—and an apology from the Burrito Buggy man. 'Cause I fight for *you*!"

Yolanda looked down at the pad to see how the score came out. She noticed that she had written her sister's name twice on the left side and had re-written *charm* on the right. For some reason she had written her father's name as well. On the left side. Why there, she wondered? She always felt close to her father when doing this. He had done it in his time. He had shown her once. She guessed that he had always been doing this when he wrote on those yellow pads to the sound of the news. That was part of the reason she could not accept what the D.A. had claimed to find on hundreds of sheets of yellow paper.

Duke Dawson: "We turn now to a breaking story in West L.A. Dan Mi the Traffic Guy is in hot pursuit of a green Toyota fleeing police. Dan?"

Yolanda looked up and watched the over-head shot of a green car moving down the freeway with twenty police cars in pursuit. She supposed that now she would never find out what extraordinary tricks the psychic dog could perform.

Dan Mi the Traffic Guy: "Oh my gosh! He almost hit that car! This is very dangerous. Ooohhh my! He almost hit that officer!"

The green Toyota exited the freeway and drove down side streets. A handful of people, obviously following the chase on one of the five local stations covering it, had made some signs. One encouraged the driver to "Step On It!" Another, held up to the helicopters, read: "Squeeze Me!" Yolanda thought she recognized the neighborhood. After a moment it dawned on her that the Toyota would soon pass by Nick Sabernail's place. Which side of the sheet did that belong on?

Car chases in L.A. are not just for the movies anymore. At least once a week the local news manages to cover a felon's desperate pursuit by the law. The chases could last hours, cover many miles of ordinary freeways, and transpire in utter darkness; still the news carried the event as if the fate of the Republic hung on the outcome. College students formed *chase-tracker* clubs to rate the daring do and tactics of police and felons. Those chased understood their role in the popular circus of L.A. street life. They would wave at the cameras, call their friends on cell phones to advise them to tune in, cruise past the old neighborhood with their train of twenty police cars, and generally revel in their fleeting fame.

One car thief, who led the police on a three hour tour (total score: four smashed police cars, two spike strips avoided, two tires blown out, eight freeway changes, twenty-seven cars in pursuit, five encouraging signs from pedestrians, and thirty-seven stoplights run—this last a record) actually sued the producers of *World's Most Violent Police Videos* for using footage of the chase. He claimed a property right in the images. He had, after all, created the entertainment value they contained. The courts threw the case out but acknowledged the fellow's point. Car chases in L.A. are street theatre now.

So when Nick looked out his kitchen window and saw helicopters hovering slowly overhead, like buzzards following the progress of a wounded water buffalo, he knew what it meant. He clicked on the TV in his kitchen and saw the chase transpiring. Recognizing the street, he walked out onto his porch to watch the hounds chase the fox. He wanted to see if he knew the driver.

The Green Toyota passed by Nick's place. Its driver sat hunched over the steering wheel concentrating on this his grand moment. The police passed by in a line. Ahead of the driver, a police car blocked the street to keep other drivers out of the way. They opened a channel for the Toyota to move through. Nick returned to his kitchen and watched the coverage unfold. He turned down Guy Mi's play-by-play. Nick made up his mind. He picked up the phone and dialed. He heard a voice on the other end of the phone:

"Hello?"

"Sid? Nick. Got the tube on?"

"Uh? No. Just a sec."

"We got a player." Nick waited.

"I don't know Nick, I don't think he's got legs."

"I say he's shaken the booze off and will stay in the game. So we have a bet? Two hundred dollars?"

A pause while Sid thought, "For how long?"

"I say he has thirty more minutes at least."

"Not for two hundred. I'll need at least an hour for two

179

hundred. And no time on foot pursuit."

"Bet. Two hundred dollars says he's still rolling in an hour."

Nick hung up the phone. The no-foot-pursuit provision of the wager did not entirely please him. The Toyota drove down surface streets that afforded many opportunities for ditching. But since night remained hours away, Nick thought it unlikely the guy would try to leg it within the hour. Poor Sid, he didn't even think to check the pursuit location. He didn't know that Nick had seen the guy, sober and intense, just moments before. Poor dumb Sid.

Twenty minutes later the Toyota spun out and hit a light post. The police dragged the driver from the car, and Nick kissed another two hundred bucks goodbye.

Nick nursed his wound with a Scotch, which helped his attitude a bit but did precious little for his wallet—which was where the wound lay, after all. Nick sat at his Formica kitchen table—a table worthy of the Marion Wright collection he thought—and built a house of cards while he drank. He used Tarot cards. The house grew higher. Nick always built card houses when he drank. His rule: when he could not see well enough, or hold still enough, to put a card on without toppling the construction, he hung it up for the night. Nick's card-house building skills had grown greatly over the years. Yet they still always failed him early. The house fell down before he had completed the second story. Nick put the Scotch away. Nick had great discipline—with liquor.

"What do you want?" Nick asked. He must have asked himself since he sat alone. "What do you really want?" Nick drew a tarot card from those lying face down on the table. It pictured two people, a man and a woman, both naked and wrapped in an embrace. "Not bad," Nick said. "Anyone I know?" Nick picked another card. This one pictured an armored woman holding a balance in one hand and a sword in the other. Nick studied the card and thought long and hard. He weighed the pros and cons. This became painful after a bit, so he stopped that and decided to hell with weighing things.

Just do it. He had heard that somewhere—he'd forgotten where—but surely it encapsulated all the wisdom relevant to his circumstance. Just do it. "After all, what's to stop us?"

Nick got up and made another phone call. He needed an address. After the call he took a shower, got dressed in clean clothes and called a florist. His phone rang and he answered it. He had the address now. Nick grabbed his keys and headed for the back door. On his way out, he passed the kitchen table still strewn with tarot cards. He lifted one of the ones still lying face down. It pictured a skeleton with a sickle, riding a white horse over corpses rising from the ground. Nick tossed it on top of the other two. Nick was a superstitious man—all gamblers are—but like all gamblers he knew how to face a risk. If the prize were great enough. Nick left.

◆ ◆ ◆

Evening fell at Yolanda's home. She had turned down the volume on the TV, which now only cast blue haze about the room. She poked at Chinese takeout. Her legal pad lay on the kitchen counter, now covered with words, doodles, and scratch marks. She looked over her bare walls. She poked at her Fu Yong Chow Mein. The doorbell rang. She stood up and walked to the door. She opened it.

Cold fear gripped her for just a moment. The devil smiled at her. Her body felt limp—a sensation she was not used to and did not like. She felt trapped and immobilized. The devil opened his mouth to speak. On seeing his teeth, feeling returned to her limbs. She had to get protection! She slammed the door in the devil's face and turned the lock violently. She careened to the side table in which she kept her gun. What was that he had in his hands? A knife? A cattle prod? Yolanda checked to see that the gun was loaded and ran back to the door. Would he still be there? Was it a gun she saw? For a moment Yolanda thought to call for backup. That would be the smart thing to do. Later that night, Yolanda could not think why she had not done that. Her dad would not have been proud of her.

But Yolanda did not call for backup. She braced herself and put a hand on the doorknob. He had probably run, she thought, no victims here. Yolanda turned the lock with her thumb, slowly, so as not to alert the man on the other side. Though he had no doubt fled by now. Yolanda whipped the door open and leveled her gun at the space in the classic police firing position.

She saw the man. His hands empty now. He leaned heavily on the doorframe with his arms crossed. He looked at Yolanda with an expression wandering somewhere in the vicinity of extreme irritation.

"Let me see your hands!" Yolanda yelled at him.

"No. Shoot me."

Yolanda looked him over. "Your hands! What did you have in your hands?"

"Flowers," Nick said, "but don't worry, they're not for you. If I wanted to get something for you, I'd buy ammunition, or a truncheon."

Yolanda glanced down at Nick's feet. Sure enough, a bouquet of flowers rested on the other side of the doorframe.

"If it wouldn't be too much trouble," Nick continued, "you could put them in some water until I leave—so they'll be fresh for my date."

"You're leaving now," Yolanda said.

"Feet up and toe tagged?" Nick said nodding at the gun.

Yolanda held the gun on him. Nick sighed and showed not the slightest concern. "I have to tell you," he said, "being held at gunpoint by the police loses some of its intimidation factor when it happens to you all the time. Though it is an interesting way to greet the world. Do you shoot many visitors? I bet the Mormons love knocking on your door. Being greeted at the door with a gun up your snout does make a man feel closer to God."

Yolanda began to feel just the slightest bit silly. "What do you want?"

Nick lifted himself off the door jam and picked up the flowers. He took a step into the doorway as Yolanda jumped back still holding him at gunpoint.

"I want these put into water, for a start," Nick said, "I paid $57.95 for them, and I'll be damned if I won't give them to someone, so I want them fresh."

"You are in my home. I could shoot you right now and no one would blame me," Yolanda said.

Nick proceeded into the room undeterred. "On the way over I worried you might have a boyfriend here tonight—seeing as how our first date turned out to be something of a sham. But I suppose you would have shot him already. Or did you cuff him in the closet to beat up later?" Nick saw the kitchen and began walking toward it.

Yolanda spoke in a firm voice, softer now, but still firm, "I am ordering you to leave these premises."

Nick walked into the kitchen, ignoring both the gun and the firm tone. "I hear you, but you're not wearing a riot helmet, and lately I just can't find people frightening if they don't wear helmets, and body armor, and burst my door down, and hold shotguns on me." Nick opened the cupboards and looked through them. "I realize that this is *your* house and not mine, and so it must be forbidden to trespass here." Nick looked through more cupboards. "Any old SWAT team can rumble though my house and so what? I'll be busy cooling my heels at county lock-up anyway, so how could I mind? But God forbid the sacred Vasquez Estate be violated. Shoot the arrogant fucker I say. Ah ha!" Nick pulled a long, thin vase out of the back of the pantry. "Not quite big enough, but I'll put the extra in my button hole." Nick put water in the vase and began arranging the flowers.

Yolanda stood there a moment more with a service .38 trained on his temple. It then occurred to her that she was not going to shoot him. She lowered the gun. Nick looked through her kitchen drawers. Yolanda walked back to the door and closed it, locking it. Nick found a pair of scissors and trimmed the flowers, cutting one very short and putting it into a buttonhole on his coat. Yolanda sat on the stool at the counter across from where Nick trimmed the flowers.

"You're crazy," she said, "you know how easily you could get shot here?"

"Not a chance," Nick said, "look at this place, it's spotless. No woman who keeps her carpet this clean is going to mess it up with blood stains.

"There are some large plastic trash bags under the sink, mind stepping into one?" Yolanda said.

Nick laughed lightly and found the trashcan. He threw the clippings away and pushed the flowers toward Yolanda. "Here," he said, "you can have these after all. Consider it a reward for not spewing my guts all over the living room floor."

"Such a small favor to reap so great a reward," Yolanda said.

Nick reached into the pantry behind him and pulled out a bottle of wine he had seen there during his vase search. "Let's celebrate our temporary abatement of hostilities." He pulled two glasses out and poured. He handed one to Yolanda. She took it, but did not drink. Nick looked around the apartment. "Just move in?"

"No," Yolanda said. She drank a sip of wine.

"You should hang the pictures on the wall," Nick said. "I work in a museum, I know things like that. On the wall you can see them better."

"As I heard it, you *used* to work in a museum," Yolanda said.

"Yes, I had just about talked my way out of suspension when I landed in jail. That put a bit of a chill on my cause."

Yolanda took another sip.

"What is your connection to the Vampire Killings?" she asked.

Nick drank. "Why, don't you know? I *am* the Vampire Killer. So my lawyer says. Whatever the truth, when asked, I am to say I am the Vampire Killer. We are going to make a fortune on my story. Inconveniently, I'll have to spend my share before the execution date."

"It's no joke, a lot of women have died."

Nick got cross again, "Okay, it's no joke. At first I thought it was, but then the LAPD busted my door down and hauled me off to jail, so after that I realized that it was no joke. I may have a bit of a laugh now and then over it, but, really, not a joke. And if I ever meet the real Vampire Killer, I promise to kick the shit out of him. No joke. Do you have cards?" Nick poured himself another drink and looked through the drawers.

"Did you steal the Compendium? Off the record?" Yolanda said, knowing there was no such thing as off the record.

Nick continued his search. "Oh yes, I stole it. I read a chapter every night before bed. It's all in Latin, which I can't read, so I refer to a translation guide with every word. Takes up most of my time, really."

"What are you looking for?" Yolanda asked.

"Cards, I can't drink without cards."

Yolanda got off the stool and went to the hall table from which she had pulled her gun. She put the gun back there (making sure he did not see where it went) and pulled out a deck of cards. She returned to the counter. "Here."

Nick looked up and smiled at the sight of the cards. "You any good at making card houses?"

They sat for two hours at the table drinking wine and placing cards. Yolanda tried to get information out of Nick, but he refused to talk about anything that night but wine, betting strategies, and card-house building techniques. After two hours the house of cards fell, and Nick stopped drinking. At the door, Yolanda told him she would have to report this contact to her superiors. Nick asked her if she would like to go to Vegas with him.

A purely professional trip, of course.

BRINGING BACK
THE DEAD

Drakan paced back and forth before the grave of Roger Windon at the Final Gardens Cemetery. Twilight had long ago fallen into darkest night. He wore a long gray cape, a military officer's cap, shinny black boots, and a monocle. He had imagined, upon first affecting monocle wearing, that keeping it in place would prove difficult. In the event, his pinched face kept the little circle of glass tightly snug to his eye socket. So tightly, in fact, it was absolutely painful. But Drakan felt his Baron von Finkelstein persona needed the trimmings, so he wore the monocle. He could not have been more shocked at how difficult it proved to find a monocle in L.A. So large a city and so few people in need of single lens eyewear. He finally acquired one at an antiquities shop—imagine! The proprietor assured him that a German Wehrmacht officer had actually used it during the war. Drakan bought the cape, hat, and boots as further accessories. He tried to imagine what that man had felt like, standing on the Russian front so long ago. Whatever the man *felt*, Drakan knew he had *seen* very little, since the monocle obscured all vision in one eye and caused tears of pain to fill the other. (The German eyepiece held its eye so far open no moisture could pool there.) Drakan obviously needed a different prescription.

Truth to tell, Drakan had wearied of the von Finkelstein identity. Vinnie constantly quizzed him on the history of Central Europe (frankly, never a major Drakanian interest), and so Drakan forever had to devise new improvements on the family history. Just that very day he had spent four precious hours writing up the complete history of the von Finkelsteins so as to have a consistent account for any future biographers. What irked Drakan most was that he had spent so much time on the *Drakan* identity and now couldn't use it on the one person in his current circle of acquaintances in a position to understand it. But he could do nothing about that. Vinnie knew him as a Baron, and a Baron he must remain.

On other fronts as well, Drakan's projects delivered mostly tantalizing frustrations. Vinnie had demonstrated the utility of zombies at armed theft. He had brought out far more money than Drakan had expected. But somehow much of it had turned blue prior to arrival. Drakan never could make heads or tales out of Vinnie's frenzied story of exploding money bags. However it had happened, half the cash remained useless and Vinnie adamantly refused to rob another bank.

And then the problem of prostitutes. These Drakan knew served under the title of *street walkers*, but lately they could barely be found on the streets. This after the supply of fat ones had almost dwindled to nothing. Just as the supply of fresh blood donors began to dry up though, a stroke of luck occurred. The cemeteries of Los Angeles began assigning guards to patrol the grounds at night. Drakan could not imagine why other people valued these bodies so, but he thanked his stars for the good luck. Now he could kidnap donors and dig up recipients at the same location. One could not find such convenience in most cities. Unfortunately, zombies proved inept at close rope work. Drakan had to tie and gag the unconscious guards himself. So Drakan had decided to dig up this Roger Windon grave. Drakan supposed Windon must have been a sailor and thus good with knots. Windon. Wind-on-the-sail. Stood to reason.

"Dig more on that side Jose," said Vinnie to a grave-digging zombie. Drakan let Vinnie supervise tonight instead of keeping watch. Three nights before, Drakan had reanimated a young thing called "Carl Halprain," now Carl the Zombie. Carl the Zombie could keep watch and shout an alarm. Quite a feat for a zombie, especially one so recently brought to the kingdom of undeath. The alarm consisted of either: "Aaagaagaaga!" for a police car, or "Eeeeekkaaa!" for a pedestrian. Drakan felt so proud of Carl the Zombie, he could just burst. So Carl kept watch, Vinnie directed the shoveling, and Drakan struck majestic poses.

"I hear coffin noise," Vinnie said. "We got a big one."

Of course we do, thought Drakan, do we ever manage a petite-sized coffin? Drakan's finger seemed to be a divining rod for over-sized iron-lined coffins.

"I'll go check the others," offered Vinnie. Drakan had four crews running tonight, plus ghouls back at the base preparing the brew. He planned to pull out at least eight and perhaps as many as fourteen bodies this evening. Later he would take a crew out to find prostitutes for extractions—hopefully large ones, but who knew anymore? All in all, Drakan had developed a highly efficient zombie-making operation.

But what to do with it? Drakan longed for fame, notoriety, scientific respectability, interviews, parties in his honor, invitations to lecture, cameos, society gatherings, and gossip column mentions. He wanted his name recorded among the greats of science: Ptolemy, Newton, Galileo, Nostradamus. He did not much care to spend the rest of his life transforming death into undeath in noble obscurity. Surely posterity would recognize his genius, a very pleasing thought, but Drakan wanted success in life as well as memory. Yet certain unfortunate aspects of the reanimation technique precluded revealing his discovery to the world. One could kill a few rats and monkeys in the name of science, but small minds had laid down rigid rules against human sacrifice.

A criminal empire seemed an unlikely option at the moment. Zombies needed a lot of direction. Vinnie would never rise above Sergeant, Drakan knew that now. In fact, Drakan had made up his mind about Vinnie: Hedgehog. Vinnie the Hedgehog he was, and Hedgehog he would remain. Not even Moose. On the other hand, Charley Sparrow, *there* was a zombie for you. Drakan could actually talk to him. He had learned, for instance, that Mr. Sparrow liked the movies—and had worked in Hollywood as some sort of repairman. Such tidbits endeared the giant ghoul to the ghoul master. Drakan knew a bit about Charley's family as well. He spoke often of someone named Edith and someone named Dorothy. "Edi ... Edith" he would say. And: "Dor..o..thy ... my ... my Dor..o..thy." He could even say sentences: "Sergeant V ... drives the ... van ... get the ... van." Virtually Shakespearian compared to the others.

Recently though, Drakan had found ways of adjusting the reanimation booster shots so as to produce improved communication skills in the undead. The results remained modest so far, but he had great hopes. The improvement in undead speaking abilities had given Drakan a brainstorm. Soon Vinnie would get the chance to set that storm in motion. And if Vinnie excelled? Well, perhaps he could hope to be raised to Lieutenant Vinnie the Horse after all.

Vinnie bustled among the opening graves; a foreman to the half-light of the undead. He cajoled, carped and threatened them to ever-greater feats of unearthing. Here at last he had found men, strong men, who would obey him without question. So long as the Baron told them to. Vinnie would point one to a grave the Baron had selected and order him to "dig." Another to a crypt to "lift." Sometimes, when the Baron wasn't looking, he would order a couple to chase each other in a small circle. The Baron would spout fury when he found them lumbering after each other in stupid obedience. Unable to talk worth spit, they couldn't squeal Vinnie out, and the Baron just chalked it up to stupid zombie antics. Vinnie just had to be careful not to let Mr. Sparrow see. Otherwise:

"Sergeant V ... ordered ... them ..."

This night they virtually cleared a section of the little cemetery. On arrival, Vinnie had nearly panicked to find two guards watching the place. They approached the hearse (the Baron had added a hearse to the organization's fleet of cars—made sense really) and asked Vinnie what he wanted. Vinnie told a clever lie.

"You see fellows," Vinnie told them, "my mother, she's in the back—dead and all, so don't worry. And the guy at the mortuary said 'Hey, take her to the cemetery—that little one—or I gotta charge you to keep her on ice' he said. So I just drop her here for the night and all." Vinnie thought that ought to hold them.

Then one asked, "How come you got all those shovels?"

Damn. Vinnie had forgotten he had twelve shovels sitting in the front seat with him. Still, his wit did not fail, "These? These shovels? Well, see, I figure I could pick Granny a good spot—sort of, stake it out. Might as well get a little digging in before the services tomorrow. I bought on the discount plan. I dig my own grave for her. You guys should look into that. Great discount for us working guys." Vinnie felt sure the appeal to working class solidarity would snow them. Vinnie had never worked an honest job in his life, but felt he must be working class nonetheless. After all, he stole at Wal-Mart.

One guard said, "I thought you said it was your mother?"

The other said, "How come you have so many shovels for just you."

Damn, these guys were smart. Vinnie launched on, "Yeah, well, she's my mother *and* my grandmother. She had me, see, and so I'm her son and she's my mom. Was my mom. And then she married my granddad—on my dad's side of course—this after dad died of course. So she's my grandma too. And I just call her 'Granny' so as not to upset my granddad. Whose a nice guy really. Just didn't like to marry outside the family." Vinnie thought this at least a plausible story and felt proud to have come up with it right off the top of his head.

"And all the shovels?"

The guard seemed to be laughing a bit when he asked this. Vinnie sighed. This shit gets harder all the time. "See," he said, "I … well, I break shovels easy. I don't look it, but I'm pretty strong when I'm digging. And these new shovels they make nowadays—you lean on them the wrong way and—POW —they give out right under you." Vinnie paused to see how he faired. Not well, by the look of their faces. He pressed on a new tack, "And I got my cousin and a nephew coming to help out later. They'll need shovels too."

"What relation would they be to dear old Granny back there?" asked a guard.

Vinnie rubbed his forehead. These guys were really tricky. Fortunately, before Vinnie had to figure out the complexities of his convoluted family tree, John the Zombie smashed the head of one of the guards. Shirley the Zombie grabbed the other and started pounding him headfirst into the side of the hearse. Vinnie heard the Baron running up behind from the van shouting: "Don't kill them! Just knock them out. Killing is for later." The Baron seemed delighted that guards watched the cemeteries now. Vinnie could not quite see it that way.

Guards or no guards, Vinnie had gotten to like working nights. With the ghouls doing all the digging, and now even the watching out, Vinnie had nothing to do but shout orders. For that he felt a real calling. That the orders had to be simple made it all the better so far as Vinnie was concerned. He had even grown to like the rank of sergeant. At least digging up corpses, and shouting orders to zombies, he felt like a sergeant. The only downside occurred whenever a zombie popped up real quick from a hole he had dug. Vinnie would nearly have a heart attack and faint dead away. No matter how many times he told himself the fiends were on his side, they still scared the hell out of him whenever they did that. Graveyards were no place for zombies.

Finally the digging and hauling came to an end for the night. The Baron had contented himself with twelve bodies—

Vinnie thought one actually looked rather pretty (which you might regard as kind of sick if you did not take into account his circumstances of late). Vinnie supervised the loading of the van and the hearse. It took a lot of stuffing to get twenty-four bodies into one van and one hearse: four living (two tied and unconscious), twelve dead, and eight hovering somewhere between. Fortunately the undead do not need room to breath.

Vinnie followed the Zombie Master back to headquarters; currently called *Fort Necro*. The place swarmed with activity. The ghouls worked in utter darkness, but amazingly, they could see fine. even more amazingly, so could Vinnie, with a quick dose from his inhaler. The inhaler contained what the Baron called an *intoxicant*, and it made the world look much as it must appear to one of the zombies. Although still pitched in darkness, one had the sensation of seeing things as if some strange violet light illuminated them. Not only that, but the Baron could write things on the walls or on signs; things that could only be read by zombies or those under the influence of the *intoxicant*. Oddly, the undead responded well to anything written out for them in this manner. You just needed to write in big letters. The only side affect of the vapors that Vinnie had noted was that it tended to highlight the ghoulishness of the undead. Even Charley Sparrow, who looked almost fine even in daylight now, looked a picture of death-hell when Vinnie snorted up the intoxicant. Worse still, Vinnie had checked out a mirror once while on the stuff. He never did that again.

Fortunately, the vapors of the intoxicant did not affect one for long. Vinnie took a snort when entering the compound of *Fort Necro* so that he did not plow through any busy zombies (the undead had no sense to get out of the way). Ghouls walked about, some in small circles, clearly having lost sight of their tasks, but others to more purpose. Some carried vats or jugs. Some lugged tubs to the industrial building. A few swept up. Garish blue and red signs named the buildings: Industrial Center, Barracks, Research and Development, Ceremonial Area. Vinnie had no idea what the last would be used for. These signs helped the undead immensely in following orders. Vinnie could not even see the words except under the influence of the intoxicant.

Vinnie pulled the van into a parking space. A zombie stood in his way but Vinnie just drove over him. It was easier to pull one out from under the van than to talk them out of the way, and you did them scant harm as long as you hit them slow. Getting out, Vinnie ordered several ghouls to help him unload his bodies. Some obeyed and some did not. Only those the Baron had specifically instructed to obey Vinnie ever did as he told them. Vinnie could not keep track of which had been so instructed and which had not, in spite of the signs each wore around the neck. So he just ordered those closest, figuring some of them would obey. The Baron hated it when Vinnie pulled zombies from their assignments to help unload bodies. The Baron had a hard enough time getting them into their proper ruts, he said, without Vinnie interrupting them. Vinnie had no idea how to get them back at what they had been doing. Vinnie wanted the bodies put away fast, and it took quite a long time to get the zombies scrunched up in the van unfolded and back to work. It was like ordering morons to play twister.

The Baron pulled up and switched vans from the big brown one to the big black one. He took Sparrow and Carl the Zombie and headed out to find fresh prey. This left Vinnie to process the new arrivals. He ordered those zombies that would obey him to pull the newly dug bodies out of the van and take them into the building marked *Industrial Center*. Vinnie lead the way, trying not to look at the undead until the intoxicant wore off.

Vinnie had never worked in a factory before, but judging by those he had robbed, the Baron's operation had become pretty big-time. Forty tubs sat next to a like number of tables, with all manner of hoses and machinery connecting each tub to its table. Vinnie had never seen all of them used at once, but clearly the boss thought big. Several generators separated this section of the plant from the Booster Program. At the Booster Program, existing zombies came to get their booster shots. Here, hoses lead from vats of green goo to large enema tubes. Vinnie preferred not to dwell on how the Baron gave the booster shots.

Past the "manufacturing" area, the Baron had set up training grounds for new arrivals to the realm of the undead. Here, old zombies put new zombies through their paces. They led them in and out of large pipes, through tires, onto a trampoline (most did rather poorly with this exercise), and into a maze made of concrete blocks (they just barreled through the earlier ply-wood maze). Against the wall the Baron had erected a seeing-eye chart and children's alphabet blocks. So far no zombie had yet mastered the periodic table of elements tacked to the corner bulletin-board. Vinnie had the job of rating each new recruit after the initial training program. The Baron made him wear a white lab coat and stethoscope when doing this, though what sounds Vinnie might hear within the chest of a zombie the Baron did not reveal.

Fort Necro also contained a laundry (the clothes of the dead needed serious attention), a stitching factory, a cold storage unit for zombies not currently needed (the Baron had found that they lasted longer if frozen), and a headquarters complex. This complex included a library, a video archive of the Baron's achievements, a briefing room, the Baron's office, and Vinnie's office. Vinnie felt pride at having an office. He kept a potted plant on the desk in there. The plant died after the first week, but that seemed fitting.

Vinnie led his ghoulish helpmates to the tubs in the manufacturing plant. He made sure that the zombies properly submerged the bodies in the pre-reanimation vats, then led them back to the hearse to retrieve the living subjects. One of these had regained consciousness and struggled against his ropes. One look at Tina the Zombie and he passed out. Vinnie had him, and his partner, taken to the Guest Quarters. At first Vinnie had thought this an example of the Baron's sick sense of humor. Later he realized that the Baron had no sense of humor whatsoever. Vinnie chained the guests to the floor and locked the door. He posted a guard in the hallway. Not that the hall needed one, but Vinnie really liked posting guards.

After helping the digging crews wiggle out of the van, Vinnie decided to turn in for the night. His room lay upstairs, in the second largest building, above the Guest Quarters. He had a large room with a big screen TV, a king-sized bed, and his own kitchenette. Royal appointments compared to the guys just downstairs. Vinnie did not fancy what would soon happen to them. He stayed well away from that side of the operation. The Baron forever ran short of "living subjects," and Vinnie greatly feared the day when the Baron looked around and noticed that Vinnie had not died yet.

Against such thoughts, Vinnie tucked himself into bed. He watched some cheesy talk show re-run, and had just started drifting off to sleep when he heard screams from downstairs. He hated it when the live subjects started caterwauling. It would only get worse as the Baron brought new ones in before morning. He hated it especially when they came round and started talking to each other. "Why us?" they would always say. Not just that of course. They would introduce themselves and such. Ask how long this one or that one had been there. Sometimes, one would ask another what he or she (mostly she) "did." This got a laugh sometimes. They would sometimes hatch plots for overpowering the guards. They clearly had no conception of how hard it could be to overpower a dead person. They always made comments on how ugly their captors were —especially that pinched looking fellow, they'd say. They would cry. But sooner or later they would always get around to: "Why us."

Why them indeed? Why Vinnie for that matter, thought Vinnie. Why did his step-up into organized crime have to land him between a grave and a tub of goo? Why did he have to work for a Dr. Frankenstein Vampire instead of an ordinary murderous thug? Why did he have to end up here? One reason only: the Baron picked him and no one else. And why them? Same reason. "Shut up!" he'd yell down at them when they started all that "Why us" talk. And they would shut up for maybe a full minute. Then one of them would break the blissful silence and scream.

◆ ◆ ◆

Vinnie awoke to the sound of pounding on his door. Vinnie always awoke this way now. Were his door not made of steel, the zombie on the other end would by now have put a pulpy fist through it. Vinnie rolled over and looked at his clock as the slow pounding continued. It showed the time as 4:00 in the afternoon. Then something very strange occurred.

"Get … up … Vinnie," the zombie said in a gravely voice.

Vinnie had no windows in his room, so only the light of the clock cut the pitch blackness of the room.

"Get up Vinnie!"

Vinnie felt his heart sink. This was it. The fiends from the bowls of the earth had arisen to scratch out his heart. The door handle shook. Panic rose in Vinnie. The voice on the other side of the door did not belong to Mr. Sparrow, and certainly did not belong to any living man.

"Get up Vinnie! Get up Vinnie!"

Vinnie screamed. Outside the door the zombie screamed in return. Vinnie felt better at this. It seemed such typical zombie stupidity that it made Vinnie's world seem safe and normal again. Vinnie got up and changed his clothes while the zombie alternated between screams and demands that Vinnie get up. Once dressed, Vinnie opened the door. Before him stood a fiend with dead-yellow eyes, sallow skin, a gapping mouth, and the odor of death. He also sported a big sign hanging from his neck reading: *Roger the Zombie*. Roger looked at Vinnie and landed his next surprise. He said: "Come … with … me." Two sentences from one zombie in one day; is there anything science can't do?

Vinnie accompanied Roger the Zombie to the Baron's lab.

The Dark Lord of the Undead had nothing but smiles for the world this afternoon. He saw Vinnie and Roger the Zombie approaching. He smiled; not a good look on him. "Did he do it?" the Ghoul Master asked excitedly, "Did he do it?"

"Uh, you mean tell me to get up? Yeah, he did that."

"And the other, once you got up?"

"Yeah, I guess, he said I should come with me—I mean, him."

The Baron walked over and hugged the ghoul. Roger let off a idiotic smile. "Isn't he marvelous?" the Baron said, "I made him last night after I got back. He already talks in sentences! Doesn't tie knots though. Apparently not a sailor. No accounting for that. Still, complete sentences. Lots of them. We have definitely arrived."

The Baron put an arm around Vinnie and guided him toward his office. The walls, floor, and ceiling of the office had been painted in a black so dark it simply swallowed what little light came into the room. "I need your advice. I have done some design work. My office walls—bare. Not right. And, after all, we have the matter of credentials. So have a look and tell me the truth." Vinnie's eyes adjusted to the dark.

The Zombie Master stopped at his desk, and when Vinnie looked at him he nodded down at the papers lying there. Vinnie saw several parchment-like papers that looked to him like diplomas. Vinnie had seen lots of diplomas in his time. Nearly every house he busted into had some on the walls. He had never studied them though. No one ever hid a safe behind a diploma. Vinnie inspected the degrees on the desk. One seemed to have been written completely in a foreign language. The other two mentioned some college in Las Vegas. Vinnie did not recognize the names on any of them. "Uhhh," Vinnie said.

"I designed them myself. I want to mount one. Eventually, I will have one from Princeton and another from Harvard, but I had no samples of those to copy, so I made these for the time being. What do you think? Which do you like?"

Vinnie thought hard. "I can't read that one," he said.

"It's all in Latin. Don't worry about that. Does it *look* right?

For my room?"

Vinnie glanced about the dark room. Books, beakers, wires and papers filled the space. On a counter across from the desk lay a human arm. "Oh yeah, it looks to fit in real good," Vinnie said.

The boss smiled at him. "Perhaps I should hang all three?"

"Sure."

Vinnie watched as the Baron walked about the room holding one and then another up to this or that wall. He ordered Vinnie to hold up the Latin one above the door. Something crashed outside the room. Both men left the room and entered the large indoor training ground. A new zombie had launched himself from the trampoline and taken out a line of his fellow ghouls. Worse yet, several had lost their identity signs. It took quite a lot to get a new zombie to recognize its name.

"Fix that," the Baron said to Charley Sparrow.

Vinnie's jaw dropped when Sparrow set out to the fallen undead and commenced to sort out their name tags. An impressive feat, even for Sparrow.

"I gave him an improved booster last night," the Baron said. "It has proved a great boon to language skills. And that brings me to your next mission."

Vinnie did not like the sound of "mission"—mission usually meant something frighteningly new. The Baron led Vinnie to the briefing room. There he set his henchman down in front of the television set and began fiddling with the VCR.

"You will need to take the hearse on a long trip," the Baron said, "along with Mr. Sparrow, and two other zombies. I have a training film here for you to watch." He put on the training film. Vinnie watched *The Road to Morocco* starring Bob Hope and Bing Crosby. What this might portend he could not fathom.

As it ended the Baron re-appeared, carrying Vinnie's "civilian clothes." The Baron said, "I hope the film has given you some sense of how to conduct an open road adventure. I don't mean the comedy, obviously, just the mood of the thing. You should conduct yourself with a certain jauntiness. Good for morale. Now—ready?"

"Where do I go?" Vinnie asked.

"Arlington National Cemetery—in Arlington, Virginia. I have trip-tics from AAA and a large map of the U.S. Also some tourist information, and a recruiting poster from the Marines. I don't suppose you'll need that, though.

"Why Virginia? We have plenty of bodies to dig up here in L.A."

The Baron looked impatient. "I need particular individuals, and they happen to rest at the Arlington National Cemetery."

Particular individuals? "Like special names they don't have around here?" Vinnie asked.

"No—special persons I think we might profit by re-animating. Here is the list, including the grave site location. Arlington is a big cemetery so you will need to survey it carefully before the actual dig. Try to get all the persons here listed—but be sure to get the first one."

Vinnie read the first name on the list, "Robert Peary?"

The Baron ran a big smile across his tight face. "Brilliant notion, wouldn't you say?"

"Who is he?" Vinnie asked.

The Baron lost his smile. "Admiral Peary only discovered the North Pole," he said indignantly.

"Well, why do you want him?"

"To interview him of course."

VEGAS VACATION

"This is not a vacation," Yolanda said.

They rode on the highway to Vegas in Nick's Thunderbird; top down, wind in the face, sun on the hairline, and bugs on the windscreen. In the roadworthy fellowship of Vegas-bound roadsters they cruised along, Nick at the wheel, Yolanda pulling strands of hair from her mouth as the wind amused itself by blowing them in. She used that fingernail-of-the-middle-finger technique that finally made sense as to why God had graced humans with a middle finger in the first place. To Nick this certainly felt like a vacation.

"Not a vacation," he said, "not on your life. Pure business. Just a talk with a medieval scholar or two and a bit of necromancy research. If we should happen to spend a little time at a craps table—it won't be anything we can't justify on an expense account."

"I didn't come to feed your gambling disease. We won't need any stops at the craps table."

"We have to stay the night—unless you want to drive back with me in the dark?"

Yolanda just looked away. They had already agreed on the ground rules. The department would not spring for Nick's airline ticket (suspects do not get Vegas vacations), and Yolanda agreed that she wanted him at the Dantelani interview. So they drove, and would spend the night—separate rooms; no gambling.

"Have you ever stopped at the craps table?" Nick asked.

"If the guys had wanted the gals to stop at the table, they wouldn't have named it after the principle product of the hind end," she said.

"Not a first class name I'll concede but some of the best odds in Vegas."

"You mean you lose more slowly at it than at the other games?" Yolanda said.

"*I* don't in particular, but other people do."

They drove on. Nick whistled. No aficionado of great whistling, Yolanda turned on the radio. Desert static and wind in the ears. She noticed Nick looking in the rear-view mirror a lot. Why?

"What are you looking for?"

Nick studied the rearview mirror, "The guys in riot gear. From our first date."

Yolanda sighed. "It was not a date, and I already apologized for the deception. I won't do it again. "

"Maybe they're in helicopters—they could follow us in helicopters," Nick said, inspecting the skies above.

"Not the way you drive."

"Okay, so you have no backup. You'll just shoot me on your own if I get out of line."

"Right between the eyes."

Nick smiled. She probably meant it. "Apart from a love of terrorizing your dates, whatever brought you to police work?"

"My dad was a cop. He was one of the first Hispanic detectives on the LAPD."

Nick rode up on a large three-sectioned truck. The roar of its engines and the exhaust from its stacks reminded him of everyone's principle reason for loving convertibles: they felt so good once you got out. He pulled past the truck and broke into fresh air. He looked at Yolanda. She pulled another strand of hair from her lips. She wore sunglasses, and lipstick, and she looked like she had been born to ride in a convertible. "So he encouraged you to sign up with the thin blue line?"

"He passed away on my thirteenth birthday."

"Sorry. Then how was it he led you into police work?"

Yolanda turned off the radio and straightened up. "What

leads anyone into anything? How did you become a museum curator? You don't seem the type."

"There's a type for that?"

"You seem a little bent to me."

Nick considered this. *Bent* could mean a lot of things. He let that part go. "I bummed around a long time. Did you know I studied at over twelve colleges?"

Yolanda nodded in mock admiration. "What did you study?" she asked.

"Archeology at Arizona, Biology at Brigham Young, Literature at Louisville—"

"You're kidding me," Yolanda said.

"Not in that order, but after ten or so, it helps to alphabetize."

Yolanda shook her head as Nick continued: "I studied Southern Gothic literature at Louisville; read William Faulkner and wrote papers on cultural colonialism in mid-twentieth century literature. You'd never guess what harm a Faulkner novel could do to people who can't even read English. I flunked my 'Literature of American Imperialism' class by pointing out how few Tahitians had read Faulkner. Then a term at Baton Rouge Community College."

"Quite a fall there," Yolanda said.

"Hey, hey! No cracks about the fighting possums of BRCC. Anyway, I had some tuition problems."

Yolanda settled back down in the seat and looked at him again. "Mommy and Daddy cut you off?"

"I've been an orphan since I was seven."

Yolanda blushed. "Now it's my turn to be sorry."

"No, no," Nick said, "I didn't grow up in an orphanage or anything. My Aunt Louise raised me. She raised me from almost three years on, even before my father died. I make no complaints."

Yolanda watched as Nick passed the car in front of them at something close to the speed of light. The doors buckled as they flew past. She noticed that Nick had stopped talking.

"How did you finally settle on art—that is what you settled on, right?" she said.

Nick smiled. "Art history. I took my masters in that. I received an undergraduate degree in performing arts." Yolanda laughed. "Don't laugh, that just meant theater studies. I considered being an actor."

"What stopped you?" Yolanda asked.

"I couldn't stand waiting tables," Nick said.

"So you thought art history would propel you away from food service?"

"Turns out I had a knack for spotting forgeries. A rare gift." Nick worked his way around a minivan with tinted windows. He wondered what anyone driving a minivan might need to hide behind tinted windows. "The department chair was desperate to put warm bodies in the seminar room. He filled my head with the idea of becoming a legendary curator, like Chick Austin, his personal hero. He talked to me night and day about how assembling an exhibit was every bit as much a work of art as painting or sculpture."

"You seem much too smart to buy that," Yolanda said.

"No, I bought it, still do in a way. Curators are among the gatekeepers of the art world. Duchamp can submit a urinal as a sculpture, but it only becomes art if a curator puts it into a museum."

"So they make the product, and you make it art?"

"Or in the case of the urinal, he didn't even make it. For all I know he ripped it out of a bordello restroom. My point is just that the curator makes it art, along with the critic, by finding a meaning another person proposed for the work."

"Sounds like a scam to me," Yolanda said.

"Right. It is a scam. But the prize, for the curator, is not money but power over the ideas in another's head. It's a scam because the original point of all that painting and sculpting was to frighten some poor medieval peasant staring at the base relief, or to impress a rich Renaissance banker looking to give his wife a picture of himself. The artist painted, cut, or carved to the taste of the buyer—a bishop wanting to terrify his flock, a banker wanting to amaze his rivals. The artist threw in whatever idea struck his nerve, but no one, not painter, not bishop, no one, got hot in the pants about *art*. The object had a function: to scare hell out of people, or send a message about the subject. The work did not express anything about the artist—as most people saw it—it just said something about the subject: and that something was what the buyer, not the artist, wanted said.

"Then one day someone decided that all these scary figures and pompous posing should be called *art*. Some would be good, and some bad, and not just based on how well they scared or how imposing they were. The works had to express the ideas of the artist. And the value of the work had to be gauged aesthetically, rather than functionally. A functional assessment just required seeing if the thing worked: did it scare the sinners to God or not? But an aesthetic evaluation required a special way of looking at the thing. This *art* stuff should be looked at *disinterestedly*. So you had to take a disinterested interest in it, or miss out on the really artistic aspect altogether. To help folks take such disinterest in art we put it into museums. After all, churches and parlors could be a real distraction to disinterest. Once they built the first museum, someone had to be in charge of deciding what got hung and what got pushed to the basement. So they found the fellow with the key to the basement, called him the curator— which I think is French for *guy who locks up the place*—and next thing you know the janitor is in charge of the whole show. We can't paint or sculpt, we even write in atrocious academese, but we say what is art, and what has meaning, and what meaning it has. All done before breakfast. Then some sharp soul invented *postmodernism.* Now we don't even need hacks to churn out paintings. I can put my dead cat on display and make it postmodern. All in all, a championship scam."

Yolanda shook her head and laughed. Nick smiled too. Yolanda said, "I can't tell when you're serious and when you're not."

"That's cause I'm postmodern, baby. Cut me and I bleed irony instead of blood."

Nick drove now behind a pickup truck leaching Styrofoam popcorn all over the road. Some stuck to the windshield wipers like dandruff from the gods. Nick couldn't pass since the pickup truck kept pace with an old Chevy, so for the moment Nick and Yolanda rode in a Styrofoam snowstorm.

"So that's me," Nick said, "delusions of grandeur vindicated by obsolete French philosophy. What about you? What makes being a detective worth scrubbing up in the morning for?"

Yolanda flicked a bit of popcorn off the wind visor. "I don't know yet, I haven't been a detective very long. I liked being a patrol officer because they let me nightstick smart assess like you. But, to be honest, your book theft was my first case as a detective."

"They had promoted you that very day?"

"No, I had worked decoy as a detective for about two months prior to that."

"Decoy?"

Yolanda pulled a piece of popcorn off her hair. "Vice squad work," she said. "I stand out on a street corner luring in the johns. We agree on a price and I lead them back to the motel room. After they hand over the money, I give a signal and four policemen from the next room charge in and grab the guy. Then we give him a ticket and let him go. Not much to it after awhile."

Nick laughed. "You mean to tell me you spent two months running a badger game for the LAPD?"

"Badger game?"

"It's a con. A woman coaxes the mark into dropping his drawers for a good time, then just before the action starts, in comes daddy screaming 'how could you do this to my fifteen year old daughter?!?' The mark goes white and begs the grifters to take his money, please. They pulled the badger game back in the stone age."

"I'm talking about a police sting operation."

"How much did they have to pay?"

Yolanda thought a moment, she didn't like the direction this had taken, "The citation levied a two hundred dollar fine."

Nick shook his head, "Rank beginners. Pros at the badger game can squeeze five hundred to a thousand out of the average mark. You guys need some expert advice on this."

Yolanda chaffed: "We weren't in it for the money. We were trying to run the prostitutes out of the area by scaring off the johns. We wanted clean streets for the kids to walk on, not a profit."

The Chevy finally pulled ahead of the popcorn machine, and Nick hit the gas and drove hot on its heels. "Back in old Europe the state would hire guys to collect the taxes—letting them keep a share of the take. You cops ought to license some grifters to run the badger game in the neighborhood. They could run off the johns, clean up the street, and free the police for riot control or something."

Yolanda pouted a bit. "You don't understand."

Nick gunned the engine and cut in front of the pickup truck. "Now we have him! Get that box in the back."

"What?" Yolanda said.

"Here hold the wheel." Nick grabbed a box from the back seat. He handed it to Yolanda. "We have him now. Fire to the rear!"

Yolanda looked in the box. It contained Styrofoam popcorn. "You keep this in your car?"

Nick studied his distance from the pickup truck. "Not as a rule, but I happened to be armed today, so now it's payback time. Let him have it!"

Yolanda shook her head, "Don't be childish."

Nick allowed the pickup to tailgate him. "Just lean back and let it go all at once. Maybe it will clog up his air intake."

Yolanda put the box back in the rear seat. "You'll just pollute the desert and tick off the driver of the truck."

"So what? You're armed. Let the bum have it."

Yolanda ignored him.

Nick sighed and hit the gas; they left the pickup far behind. "Did you have any fun running that badger game?"

"Police sting operation," Yolanda said.

"Okay, but did you have any fun at it?"

"Oh sure, great fun: men stared at me like I was a big blowup doll they wanted to screw. They paid me money to piss on them. Then, after the bust, they pissed on themselves. What a joy." She pulled another strand of hair from her thick lips. She took of her sunglasses and looked Nick in the eye. "I get a lot of leering stares. I don't like it. I have a lot going on, and I don't need to always worry what the guy next to me is thinking."

Nick had the odd sensation she meant this for him in particular. The very idea that he might be "leering" at her struck him as ridiculous. Nick easily succeeded in averting his eyes from Yolanda.

"Look out for that car!" Yolanda yelled.

Okay, eye averting proved difficult, and Nick did not succeed in it. But his heart lay in the right direction. Only his eyes betrayed him. "So the whole time," Nick said, "you never liked anything about it?"

Yolanda stiffened a bit. "Well."

Nick smiled, "Let's hear it. Come on, spill, spill."

Yolanda looked out at the desert. After a moment she said softly, "I did get to let loose a little."

"What? What did you say?"

Yolanda looked him straight in the eye now: "Let loose a little. I got to do that. My mother would not have approved, but in the service of keeping the streets clean, one must sometimes cut loose a little."

Nick didn't quite get it yet, "Cut loose how? What did you do?"

Yolanda squirmed a bit in the seat. Why had she even admitted this to him? "You have to talk a little street trash to come off authentic. You have to cuss it up a bit to the johns. So they buy you as a prostitute."

Nick smiled a devil's grin, "Okay, let's have it."

Yolanda looked at him; her face formed a perfect question mark.

Nick smiled wide. "Come on, give us a sample. Let's hear it, sailor."

Yolanda shook her head and looked at him as if he were crazed. "Not a chance."

Nick smiled wider, "You came up with it, it's your tale to tell. I've got to hear it now. What does this cut loose street talk sound like?"

Yolanda shook her head.

Nick pressed, "Come on tough-cop, give me some of that street jive."

Silence reigned. Nick smiled on.

The high desert sped by. Above, Yolanda saw three vultures circling in the distance. The heat of the day warmed her wherever the stiff breeze of the wind did not touch. The vinyl seats of the Thunderbird grew hot to the touch wherever exposed to the relentless sun. The drive seared her. She glanced beside her and caught the face of Nick Sabernail now concentrated on passing a blue Corvette just ahead.

Nick crept up on the Corvette—at about eighty miles an hour—and waited till he had pulled even before pressing the gas down and moving past it. He cut into the Vette's lane just ahead of a Jeep Cherokee, then ahead of the Jeep into open road. The wind blew his hair and the sun shone above.

"Forty bucks and I will lick the hair off your balls."

Nick's eyes popped open. He tentatively glanced over at Detective Vasquez. She looked dead ahead as she spoke, punctuating her words with a fingernail daintily pointing in the air before her, "I will cunt-fuck spunk from the bottom of your ball sack and spew the jizz back into your face for fifty bucks." She cocked a hard-whore look at her imaginary john, "I will tit-fuck your dick four times its normal size. You want a spanking? I will blister your butt, you bad boy. Piss in my face? For three hundred bucks I'll suck piss out of you that you didn't know you had. I live to have cock-juice shot in my eyes." Yolanda looked at Nick. He blushed bright red and barely watched her out of the corner of his eyes. She said, "If you ever repeat one word of that vile crap in my presence I will personally shoot your kneecaps off."

Nick swallowed and said, "My lips are sealed. And may I add, you have opened up whole new worlds for me today."

Yolanda looked ahead, and now *she* smiled the devil's grin. Nick thought he needed sunscreen; his face felt very hot.

◆ ◆ ◆

Nick and Yolanda entered the heart of Las Vegas, Nevada. The city looked like a vision of the future in the overheated imagination of a 1950's teenager. Flashing lights, giant outdoor television screens, single buildings shaped like city skylines, and a giant black pyramid. It only lacked floating taxicabs. Nick cruised down the Strip until he reached the Rainforest Hotel and Casino. You could not miss the Rainforest: It's brown and green base looked like a Walt Disney version of Mowgli's jungle. Huge tree trunks appeared to support a bushy rainforest canopy that itself lay beneath the rising tower of rooms. The tower looked more or less like a tall hotel, except that the designers had superimposed the image of tall jungle trees rich with vines on the façade of windows. On the west wall of the tower a thirty-foot image of Tarzan swung from a vine. Nick wondered if anyone could actually see out of those windows from the inside.

Nick pulled into the vast covered auto entrance to the hotel. The well-oiled machine of the Rainforest snapped into motion as Nick stopped the car. A green clad valet attendant sporting ivy for a shirt collar took Nick's keys while a bellhop wearing a uniform decorated to resemble a giraffe pelt took the bags from the trunk and scurried them into the hotel. Like jungle quicksand, the Rainforest did not give those who wandered in an opportunity for second-guessing. Nick and Yolanda entered the hotel beneath a giant coiled anaconda replica. Lion's jaws surrounded the entrance. The hotel figuratively swallowed the incoming guests. A Ph.D. in industrial psychology had assured the management that these images would psychologically coerce patrons into staying in the building and away from other casinos. In fact, the subliminally panicked patrons just wondered out the rear entrances like so much diarrheic lion feces.

Inside, the hotel lobby looked like a cavernous opening in the jungle, lined on the edge by large rocks, and illuminated by ten thousand watts of fluorescent lighting. Animatronic parrots, macaws, and tiki birds fluttered in the canopy of artificial leaves overhead. Stereo speakers piped in jungle sounds recorded for a Johnny Weismuller film back in 1934. That hardly mattered, no one staying at the Rainforest had any competing notion of what a jungle sounded like.

Nick made his way around the base of a giant vine-covered jungle tree to VIP Guest Registration. Finding no line here, he marched straight up to the woman behind the counter.

"Rooms for Sabernail and Vasquez. We called ahead," Nick said.

"Who is your Jungle Host?" the woman asked.

Nick figured this was the local jargon for the fellow who smoothed the way for high rollers. Nick said, "We haven't got one yet, but we are VIP's. She's a cop." The woman looked on without a trace of amusement. "She has a gun," Nick offered by way of further evidence.

Yolanda grabbed his arm and steered him to the lines used by the proletariat. They stood in line to the catcalls of macaque monkeys. Real ones, this time, running about in a long cage behind the line of desk clerks. Nick noticed that they occasionally threw monkey crap at the bellhop station.

"I feel like I'm waiting for a ride at Disneyland," Yolanda said.

"The kids love it, I'm told," Nick said, "and since, for some unaccountable reason, the city fathers won't let kids into the casino, their parents need a lot of distractions for them. For instance, they can play in the *Monkey House*—the world's largest indoor jungle gym. Or ride Oklahoma Smith's Jungle Adventure of Doom—the world's largest indoor jungle adventure of doom."

"Oklahoma Smith?"

"Yes. I understand the licensing agreement on *Indiana Jones* fell through."

Yolanda noticed the carpet featured images of leaves and roots woven into the pattern. Also, her feet appeared to tread on something like a tarantula. "What led you to pick such a classy joint?" she asked.

"It seemed non-threatening. I figured, if you take a gun-toting cop who suspects you of murder to a Vegas hotel, you had better find a non-threatening one."

"A non-threatening jungle?"

Nick pressed on, "Sure. Besides, the jungle provides lots of cover should you decide to start shooting at me."

They made their way through the line to the registration desk; actually a massive counter worked by forty zebra-skin clad clerks, each one dodging the occasional barrage of monkey shit. Nick negotiated for the right room, "We could take a single with a king-sized bed."

Yolanda spoke up to the woman behind the counter, "Probably not a good idea since then he'd have to sleep handcuffed to the bathroom sink. We'll take the two rooms reserved."

"Did you want those adjoining with a door?" asked the woman.

Yolanda, "Not necessary."

Nick, "Definitely."

The woman said, "Would you care for our jungle drink treat?"

Nick said, "As long as it doesn't have candy in it, I'll drink it. Could you send up a deck of cards as well?"

"Gambling is not allowed in the rooms, unless you wish to

gamble on our in-house cable gaming network."

Yolanda said, "No drinks, no cards, just the rooms."

The woman typed a short novel onto her computer screen. She doubtless commanded every conceivable fact about both of them, from their net worth to their pajama preferences. "Would you care to add one percent to your bill as a donation to preserve the Brazilian rainforest?" she asked.

"What does the data base say?" Nick asked.

"She would, you wouldn't," answered the woman.

Yolanda said, "Would that be the real rainforest or a plastic simulation of it?"

Nick said, "I think we'll just keep the air conditioner off."

Keys in hand (actually "access cards" in hand—nobody uses keys in Vegas anymore), Nick and Yolanda found their way to the twenty-third floor, and by the miracle of Las Vegas efficiency, their bags awaited them, each in the proper room. Nick looked out of the window from Yolanda's room. You could indeed see out the windows, through a green haze. Unfortunately, all you could see were the air conditioner units on the Renaissance Hotel next door.

The room itself looked like any other hotel room in the world. Except that the cheap bedspread resembled a dead lion, the walls were zebra stripped, the thin connecting door looked like bamboo, the floor almost glowed from its bright leopard skin design, and the lampshades sported the colors of the toucan. All in all, a brilliant way to move the folks out of the room and into the casino where they belong.

"We belong in the casino," Nick said.

"We are off to Las Vegas University as soon as I freshen up," Yolanda said.

"Right. Okay." Nick wondered if Dr. Dantelani liked to gamble. Living in Las Vegas he must have developed a taste for the gaming life. You probably could not get a word out of him except around a blackjack table. "You know we might need to take the good doctor out on the town to loosen his tongue," Nick said.

"I'm going to freshen up now," Yolanda said.

"Right." Nick stared out the window. Pressing his face to the glass, and looking hard to his right, he could see the Strip and the Taj Mahal-like casino that sat across the strip from the Rainforest. "An academic like him, he would probably appreciate the Monsoon Casino. It's like a visit to another culture while you play. You learn about ancient India, win a few hands at the blackjack table, talk. That's the ticket right there."

"I have all my clothes off now—you don't mind watching while I take a shower, do you?"

Nick froze in his tracks. He slowly turned around. Yolanda did not have her clothes off. She had them all on. She had her arms crossed, and she looked cross.

"You want me to go to my room, right?" Nick asked.

"Give me half an hour to get all the popcorn pieces out of my hair and then we go to LVU."

Nick smiled. "Sure, half an hour. I'll wait for you in the casino, by the craps table."

"Give me five minutes to change my shirt and I'll meet you in your room," Yolanda said.

Nick left through the adjoining bamboo door. It troubled him how quickly Yolanda could sniff him out. It must be all that detective training.

They left the hotel not thirty minutes after they arrived. Something of a record for Nick. Driving down the Strip, they passed all the hotels into what must be the part of Las Vegas in which people actually lived. This served as something of a revelation to Nick. He had never considered the possibility that anyone lived in Vegas. Worked there, yes. Played there, yes. But lived there? What did they do when they ran out of money?

After just twenty minutes of driving, Nick and Yolanda entered the parking lot of Las Vegas University. Its many lots were nearly empty, but they had trouble finding parking nonetheless. LVU had no metered parking. Instead, you had to buy a permit at an automated stall as you entered. Nick had an 'AB' class parking permit ("place on the dashboard at the front left window unobscured by any other decals, permits, dated material or other non-opaque objects on window or dash"). This permit did not allow one to park in class 'A' lots nor in class 'B' lots. For a moment it seemed they had found a good lot, but on closer inspection it turned out to be a class 'BA' lot: strictly out of order for an 'AB' permit holder. Normally, at this point Nick would have parallel parked the dean's car, but he had a cop in the car and wanted to impress her with his good citizenship.

"What are you doing?" Yolanda asked.

"I'm looking for an 'AB' lot to park the car in."

"Just put it anywhere. If they ticket us I'll send it in with a note saying *police business*."

Nick just loved dating a cop. He parked right next to the science building under a sign saying: "Danger: Radiation Disposal Truck Parking Only."

They entered the science building.

A university science building is an inviting place. It invites you to run away screaming at the imponderable disasters fermenting there. Radiation symbols and cartoon images of acid spilling into eyes adorn every door. The halls hold special washbasins provided for those who failed to heed the *no acid in eyes* signs. Through glass windows one sees equipment that, while friendly and familiar to the scientist, suggest biohazards of the future to the uninitiated. The maze of cinderblock walls forms a fortress of knowledge, warding off the ignorant that might question the value of the progress of science. The walls have no murals.

Nor did Nick find any maps of the facility. For half an hour he and Yolanda wandered the halls looking for an elevator or stairs that might take them to the bowels of the building.

A Saturday, they saw no one milling about that might direct them. Nick tended to barge into any old room, warning signs or no, and look about for help. Yolanda thought that a fire in the building would likely kill most of the occupants who had worked or studied there for less than a dozen years. At last, they found a flight of stairs that led down (two earlier staircases had led only up—the basement must be a particularly hard place to escape from). Once in the lower-lower basement (the building had one still lower) they found another cinderblock maze—this one without windows at all. After a bit, Nick began to shout: "Doctor! Doctor! Oh Doctor!"

"Are you sure he's here today?"

"The janitor assured me he held his office hours on Saturday afternoon. Doctor!"

"It seems a strange time."

"Makes perfect sense—fewer students to interrupt your real work. Doctor!"

Nick gave up shouting. Sound surely did not travel through these heavy walls. Then, like seeing Livingston through a crack in the jungle, he saw a sign above the door to room LL1002: *Institute of Medieval Occult Sciences; Dr. Luigi Dantelani, Director.*

"I wonder if they got the whole institute into just the one room," said Nick as he knocked on the door. "Dr. Dantelani?"

They heard shuffling papers and the sound of a chair screeching against the hard floor. Then the door opened a crack. Half of a long-legged spider crawled through the cracked door. Just before Yolanda moved to brush the spider away, the door flew wide open, revealing a short, round man, at least sixty-five years old, with a beard. The spider, in fact, turned out to be one of his eyebrows. Sparse, wiry little things, they sat above his eyes like two fuzzy daddy longlegs.

"Dr. Dantelani I presume?" Nick said.

The daddy longlegs scurried down as the good doctor frowned, "You're not students?"

"No," Yolanda said.

The daddy longlegs ran up the doctor's forehead, "Administration! Come in, come in."

Nick and Yolanda entered the small office. Two sides of the cinderblock room held floor to ceiling file-cabinets. One held a large bookcase crammed with old books. Another, smaller bookcase, stood against the wall, preventing the door from fully opening.

Dantelani hurried behind his desk. "I have all the necessary records, you know. A complete accounting of expense and activity." He gestured toward the file cabinets. "I keep separate records for the institute's different projects. I keep expense reports back to 1976. I can account for my time with a daily log, in which I register all of my research and teaching activities." He pulled a black, bound book from one of the bookcases. "It is divided into half hour intervals. I log in conference work, teaching time, student meeting time, institute business work, institute funded research, independent research, university work, lunch, dinner—I work many nights here, reading time and writing time I log under separate headings."

A buzzer rang. Dantelani picked up an egg timer and turned the dial around again. "See! See! I'm glad you were here for that. I keep track. I am ready for an audit." Dantelani pulled out another black bound book from his desk and opened it. A time sheet. He logged in his current activity: reading: 28 minutes; meeting with administration auditors: 2 minutes. "I appreciate the importance of records and oversight. Good records are essential to success." Dantelani said.

Yolanda spoke up, "Actually, we came to talk with you about one of your research areas."

Dantelani's right side daddy longlegs eyebrow made a beeline to his hairline. "My research? *My* research. Yes. Here. Look here." He retrieved a box from under the desk. "In the box. I keep it in the box. I'm sorry, but I can't show you the inside of the box. This is not completed research. It is still in the box, as they say. But you can hold the box. Here," he offered the box to

Yolanda, "hold the box."

Yolanda took the box.

"Heavy, isn't it?" Dantelani said. "Clearly, that doesn't prove that the research is in the box, but it is in the box, and in the box it must remain." He paused a moment and looked his guests over. As further explanation he added, "Even I don't open the box on weekends."

Yolanda put the box down.

"I have log entries to show that I don't open the box on weekends. The box contains my research—quite distinct from the research of the institute. In point of fact, I do all the research of the institute. But, nevertheless, that research is quite distinct from my research. The logs show all of this."

"I think you misunderstand us, Dr. Dantelani," Yolanda said, "we are not from administration and we did not come here for an audit."

The daddy longlegs crept down to sit close together astride the doctor's nose.

"We're doing research," Nick said, "in an area you might know something about."

"Scholars?" said Dantelani.

"Police," Yolanda said. She showed him her badge, "LAPD. We are investigating a serial killer with ties to the occult."

The daddy longlegs sprang apart and up the doctor's head so fast Nick wondered if the bridge of his nose had suddenly grown too hot for them. The doctor felt for his chair behind him and just managed to find the seat rather than fall all the way to the floor. He took a handkerchief from a pocket and mopped his brow. The eyebrow spiders fled from the handkerchief. "I'm very sorry," the doctor said, "I've been expecting an audit for twenty-three years. So few people ever come down here. Police you say? I'm a medieval scholar."

"I'm Yolanda Vasquez and this is Nick Sabernail."

"We wanted to pick your brain about something," Nick said.

"Have you heard of the Vampire Killer serial murders in Los Angeles?" Yolanda asked.

"No, no," Dantelani said, "I don't read the papers."

"That's alright," Nick said, "we really came to talk to you about a rare book."

"I don't know anything about the book," said Dantelani. His right hand continued to chase daddy longlegs around his brow with the handkerchief.

Yolanda said, "How do you know? We haven't told you what book we're talking about?"

The daddy longlegs sprang up to their separate corners of the doctor's skull. "Well," he said, "I'm just reasoning it out. Millions of books published every year for centuries. I've read very few of them. You say the book is rare? Well, rare books are hard to find. So I am less likely to have seen the one of which you are speak. So surely I haven't seen it. If I haven't seen it, I haven't read it. If I haven't read it, I could know nothing about it. QED."

Yolanda looked at Nick. Nick looked back, then pressed ahead, "This one you know about. It is a major text in your area of research. A colleague of yours told me you knew its contents."

Yolanda said, "We've come a long way to talk to you about this doctor. Lives are at stake."

Nick said, "I had a copy of this book myself, until someone stole it. Perhaps the janitor told you about this?"

Dantelani put the handkerchief away and straightened up in the seat. "Well, if the book covers my area—a limited area, you understand—that would be different." He swallowed hard and asked, "What is the book called?"

Nick said, "*The Compendium of Necromantic Sciences.*"

The daddy longlegs did not move a bit.

Yolanda said, "We would like to know about the history and content of the book—especially as it might relate to the current murder spree in L.A."

The spider legs crawled down Dantelani's forehead to sit close above his eyes in a visage of seriousness. He said, "You may rest assured, and have no fear, my good lady, the formulas and rituals enumerated in the *Compendium* are pure pseudo-science and could in no way aid anyone, no matter how educated or committed, in restoring animation to the bodies of the dead."

Again Nick and Yolanda glanced at each other.

Nick said, "Well, that is quite a relief. Maybe you could take a step back and tell us what the book says. What it's all about."

Dantelani glanced up at Nick, "You said you had it, before someone stole it?"

"Yes, but I never quite got around to thumbing through it."

Dantelani leaned back in his chair and put his stubby fingers together under his chin. "I see, I see. You want to know about the book that you lost."

"What was the book about?" Yolanda asked.

The professor sat still for a moment with his eyes closed. Then in a burst he leaped out of his chair and began searching his files. After a moment, he opened a bottom file drawer and withdrew several yellowed sheets of paper. A motion of his hand, and a flick of a spider leg, indicated he wanted Yolanda and Nick to sit. They sat facing the standing professor. Professor Dantelani studied his notes a moment, then put them down on the desk before him. He looked out past Nick and Yolanda as if addressing an auditorium.

The professor spoke, "*The Compendium of Necromantic Sciences*; occult madness or ancient science? How shall we treat of a text whose origins fade into the distant recess of time? The sources for this tome affirm an antiquity that modern science claims impossible. It was vilified in the medieval world, by which time, on its own account, the knowledge it mediated from worlds long rendered to dust, had already revealed aspects of the human condition unimagined by church and science. It relates a science defunct in the annals of science before those annals themselves had yet been composed.

"But what does this text comprise? By its own account, it contains a complete history and outline of the science of necromancy, as of about 1475, the best guess as to when the book was written. Necromancy is the science of raising the dead—if such can be called a science. On some accounts, the investigation into these techniques goes all the way back to Sumeria and the dawn of civilization. The *Compendium* records Sumerian rituals—though it records these erroneously as *Babylonian*—in its first few chapters. Clearly, in spite of the Babylonian reference, the deities invoked in the early rituals hailed from a Sumerian city far earlier than Babylon. Perhaps the city of Ur itself. That first great city to sit at the head of imperial ambition. The Medieval European who compiled the *Compendium* knew nothing about Ur, so he filled in the blank of his knowledge of the ancient world before Greece, Rome, and Egypt with the Mesopotamian city most familiar from the Bible: Babylon.

"Have you ever wondered why the Ancient Egyptians mummified the dead Pharaohs? Undoubtedly, they had religious views of the after life, as all ancient peoples did. But what the Egyptologists fail to tell you is that early on they had expectations of raising the dead *bodily*. Not mere souls flung to heaven, but bodies of the dead reanimated to commerce with the living. One account, long lost now, alleges they succeeded by using the formulas of the ancient Mesopotamians. The results though, were so horrific that the priests of the Pharaoh chose to preserve the remains of the dead, until such time as they could perfect the process of reanimation.

"Egyptologists claim that attendants of the dead Pharaoh were entombed with him, alive, to serve him in the after life. In fact, according to lost sources, but alluded to in the *Compendium*, they were used in the attempt to bring the Pharaoh back physically; their blood drained to provide the elixir of life. Only when the priests failed, or could not bare the sight of their deed, was the attempt abandoned, and the bodies finally entombed. The complex of the great pyramids was essentially a research center for raising the dead. Did you know that the Egyptian priests mummified tens of thousands of dead cats? Why do you think they did that? These were experiments in raising the dead, preserved for future research. The Egyptians established beyond doubt that animal fluid could not be used to raise the dead, and that only the sentience of humans could be raised. This the Egyptians discovered.

"The *Compendium* claims that, perhaps by lucky accident, the earliest Egyptians succeeded in one case of reanimating a dead Pharaoh. This occurred in the time of the Old Kingdom. Remember that, though the Old Kingdom was furthest back in time, it was the most advanced and knowledgeable of all the ancient Egyptian civilizations. The great pyramids were built in the Old Kingdom. Theirs was the knowledge that made subsequent periods great. Do not discount ancient wisdom. According to the *Compendium*, even before the pyramids, there arose an ancient priest named Hylif the Anointing One. Hylif, working with the formulas of Babylon (actually Ur, as I said), reanimated the dead Pharaoh Thatkutmos the IV. Thatkutmos reigned seventeen years before death and one hundred and four years after. Decaying flesh sat upon the throne of Egypt, each fortnight re-enlivened by the wizardry of the head priest. Thatkutmos the Dead, as one hieroglyph refers to him (though some scholars dispute this reading), laughed at the pains of the living and made a desert of death out of the Nile Valley. He might have reigned forever had not members of the lower priesthood set fire to his palace while the head priest performed the rites of renewal.

"For more than a century, the Egyptians vilified the practices of necromancy that had achieved so great an advance under the priestly hands of Hylif. The old books were hidden or burned and those knowing the secrets of reanimation hounded from the land or stoned to death. But how long could time pass before some old Pharaoh looked out upon the green washed lands of the river delta and bemoaned the passing of all flesh? It was then that the Egyptians began again the search for the recently lost knowledge. The pyramids, and the complex around them, grew up as research centers trying to recapture the knowledge that had been lost. Some say that the head priests knew the secrets all along but refused to raise again another death-flesh tyrant. Or perhaps the earlier success had been more luck than skill. Whatever the case, never again did the Egyptians succeed in reanimating the Pharaoh. Though every mummified Pharaoh's body absorbed their exotic elixirs of undeath.

"What of the Hebrews? From Biblical accounts, we know that at one time the Hebrews were prophets and interpreters of dreams for the Pharaohs. Could they have gained knowledge of life and death in this capacity? Eventually, we know, they fell to the status of slaves. Yet Moses, perhaps a dimly remembered historical figure, freed them from bondage. How did he do this? By death magic. Plagues so selective they could discern birth order. Perhaps these are only ancient stories. Or perhaps not.

"What secrets did the Arc of the Covenant contain? Merely the Ten Commandments written in God's own handwriting? Or did the Hebrews steal out from Egypt with the secrets of the priests of Pharaoh? Secrets of an ancient science. How did the small band of Hebrews conquer the whole land of Canaan? Could they regenerate their number by means of ancient rites? Was the golden calf really a conductor of electricity that melted from overheating? Was the Arc of the Covenant itself really a tub for the fluid of reanimation? History records none of these things—but how much has history forgotten? More than it ever knew.

"Did Plato discover some hint of the secret of return from the dead, alluding to it in his allegory of the cave? Is the illusion of the cave actually the veil that separates life from death? The *Compendium* does not say. Did Alexander march armies over the whole of the ancient world, even so far as India, in order to retrieve the ancient works of necromancy? No record of this purpose remains. Did Caesar conquer Ancient Egypt in order to secure the secrets of return from the final lands? No source tells us so. But surely it is not too great a leap to think that such a quest might animate the blood of great men such as these. The history of necromancy may well be the history of the world.

"The *Compendium* does affirm that Jesus held the arts of necromancy as his own. Indeed, according to this dark book, the disciples were but fellow scientists in the arts of reanimation. Lazarus, raised from the dead (not by a shout, but a chemical brew), represented the first great necromantic success in centuries. The Romans, dreading the occult power of the Hebrews, crucified Jesus for his scientific knowledge. But his followers reanimated him. Alas, they had not perfected the method of perpetuating the reanimation infinitely. The rest is history.

"The greatest of the necromancers, and the penultimate author of the *Compendium*, was the Arab philosopher, alchemist, and scholar Salim Abu El Saluma. Saluma, by his own account, wasted years of his life in the service of the Caliph of Cairo, attempting to turn base metals into gold. Each day he worked in his laboratory mixing chemicals and slowly poisoning himself with mercury. Never once did an ounce of lead turn to gold; though, interestingly, he does report that half an ounce of copper transmuted into silver leaf for almost a minute, before reverting back to copper again. Nevertheless, Saluma could boast no victory over metals. The Caliph ridiculed him in public and cut his funding—a perfidious act of treachery, requiring Saluma to suspend most of his alchemical researches.

"It was while picking through the refuse of the library of Alexander, then deposited in Cairo, that Salim Abu El Saluma first discovered ancient texts, long forgotten and half-burned up, that hinted at the powers of necromancy. He gave them little heed at the time. He needed gold and the philosopher's stone, not ancient rites of infidel priests. While searching the ruined texts from Alexandria, he encountered a woman. Her name was Sophia, and she was a Greek, with long, raven-black hair and alabaster skin. Saluma had never before beheld such a woman. Like so many scholars, he had channeled his sexual power into arcane research and had tasted only infrequently from the spring of libidinal delight. Sophia must have detected his inner strength, and his need, for they soon became lovers. Saluma relates that she was an enchantress and could bring forth his essence of new life with the barest touch. They became the closest of lovers. He taught her alchemy, she taught him patience.

"Then one day, a plague descended upon Egypt. Not frogs nor flies, but bloating stomachs and copious diarrhea. The plague spared Saluma, but the life flowed out of his love, the fair Sophia. He prayed to Allah that He restore his love to him. Allah did not answer. So Saluma preserved the body of his love, Sophia, in the manner of the ancient priests. He found the scraps of paper from the ancient library on the raising of the dead. He began his lifelong search to complete this knowledge. He traveled to Jerusalem. He met with ancient Hebrews who held, still, a part of the puzzle. He traveled to Mesopotamia and found bits and pieces there as well. At the Indus river, he met holy men who practiced self-mummification, and they gave to him, rather slowly on account of their condition, parchments from Tibet, where renegade Buddhists Monks defied the logic of reincarnation and pressed forward the knowledge of reanimation.

"Returning to Egypt, he assimilated this vast knowledge and began his experiments. He received funding from a secret society of sinful Christians, eager to delay their date with eternity. His experiments added greatly to the now vast repository of knowledge on the reanimation of the dead. He tried new fluids and new means of injection. He discovered, as the ancient Egyptians had, that the living must be sacrificed to raise the dead. But this was not his greatest legacy. He discovered something much more profound and much more horrific.

"In the waning days of his life, having spent himself utterly on the search for immortality, Saluma realized that he must make good his efforts soon, or he would lose forever both his dead lover and his own life. Age had stolen away his health as he studied away his days. He had to attempt the ultimate reanimation without delay. In the crypt of his lover, long festooned with the instruments of his science, Saluma began the reanimation of Sophia.

"The *Compendium* records precisely the result. From the screams of the victim, as the essence of life drained away, to the first flicker of animation in Sophia. Saluma thrilled as the once dead body of his lover twitched again. When her eyes opened again to the dim light of the crypt, Saluma leaped for joy. But, oh my listener, this was not life returned. For on that day, Saluma discovered what had always stayed hidden before: necromancy does not bring life to the dead, but undeath only. The once fair Sophia rose up with death-yellow eyes and corpse-leather skin. She had no luster of life, no loving touch, no colors bubbled in her mind, nor did desire and will guide her limbs. She was a dead thing, brought back to movement. And this she could ever only be.

"Saluma burned her crypt as a funeral pyre to love and life. At first, he thought to burn the documents of necromancy with her. He decided, instead, to record his life's work as a warning to others who might tread his dread path. He gathered together all he knew of the dark art and of its history. This he wrote and copied. The text eventually passed to Medieval Europe, along with the zero and the works of Aristotle. The mathematicians took the zero, the theologians Aristotle, and the alchemist the works of Salim Abu El Saluma. The European alchemist added bits and pieces to the Arab's work and compiled it all under the cover of the tome we now know as the *Compendium of Necromantic Sciences*.

"The church frowned on the book, banning it largely for trivial reasons: it affirmed divine powers to man, claimed Jesus had been a ghoul maker, and gave instructions for the creation of zombies. It was an era of religious zealotry. A few favored copies of the book survived the fires, but the science of necromancy did not live to see the flowering of the Renaissance.

"Today, no scientist seeks knowledge of life and death from the wisdom of the ancients. Biologists do not list *undeath* as a further option to *life*, *non-life*, and *death*. Are we wiser for this? I let you be the judge."

With that the professor sat down, quite satisfied with himself. Nick hoped that Yolanda wouldn't blame him for all of this.

◆ ◆ ◆

They had questioned the professor for two hours after the lecture's end. Now they rode back to the heart of the Strip in silence. Night had descended. The streets glowed in neon light.

"Once was a time when you could count on a cheap meal in this town," Nick said. "A sort of consolation prize for the loser and a come-on to the fellow just blowing into town. Now that Vegas is all resort hotels and fun for the kids you pay through the nose when you eat."

Yolanda said nothing. Either she was lost in thought or just didn't want to talk.

Nick carried on, "They have to ship all the food through the desert. Nothing actually grows in Vegas itself. You can water sand all you want—nothing but cactus grows at all."

Yolanda sat reading her notes from the interview.

"I'm hungry," Nick said.

"So let's eat," Yolanda said.

Nick pulled into Lazy Jake's Casino Restaurant. Nick and Yolanda got out of the car and entered Lazy Jakes. A woman sat them at a table and another sat down with them and started dealing cards.

"What is she doing?" Yolanda asked Nick.

"Dealing," Nick said looking at his cards.

"I'm going back to the hotel," Yolanda said.

"Fine, fine," Nick said to her, then to the dealer: "We're just

226

going to eat for now, I'll have a house salad and water with a twist of lemon."

"Steak dinner, medium rare, and a beer," Yolanda said.

"Two of those," Nick said, "hold the salad."

The dealer departed.

"You have a strange appetite," Yolanda said.

"Just thinking of you," Nick said. "Some women feel uncomfortable eating a salad when their date orders a steak. I worried you were one of those that always watches her figure."

"You watch it enough for both of us. And this is not a date."

Nick filled in a Keno card while Yolanda inspected her notes. "Anything useful come out of all that?" he asked.

"Dantelani claims that the *Compendium* instructs users to drain blood from living victims. That fits the facts of the Vampire Killer case."

Nick ate a nut from the bowl on the table. "Yeah, drain the bodies to reanimate the dead. Very likely that."

"The task force suspects a cult—a whole group of people, not just one person. That was for your ears only."

"No, I won't tell the other members you're on to us. Cult or one person, what does it matter? Do you really think they take that stuff seriously?"

"If it's a cult, maybe they worship necromancy, or the undead, or something. They kill people, draining their blood as part of the rituals."

The waitress brought their beers. Yolanda took a sip, Nick asked for cards and ate a peanut.

"No way on the cult aspect," Nick said. "The author of the *Compendium* wrote entirely in Latin. Weirdo Satan cults are strictly Lovecraft and Alistair Crowley readers. Latin takes too much work. If you get your thrills killing people, and pretending you get great powers from their blood, you are not going to tie up your evenings learning the verb declensions of a dead tongue."

The Lovecraft comment startled Yolanda, but she held her own tongue on that. "I'm not saying they read the actual

Compendium. They might have a popular translation and just took the original *Compendium* as some sort of totem item."

The waitress returned with cards and more peanuts. "The professor insisted that no one had ever made any translation of the book." Nick started his house of cards. "He told us that almost no one even knew about it."

Yolanda reread her notes. "Did you get the feeling he was trying to hide something?"

"I think he never quite believed we weren't with administration. I really think we should have audited him. Put him through his paces. He would've appreciated that after all those years of worry."

"You can go run your practical jokes after you drop me off at the hotel," Yolanda said.

"A man keeps records and nobody ever looks at them, it's all wasted time. But if they save your bacon someday, you turn out a savvy man after all. As for me, I only hustle the wicked, and my practical jokes always benefit the victim in the long run," Nick said. "As for going back to the hotel, I thought we might do the town. No gambling, but maybe a show? I have high friends in places. I can score tickets to any show in town."

"That would be a date, and this is an investigation."

The steaks arrived. They ate in silence. Yolanda found hers tough.

Nick pulled into the valet parking of the Rainforest at around ten o'clock. He walked back to the rooms with Yolanda. At her door, she waited for him to unlock his.

"A nightcap?" Nick said.

"No thanks," Yolanda said.

Nick hesitated in the hallway. "Why do you think they call it a nightcap anyway? It's not like you put it on your head. Maybe it's just supposed to go to your head. Or maybe it just caps the evening. Whatever that could mean."

"You don't have to go to your room," Yolanda said.

"Really!"

"You can go play in the casino."

"Oh. Actually, I thought I might just tuck you in. Figuratively speaking."

"No thanks."

"We could just discuss the case some more. I've had a number of interesting thoughts about Dantelani's story. I think we should talk about it."

Yolanda nodded. "Do tell."

Nick hesitated. "Well, I hadn't so much had the thoughts as planned on having them. In the course of our conversation."

Yolanda shook her head. Nick waited. Yolanda waited. Finally Nick said, "Look, I know you're not ready to say goodnight to me, or you'd have gone into your room by now."

"It takes two hands to open this door, and I always leave one hand free to go for my gun," Yolanda said without trace of humor.

Nick's face took a hard glint. "You're tough, cookie. I bet you'd have made daddy proud."

Nick turned, opened his door and entered his room. Yolanda then entered hers. Inside her room she turned on the lights. She locked the door and checked the lock on the adjoining door. She took off her clothes and started the water in the shower. She heard Nick's door close. She took a long hot shower and put on the zebra stripped robe provided by the hotel. She sat in her bed and studied her notes. After some time she realized that she had just been staring through them. She could not remember what she had been thinking about. She curled up in a ball on the bed and felt like crying.

Next door, Nick prowled around his room. He had gone out and gotten ice, a Seven-up, two Snickers bars and a paper. He shoved the Snickers bars into the ice to chill them and threw the paper away. He heard the shower running next door. He paced the room. He calculated to the second how long it would take to reach the casino. He rehearsed the phone numbers of

Vegas friends in his head. He heard the shower turn off next door. He turned his own shower on and stuck his head in it. He turned on the television. He turned on the television! He had never before done that in a Vegas hotel room. In fact, he recalled, he had never spent this much time awake in a hotel room in his life. He turned off the television. He looked at the sliding door connecting his room with the Wicked Witch of the West. He sat on the corner of the bed, staring at the handle.

Nick Sabernail sat on that corner of that bed staring at the doorknob to Yolanda's room until his eyes blurred. Shaking his head he said, "Enough is enough." He stood up and walked slowly to the door. He tried moving the handle.

"I'm holding my gun right now," said a voice on the other side of the door.

"Sweet Jesus, I just want to see you once more before you turn in," Nick said. He rested his head against the door.

"Go to sleep Nick," Yolanda said from the other side. Her voice sounded near and calm now, almost comforting. She must have been just on the other side of the door. "We can talk tomorrow."

"I shouldn't have said that about your dad. You open up to me, tell me something about yourself, and here I throw it at you just in spite. I'm sorry about that. I would just like to apologize face to face."

"It doesn't matter," Yolanda said.

"You didn't see your face when I said it," Nick said. "It looked like it mattered then."

Yolanda almost opened the door. But she didn't. And not because she feared murder at Nick Sabernail's hands. She turned her back on the door and slid slowly to the floor.

"You should go gamble, Nick, have a good time," Yolanda said.

Nick could hear her clearly through the thin connecting door. Nick agreed with her that he should go gambling. He felt the call of the cards and the dice. He had come to Vegas intending to gamble. Nick turned around and sat down on the floor with his back to the door. "Well, anyway, I am sorry."

Yolanda rubbed her eyes and let out an ironic laugh. "You didn't mean anything. You didn't know what to mean. I didn't tell you anything important about my dad. Nothing you could use to hurt me."

Nick took the deck of cards from the restaurant out of his pocket and began turning them over and flicking them across the room. "You looked like I had said something."

Yolanda toyed with the rope to her robe. "I told you my dad was one of the first Hispanic detectives on the force, and that he died on my thirteenth birthday." She paused, but could not stop the rest from coming out, "I didn't tell you that he was the first Hispanic detective brought up on charges of corruption and brutality. That he killed himself just before the D.A. would have made formal charges. Killed himself upstairs. While I blew out the candles on my cake."

"Sweet Jesus," Nick said.

"No one heard anything. Mother found him a little later. He didn't leave a note." Yolanda began to cry. "He told me about the charges just a week before. He told me he was innocent. He made me promise to believe him. He told me he would fight the accusations. He told me to be strong. I swore I believed him, and I would stand by him. I still believe him."

Nick felt the pit of his own stomach. He dropped the cards on the floor. He looked up at the door handle.

Yolanda wiped her eyes with the sleeve of the robe. "I've always meant to prove his innocence someday. Now, I'm a detective. But I haven't tried to. Does that mean I don't really want to know? Does it mean I don't really believe him after all?"

"You can't betray him by what you believe or don't believe. No one can help what they believe."

Yolanda swallowed hard. "My sister, she was only six. You'd think it would have affected her more. But she lives like a butterfly. I feel like I move in molasses. I feel so deep. Does a person only have depth because something weighs her down?"

Nick's eyes stung. Yolanda was quiet for some time. She sounded spent. Nick turned around and spoke at the door, "Yolanda, I want to hold you."

Yolanda instantly reached for the door handle. She had both hands on it. Then she drew back in panic. She squeezed the robe around her tighter. "No," she said.

Nick stood up. He noticed a water stain on the door where his head had rested against it.

Yolanda said, "I think you had better drive back tomorrow without me. I'll take a plane. I'll call you. Goodnight Nick."

Nick said, "Goodnight Yolanda." He went to his bed and lay down. Very quietly, to himself, he said, "You're tough, Yolanda. I'm tougher."

Nick slept.

PLUMBING THE DEPTHS

"Describe to us please, the feeling of being the first man to stand at the top of the planet." Drakan read the question from his three by five card.

"Aaa, goofba, dunk," replied Admiral Peary the Zombie.

Drakan leaned forward and whispered to him: "concentrate … talk … like … normal." Drakan leaned back and gave his latest creation a fatherly smile.

"Tauk … lick … noormel …" the Admiral said.

"No, no," said Drakan, smiling at the camera, "I want you to answer the question: What did it feel like to be the first man at the North Pole?"

The zombie leaned forward with an earnest, bug-eyed look. He said, "Heneeson tooooo."

Drakan stared at him for a moment, then perked up and said for the camera, "I think the good Admiral refers here to his long time associate and co-discoverer of the North Pole, the Ethiopian Matthew Henson."

Behind the camera Vinnie cringed at the word *Ethiopian*. Why did the Baron insist on calling blacks Ethiopians? Vinnie's friends called them Nigerians, which sounded better. Or worse. Or at least more likely to bring on a fight. Vinnie looked through the camera viewfinder again. Woe betide him if he missed any of the "action."

"Yes, how did you feel when you and," Drakan looked at the camera, "Henson," he looked back at the Admiral, "stood together at the Pole?"

The Admiral lurched forward at the camera, still sitting in his interview chair across from Drakan. "Pole … good … sit … on … Henseen. Henssseeen … Pole … sit … I."

Drakan looked on at the Admiral, a bit unsure how to take that answer. Death plays hell with grammar.

Drakan said, "Well, there's an exciting revelation. Admiral Peary sat on Henson at the Pole. Landed that way jumping for joy no doubt. Next question: What are your thoughts now, so many years after the event, of Cook's claims to have pre-empted you at the North Pole?"

Drakan looked nervously on as the zombie collected whatever he had in place of thoughts. After much concentrated effort, Peary said: "Wat … r … you … r … thaats … no … eaty … yars … ferter … thhh … vent … cook … cook … clam … cook—"

Drakan broke in, "No, sorry, it was a question. You answer it. The question: What … do … you … think … now … about … Cook's … claims?"

Vinnie wondered if people would be able to tell the living from the dead on this show.

Admiral Peary looked hard at Drakan, then the camera. Then he began a vigorous nodding of his head. He said: "Cook … clams … Eskimo … clam … cook."

Drakan jerked his head back and forth as if looking for some prompt.

Vinnie could not imagine from whom the Baron might be prompted; apart from Vinnie, only zombies occupied the studio.

Drakan said, "Well, well, an interesting bit of travelogue. Eskimo clambake. Imagine. Of course, I was asking about Dr. Frederick Cook's famous claim to have beaten the Admiral to the Pole. I'm sure we will return to the episode later. For now, let me ask you this. Admiral. Admiral?" Peary stared off at a space far to the left of Drakan and the camera. "Admiral. Look this way." The Admiral turned around, gap-mouthed

234

and bug-eyed, like all the zombies (always excepting Sparrow). "Admiral, one more question. I'm sure our viewers want to know: How do you feel, Admiral, right now, about your life, your accomplishments, right now, how do you feel?"

Vinnie knew that nothing would come of this question. The Baron had managed to hit on the one point on which even Vinnie knew no zombie could produce an opinion. Admiral Peary jerked his head about randomly as if looking for help from other zombies. Finally, he said: "Ad … mir … all … one … mir … quot—"

"No," Drakan interrupted him, "it's a question: how do you feel right now?"

Peary jerked his head about looking for help again. Then he coughed up a handful of bright green goop with a ghastly "Cooophaaauut." Drakan frantically waved for Vinnie to fade the camera out.

"Make up!" Drakan yelled. Chris the Zombie strode forward sending lights crashing to earth as he came. "Slowly! Make up. Slowly. Lieutenant Vinnie! Stay on camera. We're going to try the last part of the interview over. I'll give the Admiral some lines for the last question."

Vinnie stood by the camera. The Baron had made him an officer upon his return from Arlington. Vinnie felt he had deserved it.

◆ ◆ ◆

The ride to Virginia had been uneventful. Except that it turned out that the undead get fidgety when required to spend hours in a hearse. Chris the Zombie took to repetitively kicking the head of Norm the Zombie to the time of whatever music Vinnie played. Norm voiced no complaint (zombies never do) and finally Chris broke his neck. This did nothing to help Norm's appearance, but did not impede his functioning much. Sparrow sat up front with Vinnie, a perfect gentleman, until somewhere in the middle of Arizona the radio picked up an oldies station. Sparrow kept moving the dial back to that station. Vinnie would tune in something else, and as soon as he did, Sparrow tuned it into the old folks music. Vinnie told him to leave the radio alone, but Sparrow tuned it back just the same. Vinnie decided to lick him with sheer determination. But zombies are absolute masters of repetitive action. Sparrow showed not the slightest sign of frustration at having to constantly turn back the dial. Vinnie chewed the steering wheel for five hours. The worst of it: even after the station faded away Sparrow would continue to put the dial right back on the frequency from which they had received the oldies music. Vinnie had to listen to static for two days until a country and western station came in on the dial at 98.2. By then he had cotton in his ears.

Vinnie couldn't drive all the way to Virginia without sleep. The Baron had warned him against letting the undead behind the wheel. But on a long stretch of New Mexico Highway, Vinnie had put Charley Sparrow at the controls. He did fine. Vinnie went to sleep. He woke up going a hundred and eighty miles an hour on the wrong side of the highway. Nearly paralyzed with fear, he coaxed Sparrow off the road and took over.

The upshot of that event was that Vinnie had to sleep. A hearse filled with not exactly dead bodies pulled over on the side of the road did not strike Vinnie as quite inconspicuous enough. He opted for the Galloway Travel Out Inn motel instead.

"What do you want?" asked the desk clerk.

Good question. Vinnie figured he couldn't leave the zombies in the car. "A double, two beds," he said.

"How many will be sleeping in the room?" asked the clerk.

Good question. A better question: How many whats? "Four, just four of us." Vinnie figured he had better play things straight as much as he could. Less suspicious that way.

Outside, key in hand, he directed the dead to room 201.

Norm's head now permanently cocked at a complete right angle to his body, which meant he had to take a step around for each step forward. Vinnie noted that he still made better time than Chris the Zombie who kept wanting to walk toward the road every time he saw car lights coming down it. Sparrow carried Vinnie's luggage and a bag full of equipment. Norm got stuck in a stairwell while Vinnie pulled Chris out of the road for the third time. Vinnie noticed then that the desk clerk sat outside watching them.

"Them fellows stupid or something?" the clerk asked.

Vinnie thought fast, "They're just retards. I'm a counselor, like at a summer camp. I work with them." Vinnie thought that ought to hold him.

"Ain't they kinda old for summer camp?"

Vinnie set Chris on the path to righteousness and addressed the clerk again. "Uh, it's a camp for old retards. We clean them off, give them crafts and stuff. To do, you know. They love it. I love it. I love working with retards." Vinnie felt every bit nature's own liar. Some men just have the gift.

"How come you're taking them into a motel room?"

Shit. Where do these people come from? "It's … it's … it's to teach them how to act in civilization. So they can be mainlined. We believe in mainlining … at the camp."

"You're going to do some sex to them, aren't you?"

Obviously, this guy had not taken a very good look. Vinnie shook his head.

"I don't mind you doing sex to the retards," the clerk continued, "but you got to pay more for that."

Vinnie ponied up fifty dollars more and went to help Norm up the stairs.

In the room, Vinnie found that bunking with the undead deserved a very low ranking on his list of favorite things to do. Chris kept getting up to turn the television on and off while Norm spun in place by the bathroom mirror trying to see himself.

Unable to sleep, Vinnie decided to get one unpleasant

chore out of the way early. The Baron had given him careful instruction in how to apply the reanimation booster shots. He insisted they be done every two days to insure no breakdown in function on the "stressful" trip. The booster shot had to be given enema style, straight up the anal canal. Nothing in Vinnie's experience had prepared him for the necessity of asking a seventy-year old dead man to drop his trousers and bend over. The needle itself was so long it pierced well into the body cavity. If it did not go in that far, you received a green goo spray in your face. Vinnie hated this job. After doing all three zombies, he sat back at the foot of the bed. Then he noticed the face of the clerk looking in from outside the window. The fellow just shook his head and walked away.

By the time Vinnie and his crew got to Arlington, Charley Sparrow had more or less mastered the art of driving a hearse. Vinnie figured the Baron would just burst with pride at this when they got back to headquarters. It only took constant vigilance for the first seventy-two hours.

Arlington itself proved something more of a challenge. The Baron had given Vinnie a shopping list, but navigating the sea of stones took more out of Vinnie than butt-boosting the undead. Apart from anything else, the Baron wanted specific individuals, and naturally, not one rested in peace anywhere near any other. Back home in L.A., they could have run multiple crews. Here, Vinnie ran the show shorthanded in order to save space in the hearse for the new bodies. Worst of all, the place positively swarmed with military types. Vinnie had too much experience with zombie marksmanship to hazard a conflict.

Did the Baron appreciate all these troubles upon Vinnie's return? Not a bit of it. He complained about the condition of the bodies, and Norm's twisted head, and the wasteful use of reanimation goop. Only when Vinnie told of Mr. Sparrow's new skills did he get any warmth. The Baron had raised him to lieutenant for that. Vinnie didn't know what that meant pay-wise, but just after his promotion the Baron made Sparrow a

Sergeant. Vinnie hoped that would make the big ghoul listen to him better.

What did all this blazing about come to at the end? A cable access show. The Baron had set up a mini TV studio, complete with cameras, lights, boom mics, and undead technicians gapping at it all. After re-animating Vinnie's collection of corpses, the Baron had set right off video taping interviews. He had even set up airtime with the public access office of the local cable network. He called his show: *Fascinating Facts of the Fabulous and Famous*. Vinnie thought the Baron had some strange notions about who was famous and what was fascinating.

◆ ◆ ◆

"Our guest today is mystery writer Dashiell Hammett, author of *The Maltese Falcon* and *The Thin Man*. Mr. Hammett visits us from Arlington, Virginia." Drakan stared at the camera with a fixed expression. "Now let us turn to the author. Hello Mr. Hammett."

Dashiell Hammett the Zombie sat erect and alert in his chair. "Hello … Master."

Drakan beamed at his latest creation. Hammett was far more articulate than Admiral Peary the Zombie. But then, he was a writer. "Now Mr. Hammett, tell us please, just what did happen to the Maltese Falcon?"

Dashiell Hammett the Zombie replied in a low, slow drone, "Drink … I need a drink."

Drakan folded his hands over his cards and turned nervously toward the camera. "Alluding, no doubt, to your lifetime struggle with alcohol." He leaned in toward his undead interviewee and said, "You can't drink anything, you'll leak. Now, answer the Falcon question."

Hammett the Zombie jerked his head to the camera, "Sam Spade ate the falcon … he ate it while the woman held her underwear for the Fat Man."

Drakan mused over this answer a moment. "I see."

Hammett continued, "Gutman was not the queer. Cairo is a city in Amsterdam. I have a wicked penis."

Drakan could not tell if these were personal revelations, literary insights, or just sick zombie talk. The undead could sometimes entertain pretty strange ideas. "Perhaps you'd rather talk of *The Thin Man*. Tell me, Mr. Hammett, did Lillian Hellman inspire the character of Nora Charles?"

"The Continental Op was not a fatty boy. His real name was Wilber Mench. He ate prunes and played with his pistol. He forgot his name and had to call himself the Continental Op." Hammett the Zombie lurched in his chair at Drakan and intoned: "All ... the colors ... are gone!"

Drakan stared uncomprehending at this minion. Then he turned to the camera, "The Continental Op, as I'm sure our viewers all know, was the designation of Mr. Hammett's first fictional hero."

Vinnie had not the first idea what other viewers of this mess might know, but he knew what he knew: This stuff would not make for fun TV. Who were these people? Hammett the Zombie talked better than any zombie he had ever met (and by now he had met a few), but who knew him from Adam? If you are going to dig up a famous person, dig up a famous person people know. That's what Vinnie always said.

Drakan wrapped up his interview and called "cut." Instantly the makeup zombie came over to touch up Drakan.

Vinnie walked over to his boss. "Great show, Baron, great show. You really penetrated him that time. Got in deep."

"Yes, I did rather land well there," said the excited Zombie Master. "Still, we have to plumb more; plumb the depths. Get inside the real man."

Vinnie knew for a fact that inside the real man lay mostly glowing green goo. "What's the plan with all this, sir? We've cut a bunch of these videos now."

Drakan inspected his daily schedule. Mostly it involved rigorous zombie training. He had lately found that careful training, and the proper reanimation formula, could make zombies almost completely independent in their actions. They did best when doing whatever they had done in life. Drakan had partly solved the problem of determining these occupations by checking the obituary pages and digging up the newly dead. They did not always make such good ghouls as the long buried, but you got a good selection of occupations and knew what you were getting. It also helped if one painted signs for them to follow in the invisible ink perceivable only by the undead and those taking the intoxicant.

With such hints scattered about, the best functioning of the undead could run along smoothly on tracks Drakan laid and carry on not too differently than in life. Minus feelings, sensations, and a will of their own. As a consequence, Drakan had set up two adjunct zombie factories on the grounds of two small local cemeteries. These could effectively work twenty-four hours a day. *Starting a Business For Unlimited Growth* assured him that, "unlimited growth requires constant expansion." So Drakan expanded his enterprise.

"I only ask 'cause we cut so many videos, and I wondered what for?" Vinnie said again.

"I told you, we broadcast on cable access," Drakan said.

"I know sir, a great plan, real big-time stuff. Thing is, what do we make the money on. I know you have it worked out. I just wondered where we get the payoff. They don't pay for a cable access show."

Drakan could not concentrate with all this distraction. "We build an audience. We sell advertising, or sell the show to a network. We build an audience. All things come from a strong client base. Page one hundred and thirteen. We have unlimited growth potential with a strong client based audience."

"Right, it's just," Vinnie followed the Baron around to the ghoul training grounds, "it's just, I don't know that we have the most popular celebrities for getting all those folks to watch. I don't know that this is the right bunch for that."

"Dashiell Hammett! Admiral Peary! Are you aware that

Admiral Peary discovered the North Pole?"

"Yeah, now I am, but awhile ago ... right?"

Drakan fumed. "Did you know that his mother dressed him as a girl until he was almost a teenager? Don't you think people might be just a little curious at how that made him the man he became? Don't you think people want to know what makes a man great?"

"Yeah, sure, of course. But maybe about people they know. You know?"

Drakan watched several zombies jumping rope while another tried using a hula-hoop. He noticed that Vinnie had put that odd music on the record player again; the theme from "Rocky." Drakan didn't know the movie, nor why Vinnie felt so strongly about it. The zombies didn't seem to care one way or another. Drakan guessed they did better with it than his training music; the Ride of the Valkyries. "I suppose I may not have the pulse of the hoi polloi."

"Uh?"

Drakan elaborated: "I know my taste is more elevated than the ordinary run of mortals. How could I be here now if it were not? I hoped to be a tastemaker rather than a fashion follower. But I suppose you are right. First we must win an audience. We will condescend to entertain the masses."

Vinnie could not be sure he had won the day.

"Come Lieutenant Vinnie the Warthog, I must make a list of bodies for you to retrieve."

Now Vinnie could be sure. He had opened his mouth once too often again.

THE FLY IN AMBER

Upon returning to Los Angeles, by air, alone, Yolanda Vasquez had signed in at her station to prove she still lived, and promptly took a week of vacation time. The next day, the first of her vacation, she woke and dressed. Her initial thought had been to call Nick Sabernail and try to work things out with him. She did not quite know what *things* they had to work out, but she thought she should do it. First, though, she made a quick trip to her bank. Before going home to call him, she stopped at the gym for a brief workout. Three hours later, after taking a shower and dressing again in her street clothes, she headed for home. She stopped off for lunch at a bistro in Hollywood and dropped in on her sister, who was out of town shooting a film—according to the note proudly posted on her apartment door. Yolanda tore down the note and headed for home. Halfway there, she stopped and did some shopping at a mall. She bought nothing, but did spend several hours looking. Then she headed for home to call Nick. Before getting to her apartment, she thought she should feel hungry again and stopped at a restaurant for dinner. She ordered a chicken salad and a slice of blueberry pie. She ate the pie. She read a late edition of the *Times* to catch up on the news. She read it front to back. She left the restaurant and headed for home. On her way up to her apartment, she dropped by Mrs. Rena Trumm's apartment for a chat. This startled Mrs. Trumm, as Detective Vasquez had only ever spoken to her once before. Upon seeing Yolanda through the eyehole, Mrs. Trumm panicked, thinking the police were about to report that her daughter had died in a car accident. After calming Mrs. Trumm, Yolanda went up to her apartment.

It was far too late to call Nick now.

◆ ◆ ◆

Nick Sabernail beat on the great stone statue. Flakes of stone splintered up, some as high as the ceiling. Nick stopped periodically to inspect the dents. Seeing an un-dented area on the prone stone man he smiled, picked up his meat-mallet again, and let fly. Chips of stone danced off the statue.

"Wear eye-cover for Christ sake," yelled Eddie Cinder.

Nick just closed his eyes and pounded harder.

◆ ◆ ◆

Yolanda spent Monday and Tuesday cleaning up her apartment, practicing at the gun-range, and catching up on her reading. She visited her mother and left several messages on her sister's answering machine. Answering machines leave no excuse against the accusation of ignoring calls, Yolanda thought.

By Wednesday, she had found her groove and had completely set out of her mind the idea of making any phone calls to murder suspects. She could not even imagine why she had thought to do so before.

On Thursday, she returned from her morning shooting practice to find this message on her answering machine:

"Hey Yolanda, Nick. Guess you lost my number. I'll save you the trouble of consulting the F.B.I.'s most wanted list. It's 523-7180. I'll be around this morning. Bye."

Yolanda gathered together her gym clothes and headed out the door. After a grueling workout and a quick stop for lunch, lasting two hours, she returned to her apartment at around three in the afternoon. She saw the light on her answering machine flashing.

"Hey, Yolanda, Nick. I found out you're on vacation. Guess I should get my junior detective badge, uh? Look, I want to talk to you. I'm at a friend's studio. He's an artist, of sorts. I'm helping him with a sculpture, sort of. Anyway, the number's 674-8025. Call if you can. I want to see you. We can meet on neutral territory or whatever. Bye."

Yolanda left for the grocery store. Three hours later she hauled up sixteen bags of groceries in four trips. To her consternation, she found her refrigerator and cupboards already full. What possessed her to think she needed more food? She stuffed canned asparagus and fruit cocktail under her sink, and forced the canned whipped cream in sideways atop the Tupperware refuse from earlier meals. After finally gaining a home for each and every last item she had bought, she glanced at the answering machine. It blinked with a message.

"Hey, Nick, I'm back at my place. Give a call. Bye."

Yolanda felt she should be hungry. Nothing in the apartment looked good to her, so she went out to eat. She drove for a while, finally finding a little Italian place in a strip mall. She took her time with the meal and returned home. Three messages awaited her.

"Hey, Nick here. You wouldn't go on vacation without me, would you? Bye."

"It's Nick. I'm just guessing here, but maybe you don't want to talk to me. That seems puzzling in light of everything. I won't bother you anymore. Bye."

"It's Nick. This means war."

Yolanda wondered what war with Nick Sabernail could be like. She went to bed.

◆ ◆ ◆

The next morning she heard the phone ring. She closed her eyes and waited to drift back to sleep. She heard the answering machine picking up the call. You could hear the incoming message anywhere in the small apartment. The machine paused as the recorder clicked on. Then ... music. A blues tune sung by a familiar voice:

"I got the call-screening blues,
I don't know what to do,
To get through to you,
I'm gonna sing to you,
Till my face turns blue,
—oh yeah, bring it on home now!—
I got the call-screening blues,
It's worse than having the flu,
I ought to cook up some stew,
Or maybe drink me a brew,
—Oh yeah—the call-screening blues, baby."

Yolanda caught herself smiling. She stayed in bed another hour, but could not get back to sleep. She got up and drew a bath. She entered the tub and let the hot water surrounding her body. She thought she might just stay there all day. Her phone rang. The machine picked up.

"A Poem, by Nicholas Sabernail

Shall I rhyme, to win the love of you?
Perhaps blank verse, or a little haiku?
If I recite a ditty,
would you show me your ... affections?
What form of verse will win your confections?
Can a man mark your diameters,
In iambic pentameters?

Can your walls be breached,
With prettified speech?
Give a sign,
Make a show,
Inquiring minds,
Want to know."

Yolanda got out of the tub and dried off. She caught herself in the mirror. The face seemed vaguely unfamiliar. It looked relaxed. Vacation must be suiting her. She took her time dressing and fixed breakfast. She did the dishes.

Yolanda sat down in the plush embrace of her favorite chair. She began a book on police technique (*Managing Suspect Discomfort in Legally Optional Conversational Contexts for Police Interrogators*; a classic). An hour later, the words finally finding a place in her thoughts, the doorbell rang. She hurried to the door. She stopped herself. She drew her gun from the drawer. She looked through the eyehole. She saw a bouquet of roses. She put on a determined face and opened the door.

The poor, big-nosed teenager in the brown uniform nearly dropped the arrangement when he saw the .38. Yolanda apologized, but he fled while she looked for a tip, leaving the flowers behind. Yolanda took them to the kitchen counter. She found a card. It read: "Did you shoot him? Did you? N." The flowers came in their own vase, so she added a bit of water and put them in a cupboard behind her Tupperware.

Yolanda returned to reading.

At one o'clock she felt hungry. She made a ham and cheese sandwich, a salad, and heated up a spinach pastry she had bought the day before. As she finished her pastry the phone rang. She almost reached for it, but stopped herself. The machine answered it.

"Yolanda, it's your sister. The shooting was great! I had lines! I am so going to stay Tina Yamato! I can't wait to tell you all about it. Let's do lunch. Ciao!"

Yolanda thought that something in her sister's voice sounded disappointed. She replayed the tape, but could not put her finger on it. She returned to reading. After a bit, she put down the book and entered her kitchen. She retrieved the flowers from behind the Tupperware and put them on the table. Flowers needed light.

Later, Yolanda swept her back porch and vacuumed her floors. She heard the phone ring. She let the machine pick it up:

"You've won! That's right Yolanda Vasquez, you've won an all-expenses paid vacation in Puerto Vallarta! You didn't need to enter. You didn't need to call. You're a winner! First, you'll go para-sailing high above the exotic cliffs of Puente del Fuego. Then, it's off to the Canyons of Caldera on your very own moped! You'll luxuriate in your cabaña for two; you'll wile away the days on the beach while drinking mia tias and watching the waves roar in across the shimmering sea. Don't delay. Act now! Claim your prize from your personal trip coordinator and guide. Just call 523-7180. That's 523-7180. Call now! You won!"

Yolanda turned on the television. A reporter from *Action Power News* broadcast a remote report from a cemetery. From the pictures, Yolanda guessed that someone had dug up a number of gravesites. Either that, or *Action Power News* now reports on sprinkler installations. Yolanda did not turn up the sound. After an hour and a half of watching, but not listening to, the news, she heard a knock on her door. She got up and looked through the eyehole.

She saw a mariachi band.

You just don't see that everyday. Unarmed this time, Yolanda opened the door. The three men smiled and began playing the theme from *Evita*. The men sang:

"Please don't shoot us, Yolandaaa,
We come, to sing you, a love song,

It's not a long song,
I kept my promise,
Don't keep your distance,
I don't give up easy,
Don't keep your distance."

After thanking the band, Yolanda returned to her chair. She thought about calling Nick. Really, after all this trouble, he deserved a phone call. She would just tell him he was a nice fellow, but she wasn't interested. But a call might only encourage him. She would not call Nick Sabernail.

Yolanda turned up the sound and watched an old movie on cable. *The Hand of the Mummy*. Static camera, no film score. Still, not bad for the 1930s. Assuming you could be frightened by a slow moving fellow just off the burn ward. Yolanda put on a pajama top, ate a strawberry and headed for bed. She had endured a long day; quite a siege, really. But she would not call Nick Sabernail.

Her phone rang. The machine picked up. She heard the message while in her bed:

"It's Nick. In between sending flowers and hammering statues, I managed to do a bit of investigating on my own. I found a clue to your little Vampire Cult mystery. Not that it matters much to me. I'll be over at Eddie Cinder's all day tomorrow. He works at 3400 Sunset, Studio C. Just follow the sounds of hammering. I unplugged his phone, so you'll have to come in person. And alone please—no armored escort. By all means, bring your gun—just not your SWAT team."

Yolanda thought this a poorly baited trap. If this couldn't move her to even pick up the phone, how did he expect to move her all the way to Sunset Boulevard?

"Incidentally, does the address *1800 Pilot Way* mean anything to you? Bye."

Yolanda shot out of bed. The task force had suppressed that

address. Nick should not know anything about it. Yolanda raced to the phone and dialed 523-7180. The phone rang three times and then picked up. She got an answering machine:

"Hi. You've reached the home of Nick Sabernail. I'm not in right now. And Yolanda: you know what you must do. See you tomorrow."

Yolanda hung up the phone.

FLAWLESS FAILURE

She could hear the banging noises from the street. Someone positively laying into stone with a hammer. Her man, no doubt. Yolanda headed to the third floor to find *Studio C*. She had a gun, but no SWAT team. She had a radio. At the door to Studio C she knocked. This would clearly bring no one, so she pounded. This still could not overawe the sounds of hammering from within, so she stood outside the door and waited for a pause. She considered firing off a round, but that would require several hours of paperwork back at the office, so she just waited. After a bit, she noticed a lull in the hammering and hit the door again. A moment later it opened, revealing a skinny man in a goatee.

"Yes?" he said.

"Eddy Cinder?" Yolanda asked.

"You're the cop," Eddy said. "Yeah, I'm Eddy. But you can call me Formosa Van Dyke."

"Why would I do that?"

"I'd like it better."

Yolanda heard a voice behind Eddy. "Let her in Eddy. And don't give her any of that crap about being the Great Formosa."

Eddy moved from the door letting Yolanda pass. She took care that he never got behind her. Once inside she saw Nick, hammer in hand, standing atop the chest of a giant stone statue lying on the floor. The figure must have been twenty feet tall if stood upright. The statue didn't look like much; crudely carved and mis-proportioned. It had dents and chips all over, and Nick appeared to have been tasked with adding yet more.

"You left a message for me, Mr. Sabernail," she said.

"*Mister* Sabernail," he replied, "get that. I thought you'd finally learned my name."

Yolanda inspected the room. One large artist studio filled with stones and sculptor's tools. It had a small kitchenette at the back. "I came in response to your claim to have evidence in the Vampire Killer case, not in response to your mariachi band."

Nick hopped down off the statue, but kept the hammer in his hand. "You sound mad at me Yolanda. What did you say to me, through a door, in a hotel room, that now you're mad at me? Get caught without your flak jacket?"

Yolanda didn't like his tone. "If you haven't any evidence relevant to the case, I'll be off." She turned around, but his next words stopped her.

"Bullshit. That address means something or you would never have come here."

Yolanda turned around. "So, if as you say, you couldn't care less about the Vampire Killer case, why share any information with me?"

Nick threw the hammer at the statue; Yolanda nearly grabbed her gun. "Why do I bother with you at all? It's not like you encourage a man, what with coming armed to every date and only talking frankly with a wall around you."

"How many times do I have to tell you? We have had no dates. I don't care for you. I'm a detective, you're a suspect. Or a contact. That is all."

Eddy Cinder cleared his throat. "Maybe, uh, maybe I should go?"

To Yolanda, Nick said, "That's bullshit too. I mean more to you than just a suspect or a contact."

Yolanda stiffened; how could he know what she felt? "What makes you think that?"

"Because, if I were just a suspect or a contact to you, why tell me so? That's not how to string a mark along."

Eddy Cinder said, "I'll just get a bag together and let you two stay here."

Nick said, "Eddy, don't you have to go to the bathroom or something?"

"Yeah, right," Eddy said, "I'll be in the bathroom. You won't be long?"

"Not long," Nick said. He turned away from Yolanda as Eddy hurried off to the bathroom. Awkward silence reigned.

Yolanda walked around the statue. It had been polished to a fine glean before Nick's hammer had done it's work. She ran her hand along it feeling the rough divots in its smooth surface. She ran her hand all the way down the length of the statue's leg. Nick looked away from her.

"I'm sorry," Yolanda said, "The band was charming. A bit in fear for their life, perhaps, but charming. I put the flowers in water."

Nick looked at her at last. "Why didn't you call me?"

Yolanda removed her hand from the statue. "Why are you putting chips in this statue?"

Nick sighed. He had once played a poker game fourteen hours waiting for the right hand at the right time. Patience, Nick, patience. "It's a Cardiff Man."

"An average sized Cardiff Man?" Yolanda asked.

Nick recalled that he had lost that poker game. "Some huckster back in the 1860s buried the original Cardiff Man. He then dug it up to display it for money as a petrified mummy from a lost race. Eddy, that is, Mr. Formosa Van Dyke, got busted seven years ago pushing a similar scam. He made a fake statue and planted it at an archeological site. He excavated the dirt and placed the statue in it, properly aged and packed. Fooled everybody for about four weeks. Made the papers worldwide. Some art historian in upstate New York spoiled a fine career declaring it authentic. Seems he wrote an article rushed to press called: "The Epic Statuary of Ancient Man." Some scientist blew the lid off the whole thing. Eddy did sixteen months."

"You realize I have to report you to bunko for this," Yolanda said.

Nick walked over to a table and picked up a piece of paper. He handed it to Yolanda. "Sorry to disappoint you, officer, this one's legit."

Yolanda read the paper. "An authentic fake?"

"Good old Eddy's fraud is so famous in art and archeology circles that now he can sell his fakes as real fakes. *TheoryCraft: the Journal of Postmodern Craft Theory* voted him the most postmodern non-artist artist of non-art in the art world. That's why he wants to be *Formosa* now. He's an artist, not a hustler."

Eddy exited the bathroom. "All clear?" he asked.

"We've declared the statue a demilitarized zone," Yolanda said.

Nick laughed. Yolanda smiled at him. Eddy turned back toward the bathroom.

"We're leaving," Nick said to him.

"Where to?" Yolanda asked.

"To visit a man with a letter."

"Who is this person?" Yolanda asked as they drove along L.A. streets in Nick's car.

"Israel Hyfets Shalom Cohen," Nick said.

"He wouldn't be Jewish by any chance?" Yolanda asked.

"Watch that, no cracks about being Jewish," Nick said.

Yolanda laughed at the thought, "I'm no bigot," she said.

"He's just really sensitive about it. He doesn't want anyone to know his ethnicity," Nick said.

"With a name like that?"

"He introduces himself by a different one: Yespil Benjamin Goldbach," Nick said.

"And he thinks that fools people?" Yolanda said.

"Okay, so he doesn't quite live in the world. My point is, you should probably not mention you know he's Jewish."

Yolanda felt the wind in her hair. She liked Nick's car.

"What's wrong with being Jewish?"

"Nothing," Nick said, "Israel loves the Jews. He just feels he let them down, that's all."

"Okay, spill," Yolanda said.

"I shouldn't say, I'd be breaking a confidence."

Yolanda poked him in the rib, "You brought it up. Isn't that the rule? So spill."

Nick smiled. "You didn't hear it from me. Do you remember the Hitler Diary scam some years ago?"

"Vaguely."

"A German forger named Kujau sold a collection of diaries supposedly written by Adolph Hitler. Kujau sold them to *Stern Magazine*, this back in 1983. *Stern* paid top dollar, or mark rather, and planned to publish them as the most important historical documents in the world, which they would be, if Kujau hadn't written them all himself. *Stern* even had the diaries authenticated by the English historian Hugh Trevor-Roper. Trevor-Roper knew his Adolph, and any English scholar with a hyphenated name adds real cache to one's project. The whole deal hit all the papers."

They stopped at a light and waited while several ambulances passed, then drove on. Yolanda said, "I remember this, I think. But they were all fakes."

"Yeah, pathetic fakes in fact. Kujau mostly plagiarized James O'Donnell's *The Bunker,* and copied text from the book *Hitler: Speeches and Proclamations* by some other scholar. O'Donnell noticed the similarities, and other scholars showed that the diaries repeated the mistakes in the book on Hitler's speeches. Chemical and handwriting analysis blew the lid completely off. Kujau even got the monogrammed initials on the cover of each diary wrong. Kujau had used an old English typeface and had mistakenly picked an *F* that looked like an *A*. All in all, not the high point of the forger's art."

Nick stopped at a light while a funeral procession passed. Four hearses, no cars. "I guess each one lost all his friends at the same time," said Nick, "lightening struck a poker game."

"What has all that about the Hitler diaries to do with Mr. Cohen?" Yolanda asked.

"He wrote his own."

"Hitler diaries?"

Nick drove on. "Great ones. Worked on them for decades. He read every book on Hitler written in English, French, and German. He studied films and speeches, kept track of the critical historical literature from the journals, visited the actual cites of Hitler's life, and read *Mein Kampf* over a hundred times. He studied Hitler's handwriting from every known sample. He bought, at great expense, a set of expensive diaries, unwritten in, bound in 1932. Thus, wholly authentic paper. He studied the chemistry of ink till he could test for a Ph.D. in the subject. He read authentic diaries of Nazi officials and famous political figures, in the original, to get a feel for what they contained and how they were written.

"And more than that. He sat down and thought his way through every single day of Hitler's life from the day the 'diaries' would start till the day Hitler died. He noted on index cards what Hitler was said to have done on that day, and what he might have known that day. One card for each day of Hitler's life from 1932 to the last day in the bunker. Then he read each card and asked himself if Hitler would have had the time or inclination to write in a diary that day, and what he might have said. He roughed the entire diary out and then tested his account against all of his sources and the latest scholarship. He even did original scholarship, interviewing some former servants of Hitler for some authentic details to add to the diaries. He wouldn't include these details unless the old servant died without revealing them to anyone else.

"Then he set about writing the real article. He used the inks Hitler used on other documents. Not at all easy to fake this stuff, but he did it. Cohen wrote volumes of diaries. Every other day he would re-read the last day's work and, if it did not measure up, he'd scrape it. Start over with a whole new blank diary if he had to. It was the most perfect historical forgery any person had ever conceived.

"And make no mistake, Cohen didn't just want money, he had a personal mission. He portrayed the inner life of Hitler as depraved and cowardly. His Hitler let slip facts in the diary that confirmed his complicity in the Holocaust and revealed the great dictator as a coward and a mamma's boy. All very subtly done. You see, Cohen meant to *indict* Hitler in these diaries."

Yolanda kept close track of where they went as she listened to Nick's story. "I would think Hitler needed no further indictment beyond what history already provides," she said.

"Quite true," Nick said, "but Cohen figured after he was done with the man, no one would ever join a neo-Nazi group again. The Holocaust deniers would be silenced forever. He was naive to think that people who like to carry swastikas or who believed mad ravings about Auschwitz ovens being made for industrial bread production would respond to any argument or evidence, but there you are."

"So what happened to it all?" Yolanda asked.

"Kujau and *Stern Magazine* happened to it all," Nick said. "Cohen had finished the diaries. He was just setting up the finding of them, a brilliant plot as well, when *Stern* announced they had bought someone else's Hitler diaries. After that whole thing blew up Cohen could not have passed his Hitler diaries off as real even if Old Adolph himself rose from the ashes and verified them. If real Hitler diaries surface, no scholar will risk his reputation authenticating them. The market for Hitler diaries is absolutely and permanently dead. Cohen's life work died with it."

Nick pulled into a small apartment complex and parked next to a dumpster sitting in it's wooden cage. The smell told Yolanda that tomorrow must be trash day.

Nick said, "Remember, it's Mr. Goldbach, and he does not seem the least bit Jewish." They got out of the convertible and climbed the stairs to apartment B-2. Nick knocked on the door. A man opened it.

"Hello Yespil," Nick said.

"And the little lady? Who would she be?" asked the old man in a thick Yiddish accent.

"I'm Yolanda Vasquez," Yolanda said as she offered her hand.

"Well, come inside then," said the old man, "you can't just stand there; the smell of the trash will knock you out. Come in, come in."

Nick and Yolanda entered. The old man had all the windows covered. Only a few dim lamps illuminated the crowded space of the apartment. At first, Yolanda thought that curtains covered the windows, then she saw that bookcases and filing cabinets covered every wall, obscuring all the windows from which only small shafts of light found their way into the dark room. The old man led them into the apartment to a folding card table around which three folding chairs sat, and upon which sat a mountain of papers and several books.

The old man addressed Yolanda, "My name is Yespil Reynolds," he said, pronouncing *Reynolds* in a way no actual Reynolds had ever done. Yolanda glanced at Nick who just shrugged. "Perhaps you doubt I am Yespil Reynolds?" the old man shouted while jabbing a finger in the air at Yolanda. "I will show you."

The old man retreated to a filing cabinet and returned a moment later with documents. He cleared a space on the card table by handing several stacks of papers to Nick and then displayed his proofs before Yolanda. "Look at this, little lady. I have documents." The old man placed a driver's license in the name of Yespil Reynolds on the table before Yolanda. He followed this with a birth certificate, several credit cards, a Statement of Employment assuring the reader that the bearer, one Yespil Reynolds, had worked for the Treasury Department, and a veteran's service card giving Yespil Reynolds the right to all privileges accorded to veterans of the United States Armed Forces.

"It's really not necessary to prove that you are Reynolds," Yolanda said.

"Reynolds!" the old man shouted. "And why should *Reynolds*

be the thing I'm trying to prove and not Yespil? Do you think I am more Yespil than Reynolds? You have reason perhaps to doubt Reynolds and not Yespil?"

"I just meant that I'll call you by any name you like," Yolanda said.

"This fool here," the old man continued, indicating Nick, "has probably told you my name is 'Goldbach.' This is a slander and he knows it. Of 'Goldbach' there would be no doubt—this I know—but Reynolds ..." the old man looked away with a knowing smile still waving his finger at Yolanda.

Nick said, "Maybe you could just show her the letter we talked about."

The old man sat down on a folding chair and inspected his proofs of Reynolds. After a bit, he looked up at Yolanda. "If I were to tell you my name was Israel Cohen, what conclusions would you draw?" he asked.

Yolanda stood thinking how to answer that question in light of her briefing.

The old man carried on, "I know what you are thinking. I know how people's minds work. But a man named Coven, or Colen, might change it somewhere along the line with an *h*, and who would know? If he had no idea, who would know? And anyone can love Israel. It is the name of a country you know. It sounds lovely on the tongue. Anyone could have such a name."

Yolanda's eyes had finally adjusted to the dusty dark of the room. She saw the old man looking at her half angry, half pleading. "Mr. Cohen? I assure you I have no objections to your ... ethnicity."

Nick groaned. Cohen leapt up. "Objections to my ethnicity! What you don't know about my ethnicity could fill the Library of Congress. To my ethnicity! I can have documents to prove any ethnicity you like—in just a few days work. Give me a name, go on, give me a name."

"Israel, you are impossible," Nick said.

"She is so sure she knows about ethnicity, I'll have proof I'm

Robert Redford by noon tomorrow."

Yolanda looked away and scanned the room. Her eyes had just landed on a Nazi flag hanging on a wall when the old man pushed his face an inch from hers. "The little lady has perhaps found something curious?" he asked.

"No, I just—"

"Where does the little lady look? She looks at a flag. And if there is a swastika flag on the wall then surely the man must be a Nazi. That is what the little lady thinks?"

"Not at all Mr.—"

"Let me show you something," the old man said as he walked to a file cabinet to retrieve further documents. Returning, he bid Yolanda sit down in a folding chair next to him. She did. The old man placed a thick manuscript before her. "This is a declaration of my beliefs," he said, "You may not look at this now. It is not for now. But if God should strike me dead in the middle of the night, they will find this right in that cabinet under the flag you pretend not to look at. All of this is explained. I am not a Nazi. The flag is part of my research and a reminder to me of what I oppose. I am not a Nazi. If you do not believe that, we have nothing we can speak of on other documents."

"I think it only fair to tell you that I am a police detective. I am not here to investigate you but—"

"This she tells me: that she is a police detective?" the old man said to Nick. "Does she think I let just anyone in here? Does she think I don't know she's a lady detective?"

Nick said, "The letter, Israel, just get her the letter you told me about."

"Nick tells me you might have some information regarding the Vampire Killer case?" Yolanda said.

The old man looked intensely at Yolanda, "About this Vampire Killer, I know nothing. Mr. Sabernail asked about certain things—to do with dead bodies and such, and of this, I have a letter. I just want you to understand that nothing else you see here in my home is of the slightest interest to you. My

260

work: you will not see. Mr. Sabernail has no doubt told you I have been arrested for forgery from time to time. These are slanders. I am a researcher. You will not see my research."

Yolanda nodded solemnly. What else could she do?

"The letter," Nick said.

The old man got up and walked over to a filing cabinet. He retrieved a folder and then pulled a black book off a shelf full of similarly bound black books. He returned to the table.

Nick shook his head and left for the kitchen. The old man opened the folder and began to arrange its contents before Yolanda. Then he opened the bound volume and put it before her as well. The book contained handwriting in a foreign language.

"When you are going to write something that will convince and persuade people, you must practice and research, research and practice, practice and research. Look at this paper. This looks good to you, uh? It is not good. Not as good as this paper. But look in the book." His eyes moistened with awe and pride. "This one is perfect. Look at the photograph. Which of all these looks exactly like the photograph?"

Nick shouted from the kitchen: "She is not interested in a lesson on the forger's art, Israel, just show her the letter."

The old man sighed and shook his head. He gathered his papers back into the folder, and took the folder, and the book, back to where he had retrieved them. He took another folder, from a different file cabinet, and returned to sit down next to Yolanda. He looked at Yolanda for a long moment, then said, "I can trust you, little lady? You will keep quiet what I tell you when I tell you?"

Yolanda said, "I am an officer of the court. I have to act on any information about a crime, but—"

"Good!" the old man yelled, "good! This is a crime. Look at this." He opened the folder and revealed black and white photos of dead bodies, hundreds of them. For a moment Yolanda stared at the pictures. Then she recognized them.

"Did you know, little lady, that some people say this did not happen? What would be the importance of a document, a set of documents, that refuted these people? Do not look to me to have such a document, but if such a document had come forward, what importance could it have had?"

Nick returned to the room. He leaned down and spoke to Cohen just an inch from the old man's nose, "The letter, now, or I publish your Nazi fixation in the *Journal of Abnormal Psychology*."

The old man rose and went to yet another file cabinet. He retrieved yet another folder, this one very thin. He returned to the table and opened it for Yolanda. It contained a single typed letter:

Dear Unfortunately Incarcerated Supposed Criminal,

I write to you a personal letter on a matter of possible business. This letter is to get to know you and not to propose to you a possible business venture that would not be illegal in the same way that you are only a supposed criminal. My organization has records. You are listed as on record as having a record. The record of your supposed criminal activities suggest the possibility of your joining our organization for activities not necessarily of a criminal nature.

Have you ever wondered about your full potential? Arrangements may be made for you to realize your full potential (I write this sentence fully knowing you are incarcerated as a criminal). Regular work can be had by you from us in your field of expertise (I know of your supposed status as I write this) and in similar fields.

This work may require some digging and it is very important that YOU DO NOT MIND DEAD PERSONS. I mean here that dead bodies (those dead already) should not upset you greatly. If you have seen "Night of the Dead Hand" or "Voodoo Glue" you will better understand me. We pay money and file all the necessary forms when the time is right.

If you are interested in joining an organization that is a business or know someone of your caliber (referring here to the sub-class of potential criminals of your acquaintance) then please write to us at 1800 Pilot Way, Los Angeles, California. We can talk by phone if you write.

Nothing said in this letter is meant to imply anything not said in this letter.

Signed,

One Who Does Not Sign

The letter had actually been signed in a shaky scrawl: *One Who Does Not Sign*. Yolanda read the letter three times. She looked up at Nick Sabernail. He smiled. Why does that man's smile always bring more trouble?

On the east side of the City of Angels, in a tiny apartment fitted with low sinks and extra wide doors, a small old woman fingered through her old photographs. These pictures, yellow with age and crisp at the corners, sat in boxes, or lay pressed into old photo albums. The albums held each picture fast at the corners by triangular bits of glued paper. The paper of the albums themselves cracked as the old woman turned them. In times past, she could turn these pages with barely a hint of sound. Now, their age, or hers, had them bring forth a symphony of desiccation.

The pictures showed celebrities of a long-gone era. An amazingly young Clark Gable smiled forth from one. Another showed Pola Negri dressed as Pharaoh's concubine and standing next to a dark car. Charley Chaplin, wearing a tennis outfit, mugged for the camera in another. What all of these pictures had in common though, was not the presence of a past celebrity, but the hulking presence of a large man, always standing beside the famous face. In every picture the man stood, slightly stooped, as if trying hard not to loom above the other person. No collector of memorabilia would ever recognize the man who served as the common denominator in the old woman's picture collection. Like most of those from the past, he was long forgotten by all but the few who knew him in life and recalled his face and name from old and crackling pictures.

Dorothy Margrove had looked many times at these pictures over the years. In the past, they had reminded her of what she imagined must have been better times. As a young woman, she had put them entirely away. But once her own son and daughter had grown up and moved on, she had found herself returning to them more often. When her husband died ten years ago, she virtually banished his pictures from her sight, but these old ones of her father rose up to take their place. All pictures seemed to speak of loss to her in one way or another. But these old ones, at least, spoke of loss so long ago that the loss felt like it belonged to another person. She could look at these pictures and remember a little girl who was perhaps only just barely herself. The big burly man in them was an artifact of history; her personal history only, but safely historical nonetheless.

Until several weeks ago.

For on a Tuesday, like any other Tuesday, she had gone to the bank. She banked at First Metro because they still had polite tellers and did not add a surcharge for talking to a person rather than using a machine. Dorothy remained sharp of mind, but liked to take her time about moving her body. They didn't rush at First Metro; at least they didn't rush her. On that Tuesday a gang of grotesquely dressed outlaws had robbed the bank, shooting their way out and nearly killing a young armored-car guard. Before that day Dorothy had twice been shot at, or had at least been near those being shot at. Once in Korea, while working as a nurse, and once on a street in L.A., while doing volunteer work for a youth intervention group. The day at the bank had disturbed her more than the time in Korea. Not because of bullets. She did not fear bullets anymore. Now, she only feared for her sanity.

On that day, in that bank, during the robbery, she saw the

big man in the pictures. He looked exactly as he did in the pictures—right down to having yellow skin, which he never had in Dorothy's memories or dreams. When she saw him shot by the bank guard, she thought she must have hallucinated her own family history; bringing it into existence right there in the First American Metropolitan Bank. Her first thought at the sight was to feel sorry for all the other bank patrons whom she had put through all this by dredging up this phantom from her past. Only after so many policemen, and so many F.B.I. agents, had filed past on that Tuesday, did she finally come to accept that she had not dreamed the day's events. Since then, she had spent most of her waking hours thinking over that day and looking over her old pictures.

As she sat in her kitchen, looking at her photographs, she could think of only two things. The first: To whom should she tell her story? The second: How could she find the man from her pictures again?

AUTEUR
NECROMANCER

From the hallowed blue light of overhead TVs, the voice of Duke Dawson rang out:

"Now we go to a live report from our own Venice Whimsey at Graceland in Tennessee."

Venice Whimsey: "Thank you Duke. Fans of the King continue to gather here to mourn the loss of the body of their beloved Elvis. Local police are still uncertain how grave robbers managed to extract the body in the dead of night without alerting anyone. The State Police believe that deranged fans of the late performer committed this bizarre theft. One thing everyone agrees on: grave robbery is no longer just a Los Angeles phenomenon."

Twenty people lay strapped to tables watching this report from the overhead TVs. Machines drained away their blood. Drakan had strewn Christmas ornaments around the televisions in an effort to give his assembly line of death a "festive sports-bar atmosphere." The effect seemed entirely lost on the patrons.

Drakan directed the efforts of twenty zombies as they processed old life into new undeath. His zombie goons now wore white lab coats, and they could almost run the whole operation in the smooth detachment that passed for efficiency among the undead. Most of those working the assembly line would be moved on to other facilities in a few days time.

Fort Necro served now more as a training center for zombie factory workers than as the center of ghoul production itself. Following the best business advice, Drakan had diversified production and moved operations closer to supply.

As to skilled labor, here Drakan continued to have a few hiccups. Although he could raid the Hollywood trades for production workers, criminal talent remained harder to find. Obituaries did not brag of the felonious successes of the recently departed. So today he had scheduled a meeting with an old friend of Captain Vinnie the Llama. The man purported to be a safecracker. Drakan was to meet him in his small office off to the side of the main area of Fort Necro. This would keep the man from seeing any ghouls prematurely—Vinnie had assured Drakan that seeing the undead too soon would chill the man's enthusiasm.

His minions steady at work in the conversion facility, Drakan now sat in his swivel chair behind a desk, in what had once been a dispatch office for the long-defunct taxi company that had operated on the site of Fort Necro. He worked on how best to present himself. He had a large bronze eagle in the center of the desk to give the impression of confident power. He placed Charley Sparrow first on the right behind him and then on the left. He preferred left. He had hung the skull shaped *Seal of Fort Necro* above his seat. He now pushed the desk and chair back and forth. He hoped to insure they rested precisely centered beneath the Seal. He sat in the chair practicing bidding guests into his presence with a nonchalant wave.

He still practiced nonchalant waves when Vinnie knocked at the door. This irritated Drakan, who had not practiced nonchalant voice commands. "Enter," Drakan called. As the doorknob turned, he said, "I bid ye enter."

Vinnie opened the door and motioned for his friend, Tony Rodriguez, to enter.

Drakan called out, "Enter and approach, Captain," and, almost as an afterthought, threw the two men a nonchalant wave.

"Tony," Vinnie said, "This is the Baron von Finkelstein. Baron, sir, this is Tony—a great cracker."

"Yeah, hey," Tony said.

Drakan placed both his hands palm down on the arms of the swivel chair in the fashion of a Lord of Undeath. He paused ostentatiously and surveyed his new minion.

"Hey," said Tony, "We got fuckin business here or what?"

Drakan frowned. "I assure you we have several businesses here, good fellow, and all ready for unlimited growth. We mix our portfolio of activities. Page eighty-seven. We have a question here-now. Your possible place in our ever-expanding enterprise."

Tony glanced at the skull seal above Drakan. "Fuckin sicko shit here," he said with a snort.

Drakan looked at Vinnie who looked rather panicked. "Tony, Tony," Vinnie said, "a little respect for the boss."

"Fuck the respect. What's the job?"

Drakan shot a angry look at Vinnie and then addressed Tony in a magisterial voice—or at least as close to such as he could manage, "Mr. Cracksman, your mission will be to open the vault containing the body of one Marilyn Monroe—located at Forest Lawn Cemetery. Upon which time, after that, others of my employ will remove said body for purposes not within your brief."

Tony smiled a wicked grin. "You fuckin sick fuckin fuck! You gonna fuckin fuck the fuckin dead body of fuckin Marilyn fuckin Monroe!"

Drakan had never had much luck dealing with living people. He had found, much to his surprise and delight, that once one cleared a few early hurdles, the undead turned out to be far more understandable and easily managed than the living. Drakan positively liked working with the undead. So this Tony problem would be no problem at all.

"Mr. Sparrow," Drakan said, "take Mr. Tony to processing, B unit."

"Hey, Baron! Sir! He's a friend of mine!" said Vinnie.

Drakan fumed, "Don't worry Captain, you'll get plenty of opportunity to work with Mr. Tony. You can even share quarters if you like."

Charley Sparrow walked from behind the desk toward Tony. "Whoa, Whoa!" Tony said *Whoa* right up until Sparrow cracked him across the head, sending him to the floor.

"Mr. Sparrow!" Drakan shouted. "How many times must I tell you? Not in the head. It scrambles their brains. We don't hit the keepers in the head."

Sparrow hauled Tony out to Unit B while every pore on Vinnie's body drenched his clothes with fear-sweat. "Mr. Baron, sir, it's gonna be hard to get help if all the guys who come to see you disappear into zombies."

Drakan waved his hand dismissively, feeling quite proud of how it came off—he had practiced dismissive hand waves for several hours last night. "Captain Vinnie, I am far too busy to deal with the uncooperative living. And so are you. You will find your work schedule at the administrative office. You have a lot of specials tonight."

◆ ◆ ◆

Building Three of Fort Necro now comprised not only a studio for shooting the increasingly popular cable access show "Meet the Late Great," but also a veritable Studio City for zombie productions. Drakan's current project was a feature film staring Elvis Presley and Marilyn Monroe. Once completed, he planned to market it as a lost masterpiece. He had not yet worked out what name he would use as director. He currently leaned toward *Eric von Sedown*; that sounded right, but maybe a bit too German. On the other hand, he still had the monocle.

"And action!" Drakan called.

Marilyn the Zombie, so recently liberated from Forest Lawn, spoke Drakan's lines, "I vant to vamp you … come up and see me sometime." She wore a negligee that barely concealed her still rather rot-ridden, fleshy breasts. These Vinnie had been forced to inflate with a bicycle pump. This gave Marilyn the Zombie a less than alluring appearance. Drakan insisted he could fix this in editing.

"Cut!" Drakan yelled. He consulted a book entitled: *The Art and Craft of Filmmaking*. He jumped down from his folding chair, adjusted his beret and approached his star. "Marilyn Baby. This is your classic line. Put a bit more life into it. You *want* him to come up and see you, *sometime*. Try it again." Drakan retreated to his chair again. "Roll um!" he shouted, then, "action."

Marilyn the Zombie delivered the lines just as before, only louder. Drakan yelled, "Cue Elvis!" and Fred the Zombie pushed a portly Presley out onto the set. Drakan waved in a silent frenzy for his male lead to come forward. Slowly, the King walked toward his co-star. *Say it, Say it!* Drakan motioned.

Then the King spoke: "Since my baby left ... I found a new place ... in Hell!"

"Cut!" yelled Drakan. "Cut! Cut!" Drakan approached Elvis. "Not *in hell*, your majesty, *to dwell*, the line is *to dwell*. Just like in the records."

Elvis looked perplexed.

"Alright," Drakan continued, "Let's just move on to your next lines."

Elvis the Zombie gaped at the Zombie Master.

"Your next lines, *your next lines!*" Drakan repeated jabbing at the script.

Drakan retreated to his folding chair and yelled "Action!"

Elvis the Zombie gathered his forces and yelled at Marilyn the Zombie: "You ain't nothing but a hound dog ... just ... dying ... all ... the time!!!

"Cut! Cut! Lying! Not dying—lying all the time!"

And in such manner, Drakan proceeded to film his lost epic. For later, he had scheduled to film lost episodes of "I Love Lucy" and further lost episodes of "The Honeymooners." He had Vinnie planning a wrap party. Lots of little pastries for cast and crew—even though all were zombies and thus incapable of actually eating anything. Drakan suggested a solution to this problem. Buy some rats to eat the food off the plates. In the meantime, Vinnie spent his nights recruiting further technicians from an old-folks home dedicated to Hollywood workers. Each one properly processed at Unit B before joining the permanent staff. Drakan worked on how to distribute his newly filmed old masterpieces. Undeath would be made to pay, one way or another.

DARKNESS ALL
OVER TOWN

On Monday, returning to work, Yolanda filed the Israel Cohen letter (received by him while the forger did a short stretch for passing a rather sub-par two dollar bill) with the rest of her papers on the Vampire Killer. Forensics could find no fingerprints or other useful evidence on the letter. Detectives Harmon and Washington could not see how it fit into the picture they had formed about the death cult. They did show renewed interest in Nick Sabernail as a suspect. He had, as Harmon put it, "injected himself into the police investigation." This fit the profile of a serial killer.

Yolanda sat digesting this idea at her desk when she received a call from Detective Louis Toddall of the Las Vegas Police department.

"Officer Vasquez, you notified our department that you were interviewing a Professor Dantelani at Las Vegas University. You asked for any background information."

"That's right," Yolanda said over the phone, "I interviewed him Saturday before last."

"It seems he has gone missing. The building custodian at the Science Lab saw him on Wednesday afternoon, and no one has seen him since. Someone wrecked his office and most of his files are missing. We found blood on the floor."

"His blood?" Yolanda asked.

"No way to know. May I ask what you interviewed him about?"

"The Vampire Killer case. He is not a suspect. I consulted him as an expert on the occult." Yolanda worded her next claim carefully, "His information has not yet proved relevant to the investigation."

"You have no ideas as to what may have become of him?" asked Detective Toddall.

Again Yolanda spoke with care, "I know of no information I have that might help you. Were there any other clues at the scene?"

Detective Toddall seemed a bit reluctant on this point. "Well, we found a note, typed, at his office. But it doesn't make much sense. Not to me, at least."

"Could you read it to me?" Yolanda asked.

Detective Toddall found the note and read it to Yolanda:

To He Who Finds This Note,

I who write this note, who am Dr. Dantelani, write to inform you I resign from the University and travel very far away on research not of your concern. I do this of my own freewill, which I have. In thanks to many years service the University may keep my pay or if this proves a problem give it to such workers of good works (called charities) that they, which is it, would find worthy.

I stress my freewill, and invite full scrutiny if need be, but do not think it is.

Sincerely and Professionally Yours,

Dr. Dantelani

Toddall cleared his throat at the end. "Make anything of that?"

Yolanda felt something stick in her throat. Why could she not just tell her colleague what she thought? Yolanda tried to think what she thought. "Nothing," she said.

Yolanda hung up the phone and quickly wrote down the note as Toddall had read it to her. She compared its fractured sense to that found in the note to Cohen. She should immediately ask the department for a comparison of the two notes. Perhaps the same typewriter had been used to write them both. The Dantelani disappearance might add a whole new dimension to the case. She could put herself back at the forefront of the investigation. But it would also propel Nick there too. Why should that bother her? It shouldn't. But it did.

◆ ◆ ◆

Nick stood in line at the 7-Eleven reading the latest issue of *Newsweek*. It had to be a slow week in the world because the cover story related the latest in L.A. lifestyle fashion: The Death Glare Look.

"The most fashionable look out West today? The Death Glare Look. You don't need a huge budget or a toned body—just some yellow face paint and a willingness to keep your eyes wide open and stare at folks like a corpse."

The article included pictures of teens and twenty-somethings glaring blankly at the camera. The caption under one read: *Not much to say, but a look to die for.* Nick's turn at the counter came. He noticed that the clerk affected the death glare look himself. The clerk stared at Nick with wide-open eyes and a gaping mouth. He slowly rang up Nick's milk, plastic wrapped brownie, and magazine, without looking down once. That explained what took so long. Obviously, the Death Glare Look played hell with efficiency.

Nick held up the cover of the *Newsday* to the clerk and said, "Don't you think body piercing would be easier to maintain?"

The clerk pulled down the neck of his shirt and revealed a row of safety pins seemingly holding on part of his head.

"Jesus!" Nick said. "I think you have the makings of a law suit there, pal."

Nick left the store more determined than ever not to follow fashion.

♦ ♦ ♦

Yolanda still sat at her desk debating the matter of proper police procedure, and the increasingly vague lines between contact and suspect, when Tom Delaney escorted an elderly lady to her desk. The woman carried a shoebox and a photo album. Tom grinned a wide grin and showed her a seat in front of Yolanda.

"This is Detective Vasquez. She takes care of folks like you. Those with interesting stuff to show us," Tom said to the woman. Tom grinned a Cheshire cat grin at Yolanda and walked off. The woman smiled. Yolanda smiled back.

"How may I help you?" Yolanda asked.

"My name is Dorothy Margrove. I think I might have information on a crime. Or perhaps a missing person. I don't know which."

"Oh?"

Dorothy continued: "I've been seeing people all day. No one seems to know what to do with me."

Yolanda knew Tom had sent the old lady over as a way of hazing her. Men could be such boys, she thought. "Well, maybe just start wherever seems reasonable and we'll see what we have."

Dorothy smiled, opened her shoebox, and began pulling out yellowed pictures. Yolanda watched as Dorothy spoke in a soft and lilting voice, "These are my pictures. My mother gave them to me when I was much younger. I've been told some of them might be worth money because of the old movie stars in them, but they are precious to me for another reason."

Yolanda noted that most included a large man standing in front of a black car next to one or another celebrity from long ago.

Dorothy continued, "You see the man in all the pictures is my father. His name was Charles Sparrow. Sparrow is my maiden name. Mother always called him Charley. He used to

275

drive movie stars in the old days of Hollywood. He would have his picture taken with them. I'm so glad he did, otherwise I would have only a few pictures of him, as most of my friends have only a few of their fathers."

Yolanda found the old photos interesting. Dorothy showed each one to her, one at a time. Yolanda would search the face of each person in the photo to see if she could identify the star from an age gone by. Dorothy would simply point out her father in each one, as if the other person in the picture were but an adornment to him. Finally, Yolanda tired of the game and asked, "These are very interesting, Mrs. Margrove, but what have they to do with any crime?"

"Please call me Dorothy. I do so prefer the friendly sound of a first name."

"And please call me Yolanda, but I am curious what crime might be connected to these photos."

Dorothy said, "I'm afraid I saw my father, the man in these photos, robbing a bank last month. The First American Metropolitan Bank. A man was shot, not by my father, and not badly hurt I'm told, during the robbery."

Yolanda restrained a tired sigh, "Your father must be very old to be robbing banks."

"That's part of what disturbs me so; my father passed away in 1937. Shot while robbing a bank I'm afraid." Dorothy paused.

Yolanda, noticing how hard this must be for her, remained silent while the elderly lady collected herself.

Dorothy continued, "You see, Yolanda, my father was never a bad man. He came on desperate times and made a terrible mistake. It cost our family dearly. But I know he was a good man."

Yolanda responded kindly, "I understand, Dorothy, but surely you see that your father could not have robbed the First Metro Bank last month if he died in 1937."

Dorothy nodded in agreement. "I quite agree. It is not possible. But I saw him. As clear as I see you. He passed right in front of me carrying a bag of money. The young man shot him, but father kept on walking. I didn't tell the F.B.I. men at the time, because I know how very strange it must sound. But I saw him. I wish now I had called to him. Perhaps he would have stopped and spoken to me."

"I'm not sure what I can do for you, Mrs. Margrove," Yolanda said.

"Please, take some of the pictures, see for yourself. The bank teller told me the F.B.I. has film of the robbery. Take some of my pictures and see for yourself if the man looks like my father or not. If not, you can put my mind at ease that I am just a silly old woman. Would you do that for me?"

Yolanda's first instinct told her to find a polite way to turn the woman down. Her second instinct told her to agree to the woman's request and then forget about it. She said, "I'll look into it for you, Dorothy."

◆ ◆ ◆

Nick sat at home watching cable TV. His cable supplier boasted of six all-news channels. Three of these delivered virtually nothing but business news. If the President of the United States were shot dead in his underwear, exiting a bordello in Thailand, these channels would lead with the market reaction. The other three, including the old man of the bunch, CNN, mixed business news with whatever else happened. Since most of the time not much happened that interested the cable news channels, they typically filled their wire-ways with denouncement and hectoring from political "insiders" and journalists interviewing each other about the inside of politics.

This evening, on *Tony O'Flannigan Takes On the World*, the indefatigable O'Flannigan interviewed Kasumi Sasaki, a sociologist from Columbia University, and Paul Baggity, a leader of *Christian Right Action Patrol*, a watchdog group. The topic: The

Alarming Rise in Grave Robbery.

O'Flannigan led off with the startling stats, "Grave robberies are up 4000 percent. These are crisis numbers. In L.A. alone, if trends continue, nearly twenty percent of the buried will soon be dug up. Not only that, but the trend is growing. Even in sleepy Akron, Ohio, the police caught some kids shoveling away at an old grave. They said they heard about it on TV." O'Flannigan wanted to know what gets into kids these days.

Kasumi Sasaki began a long monolog on the cultural significance of death, the disposed feelings of youth, and the social science literature on copycat phenomena. She got through just forty-five seconds of this treatise when O'Flannigan cut her off.

O'Flannigan asked, "So you think it's just rotten kids?"

While Professor Sasaki recovered from the question, Mr. Baggity broke in to point out that, "The rot in the soul of today's teenagers originated in the socialist death-lust the public schools pound into them every day. When this country had prayer in schools, dead folks stayed buried."

Dr. Sasaki recovered her wits and demanded Baggity produce statistics correlating school prayer and grave-robbery. After a minute of incoherent shouting O'Flannigan broke in to ask Professor Sasaki her opinion of gun-control laws. While she tried to piece together the relevance of that question, Baggity broke in to point out that prior to the nation's crazed enthusiasm for confiscating guns, grave robbery rarely occurred. Professor Sasaki leapt on this demanding to know if Baggity asserted that the Bible prescribed gun ownership. Baggity began hurling Bible quotes to the effect that it did. O'Flannigan, knowing how hard religious topics hit his ratings, segued into commercial by asking his "panel" to consider whether L.A. and other major cities should consider "shovel control laws."

"Right," yelled Baggity, "it's people that dig up bodies, not shovels!"

After a commercial touting backyard wrestling videos,

O'Flannigan's show returned. Professor Sasaki had clearly steadied herself and could be seen reviewing her hastily scribbled notes on the subject of shovel control laws. O'Flannigan launched in, "Did you know that Elvis sightings are up 1000 percent? What are people looking for when they see the King at a supermarket?"

The professor stared at him like a baseball catcher hit by a fastball in the locker room. "Oatmeal?" she meekly offered.

Baggity grabbed the issue like a pro, "God. They are at the supermarket looking for God. And what does our celebrity-deifying culture offer instead: Heartbreak Hotel."

O'Flannigan turned again to the professor and asked: "what is this heartbreak that has no name?" The good professor sat motionless so Baggity launched in with: "Jesus envy."

Nick turned off the TV.

◆ ◆ ◆

Yolanda sat watching the television set. The figures moved in slow motion. She looked hard at the faces of the men, at their awkward movements, at their eerie stillness. Then they dropped to the ground. A gun melee followed. At one point, the largest of them passed right in front of the camera, so close you could see the pores on his face. Yolanda checked that face against the pictures she had brought. Same face.

"Why do the perps drop to the floor?" Yolanda asked.

"I have a theory on that," Special Agent Lansdown said, "Agent Parker doesn't agree, but I think Cowboy is so crazy and erratic; even the members of his crew are afraid to stand up while he lets off a round. They duck because they are just that scared of him."

Yolanda pondered this a moment, then asked, "Why does the one fellow walk into the wall?"

Parker spoke up, "If you start asking questions like that it just never stops. You said you had possible information on this crime. Do you?"

Lansdowne shot a harsh look at his partner and turned to Yolanda, leaning down as if to impart a professional secret. "Hotdog's been under a lot of pressure lately. Thing is, we don't really get what these guys were doing at all."

Quietly, Yolanda asked Lansdowne, "You mentioned a note, could I see it?" Lansdowne suggested Parker get a cup of coffee. Once he had left, Lansdowne took a note out from a cabinet and showed it to her. Yolanda read it. Finally she asked, "Did the perps say anything helpful while in the bank?"

Lansdowne replied, "They used some fake names, according to the witnesses. At least, we assume they're fake. I think maybe they drop to the floor so Cowboy can order them up using the fake names. Maybe trying to throw us off. Agent Parker doesn't want to talk about it." Lansdowne reached into his pocket and retrieved his notes. He read from them: "Cowboy calls out the names: Leo, Randall, John, and Sparrow."

Yolanda held her breath for a moment, "Which one did he call *Sparrow*?"

"The big one," said Special Agent Lansdowne.

That night Yolanda sat at Mama Tuscan's Italian Eatery. Jesus Havier owned and operated Mama Tuscan's. He had never been to Italy in his life, but he cooked some mean pasta just the same. He spoke no idle boast when he claimed to be the best Mexican cook of Italian food in West Los Angeles. Like most waiters at Italian restaurants, Mama Tuscan's (i.e., Papa Havier's) waiters all hailed from south of the border, but they faked those Northern Italian accents well enough to fool a Hollywood voice coach. It helped that the food tasted authentic.

Yolanda ate eggplant Parmesan and bruschetta. Normally she ate alone here, and it rather stunned the staff when she brought a date. She told the waiter that this wasn't a date, but no one believed her, least of all her date. Across from Yolanda sat Nick, not quite her date, eating salmon. "The eggplant looks good," Nick said.

"I told you to order the eggplant," Yolanda said.

"I felt fishy tonight," Nick said.

"I didn't notice, you always look that way to me."

"I don't have to be straight man all night, do I? We're going to trade places and you feed me some lines too, right?"

Yolanda savored her eggplant, rather too obviously, Nick thought. "Is that bread for both of us?" he asked.

"Separate checks, separate bread," she said, "it is good though." Yolanda savored a piece of the bruschetta. Her tongue steadied the tomato and cheese until her lips could engorge the bread and her teeth tear off a small piece; all in slow motion. That woman really can savor, Nick thought.

"Salmon's good, though," Nick said, "No complaints at all."

Yolanda smiled at him as she ate another bite of eggplant.

"Would you like to try a bit of salmon?" Nick asked.

"Love to," Yolanda said.

Nick picked up an unused bread plate and set it between them. "Let's call this the Brandenburg Gate, just like in the cold war," he said. He cut off a piece of fish and set it on the side of the plate closest to him. "Now, you put a bit of eggplant on your side of the Brandenburg Gate, then we rotate it, and everybody eats happy."

Yolanda smiled, cut a portion of eggplant and set it on the plate between them. Nick slowly rotated the plate until the salmon piece lay before Yolanda and the eggplant piece before him. "A successful exchange," Nick said. They each ate from the plate.

"Not bad," Nick said.

"The eggplant's better," Yolanda said.

"All the more reason to share your bread," Nick said.

Yolanda pushed the bruschetta to Nick who ate one lustily. Then she said, "Cohen received the note he showed us while in jail, right?"

"Right," Nick said.

"And this other friend of yours got one there too?"

"Hunter did, right, same note exactly."

Yolanda pulled open her bag and brought out seven pictures and set them before Nick one after the other.

"Wow, that's Clarke Gable," Nick said.

"In your professional opinion as a curator, are these pictures authentic?" Yolanda asked.

"In my opinion as a *former* curator, that's Clark Gable next to the big fellow there," Nick said.

Yolanda shook her head, "For one moment, be serious, can you tell me if these are fakes or not?"

Nick put down his fork and picked up the picture. He examined the back of the photograph. He stared hard at the edges of each image.

"Here," Yolanda said, pulling a magnifying glass from her bag, "will this help?"

Nick took the magnifying glass and just stared at it in amazement. "You mean detectives really carry these things around?"

Yolanda dropped her head into her hands.

"I thought that was just in movies," Nick said. "Do you have a deerstalker hat in that bag?"

"Is the picture real?" Yolanda said.

Nick examined it closely with the magnifying glass. He did the same with the others. Finally he said, "They show no signs of cut-and-splice work with the faces. The discoloration is consistent with what I guess to be the age of the photos. The paper looks authentic. The backgrounds are plausibly varied." Nick looked at one showing the big man and a woman he did not recognize, standing before a car. "You know, that looks like the old Hollywood Palace Theatre in back of this one. I did a show on the vanishing architecture of Los Angeles. They knocked the Palace down in 1946. I can't think anyone faking celebrity snaps would bother faking the old Palace Theater. So this one has to be pre-forty-six at least. The background anyway."

Yolanda took the picture and studied it. "Is there a market for old photos like this?"

"You're asking me as a curator?"

Yolanda shot him dirty look, "Curator or black-marketeer, take your pick, are photos like these valuable?"

"They sell, but not for enough to make this level of craftsmanship pay—if they're fake. You think they're fake?"

Yolanda drank a bit of wine. "They belong to a retired old woman named Dorothy Margrove. She claims the big fellow in all the pictures was her father, named Charles Sparrow. Says he died in 1937 during a bank holdup. I'm trying to check on that, but no one but the F.B.I. keeps records back that far. So far, all I know is that Mrs. Margrove's maiden name was Sparrow."

"So what has all this to do with the price of tea in China?"

Yolanda continued, "Seems Dorothy saw her father robbing a bank downtown, just last month."

Nick chucked, "Old folks do like attention."

"I saw him too, in the video record of the holdup."

Nick stopped laughing. "Then again, old folks do get around, they sometimes know more than you'd think."

"The bank pictures were very clear," Yolanda said. "I could swear it was the same man—only … a bit …"

"A bit?" Nick said.

Yolanda set her jaw, "He was a bit … dead-looking. Don't smirk! He and the other perps looked like death-warmed-over. All but the gang's leader. I wasn't the only one to notice. The Feds think the gang members had makeup on to conceal their faces. I say they just had horrid looking faces."

"What did the G-men say when you told them your theory?" Nick asked.

"How crazy do you think I am?" Yolanda said, "I didn't tell them anything. I have enough trouble getting my peers to take me seriously without telling ghost stories at the Federal Building."

"Speaking of the F.B.I., those fellows over there look like Hoover boys if I ever saw any." Yolanda turned around to look at the door where Nick had pointed. Nick deftly swiped a piece of eggplant from her plate. Yolanda turned back.

"I don't see anyone that looks like a Fed," she said.

"Oh," Nick said, still eating the eggplant, "they just ducked out. Did you find out anything else?"

Yolanda gave Nick a skeptical look and picked up her bread knife to better guard her dinner. "Dr. Dantelani disappeared. The Vegas police suspect foul play."

Nick stopped chewing. "You're kidding me?"

"No. Just a few days after we saw him. Look at this." Yolanda pulled her bag into her lap from the floor and retrieved a piece of paper, all without ever losing sight of her remaining eggplant. She handed Nick the paper. Nick read it.

Yolanda said, "The Vegas police found a note in Dantelani's office saying exactly that. The office looked ransacked. They found blood on the floor."

"The professor's blood?"

"They don't know—you need a tissue sample to identify a blood sample. What do you think of the note?"

"Well, for a start, tenured academics do not up and leave their positions. He may have been killed, but he did not quit. And clearly no one with a Ph.D. wrote this."

"Right, but what else? Do you notice anything else?" Yolanda asked.

Nick read the note again. Then it dawned on him. "It sounds a lot like Cohen's letter; the fractured syntax, the over-earnestness. Creepy."

Yolanda pulled another paper from her bag. "That's what I thought when I heard it. Now look at this. This is a copy of the holdup note left at the bank Mr. Sparrow's doppelganger robbed."

Nick read the note. "This is a holdup note?"

"Yes. The longest and most confusing holdup note on record, according to the Feds. What do you notice about it?" Yolanda said.

Nick reread the note carefully. Yolanda scooped up a bit of

cut salmon from his plate—Nick failed to notice. Nick said, "You think the same person wrote this, and the Dantelani note and the letters sent to jailbirds. I admit they sound similarly odd, though that is hardly a scientific judgment. You have Cohen's letter and a copy of the bank note, and the Vegas police have the Dantelani note. Why not test them to see if the same typewriter typed them all?"

"That would require a work order, and getting that would require letting my superiors know what I'm thinking. I'm not ready for that yet."

Nick pondered his spontaneously shrinking salmon for a moment. "So what are you thinking?"

Yolanda savored the salmon. "Where's the hustle in all this? Why would someone want to connect a Medieval scholar, a bank holdup, an obsessive forger, and antique celebrity photos?"

"You think they're a part of some giant scam?"

"Let's just say I want to eliminate the possibility. What sort of scam could it be?'

Nick waved a waiter over and asked for a desert menu. "I'm not sure I like what sort of expert you're taking me for now." The waiter brought a dessert menu.

"Does someone want to trick the police into authenticating the photos? Could someone pull all this to embarrass the LAPD? Could Dr. Dantelani use any of this weirdness to get publicity?"

Nick studied the desert menu as the waiter looked on. "What's good here?" Nick asked Yolanda. "You like the cheese cake?" Yolanda just looked on. Nick said, "I'll have the cheese cake."

"I'll have the crème brulee," Yolanda said. Nick gnashed his teeth.

"Now we have to fight over the crème brulee," Nick said.

"You might like the cheese cake," Yolanda said.

"And what would it take for you to tell the new guy that crème brulee was the real treasure here?"

"What does it take to get a straight answer from you?"

Nick leaned back and said, "Police authentication of antiques holds no interest to collectors, besides which, the photos aren't valuable enough to pay for faking, much less the elaborate plot you're considering. No one needs to go to this much trouble to embarrass the LAPD. With a little bit of patience, the L.A. cops will embarrass themselves without help from anyone. Why would Dantelani want publicity? He is the academic equivalent of a made-man. I suppose he could go into cahoots with Cohen, forging some medieval document the professor might use to land himself on the cover of the *Medieval Scholar Times*, but he sure isn't out robbing banks to pull off that project. Nor would he have reason to stage a disappearance. Nor would Cohen be the sort of fellow to make him disappear over a forging dispute. And Hunter Coyote couldn't forge his way out of detention, so why send the weirdo note to him if the good doctor wanted to recruit a forger? But then you already thought of all this."

Yolanda nodded, "I just need to hear it from someone else. This case begins to grate on my sanity." Yolanda rubbed her temples a moment. "Just like you, those were the most likely sounding explanations I could invent. What other sort of scam could someone be running that might include all these elements?"

Nick thought that over for a moment. Then the desserts arrived, and Yolanda's crème brulee momentarily captured all his attention. She dipped a spoon into the confection and raised a bite to her lips. With the tip of her tongue she arranged the crystallized topping delicately on the spoon. Then she held the spoon up to Nick's lips saying, "Answer the question and you can have a bit of my cream."

Never in his life had Nick so wanted to answer a question. Think Nick. Think hard. "The trick to seeing a scam lies in identifying the mark. Who would all this weirdness be scamming? Dantelani has no money, so he is not the mark. They just took what they wanted from the bank, so no mark there. What could you scam off of folks like Cohen and Coyote? The only mark they've hooked so far would be you. The whole crazy scheme revolves around keeping you—L.A.'s most promising young detective—from cracking the Vampire Killer case. There, you have it!"

Yolanda ate the cream herself.

"You didn't like that one. I can tell. But look, have pity. People pull scams for money, and sometimes for publicity, but no boodle hangs at the end of all these notes. Grifters don't rob banks. That's a whole other category of criminal. Maybe the notes aren't as similar as we think. Anyway, I don't see any scam here at all."

Yolanda thought about that for a moment. She offered Nick some crème brulee. "I couldn't see a scam either. But what does that leave? Charles Sparrow, dead in 1937, robbing banks? Bank robbing ghosts kidnapping medieval scholars?"

Nick dove into his cheesecake. The crème brulee tasted much better. "You are not thinking of ghosts, and I know it."

"I won't get into crazy talk."

"Come on, you're missing the key link to all this: the *Compendium*. That's the Dantelani connection to your investigation. And the only thing that connects up to long-dead bank robbers. Maybe they are undead bank robbers."

Yolanda could tell from his voice that Nick did not really consider this a possibility. She said, *"You're* the connection between all this. You put me on to Dantelani, and you were prime suspect in the theft of the *Compendium*. You introduced me to Cohen and told me about Coyote's note. *You* are the common link here."

"Right," said Nick, "and I used the Latin tome to resurrect dead stickup men and knocked over a bank. All while cruising the tables at Vegas. I'm the man."

Yolanda didn't know what to think.

They ate their desserts in silence and paid their separate checks. Nick held the door open for Yolanda when they left. The street outside Mama Tuscan's had grown dark. Yolanda had parked in the back lot, Nick across the street. "I could take you home—we could pick up your car in the morning."

"Generous of you." Yolanda noticed an elderly couple walking toward them holding hands. They walked stiff, in a manner that seemed to Yolanda both wrong, and yet, frighteningly familiar. Though a cool breeze blew, they wore far too many clothes for early fall in Southern California. They did not look ahead of them as they walked. Both stared wide-eyed at Yolanda.

"We could just play cards. As long as we had cards out, have a drink," Nick said.

The couple hobbled forward, never moving their eyes off Yolanda. They never blinked. The light of the streetlights played off their faces, showing them, then concealing them.

"We could just spend more time together. I'll sleep on the couch. You can sleep there too, if you like," Nick said.

The couple was almost upon them. Yolanda grabbed Nick's arm hard and nodded at the couple as they passed, staring at the two of them, wide eyed. Nick looked over at them. To Yolanda he said, "Yeah, weird, uh. That's the *death-glare look*. Read about it in *Newsweek*; all the rage among the trendy set. You'd think that older folks like that would be past such fashionable nonsense."

"Nick, that look, their faces—those were just the expressions of the bank robbers on the F.B.I. video."

Nick looked again, but the couple had walked on. More than at any time since she met him, Yolanda wanted more of Nick's company. Still, she went home alone.

DRAKANIAN ECONOMICS

Deputy Mayor Joe Stafford sat on the platform outside the Upper East Side Community Service Center. He came today to give a plaque to the head of the Community Center, who would accept on behalf of the entire community. It seems that the Upper East Side had achieved the unheard of distinction of having a zero crime rate. This after a rash of bizarre missing persons reports. For a few weeks or so, no one at City Hall, or the police department, could make heads or tales of this neighborhood. Now the city considered closing down the police substation, since so little happened here.

Not only that, but this neighborhood could also boast complete independence from most city services. They used little electricity, virtually no water, and produced stunningly little garbage. Social services received no calls for assistance from this neighborhood, and all of its parole violators reported dutifully to their parole managers, and held fulltime jobs in the community.

They didn't even complain about potholes.

So the Mayor decided that a plaque was in order, along with a special visit from his deputy. Joe Stafford met the Community Center director that morning. The fellow was a sallow skinned, soft-spoken man of few words. But, evidently, he knew how to get things done. By the afternoon he had arranged a platform, podium, and chairs. The Mayor had instructed Stafford to give the plaque to "someone in charge of the neighborhood." Stafford had initially thought to give it to the district's councilman, but he had gone missing the day before, and his staff had yet to find him. Not wanting any delays, Stafford thought perhaps the director of the Community Center might accept the plaque. On arriving, though, he found that the director insisted on Stafford handing it over to someone called *Mimaster*. Asked about details of Mr. Mimaster's association with the Community Center and the neighborhood, all he could get from the fellow was the constant repetition of the name. None of this mattered to Stafford. The plaque only named the neighborhood, so anyone could accept it. If they liked this Mimaster guy so much, he could accept it.

Stafford sat on the platform while the other minor neighborhood dignitaries took their places. Below him he noticed an incredible turnout by the civic-minded people of the community. He guessed over a thousand people sat in chairs or stood in the park around the platform. Such nice folks too. They all wore large nametags (which Stafford thought might be taking civic-mindedness a bit far). They didn't push, or shove, or jostle for a better view. They didn't block traffic, or even so much as cross against the light. "Don't Walk" meant don't walk to them, and there was the end of it. Even the children sat or stood without fidgeting or complaining. In fact, none of the people waiting for the start of the ceremony so much as spoke a word. Stafford had not noticed this at first, being preoccupied with talking on his cell phone, but now that he had put the phone away, the silence started to creep up on his nerves. He leaned over to the Community Center director and asked, "Why doesn't anyone talk?"

The director lurched over at Stafford in that disturbingly unbending manner he had, and upon processing Stafford's question, immediately got up and walked over to the microphone on the podium. He said to the assembled crowd: "Talk."

At once each of them began to speak. Stafford noticed they

did not talk to each other. Rather, each one, independent of anyone else, began talking out loud. Stafford found this more disturbing than the silence. The director sat down again next to Stafford, now to a cacophony of monotone murmurs. Stafford leaned over to the director and tried to distract himself with some small talk. "You seem to have a real neighborly community here. What sorts of things do folks like to do?"

The director jerked his head around to face Stafford and said, "Watch TV."

Stafford nodded politely. "I see, I see. Well. Anything in particular?"

"Public access, channel sixty-two. Four o'clock. Eight o'clock. Twelve o'clock. Tuesdays and Wednesdays. Repeats at two a.m. on Saturday," said the director.

"Oh," said Stafford, who decided thenceforth to distract himself with his cell phone.

Fashionably late, Mr. Mimaster arrived. Stafford guessed he was some sort of mortician. He certainly didn't get much sun, and he looked like he spent a lot of time hunched over something or other. Mostly though, Stafford supposed he worked at a mortuary because he arrived in a black and silver hearse. He had a driver, a huge fellow, and several hangers-on. Mimaster himself came dressed in black, wearing a cape and twirling a monocle in his left hand. Stafford identified him instantly, since everyone in the audience began repeating his name. "Mimaster, Mimaster, Mimaster," they said.

Mimaster worked his way through the crowd, nodding like some mafia don to the people, who dutifully nodded back. Once on the platform, the director introduced him to Stafford. Stafford missed most of the names and titles the fellow hurled at him in a torrent of words. He caught "Necro-Master," and "Re-founder of the Arval Brotherhood," but Stafford missed the rest. Mimaster kept the rest his introduction to the Deputy Mayor brief, "Great honor, Deputy Mayor, great honor. Long awaited; quickly given. Most appreciated. I have a few words to speak, not many. Stitchers to train today, not your worry; just a few words and fine plaque, fine plaque."

The ceremony began. The crowd quieted to a death-hush. Stafford gave a brief speech on what a fine neighborhood they had and then presented the plaque to Mr. Mimaster. Mimaster gave a forty-minute speech that covered everything from the dead of ancient Egypt to always following your dream. Stafford could not make heads nor tails of any of it, but the crowd hung on every word. At the end Mimaster said, "Now, you may clap," and they did—not stopping until Mimaster had left and the director told them to stop. Stafford figured the whole neighborhood had joined some weird cult and hoped the press did not find out that the mayor's office had just plaqued the cult leader.

On the other hand, they did have a low crime rate.

Drakan adored his new plaque. He hung it just below the Great Seal at his new headquarters at Forest Lawn. Having converted the entire staff, and most anyone who happened by, into zombies, he pretty much owned the place now. Grave-robberies had dampened the burying business to nothing (cremation was all the rage lately—much to Drakan's chagrin), but the hills of Forest Lawn were alive with the sleeping dead. Zombie teams worked night and day digging up new companions. To lighten the mood, Drakan had Vinnie teach them a working song. Vinnie chose one that went "The ants go marching one by one, hurrah, hurrah." The song seemed oddly familiar to Drakan, though the zombie rendition probably did slim justice to the original. In addition to the digging, Drakan had set a zombie construction crew loose building a Great Hall, in which he meant to install his throne room, and from which he would direct his empire. He had designed it himself, right down to the gargoyles. The original Fort Necro continued to operate as a zombie factory and movie studio.

The building of the Great Hall proceeded far more smoothly and swiftly than Drakan had any right to expect. Zombies had many advantages. They had no union, worked night and day without breaks or meals, and had no concern over safety. Once trained in some repetitive act, they would proceed to do it without the first hint of malingering. So long as you used undead for tasks they had performed in life, they could re-learn their old trades without much ado. Just don't ask a zombie carpenter to lay bricks. He will only hammer away at them mindlessly. The bricklayers also needed clear markings as to how far, and how high, to build, or they would construct a Great Wall of China from Forest Lawn to the freeway.

Drakan would write out his instructions to the crews in his invisible zombie paint, and they would stop building where he wanted. In this manner they made great progress, although the Gothic building they constructed looked a bit ramshackle. It listed over a bit, as if leery of standing up too high and attracting unwanted attention. Drakan thought it would turn out grand.

Drakan used the offices of Forest Lawn as his new administrative headquarters. He had, already, quite an empire to administer. Making movies required cameras, film, editing equipment, enough lights to illuminate the Mojave Desert, props, sets, and the constant processing and booster-shooting of new and old technicians. Drakan's various construction projects required a constant stream of raw materials and tools as well. He found it most efficient to simply take over his suppliers by converting their staff into ghouls—including their families and neighbors. These new zombies could then be kept working in their old occupations contributing their salaries to Drakan's expanding empire.

Drakan had worried at first that converting people into zombies while leaving them in the homes they had used while alive, might appear suspicious. He still wanted his empire to remain secret. Surprisingly, most people managed to continue in undeath much as they had in life, and do so without attracting much attention. Neighbors rarely knew each other's names anyway. If people were not seen in public, everyone just assumed they were at home watching television.

Drakan and his minions constituted a true underground economy. Ghouls would continue to work, either at their old jobs—now fully populated by other ghouls, or on Drakan's various projects. What money they might make in the regular economy, they funneled uncomplainingly to Drakan. He, in turn, supplied them with reanimation fluid boosters. To receive these he had devised a careful schedule, constantly updated as his empire expanded, which cycled all of his many minions through local booster stations at least once a week. Any alterations to this schedule, or other instructions to his horde, could be announced on public access TV. Apparently, only zombies watched this.

In addition to booster shots of the serum of undeath, Drakan provided his followers, quite literally, with direction. In his invisible zombie paint, he marked the walls, billboards, mailboxes, lampposts, street signs, windows, doors, and traffic lights with words and directions that he and his ghoulish aids taught each zombie to understand. For the undead, L.A. became a sea of signs, just as for the living, and they traveled in their appointed paths without hesitation or thought. Drakan only had to brief the zombie painters carefully and use the intoxicant periodically to check their work.

His principle difficulty lay now in administration. The undead were not self-starters. He had to set up their tasks for them, either directly or through undead intermediaries. These intermediaries themselves had to be carefully briefed. On the other hand, undead administration required very little paperwork. Invariably honest, the undead could be counted upon to keep doing whatever you started them doing, without slacking. Drakan had found that most paperwork revolved around discouraging indolence and discovering deviousness. The undead, lacking these vices, made up the modern world's first true paperless economy. Drakan prided himself on being an innovator in business as well as science.

His empire remained unknown to the living. He had yet to find a way to present his momentous discovery to the world, and thus reap his measure of fame. Certain issues of so-called ethics still dogged his achievements. But as his empire grew, it dawned upon him that if he could not go forth to the world and declare his greatness, he could make the world come forth unto him and declare him great. If a punctilious nit-picking about not killing people prevented the living from seeing him as a true heir to Aristotle and Newton, then he would make the whole world undead and bustle in it as The Master. Not a bad thought, but he needed a better name than that. Something that would really sing.

◆ ◆ ◆

Vinnie had new quarters. He had a full suite at the Necronic Palace, as the Baron now called their Forest Lawn Headquarters. He had a kitchenette to cook his meals in (he had declined the Baron's offer of a personal undead chef), a living room for his TV, and a separate bedroom with a king-sized bed. He suffered only one deprivation. Privacy. For reasons Vinnie could not penetrate, the Baron insisted on Mr. Tony the Zombie sharing Vinnie's quarters. The Baron said that Vinnie could train his former friend into becoming another Charley Sparrow. In actuality, Vinnie did his best to keep the zombie cracksman marching mindlessly into a corner of the room.

Vinnie had once been terrified of the undead. But like a ghost that stays too long, undeath had gone from terrifying to merely irritating. Mr. Tony the Zombie left green slop in the bed and on the living room floor, he moaned at night while Vinnie tried to sleep, he rocked back and forth on his heels when he had nothing else to do, and he always stared at Vinnie with big eyes that seemed a constant indictment. "Why, Vinnie, why?" those eyes said. Mr. Tony the Zombie *himself* said nothing except occasionally, "Fuuu … ken … a," which Vinnie found aggravating and always inappropriate. Beyond that, Mr. Tony the Zombie provided the Baron with a constant source of complaint, "Made any progress with your friend?" the Baron would ask. And, "Why can't your friend be more like Mr. Sparrow?" Vinnie had half a mind to tell the Baron that his friend could have been more like Mr. Sparrow if the Baron hadn't had Mr. Sparrow smash his brains to pulp. But Vinnie held his tongue. Tony had reached his present condition by mouthing off too much.

Tonight Vinnie had a function to attend. That's what the Baron called it. So Vinnie wore a tuxedo, recently liberated from one Alfred C. Knox, now Alfred C. Knox the Zombie. This would be a big event for the Baron. He and Vinnie had spent much of the day arranging matters. The guests were all dug-up and re-animated—that proved the easy part. The hard part was rehearsing them for the party.

Vinnie arrived at the Great Hall, still without a roof, and helped direct the paint crew in its last minute preparations. Undead celebrities did not mingle right if left to their own devices. The Baron's first celebrity party had ended rather quickly and rather badly. The Baron had arrived and noticed that while all his guests held champagne glasses (with strict instructions not to drink lest they leak on their clothes), none of them moved or talked. The Baron ordered general moving about, and within ten minutes every ghoul in the place, from Jimmy Stewart to Red Buttons, had piled into one corner of the room, nearly crushing the Baron, who had to beat a hasty retreat. It had taken Vinnie and a couple of construction zombies over two hours to pull everyone apart. The Baron did not want a repeat of that fiasco.

So this time the Baron had painted footprints on the floor in zombie paint, along with detailed orders instructing each guest where to move when the appropriate signal sounded. He had selected a gong to sound the signal. Each time the gong sounded, the ghouls would walk in the traces of the footprints to their next conversational partner—careful not to spill any champagne. So that mirth and revelry would reign, each guest had been given a script instructing them what to say at the party and when to laugh.

The Baron assured Vinnie that the guest list could not be improved upon. Lana Turner laughed (rather frighteningly) with Raymond Chandler and D.W. Griffith. Buster Keaton did pratfalls (407 on the night) while Katharine Hepburn and Spencer Tracy raised champagne glasses to their mouths, careful not to spill any fluid down their undead throats. Errol Flynn flirted with Douglas Fairbanks (whom the Baron had put in a wig—the guest list had included too few female zombies, and Fairbanks was a great actor after all—or so the Baron had assured Vinnie). A short Humphrey Bogart the Zombie traded tough-guy talk with a hulking undead John Wayne. Laurel and Hardy the Zombies listened raptly as Lou Costello the Zombie repeated his trademark "Hey Abbott!" over and over and over. The actual Bud Abbott could not attend, due to cremation.

The gong sounded, and each reveler proceeded mechanically to the next station and repeated their party routine in new company. W.C. Fields the Zombie could not resist drinking the bubbly. Groucho Marx and Lucille Ball held glasses beneath his portly frame and gathered in the now green-tinted champaign as it flowed out again. To this Fields murmured, "I am punctuated, I am no single souse—I am a river to my people." The only witticism not scripted by the Baron himself. More typical was Bela Lugosi's line: "I vant to zip your champaign!" Lugosi, incidentally, was the only zombie in attendance who wore the clothes he had been buried in: his Dracula costume. If only Boris Karloff had not been buried in England.

Again the gong sounded, and again the party rotated, as if a part of some macabre square dance. Alan Hale Sr. said, "I'm proud of my son, I really am," 232 times. Clark Gable said, "Frankly my dear, I give a damn if I give a damn," 307 times. Harold Lloyd continuously cleaned his glasses. The

Baron showed up fashionably late. He mingled happily with his guests. He would motion for the gong to sound and watch as they traced their steps.

After the party ended, and the celebrities had been put away, the Baron gushed at Vinnie over the success of the soiree. Next time they would have to include society people. And more intellectuals. Vinnie figured this meant a road trip to New York City in the near future.

Two days later though, Vinnie found the Baron newly obsessed with a different matter altogether. Vinnie stood by while he paced frantically about in the Great Hall as the zombie construction workers tried, with little success, to put on the new roof. Vinnie dared not interrupt a determined pace by the boss, and so he just waited until the Baron spilled what had so captured his attention. Finally, the Baron noticed Vinnie standing there and walked over. He thrust a pamphlet into Vinnie's hand and said, "Uh huh, uh huh," and then returned to pacing. Vinnie looked at the pamphlet. It appeared to be an advertisement from the Los Angeles County Museum, announcing a visiting exhibit.

The Treasures of Ancient Egypt.

BOOKED FOR REVELATIONS

At seven o'clock on Sunday morning, Officer John Cavet of the LAPD forced his way into a refrigerated storeroom at the back of the Haywood Grocery Store and Deli on the upper east side of town. He had come to the neighborhood grocery in response to a patron's complaint. The man said he had found a human finger in a salami sandwich, purchased at the store. The store's door had not been locked, and Officer Cavet entered fearing a burglary might have occurred. He entered the refrigerated storeroom in case crooks had stranded the staff there. He found no staff members. He did find over two hundred dead bodies, crammed into the unit. Officer Cavet's find made the front pages.

Detective Harmon of the Vampire Killer Task Force assured the press that this discovery had no connection to their case since the bodies had not been drained of blood. Yes, the task force did have suspects in the case. No, he would not say anything more at this time.

The Mayor informed the press that, contrary to rumors, he had not given a plaque to the neighborhood in honor of its low crime rate. The Deputy Mayor had done so, quite without the mayor's consent. No, the Deputy Mayor would not be available for comment; he had just left on a fact-finding tour of the Aleutians. The Mayor had no idea where the bodies had come from, but urged the press not to assume any foul play until the LAPD completed its full investigation.

Deputy Sheriff John Crosswell, head of the Vampire Slayer Task Force, informed the press that while he did not believe the Vampire Slayer had any connection with the bodies allegedly found by the LAPD, he intended to include a full investigation of the event as part of his task force's operations. He meant by this, a full investigation of the alleged discovery, not of the cause of death of those found in the freezer, which he assumed the LAPD could handle. He did confirm that the Sheriff's Office was considering a lawsuit against the LAPD for copyright infringement in their continued use of the name "Vampire Killer."

Finally, the Board of Health declared that the grocery's deli would drop from a *B* to a *C* rating.

Detective Yolanda Vasquez checked her e-mail for the fifth time that day. She had made electronic contact with a woman at the F.B.I. in Virginia who seemed to know what she was doing. The woman worked as an archivist in the fingerprint department, and at Yolanda's request agreed to conduct a special search. At three o'clock in the afternoon, while the rest of the department traded theories on the Freezer Killer case, Yolanda received her reply from the F.B.I. The e-mail read: "One match found for fingerprints lifted from 1800 Pilot Avenue. These match one Charles Sparrow, suspect in bank robbery occurring on October 14, 1937. Suspect recorded as dead at scene."

Yolanda worked a theory: someone wanted to cover their crimes—serial murder and armed robbery—by giving the appearance that a cult had learned to raise the dead. They wanted the police to think that zombies were loose upon the land. They stole the *Compendium* from the Marion Wright to start the false trail. They dug up Charles Sparrow (Yolanda had checked: the Sparrow grave had been pillaged early in the spree of grave robberies) and placed his fingerprints at the 1800 Pilot Avenue crime scene, along with other false leads. They used a *Sparrow mask* of their own design when robbing the First American Metropolitan Bank. This, they hoped, would further mislead the police. When a detective on the LAPD (i.e., Yolanda herself) had taken the initial bait, and interviewed Professor Dantelani, they kidnapped him in order to further generate suspicion of zombie activity. She couldn't fit the Cohen/Coyote notes into the story, but the rest fit. Except for one little problem. No one, not even Yolanda, could possibly believe such nonsense.

Serial killers who rob both banks and graves, while faking zombie resurrections? The only explanation for her data that seemed to Yolanda less likely than this was the one she could not bring herself to express. That someone had killed a prostitute to bring Charley Sparrow back to life in order to rob a bank. And not just Sparrow, but many others as well. Apart from the obvious scientific absurdity of the idea, Yolanda could not fathom the psychology of someone who would actually try to pull off so unlikely a scheme. Still, everything should be checked out.

She contacted Lawrence Seward of the University of California, Los Angeles, Department of Biology. After finally convincing him that she worked for the LAPD, and that she meant to play no prank on him, he confessed to never having considered the possibility of bringing the dead back to life.

"Technically, *undeath*," Yolanda corrected him. She felt hugely silly the moment she said that, but this is just the sort of thing you get into when you bandy about necromantic notions. Dr. Seward said he doubted anything that the alchemist of the Middle Ages had come up with would have the least legitimacy from the point of view of modern biological science—least of all raising the dead. "To life or undeath," he had said. The soul of politeness, he had referred her to a college in the anthropology department of USC who studied the phenomenon of zombies in Haiti.

Yolanda called professor Dakota Tennor at USC. After convincing the good doctor of her bona fides, she asked about the possibility of raising the dead or the viability of the concept of *undeath*. Dr. Tennor spoke at length on the subject of voodoo—especially its legitimacy as a true religion and its unjust vilification in movies. Dr. Tennor also assured her that Hollywood and the press greatly exaggerated the frequency of actual Haitian zombie making.

"Then there are real zombies?" Yolanda had asked. Within minutes Dr. Tennor made her sorry she had broached the question. She gave Yolanda a twenty-minute lecture on the semantics of the term *zombie*. The doctor followed this with nearly thirty minutes on the symbolic nature of the zombie in voodoo ritual. This tendency to bludgeon with lectures dissuaded Yolanda from asking any further questions. Yolanda had, in any case, found out what she needed to know. So far as modern science knew, Haitian zombies, what real ones there might be, were persons who had never actually died, but only been drugged and then revived. Modern science did not recognize any such thing as *undeath*. Unless Yolanda got a lucky break in the case, she had nowhere left to go.

Detective Harmon readied himself for the battle. He would meet the foe with Tom Delaney and with partial assistance from Lieutenant Washington. He would also have an audience. He would conduct the interview in a room with a one-way mirror. On the other side of the mirror, members of the Vampire Killer Task Force would watch and take notes. These detectives gathered now in that room. Harmon sat on a table blocking their view of the interrogation room. He wanted to preserve the drama of the moment when he would step away and they would get their first look at the man he had to take apart. Harmon looked to this morning's exercise not only as a possible break in the case, but also a lesson in the art of police interrogation. Washington entered with Detective Mammon and Detective Vasquez. Then Detectives Johnson and Verlet entered. Then that pudgy kid that transferred over from CSI entered. Finally, Detective Grice, just promoted from patrol, and his partner, Detective Peterson, arrived. Harmon had pretty good attendance for early in the morning.

Harmon drank some Maalox and began his talk. "What we have here, gentlemen—ladies and gentlemen—or lady and gentlemen," Harmon hated the verbal politics of a gender diverse detective force. "That is, what we have here, is a possible break in the Vampire Killer case. Yesterday, I told the press that the Freezer Killer had no connection to the Vampire Killer. We all know that our evidence in the Vampire Killer case points to more than one killer. A cult or something, in fact. One theory, one I happen to subscribe to, holds that the killers like to freeze the blood and some of the internal organs of their victims. Jeffery Dahmer did this, we know, and it fits the Behavioral Sciences profile. Trophy taking they call it. Now maybe, just maybe, they have gone over to just freezing the whole dead body—not just blood or parts. If that were so—why, we have a whole new ball game."

No one in the room seemed too interested. Some drank coffee, one detective talked quietly on his cell phone. Harmon hated the invention of the cell phone. It seemed designed to insure that no one could ever again be forced to listen to anyone else.

"Whose the perp?" someone asked. Probably that jerk, Detective Verlet. Harmon continued, "This guy, the one Detective Delaney and I will question this morning, he was a gimme." Harmon had just now made up "gimme" as a police slang term. He found that the young detectives tended to pay more attention, and accord more respect, if you peppered your speech with new slang. No one would ever ask what the new term meant, for fear of seeming out of the loop and unprofessional.

"What's a *gimme*?" asked Detective Vasquez.

Harmon grimaced and drank some more Maalox. Vasquez: a loose cannon. "I just mean he walked into a police investigation and immediately aroused suspicion. This occurred about noon yesterday while CSI documented the Haywood Market crime scene. The media boys had left, and the officer controlling admit took a brief potty break cause no one in the neighborhood showed any interest in the crime scene. It was kinda weird, but no one hung around gawking or anything. So no one manned the police line while CSI dusted the refrigeration unit. This was *after* all the bodies had been removed. Well, seems this fellow just walked in and asked one of the crime scene investigators who had ordered the bodies removed. Didn't take but a minute for the investigator to figure out the guy asking wasn't a cop. A detective arrived and interviewed the guy. He seemed suspicious so we brought him in and printed him.

"The guy's name is Vincent Ramano. He has a long rap sheet, mostly second story work. We faxed his picture around and got some more interesting results. Nothing violent and no crazy stuff, but he sits pretty crooked. Ramano doesn't live in the neighborhood and has no business there. We think maybe he knows something about these bodies. I'm going to find out what."

Harmon moved from the table and revealed Vincent Ramano standing at the one-way mirror poking at a zit.

◆ ◆ ◆

Vinnie hated the fact that his acne always exploded whenever he went into police custody. Stress, the doctor said. Bullshit said Vinnie. All day, everyday, working with dead people—plenty of stress there; no zits. Now, less than twenty-four hours with the blue goons, and he could be an acne cream *before* picture.

The door opened and two men entered. "Sit down!" one yelled. Why do cops always yell? Vinnie sat.

"I'm Harmon, this is Delaney." Vinnie nodded politely to the two detectives. Harmon said, "You have been informed of your rights and have waived your right to an attorney, that right?"

Vinnie nodded. He sure as hell did not want an attorney. What on earth could he tell one? Vinnie could handle these guys smooth and easy.

"Now, Vincent," Harmon said, "Should we call you that? Vincent?"

"Vinnie."

"Fine, Vinnie. Now Vinnie, could you tell us just what you were doing at the Haywood Market and Deli yesterday?"

"Sure," Vinnie said, "I just stopped in for a pint of milk and a Twinkie." Always provide details, Vinnie thought, not just *food*, but some particular item of food.

"Milk and a Twinkie," Harmon said. "Thing is Vinnie, according to your driver's license, you live forty miles away. Why come so far for milk and a Twinkie?"

Vinnie could handle this. "I'm thinking of re-locating. You know how it is. You want to get the feel of a place before you settle down there." He looked at Delaney, who seemed a sympathetic sort—Vinnie had a sense for people and could tell things like that. "You know, you want to see what the folks are like, that the grocery stores have the food you like, that there aren't too many spics living there. Stuff like that." Detective Delaney nodded sympathetically.

"So you were just checking out the Twinkie supply at the local grocery store?" Harmon said.

"Yeah."

"Before you bought into the neighborhood."

"Right," Vinnie said, "bought or rented. Probably buy. Time to settle down and all."

Harmon nodded. Vinnie thought all this was going well.

"So, Vinnie," Harmon said, "how come you had a key to the front door in your pocket?"

"Key?" Vinnie said. He thought that by saying *key* right then he could buy himself some time.

"Yeah, key. When we searched your pockets, we found a key. We tried it on the front door of the grocery store. It fit. Why did you have that key on you, Vinnie?"

Vinnie had rather hoped to buy more time than that by saying *key*. "Well," Vinnie said, discouraged at how little time saying *well* bought him, "see I found the key, I was returning it. To the rightful owners." That should do.

Delaney spoke up, "Where'd you find the key, Vinnie?"

Vinnie hit his stride, "In an alley. I'm looking in this alley, to see if they're clean and all—for if I want to live in the neighborhood. I find this key. The one to the grocery store. So I go there to give it back to them. I want to be a good citizen in my new neighborhood. If I go live there, you see."

Harmon leaned forward, "What I don't quite see is how you knew from looking at it that the key opened the grocery store. How did you know to take it *there*?"

Cops. You had to work everything out for them. "I used to work in a grocery store. Not that one, another one, a long time ago. I know what those keys look like."

The two detectives just looked at him.

Vinnie gave a little chuckle. "Ha, okay, you got me, just a joke there. Lighten the room a little. See, really, I didn't know it would open the store. I just found the key and took it there. Figured they could find the owner. Stores do that, you know?"

Harmon said, "Did you know that the freezer there contained two hundred and two dead bodies?"

"Hell no!" Vinnie said. "I was just returning a key. I found a key and I was turning it over. Get my cookies and milk, and I was out of there."

Harmon said, "So why'd you go to the back and ask the investigator where the bodies had gone?"

Delaney said, "I thought you went in for Twinkies. Was it Twinkies or cookies?"

Vinnie jerked his head back and forth at the two men, wondering which question he should concentrate on. Finally, after some thought, he said, "I went in there looking for

Twinkies. Only just now, I wished I had some cookies. Twinkies are my favorite, but I like cookies too. So just now I wanted some cookies and so I said cookies. But yesterday at the store, I wanted Twinkies. Definitely Twinkies."

The two detectives seemed unimpressed. Vinnie pressed on, "About going in the back. I was looking for someone, about the milk—in the freezer maybe. So I go in the back. And, you know, about asking about bodies," Vinnie gave a little laugh, "well that was a joke—you know, *who took the bodies pal*? Like a joke. Just a thing you say." Vinnie could tell the detectives didn't buy all that. But they had not raddled him, and he could see the end of the tunnel now.

"Okay, let's forget about the grocery store for now," Harmon said.

Vinnie felt better, almost through the woods, free and clear.

Harmon said, "I want to ask you where you were three weeks ago Tuesday."

Vinnie concentrated, he had no head for dates.

Delaney said, "Let me help you out with that, Vinnie," and he put a picture in front of Vinnie. Vinnie's heart sank. The picture showed the front of the First Metropolitan Bank. Vinnie thought fast.

"I don't bank there."

The detectives laughed. "Now Vinnie," said Harmon, "we have your rap sheet right here. We know your record. You robbed that bank. We want to hear about that."

Vinnie shook his head vigorously. "You've seen my sheet. I never robbed with a gun before in my life. I work nights, creeping. You got no way to pin that on me."

Delaney said, "Who said they used a gun?"

Harmon said, "Who said they robbed it in the day?"

Vinnie felt he had started to lose control of the situation. "I just mean, you have no proof I did it."

Delaney put another picture before Vinnie. Vinnie saw himself in a cowboy hat pulling a mask down over his face. Now, that had to look bad. Vinnie gave a long hard think on this one.

"That's you, Vinnie," Harmon said, "The F.B.I. has a whole video tape of the robbery. We faxed them your picture. They seemed pretty pleased when they got it."

Delaney said, "When we're done with you, we send you to the Feds. They have a lot to talk to you about."

Vinnie shook his head for a moment. Then he pounded the picture on the table and shouted, "Oh Lenny! Why, Lenny? Why? When Mother gave you so much? Lenny! Lenny!" Vinnie wept on the table, his shoulders heaving with sobs. For once, the two detectives seemed at a loss for words. Vinnie wept on, face on the table, hands over his head. Only once did he peak up to see what effect all this had on the detectives.

Finally, Delaney asked, "Who's Lenny?"

Vinnie collected himself. He choked back a sob. He said, "Lenny," he chocked back more tears, "is my long lost twin brother. No, no, don't interrupt me. This is hard enough. I haven't seen Lenny in years. He was a good kid. My kid brother. I mean, not much more of a kid than me, of course, but I was the older. Three minutes older. So I've always felt responsible. And Mom! She did so much for him. But Lenny. I hate to say this, but Lenny, he's a bad kid. He went wrong. So many things. But I never expected this! Lenny! Lenny!" Score.

"So," Harmon said, "you're saying that this is your twin brother, Lenny, in the picture."

Through his sobs Vinnie said, "We're identifiable twins, so we look alike and all."

Harmon continued, "And you're saying that it was Lenny, your evil twin, and not you, that held up the bank?"

"How could he? He did. But how could he?" Vinnie sobbed.

"And you say you haven't seen Lenny in years?" Harmon asked.

"If only I had been there—with Lenny I mean—maybe I could have set him right!"

Harmon leaned in, "Vinnie. Vinnie. Look here. In the picture. Vinnie? Look here."

Vinnie collected himself and looked at the picture where Harmon pointed.

"Look here Vinnie," Harmon continued, "see that shirt Vinnie, the one in the picture? It's the same shirt you're wearing right now Vinnie. Now, how is it Lenny's got your shirt Vinnie? I mean, if it's Lenny and not you robbing the bank there? How is it he has your shirt?"

Vinnie studied the picture and yes, goddamn it, it was the same goddamn shirt. If only Ethel the Zombie hadn't gotten the damn blue stains out he would have thrown the damn shirt away. Lucky cops.

"Let's cut the crap, Vinnie," Delaney said, "you play ball with us and we can help you out."

"You guys ever heard of multiple personalities?" Vinnie asked.

"Just don't call one of them *Lenny*, okay?" Harmon said.

"Fuck it, I give," Vinnie said. "The truth, you guys will never believe it."

"Try us," Delaney said.

"You guys ever heard of *undead*?"

Right up until Vinnie had said the word "undead," Yolanda, sitting behind the two-way mirror with the other observers, had paid almost no attention. That one word shot through her like a static charge. She listened as Vinnie told the two detectives that he worked for a man called Baron von Finkelstein, who sucked the blood out of people to make zombies. How he, Vinnie, was actually Major Vinnie the Yak, number two man in the organization. Vinnie went on to relate that he and the Baron robbed graves to find bodies to *reanimate*. He also told the men that his master was shooting movies staring Clark Gable and some North Pole explorer, and had a TV show. They ran a dead body underground railroad that channeled the bodies of dead war heroes from Arlington

National Cemetery to "Fort Necro" and the "Necronic Palace."
At this point, Harmon terminated the interview.

The other detectives behind the two-way mirror filed out
of the room, slightly amused and mostly bored. Yolanda sat
pinned to her seat. She quickly wrote down everything she had
heard from Vincent Ramano. Then she got up and went into
the hall. There she got a glimpse of the little cat burglar being
hauled away to the upstairs holding-cell. Harmon and Delaney
talked, huddled in a corner. Yolanda caught some of their
conversation as she approached.

"I thought we had him for a minute there," Delaney said.

Harmon said, "He's tougher than he looks."

Yolanda interrupted them. "Sir," she said to Harmon, "I'd
like to question that suspect further."

Harmon waived a dismissive hand at her, "Not till we get
a psych evaluation. Delaney has dibs anyway. You want to
question him, you have to do it with Delaney."

Delaney cast a wicked smile at Yolanda. She chased Harmon
down the hall. "How much of that last bit did you credit?" she
asked.

Harmon stopped and turned at her. "Don't insult me," he
said.

◆ ◆ ◆

Yolanda poured over her list. She could find no *Finkelstein*
or *von Finkelstein* or any variant spelling. Nor any *Baron*. Nor
anything similar. No one with those names had checked out
large numbers of books on the occult from the L.A. County
Library system for the last four years. She hoped to have more
luck with a second visit to the Grandmaster Ghoul.

Yolanda heard the first shots while she locked her lower
desk drawer. Gun shots in a police station demand an
immediate response. Yolanda gripped her service revolver.
Around her, cops stopped what they were doing and froze in
place, listening. Then more shots, and everyone came alive.

Several officers rushed to the window while some headed for the stairwell. At the window one of them shouted, "We're under attack!" Yolanda had a hard time processing that bit of information. Police stations just don't normally come under attack. Then the windows exploded from gunfire. The officers standing at the windows ducked for cover. Bullets punched holes in the walls. Aquariums exploded everywhere.

"God damn!" someone shouted.

"I'm hit! Christ!"

Several officers at the window began returning fire at the street below. Yolanda crawled over to the detective lying in a pool of blood holding his leg. She took off her jacket and wrapped it around his bleeding leg. She thought it very odd that her only thought at that moment was to notice that no one cared what her breasts look like as she took off her jacket. In violent adversity, she had finally obtained full membership in the fraternity of police.

Detective Peterson joined her next to the wounded cop. "Damn," he said. Yolanda knew that Peterson had been an army medic and she let him take over caring for the wounded man. She heard the sound of gunfire growing louder at the stairwell door. She pulled her gun and half crawled, half walked, toward the door. Glass exploded over her head, but she could see only the stairwell door. She felt like her legs trudged through molasses and that thick mud clung to her shoes. Her breathing sounded louder than the gunshots blasting out the window. She closed on the door.

The door flew open. A vision from hell, mouth gapping, eyes open wide in angry terror, appeared in the doorway. The gapped-mouthed man wore an old marine uniform, such as one would see in a World War II movie. Yolanda absolutely froze. The ghoul raised an M14 rifle and Yolanda snapped back to the world and opened fire on him. She hit him twice in the chest. The horrid marine fired the M14 and she aimed again, this time at his head. She kept firing her gun until she heard the metallic click of the hammer falling on an empty chamber.

The man at the stairway door took a step forward. He seemed to have noticed Yolanda for the first time and aimed the gun at her. Yolanda's blood froze. She would die here, killed by god-knows what and for no reason she could understand.

She watched as a large chunk of the ghoul's head popped off. Crouched on the floor, just below the ghoul, Tom Delaney fired up at the man. The ghoul turned about and fired two bullets straight into Tom's chest. Yolanda jumped back behind a desk and began to reload her revolver. When she popped back in view of the stairs, ready to make her own last stand, the ghoulish marine had left. Yolanda rushed to Tom who lay on the ground bleeding. He looked at the ceiling with a stunned expression.

"I hit the fucker in the head," Tom said in a voice giving way to darkness.

Yolanda shouted at him, "Tom! Listen! Stay with me! You'll be alright! Medic! Peterson! By the stairs!"

Yolanda frantically worked to stem the tide of blood flowing from Tom's chest. Tom looked into her eyes. Peterson showed up and began what treatment he could. Yolanda never took her eyes off Tom's. Tom Delaney died, searching for his mother's features in the face of Yolanda.

The press reported that a large gang of thugs dressed in Halloween masks and old army surplus uniforms attacked the Fountain Avenue Precinct at 3:40 in the afternoon. The culprits wore body armor and briefly took over the precinct house. They freed all the prisoners kept in holding cells, many of them taken by the attackers against their will. One detective died in the melee, and over fifteen others had been wounded. The police had no idea why the attack had taken place or who was behind it.

FALL BACK, LEAP FORWARD

Justin Case read the morning paper, and he did not like what he didn't see. The police station attack of the previous afternoon dominated the front page. The paper claimed that the leader of the attack wore an *Audie Murphy mask*. Apart from that, the papers said nothing that the twenty-four hour TV news coverage had not already covered. This all read like old news to Justin Case.

What most concerned Justin Case was the complete lack of mention, for weeks now, mind you, of Justin Case. Three weeks earlier the papers crawled over each other to report him, and his lawsuit against Marlon Brando on behalf of the hefty method actor's former maid. Justin Case wanted justice for this maid, whom Brando had seduced, and by whom he had fathered two children, twins in fact. Brando denied all these allegations and thus proved his perfidy. The press ate it up. Then the stupid DNA tests came back and proved (if you believe in proof, which Justin Case did not) that Brando could not have been the father of the children. Imagine that. With two of them, you'd have thought the odds favored his fathering at least one. Then the maid failed her lie detector test, which indicated that she lied when she said "yes" to the question: "Have you ever been employed by Mr. Marlon Brando?" Justin Case could not see the relevance of this question, since obviously the woman could have cleaned Brando's house for free and thus never *technically* been employed by him. But, perversely, the press moved on to other stories.

Now Justin Case needed a new jump-start to his legal career. A few weeks ago it looked as if he had a quick ticket to Hollywood lawyer heaven. He, and he alone, represented a serial killer. And a photogenic one. But Nick Sabernail had gone from being a prime suspect in one of the biggest murder cases in the city's history, to being no one anyone cared about. Had the murders stopped? Not by a long shot. And now the papers suggested connections between the murders and the rash of grave robberies. Not only that, but they talked of a *death cult*. A death cult! And where did Justin Case fit into all this? As attorney to prime suspect Nick Sabernail he ought to be in the middle of the firestorm. But it seemed no one still thought Nick guilty of organizing mass serial murder. This struck Justin Case as quite absurd. One look at Nick Sabernail ought to set alarm bells ringing. With a guilty face like his, it was a wonder they let him walk the streets at all. What to do, what to do.

What Nick Sabernail needed was a clear and public denial of guilt. Justin Case needed to set this city straight and protect his client from any rogue stories that might encourage ... who knows? Spontaneous vigilante acts? Justin Case would look out for his client. Justin Case was on the case.

Nick Sabernail awoke to a wild blend of orange and brown and muted red. He closed and opened his eyes hard several times and the swirl of colors resolved themselves into the pattern of textile flowers. Nick rubbed his eyes and shifted his weight. He lay on a couch in a room clearly not his own. He raised himself up and felt his sore muscles realign themselves in some semblance of the human muscular system. He looked around at the room, illuminated by shafts of light, heralding the day through partly drawn brown curtains. The room smelled of lilacs. Not the fresh, wafting scent of lilacs in the wild, but the soapy, unidirectional scent of a lilac odor dispenser plugged into a wall.

"Awake at last," a woman's voice said. Nick turned around and saw the attractive features of Yolanda—aged thirty years or so.

"Mrs. Vasquez," Nick said.

Yolanda's mother smiled. "Yolanda takes a shower now. When she's done, I must go out and pick up a few things, if you think she's up to it?"

Nick noted that Mama Vasquez wasn't about to leave the house till her daughter got out of the shower. Nick wondered which one had that idea.

"It's almost noon," Mama Vasquez said, "but I made some coffee."

Nick rubbed his forehead and accepted the coffee. He remembered the night now. He had tried frantically to find Yolanda when the news of the police station attack first broke. He finally caught up with her messages at about nine o'clock last night. She had gone to stay the night at her mother's. Nick called her there, and to his surprise, she asked him to come over. Nick arrived at about ten. Yolanda's mother talked to them for about an hour and then went to bed. After that they talked till the sun began to seep light into the morning sky.

Yolanda told Nick about her suspicions, and especially about a fellow named Vincent Ramano, who had been taken (kicking and screaming it seems) from the precinct house during the attack. She also spoke at length about the death of Tom Delaney and how frightened she had been. She wondered if her dad would have been proud of her. For once in his life, Nick had nothing he could say. So he just listened. She would sometimes pause for ten minutes lost in thought, and then speak again. Nick said very little. During these long pauses he would just watch her and wait till she again felt like sharing her mind with him. Once, at around four in the morning, she began to cry and put her head on Nick's chest. Nick thought it the most beautiful experience of his life. At just before dawn she fell asleep and her mother entered the room and helped Nick put her in bed. Nick slept on the couch.

Now Nick felt like a man who had made a major breakthrough with the woman he loved yet had still managed to end up sleeping on the couch. Whoever had written that crap about being lucky in love when unlucky at cards did not have the first idea how the world worked.

Mrs. Vasquez turned on her soaps and Nick ate the scrambled eggs she had cooked for him. Yolanda appeared from the bedroom. What that woman could do with six hours sleep just boggles the mind.

"Good morning Mom," she said, "good morning Nick."

Nick smiled and presented her with scrambled eggs. Yolanda watched Nick while she ate them, for once not like a woman about to go for a gun.

Nick said, "I just love ending a date with breakfast."

Yolanda took a bite, smiled, and said, "That was not a date."

Nick's smile and fond feeling lasted all the way to the noon news. Then, over Yolanda's shoulder he saw a familiar face. "Mrs. Vasquez, could you turn that up?"

Nick went to the TV set. On it he saw the smiling face of his old friend Mike Beligesi; aka, Justin Case. Justin Case addressed a bouquet of microphones, "I want to make it absolutely clear that my client, Nick Sabernail, formerly a curator at the Marion Wright Museum, is in no way connected with the Vampire Killer case. In particular he is not himself the Vampire Killer, nor is he the leader of a death cult of Vampire Killers. Police allegations to the contrary remain completely unsubstantiated. Mr. Sabernail's lack of an alibi for some of the early killings, and his known interest in the occult, and his fixation on death, in no way warrant current police interest."

"What is he trying to do to me?" Nick asked the smiling face on the screen.

A reporter asked Justin Case, "Is your client currently a suspect?"

Justin Case continued his public defense of Nick Sabernail, "You'd have to ask the LAPD that question. I know they have recently detailed a large portion of the task force to an

316

investigation of my client. This amounts to police harassment, and I am considering litigation against the LAPD."

A reporter asked, "Where is Mr. Sabernail now?"

Justin Case said, "Mr. Sabernail's whereabouts are currently unknown, but this does not indicate any guilty consciousness on his part. Mr. Sabernail often disappears for long stretches of time. I am not here today to urge people to be on the lookout for Mr. Sabernail. I am here to challenge the LAPD to step up its investigation of Mr. Sabernail and his alleged murder fixation. We have nothing to hide and welcome further investigation."

At this point the news broke away to a car chase. Nick yelled at the TV, "I'll kill that little rat-weasel!"

"I'm not sure that's the way to demonstrate your innocence of murder charges," Yolanda said.

Nick gathered his things to go. "You'll be alright, Yolanda, while I take care of this?"

"I'm a big girl, but I think you should cool down before you confront Mr. Case," she said.

"Don't worry, I'll be cool by the time I find him. He's hiding now," Nick said.

As Nick left, Yolanda called out to him, "I wouldn't worry too much Nick, no one much watches the noon news."

◆ ◆ ◆

Drakan watched the noon news. It played on a row of televisions set above his extraction tables. He stood above a special subject, whose processing he intended to supervise himself.

"Baron!" Vinnie said, struggling against his restraints, "Please!"

"I am Drakan, and this is for your own good," Drakan said.

"Yes, Drakan. Drakan. Of course you are. But Drakan, why this? Why me?"

Drakan tried to concentrate on the news report. His attack on the police station had gone quite well. And why should it not? He had used the best marines in the country's history, lead by the Second World War's most decorated soldier. Yet he worried that the high media profile of the attack might garner too much police attention. He did not as yet know what Private Vinnie the Flea had told them.

"Please boss, I didn't tell them anything. I know the code. I leave the singing to Sinatra and all that. Really, please."

The pumps started. As a courtesy Drakan had left the gag off Vinnie. Also in case of any last minute confessions.

"Please Baron ... uh, Baron Drakan ..."

"I'm not a Baron," Drakan said, "I hate that stupid monocle. I'm glad to give up the Germanic title. Another good reason for this." Drakan noted with interest that the police suspected a fellow named Sabernail of crimes connected with Drakan's projects. This could be useful.

"Boss, Baron ... I don't want to be one of them ... I ... don't want ..." Vinnie died.

Drakan used Vinnie in an experiment to see if death by blood draining, without using the blood as a reanimation elixir, might not produce a higher quality zombie. Vinnie would be a trial subject. "Don't worry, Private Vinnie, I think you might rise quicker through the ranks once undead. I really much prefer working with the undead anyway."

Drakan called for Mr. Sparrow. He wanted Major Sparrow to drop something off for him.

Yolanda reported to the precinct house around one o'clock. Chaos had barely abated. Three officers were missing, possibly kidnapped by the assailants. Yolanda thought she might speak to Lieutenant Washington about Nick Sabernail. Come clean that she had perhaps developed a closer relationship to him than departmental protocols allowed. Lieutenant Washington could not be found. Detective Harmon conducted a briefing on the Vampire Killer case that she had not been asked to attend.

Yolanda decided that, as long as she had no one to confess to, she might as well go see the Grandmaster Ghoul about any von Finkelstein customers he might have had. She drove to Sepulveda and French, noting the oddly light traffic. Pulling in at O'Tenisey's shop, she saw that painters covered the nearby billboard with a clear shellac. Weatherizing it, she supposed. A painter also spread a clear liquid on the windows of O'Tenisey's store. Some sort of beautification project?

Yolanda entered the store. She called out, "Mr. O'Tenisey? Grandmaster Ghoul?" Nothing moved in the small store. She made her way to the counter, and had just touched the curtain concealing the backroom when it flew open, revealing a sallow faced O'Tenisey. Yolanda jumped back.

"Closed!" O'Tenisey said.

His voice had a hollow sound, his face a tenor of death. Yolanda felt her heart beat faster. She strained a bit for breath. "I'm detective Vasquez, Mr. O'Tenisey, remember me?"

O'Tenisey's visage had changed since their last meeting. He had no jolliness about him now. He looked like a gatekeeper to hell. "Go!" he said, raising a slow hand to point at the door.

Yolanda retreated to the door and left. Outside, she glanced at the painter covering the window with a transparent film. He turned his head to her. She gasped at his sunken eyes, and fixed, mirthless smile. Yolanda returned to her car and locked the doors. She felt almost as shaken as she had during the gunfight the day before. She started the car and wondered where to go now.

She drove home. In her apartment she changed clothes and called Nick's house. No one answered. She called the station to see if they needed her. Sergeant Tanner at the dispatch desk told her she could report in for a debriefing that night, or tomorrow if she preferred. He confided that Lieutenant Washington had been missing since the attack yesterday, and the detective division remained in a bit of an uproar. Yolanda thanked him and hung up. She took her second gun from the table drawer and put it into her bag. She left her apartment and drove to her mother's house.

It took Yolanda over an hour to persuade her mother to keep

the gun in the side-table drawer. Mama Vasquez knew how to shoot—Yolanda's father had taught her that. Yolanda and she had gone target shooting once long ago. Since that time, Yolanda's mother had cooled on the idea of having a gun in the house. Yolanda couldn't tell her why, now, of all times, it seemed important to huddle armed in one's home. Her mother took the gun to make her daughter feel better. They ate dinner, and Yolanda decided to take a walk around the neighborhood before going home. She would just feel better about leaving her mother alone if she could give the streets a quick walk through.

Night lay over the city. Streetlights cut the darkness into small illuminated islands of asphalt. Only the blue light of televisions came from the windows of the houses. A few cars drove down the street to add horizontal streams of light to the vertical shafts of the streetlights. Two men sat on a table outside an all night taco stand. Yolanda knew that they would leer at her, and make cracks, if she approached, but she did anyway. They saw her coming, but did not move from the table. Yolanda felt her skin crawl. On a slow night, a young woman should get more attention than this. Were they lookouts for a robbery?

Once close, Yolanda could see the men's faces lit by the light of the taco stand. They looked like corpses. The man in the taco stand had the same death look about him. Just then the smell of rotten food hit Yolanda's nose. The taco stand must have been full of rotten meat. Yolanda gagged and had to concentrate not to throw up. The men at the stand did not seem to notice the stench. Yolanda backed away. The men did nothing. She moved further down the street into the greater darkness of the night.

She walked until she saw a laundry mat, still open. In younger days she had brought her mother's laundry here. She saw a man through the window, standing by the row of dryers. Something about the man seemed frightening to her, something she could not put her finger on. She walked past the laundry mat looking into the window. The man appeared to be wearing an old fashion police uniform with two rows of buttons. The sort of thing New York cops might still wear, but that the LAPD had long given up. Yolanda paused. She walked to the door and entered. All the dryers had been turned on, they made a terrible din. In the far corner a bum lay sleeping across several chairs. The only other person in the place was the man wearing the old-time police uniform. Yolanda looked at him. He had a nightstick dangling from a rope on his belt. Again, unlike anything the LAPD would use today. She looked up at the man's face. His death-glare froze her. She considered running, but something familiar in his features held her feet fast. She took haltering steps toward the man.

"Father?" she said. The man turned dead yellow eyes on her. "Papa?" Yolanda said, near to bursting into tears now.

"Get along now," the man said in a soft, but hollow voice, "nothing to see here."

Yolanda backed away pulling out her gun. The man did not move. At the door she turned and moved back up the street to her mother's house. The men at the taco stand watched as she went by but did not move.

Yolanda banged on her mother's door. Mama Vasquez opened it. Yolanda almost cried she felt so relieved to see the life-filled glow of her mother's skin. Somehow, she had expected to see death there as well. Her mother instantly noticed her daughter's fear and pulled her inside, holding her close. Yolanda cried for a few moments then pulled herself together.

"Get your stuff," she said, "you're leaving."

"Why?" her mother asked.

"Get your things, you're going to Aunt Florentina's."

Mama Vasquez did not know why her oldest daughter intended for her to spend the night in the valley, but she could see that nothing would dissuade her, so she gathered an overnight bag. Yolanda escorted Mama Vasquez to the latter's car, like a Secret Service agent moving the First Lady. "Stay at

Aunt Florentina's till I tell you otherwise," Yolanda said. Mama Vasquez agreed.

Yolanda watched her mother drive off. She looked down the street. She saw no life anywhere. Yolanda returned to her mother's house and bolted the door.

She sat and collected her thoughts. Having no idea as to who one calls about a zombie infestation, she did what any sensible person would do: she called the police.

After a few moments she got Detective Harmon on the phone. "Is Nick Sabernail with you?" he asked.

Yolanda felt better that so human sounding a voice spoke to her. An angry sounding one, but richly human nonetheless. "No," she said, "Why?"

"We just recovered two Vampire Killer Victims from his apartment," Harmon said, "Two dead girls, drained of blood."

Yolanda's head whirled. "How?" was all she managed to say.

"We got a tip," Harmon said, "He is real dirty. Someone expunged his file from the computer. We think it listed offences relevant to the Vampire case. We have proof of his connection to some grave robbers. It's all coming together."

"I ..." Yolanda could say no more.

"I know you're compromised on this Detective Vasquez, just don't make any dumb moves. Report to duty at once. If you see Sabernail, do not try to apprehend him. Just report his location. You, come in now."

Yolanda hung up the phone. For almost twenty minutes she sat in silence. Then she took her mother's keys from the key tray. She walked out the door and locked it behind her. She walked down the street, trying hard not to look at the taco stand. She saw the laundry mat and stopped. Cold fear swept her, but she willed her left foot forward and continued to the door. She stepped inside. The drying machines rumbled. The room felt hot. The man in the uniform did not sweat. He had not changed position since she had last seen him; not a millimeter. Yolanda put her hand on her gun beneath her jacket and approached the man.

"What is your name?" she asked him.

"Move along now … nothing to see here," the man said.

"Who are you?" Yolanda said.

"Move … along now … nothing … to see … here," the man said.

"Don't say that!" Yolanda said, "I see you here. Look at me. You must be here, in this place, for a reason. Do you see me? Do you know me?"

The ghoul looked at her. He fixed on her eyes.

Yolanda felt near tears. "I need to talk to you. That must be why you're here. Why you are in this place. Please." Yolanda reached up and touched the man's face. It felt cold as damp earth. She pulled her hand back with a start.

The ghoul clutched tight his baton and grabbed Yolanda's shoulder hard. He raised the baton and said in a voice grown loud with some unearthly rage: "Move! Nothing to see!" He brought the baton down hard, but something struck his face as he did so. The ghoul lost his balance and stumbled backward. Yolanda saw that the base of a coat rack had hit him. She drew her gun as the ghoul rose up again.

"Papa!" she said. "Please! I have to talk to you!"

The ghoul backhanded her, knocking her to the floor. Yolanda righted herself and fired a shot at the wall. She could not bring herself to level the gun at the ghoul. The ghoul stood erect. It again raised the baton. A clothes cart flew over Yolanda's head from behind her and hit the ghoul. Hands grabbed her from behind. Warm hands; living hands.

"That's not your father, Yolanda," Nick's voice said to her, "we need to get out of here."

Nick pulled her to her feet as the ghoul lashed out again. They ducked the blow and both careened through the door. Nick practically threw Yolanda into his convertible. He jumped in and put the car in reverse screeching out of the laundry mat parking lot.

Yolanda came to her senses. Nick gunned the engine and headed down the road.

Yolanda yelled, "Stop!"

Nick said, "Later."

Yolanda pointed her service revolver and said, "Stop!"

Nick swung the car into an alley. He looked back. No one followed.

"Sometimes they keep after you."

"That was my father!" Yolanda said.

Nick turned around to face her. He ignored the gun and took Yolanda by the shoulders, gently. "That was not your father. It is just something some freak did to his remains. Listen. These things are all over town. I ran into Dantelani earlier this evening—or what's left of him. I nearly got my head squeezed off trying to talk to him." Nick pulled down his collar showing bruises around his neck.

Yolanda stared at his neck a moment. She said, "They found bodies at your apartment."

"I know. Can we talk about that somewhere else? Can I take us somewhere else?"

Yolanda looked around her. She opened the car door and backed out. "Go in front of me to mother's house," she said.

Nick sighed a tired sigh. They made their way to Mama Vasquez's. Yolanda opened the door. They entered. She faced Nick, gun in her hand. "Why are their bodies at your apartment?"

"Beats the hell out of me. Maybe Justin Case put them there as part of my defense," Nick said.

"Harmon said you have connections to grave-robbers."

Nick sat on the couch. "That would be Hunter Coyote," Nick said. "You must have missed the evening news. My lawyer vehemently denied that any reward was offered for information leading to my conviction. My friends have been lining up for pay day."

"What happened to your police record?" Yolanda said.

"Yolanda, your theory that someone is using the *Compendium* is on the money. Zombie masses are growing exponentially. Someone needs to do something, and we seem

to be the only people to even entertain the possibility that ...
I don't know what to say. That creatures come out when the
moon is blue."

A car pulled up on the street outside the house. Yolanda
ducked down to the floor. Nick joined her there. "That's a police
car," Nick said.

Yolanda saw that it was. Two patrolmen got out. One
approached the front door while the other stood by the patrol
car.

Yolanda felt trapped. "What happened to your police
record?" she whispered to Nick.

"Forget it, Yolanda," Nick said, "You can't decide that way.
I'm not a mystery you can solve. You have no bridge to cross
here; you make the leap or you don't. If you think I'm a killer,
turn me in now."

"You're wanted," Yolanda said.

The patrolman knocked on the door. Nick put his hand on
Yolanda's cheek.

Yolanda said, "You're wanted."

Nick kissed her gently. Yolanda lowered her gun to the
floor. She kissed Nick. She put both hands on his face. Tears
streamed down her cheeks. Looking into his eyes, she thought
he must be the most beautiful man she had ever seen.

Outside, the patrolmen looked around the house, searching
for traces of the Vampire Killer that had been stalking
Detective Vasquez.

Inside, Yolanda and Nick made love.

THE COLOR OF
UNDEATH

Nick and Yolanda awoke to birds chirping. They dressed quickly, and slipped out the back way of the house, feeling a bit like naughty teenagers. Yolanda made her way around to her car and saw no officers staking out the house. This seemed odd. Odd, too, that they had not tried to enter last night. But then, a lot of odd things had happened lately. She got in her car and drove around the block, picking Nick up after he had high-tailed it through a neighbor's yard. They drove and listened to the radio.

Yolanda's favorite news station had gone off the air. They found another one. The major news item of the morning covered the theft overnight of antiquities on loan to the Los Angeles County Museum. Following that, a reassuring report that officers thought kidnapped during Tuesday's police station attack had turned up alive and well. Then the newscaster said that another officer, a Detective Vasquez, was feared kidnapped by the notorious Nick Sabernail, prime suspect in the Vampire Killer case.

Yolanda and Nick had planned to drop Nick off at an attorney's office (not Justin Case) and allow him to arrange to surrender himself to police. On hearing of her supposed kidnapping, Yolanda called up police headquarters on her cell phone. She wanted to assure the department she faced no danger. After a few moments she had Lieutenant Washington on the phone.

"Come in now," he said.

"Sir," Yolanda said, "I haven't been kidnapped. I also have reason to believe that Mr. Sabernail will voluntarily surrender himself today."

"Come in now," Lieutenant Washington said.

Yolanda felt uneasy at the strange sound to his voice. "May I speak with Detective Harmon?" she asked.

"Harmon is away, come in now."

Yolanda hung up the phone. Nick noticed her concerned look. "What's wrong?" he asked.

"I don't know," Yolanda said. "He sounded odd. Like ... one of them."

They passed a car wash. The day was badly overcast, with a drizzle of rain, but the car wash did a booming business. "Pull in there," Nick said. Yolanda pulled into the parking lot of the car wash. They sat in the car and looked out at the car washers and their patrons. They dried cars in the light rain with slow, uncanny resolve.

"Could they do that? Pass a zombie off as a cop to people who knew him?" Yolanda asked.

Nick said, "You should have seen Dantelani; he looked very convincing. I drove around the neighborhoods near my house. Some seemed untouched by any of it, but others—I got the creeps."

"Mother's neighborhood seemed completely infected," Yolanda said, "but my neighbors seem normal."

"I think that's how they do it—they take over a small part of some place—a neighborhood, a business, a police station —and expand from there. I think the area around my house is starting to go over. When I went home yesterday, before anyone planted any bodies, I had thirteen messages recorded on my answering machine. Most came from neighbors I rarely spoke to, each one asking if I'd like to come over and watch some TV."

"I can't believe this," Yolanda said.

"That's why it can happen. No one can believe it. If you and

I hadn't drifted into all this gradually, we wouldn't believe it now."

Yolanda watched the eldritch car washers racing the rain to wet down the cars. "What do we do? How can we make anyone believe us?"

Nick thought a moment. "You once thought I might be the Vampire Killer, right?"

Yolanda smiled at him, "That was a simpler world."

"Right," Nick said. "How did you come to that? What clues did you follow? However you came to me, it also led us to knowing about all this."

"Well, there was the *Compendium* theft. Your lousy alibis, and—what happened to your police record? You did have one."

Nick waved his hand, "That isn't it. My record had a few minor bunko charges on it. A computer nerd friend of mine did a bit of hacking as a lark. What else?"

Yolanda fished in her bag for a moment. "This. It's a list of people who checked out books on death and the occult from the county library over the last four years. One hundred books or more. I found you on it. I also found your name on an index card at O'Tenisey's shop. You showed an unhealthy interest in newt eyes. Some were found at the Pilot Way crime scene."

"All research for the exhibit. I originally planned to focus on witchcraft."

Yolanda thought a moment, "Still, I had a sound strategy. I just focused too strongly on the handsome stranger."

Nick smiled, "What if we went to O'Tenisey's and compared his *whole* list to the library list?"

"One problem with that," Yolanda said. "He's gone ghoul."

"We'll tippy-toe."

◆ ◆ ◆

At O'Tenisey's, Nick found a back window whose bars had long rusted through. He pulled them back and crawled through the narrow space. His eyes had barely adjusted to the gloom when he saw a figure coming through the window.

"What are you doing? I can look by myself." Nick said.

"This is your idea of *tippy-toeing*?" Yolanda said, "Ripping great hunks of metal off the wall?"

"Shhh! Whisper!"

Yolanda pushed past him, "The Grand Ghoul must be mostly deaf if he didn't hear your racket."

Yolanda led Nick through the dark storeroom to the small room in which O'Tenisey had tried to initiate her. "This place stinks," Nick said.

"Zombies have no sanitary sense," Yolanda whispered. She looked around a stack of boxes and froze. In a hushed voice she said, "He's sitting in a chair, by the radiator."

Nick peered around and saw O'Tenisey the Zombie sitting in a folding chair, staring straight ahead. "I wonder if he knows he's a zombie?" Nick said.

"He's right between us and the card file," Yolanda said.

Nick considered their options, then said, "Do you have handcuffs? Give them to me."

Yolanda gave Nick her cuffs. "What are you going to do?"

"Didn't you know? I'm Cactus Jack the Zombie Trapper," Nick said. Before she could stop him, he darted out toward O'Tenisey. Yolanda pulled her gun, knowing how little good that would do her.

O'Tenisey noticed Nick coming toward him. Nick yelled, "Can you make a diorama of Dracula's girlfriend?" This question seemed just sensible enough to confound the zombie and slow his already less than alert reactions. Nick locked one cuff onto O'Tenisey's arm and the other around the radiator. "No? How about just sell me your mailing list then?"

O'Tenisey the Zombie made a try at smashing Nick's head in, but the cuffs held him fast. Yolanda jumped up and ran past them into the small cubbyhole where she had last seen the card file. Nick continued to talk to O'Tenisey, "You know, I always had you pegged for a lady's man, O'Tenisey. Is it true that zombies get more girls?" The zombie tried again to smash in the head of Nick Sabernail.

Yolanda pushed boxes and dioramas off the desk until she saw what looked like the card file. She looked through it to make sure she had the right boxes, and to insure that she had the whole alphabet.

"I've noticed the undead don't bathe much," Nick said to O'Tenisey, "were you actually buried in those clothes?"

O'Tenisey gave a mighty lunge and pulled free of the radiator. He would have clobbered Nick into the middle of next week had he not ripped his arm off of his body. Nick ducked, and the one-armed zombie careened to the floor.

"Time to go, sweetheart!" Nick called.

Yolanda grabbed the card files and vaulted over the zombie. They took off through the curtains into the shop; they could never have made it out the window with the zombie chasing them. They ran to the door. Locked. The one-armed ghoul came charging out of the back room. Nick kicked open the door while Yolanda put six rounds into the zombie's head. The impact rocked him back and the bullets completely removed its eyes. Still the ghoul charged on as if he could see them both perfectly. Nick grabbed the two card boxes Yolanda had dropped when she aimed her weapon, and both beat it fast back to the car. O'Tenisey chased them to the door; but then stopped, turned around and went back. Presumably to sit by the radiator again.

Nick stood panting at the driver's door, "Jesus. Why'd he turn around?"

"How could he see us with no eyes?" Yolanda said, catching her breath.

"We have a lot to learn about zombies," Nick said.

◆ ◆ ◆

Yolanda and Nick ate Mexican fast food at El Cantina's in Redondo Beach. A hard rain now poured outside. Yolanda had one box of cards and half the library list, Nick the other box and the rest of the list. They ate tacos and searched names. Yolanda had already determined that O'Tenisey had never had a *Finkelstein* as a customer.

"You're *sure* you didn't see any undead cooks in the kitchen?" Nick asked.

"I don't want to eat wayward zombie parts any more than you do," she said.

"I thought that was great, that health inspection thing you pulled. I really need to get me a badge."

"Crinchley," Yolanda said.

"Run that by again?"

"Crinchley, L.," she said. "He checked out one hundred and fourteen books on the occult, mostly over two years ago. He also bought from O'Tenisey; starting about six months ago. We have a hit."

Nick looked at the two names. "I don't know. Not much to hang your hopes on."

"Hell," Yolanda said, "I nearly put you in the gas chamber on not much more. Pretty close is close enough."

"Is that what they teach at detective school?" Nick said.

"That, and never kiss the suspect," Yolanda said. "I have some calls to make. I want to use a landline. Don't let any zombies spice my taco while I'm gone."

Yolanda used a pay phone just outside El Cantina's. She came back half soaked from the rain and very excited. She said something, but Nick sat transfixed by the wet shirt clinging to her body.

"Hello?" Yolanda said, waving a piece of paper in front of Nick's transfixed eyes, "Did they undead you while I was on the phone?"

"Oh no," Nick said, "I feel very much alive."

Yolanda smiled, and could not think for the life of her why *now* his attention so pleased her. "I have our man," she said.

"Just like that? A phone call and *bam*?"

"Three calls. One to the library for L. Crinchley's address. One to the Dunston Apartments where the manager assured me that Mr. Crinchley had long since moved on. Finally, to a sweet old woman in Wrightwood to confirm that she had paid all Crinchley's bills when he lived at the Dunston Apartments."

Nick looked a bit confused. "An old woman in Wrightwood?"

"His mother," Yolanda said.

"Whose mother?"

"*His*, she said, waving a piece of paper in front of Nick. Nick took the paper and read the name on it: *Lavender Crinchley*.

Three hours later, they sat in the modest living room of Mrs. Tanya Crinchley. She served them coffee cake and flavorless tea. Two large dogs barked outside her door so loudly, and so incessantly, that Nick felt his nerves fraying after just five minutes in the house. He assumed that Mrs. Crinchley must be stone solid deaf. He leaned over to Yolanda and whispered, "Maybe she should feed the dogs or something."

Mrs. Crinchley came in and sat down with her own slice of coffee cake and mug of tasteless tea. She said, "I fed them a day ago. It doesn't do to feed dogs too often. Makes them fat. No use at all, a fat dog."

"Mrs. Crinchley, I wanted to talk to you about your son, Lavender," Yolanda said.

"Lavender," Mrs. Crinchley repeated, "My only child. It's hard to raise just one, you know. No playmates. Not a one. I didn't allow any people over. Not from the neighborhood. It is important to have the right influences on a young man. You can never tell what thoughts another child might put into the head of your own. If I could raise them all, that would be different. Obviously, this place is too small for that. Not enough toilets, for a start. And you need a lot of rope to train them to the toilet. Rope costs money, and it takes time to tie and untie the knots. Three or four times a day—depending on their bowls. Course, that's just a few years—while they're young. Still, lots of rope."

Yolanda could not be sure she had followed all that, but tried gamely to keep up her end, "I suppose he had school friends?"

"Naturally. I was his school friend," Mrs. Crinchley replied. "He had the dogs, of course. Not always those two. But always two. Big ones. With lots of spirit. A dog that won't let you know he's around is not much use. No reason to have a quiet dog— might just as well buy a stuffed one. I'd insist on an active dog. If one tired out too soon and refused to bark, I'd send him right back to where he came from, or drop him to the bottom of the well out back, and go get a new one."

Nick put down his tea, wondering if Mrs. Crinchley used city water.

"Now little dogs bark more," Mrs. Crinchley continued, "but they sound like rats on steroids. A big dog is what you want. A big dog barks, and there you've got something."

Yolanda, proving her skill at weeding out the significant from the static of Mrs. Crinchley's conversational noise, asked, "Do you mean that you home-schooled Lavender?"

"Well I couldn't have him going to a neighborhood school. So many children there. He learned here. We read all the classics: Nancy Drew, Hardy Boys, back issues of the Ladies Home Journal. Lavender always favored science, so I let him read his Encyclopedia Britannica. I always thought he would have been wonderful selling those door-to-door. He had memorized practically everything in them." She looked at Nick and asked, "Do you know how many species of trees there are in the world?"

Nick answered, "No, not really."

"Me neither," said Mrs. Crinchley, "but I bet Lavender knows. Mind you, I only let him read his encyclopedia after television. A boy must have his television. I don't know how you could raise a child without it. I didn't let him watch any of the regular stuff. We had our UHS channel and that was fine. Wonderful old movies and classic television shows. Oh, Lavender loved the Foreign Legion movies. You couldn't even get him to go to the encyclopedia when one of those was on the television. Now its all cable."

Nick thought his head might split open if those dogs didn't shut up. How could their throats stand it?

Yolanda asked, "When did Lavender move out, Mrs. Crinchley?"

"Well a mother can't do everything for her son. He insisted on going to college. What could I do?"

"What college," Nick asked.

"That nice one in Las Vegas," Mrs. Crinchley answered.

"Did he ever mention a Dr. Dantelani?" Yolanda asked.

"Did he mention anyone *else*?" Mrs. Crinchley said. "He would swear oaths by that man's name. He'd say: *I swear by the name Dantelani I didn't let those dogs loose*, and such like that. He did like college. I think it a shame that he never took classes from anyone but that one professor. Lavender always did prefer reading books to dealing with people. I could never understand why that was. I always had him watch TV shows with such nice people in them." She turned to Nick and asked, "Did you ever watch that show called the Dick Van Dyke show?"

Nick admitted he had seen it once.

"Then you understand what I mean," Mrs. Crinchley said. "Such nice folks in that show. How could a boy turn out so unsocial watching TV shows like that? Why, it's hard to raise a boy all by yourself. Not now of course. Easy now. But not back then. Back then the TV shows didn't run all night. Nothing but static on late. He did love watching that static, though."

Yolanda ventured tentatively into more sensitive territory, "Did Lavender ever show any ... violent tendencies?"

"Watching all those Foreign Legion films? Why, I should hope so. Not as much as you'd think. He needed a mother's encouragement. I'd let him pitch down the dogs that had gone quiet. But he never did take to that sort of thing. Always wanting to put his nose in a book. His father would never have approved. Lavender's father worked the oil rigs, you know.

334

Died of a stroke two weeks after his big one finally came in. He never met Lavender."

Nick could stand the dogs no more. "Do you know where we might find sweet little Lavender?" he asked.

Mrs. Crinchley shook her head, "No, Lavender quit writing to me regular months ago. He has no time for his mother now. Its all those cable shows, you know, they spoil a child."

Yolanda asked, "When was the last time you heard from him?"

"I got a letter last week, first one in ages. It came with a package. Made no sense at all. He didn't give a return address in it, but he said I could use the stuff in the package to find him. Lavender always did have a funny way about himself."

"Do you still have the letter?" Yolanda asked.

"The package, too. You can have them both for all I care." Mrs. Crinchley got up and left the room.

Nick held his temples as the dogs continued their incessant barking. "Can I borrow your gun for a second?" Nick asked.

"We're almost out of here," Yolanda said.

Mrs. Crinchley returned with a piece of paper and a small brown box. "This was his last letter," she said, handing the paper to Yolanda. Yolanda and Nick read the note:

Dear Mother of Greatness,

I have not written for I have no need of mere checks now. The world is mine to roam. You may see if you have eyes to see that my eyes have seen the world that I have made in the image of my eyes. Movies have helped too, of course. If you want to witness your son's greatness and visit me, just peer into the City they call the City of Angels while taking that which you will find in this package. The signs will be made clear to you. Follow them and visit my throne.

Lavender, Now Drakan, Soon: Necronimus!

Yolanda looked inside the package. She found several inhalers like those typically used to deliver asthma medicine.

Nothing else.

Nick and Yolanda rose to go. At the door, just before leaving, Nick had a thought and turned back to ask Mrs. Crinchley, "Why did you name him *Lavender*?"

Mrs. Crinchley answered, "I think a child should have a common name. Lavender is a common color, and one of my favorites. Don't you think it a pretty name?"

Nick admitted he did.

NIGHT OF THE NECRO-HORDE

Nick and Yolanda drove back to L.A. in silence. Yolanda had read Lavender's note at least a dozen times. It said too much or it said too little. Lavender was now Drakan? What could a *Necronimus* be?

The rain had stopped and night descended. The light of the full moon gleaned off the wet pavement as they entered L.A. They could see few cars on the streets. From the windows of the houses they passed, no light emerged—except for the flashing blue light of TV screens. Nick pulled the car over to the side of the road. He looked at Yolanda. He pulled one of the inhaler's from the package.

"Don't, Nick," Yolanda said, "we don't really know what it does."

"It makes the signs clear, Yolanda," Nick said. "That's what we're looking for, right? Clear signs to the man himself? You know we have to try."

"We could get it analyzed, bring in help," Yolanda said.

"We could, but we won't. We haven't time."

"Then we both do it," Yolanda said.

"No. It should only take one."

Yolanda touched his face with the palm of her hand. "I don't much feel like going back to *one* again. We'll both do it."

Nick nodded. He let out a deep breath and pressed the inhaler to his mouth. He breathed deeply of its gases. Yolanda did so as well. For a moment Nick's head whirled, just like the first time he had tried smoking a Turkish cigarette. After a minute of this, his head cleared, and the dizziness subsided. He looked ahead and saw a world bathed in violet hues. Buildings, traffic signs, and the street itself seemed to glow in some night-light neon that Nick felt he saw not with his eyes, but with the back of his skull. He breathed in, and took comfort in the fact that he could.

"You look a wreck," Yolanda said.

Nick slowly turned his head to face her. Her features looked like cracking flesh, desiccated and ash gray. Her eyes bulged in hyper-violet rings of discolored circles. She had lips like a cadaver's. Nick reached out his hand and, almost weeping, said, "Yolanda?" He touched her. To his relief her skin felt smooth and normal, not at all as it looked.

"It only affects our vision," Yolanda said. She touched Nick's face. Nick turned his head around and started the car.

They drove down L.A.'s streets. Some of them seemed almost normal, but then they would happen upon signs and arrows and lights, all radiant purple. The signs said such things as: "New Client Processing," "Boosters for Division C-4 and above," "Unit B Full-Family Processing," "Hail Drakan," "Build Business for Unlimited Growth," "The Hour of Necronimus is at Hand," "Remember: Do Not Bite Your Tongue," "To Necronic Palace," "If you Drink, You will Leak!"

"Are you getting all this?" Nick asked.

"Yes, It's unbelievable. I saw some men—some zombies, painting billboards and windows in clear liquid, but I never imagined!"

"It's all here, only you can't see it without this stuff."

When the violet hues began to fade, they took another dose from the inhalers. "Where do we go?" Nick asked.

"Vincent Ramano mentioned a Necronic Palace," Yolanda said, "follow the signs to that."

Nick did. As they drew closer to Forest Lawn, they noticed great crowds of people, walking in a steady line to the cemetery.

Nick said, "Don't take the inhaler again, someone needs to be able to tell the undead from the living."

Finally, the car could proceed no further. Traffic had come to a complete halt. Nick and Yolanda got out and followed the crowds. They saw that many of the undead headed for a large building to the right of the cemetery proper. It looked like a recent construction made of corrugated tin. Windows of different sizes set high up on the walls. Ghoulish armed guards in purple and yellow uniforms stood on flimsy wooden towers looking down on the line of people walking towards the building. Occasionally one would yell "Halt!" to no one in particular. No one below would pay the least attention.

"The zombies are practically stepping on each other to get into this place," Yolanda said. "What could they want in there?"

"Maybe they're giving away flesh cookies," Nick said. "Let's duck out of this line and get a look at the building from the other side."

They meandered out of the line and walked a wide route till they saw a way of approaching the building's windows without being seen by the guards at the tower. As they neared the building, Yolanda noticed a policeman, gun drawn, trying to walk into the side of the wall. Nick started to walk toward him, but Yolanda stopped him. "He's one of them," she said, "I think they sometimes jump their tracks."

Nick and Yolanda made their way to a point on the wall below a window. Nick looked about and saw a large dumpster nearby. He braved the line of sight of the tower guards to retrieve it. One of the purple clad ghouls stared right at him but said and did nothing. Nick concluded that undead security guards had all the competence of the living sort.

He hauled the large dumpster over to the window and put bricks against the dumpster's wheels to keep it in place. He and Yolanda climbed onto the dumpster and looked through the window into the building. The noise their actions made would have alerted any human sentry, but the zombie policeman just marched diligently into the wall nearby, heedless of the noise.

Nick and Yolanda looked into the building.

What they saw defied their expectations, inflated as those had already become. In the center of the room lay a giant collection of vats filled with glowing green liquid, apparently pumped in by two four inch pipes stemming from the north wall. All around these vats, zombies lined up to receive enemas from long needles. They would calmly wait their turn, then walk in front of the needle, turn around, drop their pants or raise their skirts, and get a butt blast of green goo.

"I think this inhalant stuff is starting to affect my mind," Nick said.

"No," Yolanda said, "mine's worn off, and I see it too."

"People lined up for enemas?"

"Right."

Finally, Nick tore himself away from the macabre scene, and he and Yolanda descended from the dumpster.

"Do you think that's it? The headquarters for Drakan himself?" Nick asked.

"No."

"Me either."

"This is some sort of processing plant," Yolanda said.

"But not for making zombies; those folks are all zombies already. They'd have to be to stand in that line."

Yolanda thought for a moment. "Remember everything Dantelani said, he was Crinchley's original teacher. You have to kill a person to make a zombie."

"The sign on this building said *Boosters*," Nick said, "Maybe they need booster shots to keep on going?"

Yolanda nodded, "That makes sense, at least we can hope so. If they need constant boosters, then, if we can cut off the head, the zombies will all run down."

"But where do we find the head?" Nick asked. The force of the inhalant had faded and he could see Yolanda's true face clearly now. He could not see the signs that might lead them to Lavender Crinchley. So he breathed in those noxious fumes again.

"Look for signs to the Necronic Palace," Yolanda said.

◆ ◆ ◆

Drakan had gathered his finest zombies to witness his apotheosis. They stood in rows inside the Great Hall. Torches illuminated the Hall's interior. Drakan thought this a fitting touch, the torches. His zombie electricians had failed him, and the rain had shorted out the lights, so he had to use torches. It seemed fitting nevertheless. A nod to the ancients. He still had to have power for the great event. He calculated that he could get enough for the cyclotrons and the stage lights by running extension cords from the administrative office emergency generator to the Great Hall.

He looked out at his invited minions: celebrities, soldiers, writers, and officers in his zombie empire. A wonderful collection of the best of the best of the undead. Pity the roof leaked. Still, the undead didn't mind; they were very accommodating. Far more important was his cyclotron, and the corpse that tonight he would raise from the dead, to serve him as his new second in command. Drakan inspected again the straps that held the blood donor down, to make sure he would not break free. He checked the tubes and the reanimation fluid that would bring undeath to the corpse. Lastly, he inspected the corpse itself. He could see that it remained badly desiccated, in spite of Drakan's earlier treatments. He had left it in it's wrapping, to help preserve it against the elements, until the elixir of undeath brought it back to serve its new master. Drakan thought the corpse held up well considering that it had existed on this earth for over six thousand years.

Drakan saw that all was ready. And yet, in spite of the celebrity gathering, he thought he could do with a larger crowd. For tonight he would become *Necronimus*! He would fulfill his destiny and commit the ultimate act of zombie resurrection. Upon his throne he would sit, with a minion finally worthy to serve him. After that, all that remained would be taking over the rest of L.A. and getting his movies into the theatres. Corporal Vinnie had always seemed skeptical that Drakan's masterpieces could find an audience. Perhaps so; among the living. Just another reason Drakan had given up on the living. The undead would flock to see his films.

Drakan glanced over at Corporal Vinnie, now standing in the third row of ghouls. He looked very happy, Drakan thought. Drakan had ordered Vinnie the Zombie to always smile and say how happy he was as a zombie. Vinnie the Zombie did. The smile looked haunted and desperate, but he did smile.

Drakan ordered Charley Sparrow forward. Sparrow approached. "Have a crowd gather outside the great hall to cheer me at the moment of my triumph," he ordered. Charley Sparrow walked off to comply. Yes, Mr. Sparrow remained the most human-like of all his zombies. But not in a bad way.

◆ ◆ ◆

Nick and Yolanda mingled with the zombies. None seemed to notice that they were not undead. In fact, every now and then, Yolanda spotted some other living person meandering around. One of these strode up to her and said, "Hey, where's the party? Isn't this crazy? Where do you get the makeup?" Yolanda tried to tell the man to get the hell away, that he faced danger here. He ignored her and went to stand in line for the enema building.

Nick walked with Yolanda, hand on her arm, or arm around her waist. On the fumes of the inhalant, he felt just a bit too close to the zombie horde. He worried that undeath might take his mind forever. The crowds of ghouls seemed surreal enough without seeing them through a violet haze. Under the inhalant, the world looked as if the moon had turned into a black light. He found a sign to the "Great Hall of the Necronic Palace." Yolanda agreed that that must be the place to find the great king of undeath himself. If they were to find him at all.

They followed the sign through the mass of undead. As they passed into a momentary clearing in the zombie horde, Nick noticed a familiar face. "Didn't that guy ruin our first date?" Nick asked.

"We've never had a date," Yolanda said. Then she saw where Nick pointed. Ten feet away stood Detective MacGriffin, LAPD, retired, wearing a Napoleonic uniform, and mumbling some incoherent mantra of undeath.

"Jesus," Yolanda said.

"Will he recognize you?" Nick asked.

"Let's try not to pass by him," she said.

Unfortunately, a zombie crowd is even harder to push through than a living one and the ghouls streamed the two straight to the skinny Napoleon. He looked them straight on and to them said only, "Irony is the only enemy," and nothing else.

Nick tried to avoid the ghoul's eyes by staring off behind MacGriffin the Zombie. In the distance he saw Hunter Coyote hawking headsets, saying: "Give me your money—put this on," to each passing zombie. Each did. Unable to tell the living from the post-dead, Nick pointed at Hunter and asked Yolanda, "See that guy in the old army fatigues selling the headphones? Is he a zombie?"

MacGriffin had passed on now, and Yolanda looked where Nick pointed, struggling against the flow of walking corpses. "No," she said, "he's just some guy hustling the undead."

"Figures," Nick said.

Nick and Yolanda broke free of the crowd and wandered in the direction of the Great Hall by a different route. Zombies had no sense of personal space and tended to move in great crowds tightly packed rather than spreading out to take all routes to a place. Nick watched for more signs to the Great Hall while Yolanda took in the sight of industrial level grave-robbing. Teams of ghouls dug up bodies from every grave in sight. Was that a children's song they murmured as they dug?

More than the absurdity of it all, what impressed itself upon Yolanda was the scale of the thing. She could not help but think that Lavender Crinchley's hellish program must be reaching some critical mass. If not stopped tonight, would the momentum of its exponential growth make it impossible to stop at all? Had it already expanded to other cities? Yolanda shook her head to drive out such thoughts. In doing so, she cast her eyes away from the graves and back toward the throng of undead. There she saw a familiar face, and a living one this time.

◆ ◆ ◆

The cyclotron hummed, the victim screamed, the audience of attending zombies shouted "Ooohhh!" on cue from the Gong Master, and Drakan danced about excitedly. Blood left the donor and entered the tank of reanimation fluid. Reanimation fluid pumped into the ancient corpse. Drakan felt he had almost achieved the dream of the ancients. The scribes and alchemists of Egypt had been able to do no better. Drakan would surpass them all. And on video tape this time.

He glanced back at the crowed of lined zombies and caught sight of Dantelani the Zombie standing in the front row, saying "Oooohhhh!" on cue. Drakan thought it wonderful that his old teacher could be here for this night of triumph. A shame it had to be as a zombie, but the old professor liked to talk too much to be entrusted to keep their secret once the authorities had learned of him. Dantelani the Zombie smiled just the same, as Drakan had ordered.

Drakan looked at the corpse receiving the reanimation fluid. It showed early signs of reanimation. He could see that even through the wrappings. Yet something was wrong. The cyclotron had now completely drained the donor and the corpse barely showed signs of undeath. Panic gripped Drakan for a moment. He called out to his right hand man, "Mr. Sparrow! I need another living donor, quickly!"

"No more," Sparrow said.

Drakan lamented the unfortunate disproportion of undead to living at the ceremony. If he could have invited just a few living dignitaries to witness his apotheosis he would not now be out of subjects for draining. Drakan turned to the big ghoul and shouted, "Go out and find some, immediately!" Charley Sparrow led several ghouls out of the Great Hall in search for more living donors.

◆ ◆ ◆

"Mrs. Margrove ... Dorothy ... please, you have to leave here," Yolanda pleaded.

"I was told I could find Charley Sparrow here. My father. They said he would be here tonight."

"Can't you see," Yolanda said, "these people, they aren't right."

"Of course, I see," Dorothy said, "you go on and do what you must do. I have to find my father. You understand that, don't you?"

Yolanda did, she truly did, but that would not save the sweet old lady.

Under the influence of the intoxicant, it seemed to Nick that Yolanda was now trying to persuade some old zombie hag to call it a night. Weird.

Nick peered off into the distance. He saw a large building, perhaps two or three stories high, leaning over as if some giant lay sprawled out on one side of it, tilting it to starboard. Gargoyles festooned its corners. The Great Hall? Nick put his hand on Yolanda's shoulder and pointed to the building. It couldn't be too far away, just over a hill. Yolanda didn't notice him, she continued to plead with the old zombie.

Just then, Nick saw trouble coming. Two zombies, one of them quite big, came out of the crowd of meandering undead, striding with a purpose toward himself, Yolanda, and the old woman. The zombies Nick had seen till now did not stride with purpose—meander, limp or trudge with purpose, yes—but not, till now, stride. "Trouble on the rise," Nick said.

Yolanda looked up. The sight stunned her. Charley Sparrow headed straight for her. Even in the moonlight, she recognized him. Large and imposing, with dead yellow skin and a fixed expression identical to that she had studied in the bank-photos. Nothing she had so far seen, not even her father's walking corpse, had so pressed home the reality of undeath as seeing Charley Sparrow walking toward her. He served as the bridge between the world as she had known it, and the world as she knew it now.

Dorothy, her eyes not as good as Yolanda's, had not yet recognized the man headed for them, but she did notice Yolanda's look of awe. "What is it child, what do you see?" she asked.

"Daddy's here," Yolanda said.

What happened next, happened fast. Yolanda pulled her service revolver. Dorothy looked at the approaching men and recognized her father at last. Yolanda yelled "Run Nick," and fired at the zombie; she missed. Dorothy grabbed her hand and yelled "Please!" Charley Sparrow raised a two-by-four and laid it hard against Yolanda's hands knocking her to the ground. Nick lunged at the great zombie and caught a backhand straight across his head knocking him cold. Sparrow raised the board again to bring it down on Yolanda who still lay dazed on the ground. The blow would surely turn her head to putty. Dorothy stepped between the board and Yolanda and said, in a voice almost too soft to hear, "Daddy, it's Dorothy. Please don't hurt her." Charley Sparrow stopped in mid motion. His expression did not change—but he did drop the board. Yolanda breathed again. Sparrow turned around, scooped Nick off the ground, and headed back to the Great Hall. Dorothy followed him under her own power.

The second ghoul grabbed Yolanda in a bear hug and picked her up till her face was only inches away from the zombie's. His skin felt cold and he had no breath at all. Yolanda felt the air being crushed from her lungs. In a moment she would pass out. She still held her gun, but she could barely move to point it at the ghoul, and what, in any event, should she shoot? Yolanda struggled to inch her hand up till the gun rested against the underside of the zombie's chin. The ghoul's grip tightened. Stars appeared before her eyes, she grew faint. She pulled the trigger and the zombie's head exploded. Yolanda passed out.

◆ ◆ ◆

Drakan coaxed his new donor into some semblance of cooperation. "You'll be a legend," he told the man. "What's your name? I'll record it in my annals."

The man struggled enough that Claude the Zombie had a hard time getting him strapped in. Strength wasn't the issue, Claude the Zombie could easily overpower the man. But zombies lacked finesse, and Drakan's strapping system tended to tax their coordination. If Drakan could just distract the fellow for a few moments, Claude the Zombie could get him strapped down well and good.

"What's your name?" Drakan asked again, in what he hoped was a soothing voice.

"I'm Jake Schwartz!" the man shouted, as if upon hearing the name, his captors would realize their mistake and free him, "I'm from Indiana! I'm just looking for the attractions!"

That sounded like a singing group to Drakan so he ran with it, "They'll be playing here later. This is your front row seat, Legend Jack Schwartz."

Finally, Mr. Sparrow returned carrying his own live subject, unfortunately unconscious. "Mr. Sparrow," Drakan called, "help Claude the Zombie strap in this subject." Sparrow dropped his load and made short work of strapping down the increasingly panicked Jake Schwartz. Schwartz had been looking for the Universal Studios Tour when he happened upon what he thought was a movie shoot in progress. It dawned on him now that this was not some new catapult ride. The people at Universal Studios would hear from his attorney.

Drakan ran his tubes and began his cyclotron. He would take no more chances. He had three additional living donors on hand now, including the unconscious fellow and the old woman tending to him, though she might be a bit fragile for tonight's work. Drakan's empire now included over fifty old folks homes. He had found the elderly to be better zombies than donors. They sometimes died too fast. The whir of the cyclotron caught Drakan's ear. Such music of science.

◆ ◆ ◆

Yolanda shook off the dizziness. Looking up, she saw a headless zombie flailing around aimlessly. She felt better at the thought that they could be incapacitated. Not that the technique recommended itself very highly. She remembered Nick. She jumped to her feet, too fast, and the dizziness overtook her. She fell down again to the hard wet earth.

Then she did it right. She stood up slowly and checked her parts. Her left wrist had taken most of the blow—it hurt like hell and might be broken. She took two deep breaths and felt no great pain. Her ribs had held up. She jumped back as the headless zombie nearly trampled her in its flailing.

How to find Nick? She looked for footprints on the ground, but she had no tracking skills and could make out nothing useful. Fighting back panic, and trying not to hyperventilate, she scanned the area. Then she saw it: a giant leaning building. This one had been built of brick and wood, with many long and narrow windows, still missing glass. It formed a wobbly rectangle three stories high, and might pass in the dark for some sort of demonic cathedral, complete with gargoyles. She had not experienced much of the world of the undead, but from what she *had* experienced, that listing edifice seemed to her just the sort of Great Hall zombies would build. She picked up her gun and headed for it.

Yolanda approached what she guessed was the front of the building. She saw two giant doors, each two stories high, into which ghouls packed themselves too tight to breath (not a problem for them, she supposed). A huge crowd of zombies stood in a thick semicircle around the doors, pressed just as tight. Yolanda went around this mass in a long circle to the right of the Great Hall. Here, along the long side of the rectangular building, with the roof listing menacingly over her, she found ground free of the undead.

The ghouls had clearly not finished building The Great Hall. Construction materials lay all around. Boards covered many of the windows. As she approached the back of the Great Hall she could look through the long, cathedral-like windows that stretched from floor to ceiling. They had not been boarded up, so *someone* in there must need fresh air. The windows were so wide and numerous that the backside of the building had as many gaps as pieces of wall.

Looking into the building, Yolanda saw rows and rows of pews, packed with the undead, each of them standing and staring at a stage centered at the back wall of the Great Hall. On the stage, she could see a giant glass cylinder filled with liquid and surrounded by machinery she could not identify. She could not see anything else from where she stood. The wind picked up behind her, blowing cold, damp air. A gong sounded. The ghouls inside let out a hideous "Oooohhhh!" Yolanda held steady to her nerve.

Scaffolding still remained on the outside of the building a little to her left. It looked almost as unstable as the rest of the building. Obviously the contractor didn't have to worry about workers comp claims. To see more of the inside of the building she would need to climb scaffolding. Yolanda climbed the creaking metal until she could look down from the framework at the scene inside the unfinished building. Now she saw that the stage held a table, opposite the cylinder. On the table, a man lay screaming. Given her experience with the Vampire Killer case, she could guess what was happening to him. She could not think of what to do to stop it. The zombie to policewoman ratio did not favor a frontal attack. The man on the table seemed to be past the point of helping anyway.

A greater shock to Yolanda's senses lay in the cylinder itself: a mummy. A real honest-to-god Egyptian mummy. It lay in liquid and had tubes running into it. Salvador Dali could not have concocted a more absurd scene of man, corpse, and machinery. Between the mummy and the table, jumping about frantically, she saw a thin man dressed all in black, yelling something about legends and raising the dead of Egypt. Lavender Crinchley, no doubt about it. Further into the building, zombies stood in disciplined rows. A gong sounded again from the front of the room, just behind the frenzied Zombie Master, and as one, the assembly of ghouls said "Oooohhhh!" Yolanda could feel sanity slipping away. She focused on her principle task. She searched the room for Nick. She saw him at last, just coming to his senses at the bottom of the stage on the far side away from Yolanda. Dorothy tended to him. Charley Sparrow stood there too, looking at them. Nearby stood the fellow Yolanda had tried to send home earlier.

Now what to do?

Drakan watched for signs of undeath. They increased; they grew. Still, the Pharaoh did not rise. Drakan checked his tubes and cables. He needed more blood. "Prepare another subject!" he yelled. Sparrow grabbed a man and brought him to the table.

"Alright, I'm going, I'm in," the man said.

Drakan found his cooperative attitude cheering. "What is your name that we may record it for the annals?"

"They call me Dude," the man said, "Hey, I'm on the stage! Dude made the stage!"

Sparrow tied him down. The man did not resist. He seemed to think this all some sort of theatrical production. All well and good for the strapping down part, but inappropriate for the actual extraction, "Only through agony, terror, and hopeless pain can undeath be born," Drakan intoned—proud at how good his intoning had become. The tourist just smiled and nodded. Once Sparrow had secured the man well, Drakan addressed him again, "You are going to die—meet your death with terror!"

"Oh yeah! Aaaahhh. Like that, right?" the man said.

"No!" Drakan shouted. "You really are going to die! I need real terror!"

"Okay. I'll try," Dude said, "but if you want great acting, you shouldn't take audience members, pal."

Normally Drakan liked to have them nice and terrorized before he cut in the tubes. It appeared that he would not get that this time.

Yolanda considered taking a shot at the tight-shouldered man in the black cape jittering about the stage giving orders. Even without an injured hand, in the dark, at this distance, she could easily miss. The ghouls that had attacked her and Nick moved fast—real fast. She knew she had slim chance of stopping them with bullets. She needed something altogether bigger. She climbed down from the scaffolding and inspected the material at the site. She found no bazookas. Behind the Great Hall she saw a building that could not have been built by zombies, it looked too sturdy. An original Forest Lawn edifice, she guessed. Large power cables ran from the stage, through a gap in the back wall, and into the building behind the Great Hall. The power source for the floorshow evidently came from that building. Following the cables, she found the electric generator powering the equipment on the stage. A ghoul in a purple jumpsuit stood guarding the generator. Yolanda considered trying to shoot his head off as she had done the earlier zombie. The sound of the shot might alert help. Knocking the guard unconscious was out of the question. (What anyway was his state of consciousness?) Then she recognized the odor in the little building. The generator ran on gasoline. Cans of gas lay against the wall. Old clothes, presumably once covering dead bodies in coffins, lay in large piles in the equipment shed housing the generator. She tried a quick experiment—she walked over and picked up a can of gasoline in full view of the zombie guard. He saw her and did nothing. Yolanda surmised that he had been instructed to guard the generator, and the generator alone he would guard. Now Yolanda had a plan. Although the ground remained wet from the rain, she knew from close experience that zombies were a dry bunch. Yolanda gathered her wits and gathered her rags.

◆ ◆ ◆

Nick's head hurt, and he was glad of it. A hurt head meant he had not been decapitated. Just the same, he flexed his neck muscles to move his head around a bit. Yep, still on the shoulders. He looked up and saw the old woman to whom Yolanda had been talking prior to the world caving in. She did not look like a zombie. The intoxicant had worn off—but that did little to improve the aesthetics of Nick's surroundings. Nick looked about and realized that he had somehow been dropped off at a movie lot during the filming a cheap re-make of *The Mummy Rises*.

A pale, pinched looking man, dressed in black, shouted for the cameras: "Arise dead of Egypt! Arise and fulfill my destiny! I am your lord and master!" Then a gong sounded and Nick heard a loud "Oooohhhh!" Nick then noticed that he could not see any movie cameras, just a zombie holding a camcorder. So much for the movie theory.

The pale man dressed in black spun around and looked dead on at Nick. "You will be next! The Pharaoh may rise even without you, but I shall take no chances and have you prepared at once. Glory in your privilege!" He gestured at Nick with both palms up, offering a ceremonial dedication to the sacrificial victim.

It takes very little to end the world. A portly fellow with a damaged slide-rule misreads a monitor. A panicked politician not yet recovered from his Ambien dose thinks some common phrase like *Pearl Harbor*, or *Munich*, or *Strategic Vulnerability*. Identities are confirmed, launch codes are sent. Then everyone sits at their desk, job done, mission accomplished, and asks, "Should I call my kids now?" These thoughts passed at light speed through Nick's head as he looked at the world-mastering "Drakan." He might not seem suitable material for a Necronimus, but really, it doesn't take much. Nick thought all this, but he said, "You must be Lavender Crinchley. I have a message from your mother."

Drakan's shoulders dropped along with his mouth. His expression suggested a man who had expected to bite into mild custard but had just chewed ground glass instead. A message from mother? He just gapped at Nick like a teenager caught spanking the monkey in the closet. "How do you know my mother?"

"She says you don't write enough, and you watch too much damn TV."

Behind Drakan, the mummy began to shudder and twist. It's hands flailed up in the tub. Drakan didn't notice. He remained transfixed by the fellow on the floor below the stage. "Who are you, your face looks familiar?"

Nick made his way to his feet. This took effort, and he had to fight off the dizziness that threatened to engulf him. He looked around but saw no avenue of escape. He knew better than to try fist fighting with zombies. He would try sweet reason, "I ought to look familiar. You dropped off some bodies at my place yesterday. I appreciate the gesture, but I don't share your hobbies."

Drakan said, "You're that Sabernail person! The Vampire Killer on the news!"

"It would just tickle my lawyer blue to hear you say that," Nick said, "but for the last time, I don't vamp and I don't kill. Speaking of my lawyer, I think he'd fit on that table real good. I could just pop out and get him for you if you like."

Drakan began frantically looking around for Nick's lawyer; or the cavalry, or anything else. Then he noticed the splashing in the mummy's vat. "The dead of Egypt arise!" he said. The fluid in the vat glowed with a green luminescence, a phenomenon that Drakan had never before encountered. Could earlier efforts at reanimating this long dead Pharaoh have left its traces in him? Might he be even more a special case than Drakan had suspected?

Drakan looked at his donor: dead. Although the process seemed near completion, and the mummy reanimating well, Drakan wanted to be certain. He turned back toward his remaining live subjects. Perhaps he should hold onto this Sabernail person until all this mother business got settled. "Mr. Sparrow, bring the old woman to the table for extraction."

Charley Sparrow walked toward Dorothy. Nick tried to block his path, but the big zombie just knocked him to the ground. Sparrow reached down for Dorothy.

"Father, I'm Dorothy," the old woman said in a gentle voice. "Please don't do this. Please don't hurt anyone else." The old woman looked into his long dead eyes—yellow and empty.

The undead do not feel. They do not remember. They do not have pity. They are bound by the will of their creator and have no will of their own.

But Charley Sparrow stopped dead in his tracks.

"Bring her to me Mr. Sparrow!" demanded Drakan.

"Dor ... o ... thy," Charley Sparrow said. Dorothy touched his giant hand and smiled.

Drakan could not fathom what circuit Mr. Sparrow the Zombie had blown. For some reason he was reluctant to bring him the woman. "Then bring me the man," Drakan shouted. "Bring me Sabernail!"

Charley turned and grabbed Nick and hoisted him up onto

his shoulders. Dorothy yelled "No!" but another ghoul grabbed her and held her back. Nick fought hard to free himself. His struggle came to nothing. The big man's grip could not be loosened. Sparrow heaved Nick onto the hard wooden table. The impact of the landing knocked the wind out of Nick, stunning him for a moment. Sparrow strapped Nick onto the table. Nick could do nothing against the zombie's incredible strength.

A pinched pale face thrust into Nick's limited field of view. "Die in fear!" Drakan screamed.

"Your mother needs you to drown some more puppies, freak!" Nick shouted back.

The dead Pharaoh struggled into undeath. It needed no new blood now. Drakan didn't care. He would suck this foul-mouthed man dry anyway. He would make him regret his words. He could even have him say so, later.

Drakan looked over at his glorious creation. The Dead of Egypt seemed ready to burst out of its glass chamber. Apparently the great resurrection would not wait. Drakan turned to the glass cylinder. He took a ceremonial posture towards it in preparation for the establishment of his authority as Lord of Undeath. "Rise and obey," Drakan intoned. "Rise and obey."

Drakan watched as the mummy placed his hands on the sides of the cylinder. He heard the splashing of the fluids subside as the dead Pharaoh steadied itself. Drakan smelled ... smoke? Drakan jerked his head around. The gong sounded. The crowd said "Oooohhhh!"

Drakan saw smoke billowing up from the left side of the Great Hall. It then occurred to him that he had neglected to give any fire safety lessons to his minions. None had been briefed on putting out fires; a complicated contingency to write in invisible ink in any case. Drakan jumped back from the rising Pharaoh, trying to think of what order he could give. A shot rang out. Drakan realized that someone had tried to shoot him. Someone had tried to shoot Necronimus! Panic welled up in Drakan's chest. Then more shots sounded from where the smoke came.

Drakan yelled out, "Get the one with the gun!" and pointed to where the sound had come. As if of one will, the mass of attending zombies charged toward the smoking side of the building in obedience to Drakan's ill-considered command.

Nick now lay completely strapped down to the table. Charley Sparrow above him. The giant ghoul looked back at Dorothy. He saw her clutched by a zombie goon, her face a mask of pain.

Charley Sparrow had made a lot of mistakes in life. But alone among zombies, he found the will to correct one of them in undeath. Staring into the pained and frightened eyes of Dorothy, he did something no necromancer would have ever thought possible. He remembered. Not skills from life, nor instructions from his master, but something altogether more human. He crossed a veil between life and undeath that the masters of necromancy had always thought absolute. Charley Sparrow was indeed a most unusual zombie. He *would* take care of his little girl Dorothy.

Sparrow leapt from the stage and landed a foot away from Claude the Zombie, who held Dorothy tight. Sparrow put one arm beneath the old woman and with the other he pulled loose Claude the Zombie's iron grip by ripping the ghoul's arm completely off his body. Sparrow guided Dorothy softly to the ground, looking into her eyes, and at the smile on her lips. The armless ghoul tried to grab her with the other arm. Sparrow lifted him up and threw him into a wall so hard that Claude the Zombie turned to dust on impact.

Nick saw none of this; not the undead charge into the smoke, not Drakan/Crinchley's address to the Pharaoh, not Sparrow's rescue of Dorothy. Nick had a very bad seat. Then the view got much better: Yolanda Vasquez's face appeared.

"Kinky dog!" she said, "why didn't you tell me you liked this sort of thing?" Yolanda began pulling the straps loose.

Just halfway to freeing Nick, they both heard the most

unearthly cry ever to emerge from lips ever human:

"PHARAOH ANKTA!"

They looked toward the sound. The mummy had lost much of its wrappings. It stood, half-man, half-corpse, now over eight feet high, and almost iridescent in the growing flames of the building. It's arms stretched out as new undead flesh grew round them. The giant undead Pharaoh's skull-like face took on a hideous mask of sallow flesh. The liquid in the glass cylinder boiled beneath the Pharaoh's feet.

Drakan stammered at the beast before him. "Obey your master," he whimpered.

From where Nick sat, this seemed an unlikely prospect. Death-Glow Pharaohs do not obey little pinched men.

The giant corpse smashed out of the glass cylinder. In a hellish voice, it let loose a cry so fierce that Yolanda momentarily stopped struggling with Nick's straps to cover her ears.

Drakan yelled, his voice cracking with the strain, "Obey me! I'm your master! I am Necronimus! I am! I am!"

Pharaoh the Zombie turned a slow head toward Drakan.

"I am," Drakan said.

The Pharaoh smiled. The smile of the dead. It leaned forward to face the Zombie Master.

"I am Necronimus," Drakan whimpered.

The Pharaoh's corpse, recipient of a thousand and one experiments in reanimation, paid no heed to the meek alchemist's demands. The giant mummy's jaw gaped open and from it spewed green gel as if from a fire hose. The green liquid smelled like liquid fire. It hit Drakan, covering him head to toe. Drakan screamed.

Nick could smell the pinched man's burning flesh. "Damn! Acid spewing mummies!" Nick said. "I think we should leave."

They worked the straps even harder, but the Pharaoh had seen them. The green glowing mummy moved closer. They could not free Nick in time.

"Run!" Nick shouted to Yolanda.

But the thought never crossed her mind. She worked to free Nick.

Below, at the foot of the stage, Dorothy looked one last time at the face of her father. "Help them," she said.

Charley Sparrow set Dorothy down. "Dorothy," he said.

The mummy closed on Nick and Yolanda. The re-animated Pharaoh let out a demonic laugh that echoed throughout the teetering hall. It opened wide its hideous mouth. It leaned forward toward Nick and Yolanda to vent its hellish spray. They covered their faces and prepared for the worse. Just at that moment, Sparrow tackled the great beast, bringing it down.

"Why didn't I think of that?" Nick said.

Yolanda pulled loose the last strap. Nick leapt from the table. They bolted from the stage.

Sparrow and the Pharaoh remained on the stage in a death-lock of undeath. The mummy spewed Sparrow with his fiery venom, but the big man would not let go. Sparrow's body dissolved. His grip held.

Nick and Yolanda gathered up Dorothy. Her face radiated an inexplicable serenity. Yolanda assumed she had gone mad. Nick carried Dorothy in his arms as Yolanda navigated a path through the zombies. The obedient zombies in attendance at Drakan's ceremony were adding their dry mass to fuel the flames of the building. Those at the back pressed their fellow ghouls forward into the growing flames.

Yolanda felt the building shudder. The Great Hall, never a very stable construction, listed badly to starboard now. This is why we have building inspectors. "We have to go!" Yolanda cried.

They fled. As Nick carried her, Dorothy got her last glimpse of her father, no more than a skeleton now, still holding the mummy fast. It's green acid dissolving both Sparrow and itself.

The three of them cleared the building by only a few seconds before the whole sloping mass fell in upon itself. The falling masonry crushed to powder the dry bones of the zombies inside. A great ball of fire rose over the collapsing edifice. It looked to Nick like the Great Los Angeles Zombie Roast.

◆ ◆ ◆

The three, Nick, Yolanda, and Dorothy, made their way from the remains of the burning building. They walked apart from the undead. Nick and Yolanda held each other tight as they walked. Dorothy declined any help. She seemed calm and content. To their right a stream of zombies marched toward the burning palace of death, as patient as tourists in line at Disneyland. The undead marched in obedience to those that marched ahead of them. Heat, rubble and fire did not deter nor divert them. Zombies piled onto the flames, like volunteer kindling.

Yolanda lead the way to a hill near the road. It remained largely free of the undead, but for a few spinning in circles. Nick helped Dorothy sit down on the grass. Dorothy thanked him politely, and continued to look unaccountably pleased with the evening. Nick and Yolanda sat a few feet away. Nick beat zombie dust off his clothes, happy to be freed from bondage. Yolanda picked dried flesh-flakes out of her hair, happy just to be. The occasional confused zombie ambled by and stared a moment as if waiting for instructions. Nick just waved them on.

"Yolanda," Nick said.

"Yes," she replied.

"Can we just call *this* our first date? I'd really like to get on with this romance."

She lay her head on his shoulder.

◆ ◆ ◆

By dawn, all the proper authorities had arrived. The police, the Mayor, and the reporters, began sorting out the mess.

Paramedics attempted to treat injured zombies, but found they could benefit little from the resources of modern emergency medicine.

Paramedic: "I have no vital signs! I need plasma, stat! Lots of it! Sir, if I could just have you lie down. Sir. So I can get your heart to beat again. Just lie down. And breathe maybe. If you wouldn't mind, sir."

Emergency Services called in to hospitals on patients "covered in death." "Blood pressure: zero over zero. But he's looking at me! He's picking his nose!" "He seems to want an enema!" "You need to come down here and see it yourself!"

The police managed the zombie crowd. Many officers marveled at the compliance of these riotous arsonists. Especially when compared to the norm.

Riot Officer: "If I could just get you folks to step back. Wait, you're crushing the people at the rear! Just come forward. Stop! Good. Just stand there." He thinks a moment, "On one foot. Wow."

Reporters made valiant attempts to interview the undead, but they lacked Drakan's knack for it.

Venus Whimsey: "Tell us about this tragedy. How horrible it felt. How did it feel? Horrible?"

Paul the Zombie: "Horror ... feel ... butt ... feel ... goop."

Venus Whimsey: "There you are Duke, straight from one of the victims. Everyone here is in a state of shock at whatever it is that has happened. Just looking at these people's faces, you can tell the hell they've been through."

Occasionally, when a zombie reporter would stick a microphone into the face of a zombie, the interview could almost pass for a conversation, allowing for its incomprehensibility.

Zombie Reporter: "Mimaster ... who ... burn ... whaaattt???"

Emma the Zombie: "Mimaster ... nomaster ... go ... boooom!!!"

Zombie Reporter: "Aaaarrraaggaahhh!!!!"

Emma the Zombie: "Aaaarrraaaggaahhhh!!!"

Sheer poetry.

The press conferences lasted for days. The Mayor declared a state of emergency, only to find things strangely calm. The Sheriff declared himself vindicated on the matter of the Vampire Slayer naming controversy. The Chief of Police vigorously disagreed, or at least the press assumed that to be his intent. As the Chief had apparently "gone zombie," his attempt to eat Channel Two's microphone had to be subjected to a good deal of interpretation.

For three days the undead continued working their ruts. People (the living ones) found them to be quiet neighbors and efficient co-workers. Some living citizens even missed the undead as they dropped in their tracks. The undead never turned their music up too loud or asked for raises. They didn't even smell half as bad as you would think.

For weeks, the pundits would opine on the political fallout, military leaders would fret over a zombie gap, management gurus would marvel at Drakan's labor force compliance, philosophers would speculate about the metaphysical meaning of *this* sort of zombie, and Hunter Coyote would sell "authentic zombie parts" for ten bucks a limb.

The scientific community agreed that Drakan's research showed promise, but was not yet ready for publication. The art house cinemas played the lost films of Clark Gable, Marilyn Monroe, and other undead stars. Film scholars wrote learned articles on that great auteur, Lavender Crinchley.

◆ ◆ ◆

Nick and Yolanda took a long vacation in the Cayman Islands. They sat on beach chairs and drank colorful drinks named after extinct parrots. There they considered what it all meant as they worked on their now much in demand memoirs.

"I think it's the story of a man who saves a woman from the dead hand of her past," Nike said.

"*He* saved *her*?" Yolanda replied.

"Sure. Emotionally. Metaphorically. Very metaphorically," said Nick.

Yolonda thought on this a moment, "I think it's the story of a brave policewoman who burns out a zombie infestation, and incidentally saves her feckless lover from becoming a human sacrifice."

Nick grimaced, "Conceding your point, I still don't think that that will make it into the movie version."

"So you think the story could be a movie?" Yolanda asked.

"It's very cinematic," Nick said.

"But the studio would never accept the ending," said Yolanda.

"They'd insist on artistic license, for the sake of commerce." said Nick.

Yolanda pondered the wisdom of his words, "Yes, they would. So maybe it isn't a movie after all. Maybe just a book. More scope for the author's vision."

"But would the public buy the ending, even in a book?" Nick said.

"Perhaps if it had just a limited public, a select readership," Yolanda said.

"Right," said Nick.

They sat on the beach and watched the waves roll to shore.

ABOUT THE AUTHOR

Whip Lipsey

Whip Lipsey grew up in Georgia, came of age in Missouri, and dropped out of high school in California. He holds a bachelor's degree in history from the University of California at Irvine and a PhD in philosophy from the University of Rochester. He left academia to work as a screenwriter (and was shocked to learn that writing for Hollywood does not require a doctorate). After twenty years raising his three children as a full-time father, he has returned to writing.